THE

than ever!

We're celebrating our fourth anniversary...and thanks to you, our loyal readers, "The Avon Romance" is stronger and more exciting than ever! You've been telling us what you're looking for in top-quality historical romance—and we've been delivering it, month after wonderful month.

Since 1982, Avon has been launching new writers of exceptional promise—writers to follow in the matchless tradition of such Avon superstars as Kathleen E. Woodiwiss, Johanna Lindsey, Shirlee Busbee and Laurie McBain. Distinguished by a ribbon motif on the front cover, these books were quickly discovered by romance readers everywhere and dubbed "the ribbon books."

Every month "The Avon Romance" has continued to deliver the best in historical romance. Sensual, fast-paced stories by new writers (and some favorite repeats like Linda Ladd!) guarantee reading *without* the predictable characters and plots of formula romances.

"The Avon Romance"—our promise of superior, unforgettable historical romance. Thanks for making us such a dazzling success!

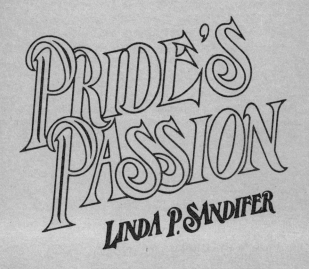

PRIDE'S PASSION

LINDA P. SANDIFER

◆ AVON
PUBLISHERS OF BARD, CAMELOT, DISCUS AND FLARE BOOKS

PRIDE'S PASSION is an original publication of Avon Books. This work has never before appeared in book form. This work is a novel. Any similarity to actual persons or events is purely coincidental.

AVON BOOKS
A division of
The Hearst Corporation
1790 Broadway
New York, New York 10019

Copyright © 1986 by Linda Prophet Sandifer
Published by arrangement with the author
Library of Congress Catalog Card Number: 86-90767
ISBN: 0-380-75171-2

First Avon Printing: December 1986

AVON TRADEMARK REG. U.S. PAT. OFF. AND IN OTHER COUNTRIES, MARCA REGISTRADA, HECHO EN U.S.A.

Printed in the U.S.A.

K-R   10   9   8   7   6   5   4   3   2   1

To my parents, Dave and Virginia Prophet

Dad, a storyteller in your own right,
      thank you for sharing your knowledge
      and experiences of life.

Mom, thank you for reading all those early
      manuscripts and for having the faith that my
      dream would come true.

PRIDE'S PASSION

Prologue

Colorado, 1891

The fire swelled upward and was caught by the wind and tossed across the dry grassland. The crackling sound soon became a roar as the flames rolled and tumbled, reached and searched for more fuel. The surging blaze raced toward the ranch, carrying with it the acrid smell of burning grass and animal hair.

Will Chanson, Bart Russell, and the other volunteers beat at the grass with wet gunny sacks, slickers, and blankets. But they were repeatedly pushed back closer and closer to the ranch buildings by the heat and smoke boiling out of the rapidly advancing inferno.

Will readjusted the bandana over his nose and turned his smoke-blackened face from the fire long enough to glance behind him at the distance separating the fire from the corrals, barn, and crude two-room log house. He spotted Parley Barnes, his wife, Grace, and their six children standing in the center of the yard watching them.

Will's temper rose, not only because Barnes wouldn't help to save the ranch he managed for the Kincaid Cattle Company, but because Barnes hadn't even plowed a firebreak around the place. Did he think fire was particular to what it destroyed? There'd been more than one ranch house burned to cinders this summer. It had become not a question of *if* it would happen, but *when*.

The smoke stung Will's eyes. The fire was getting too wide, and his line of men couldn't reach to the perimeters. He couldn't risk their lives any longer.

"Come on! Let's get out of here!" He tried to holler above the rumble, but only those closest heard the command. They, in turn, passed the word down the line. Will waited to see that everyone had heard, and when the last man had turned from the roaring flames, Will followed.

As the men crowded into the yard and raced to their horses, Barnes hurried toward Will. "What are you doing? You can't quit!" he cried hysterically.

In one fluid motion, Will mounted his horse. "I won't fight to save this place and risk these men's lives if you're going to stand there and watch at a safe distance! I suggest you get your wife and children out of here. This place is gone."

Barnes grabbed Will's horse's reins. "You can't quit! Everything I own is in that house."

"You should have plowed a firebreak like everybody else. We can't beat out a prairie fire with brooms and blankets."

Barnes's face was set. "I ain't no damn farmer. Never been behind no plow, and I ain't about to start now."

Will looked toward the fire again. Then, with eyes that stung fiercely, he looked at Barnes and his wife, who stood trembling by his side. Will spoke to her in a softer, almost pleading tone. "Get

2

into the wagon with your children, Mrs. Barnes, and get to safety."

She turned to him with a crazy look in her eyes. "I ain't movin'. Everything I own is here." She pointed a finger at him. "You tell those men to get back out there and fight that fire. They could stop it if they put their minds to it!"

Anger burst inside Will's head. He grabbed back the reins and loped the short distance to the corral, where one of Barnes's purebred shorthorn bulls was pacing nervously in its confines.

Will leaped from the saddle as his horse skidded to a stop. He jerked his Winchester free of the saddle scabbard. There was only one thing left to try, and he didn't like to do it, but it was the only way to prove to Barnes that they were beat this time. Will climbed over the pole fence as the bull tossed his big, white-faced head and sprayed froth from his mouth into the dirt and onto his sides.

"What do you think you're doing?" Barnes screamed while scrambling over the fence.

"Trying to stop the fire like you want me to."

"You won't go killin' my bull. That's mine, not Kincaid's. You won't use him to put out no fire."

Will pulled the lever-action and pumped a bullet into the chamber. "Are you going to take your family and leave?"

Barnes's lips thinned to a long, straight line. "You boys find another way. You're just givin' up and threatening me. I'll tell Kincaid you didn't even try."

Will's eyes narrowed. "We aren't doing this for Kincaid. We're doing it for ourselves and for you. Go ahead and tell him. He doesn't pay my wages."

In the distance, the flames rose against the blue

sky, danced in a mirage, and then drifted away on the thinning smoke. The absence of smoke was a sign in itself that the fire was building in ferocity.

Will put the rifle to his shoulder, stared down the barrel at the bull, and squeezed the trigger a split second before Barnes hit the rifle, nearly knocking it from his grip. The bull dropped, and the other men automatically raced to the corral, knowing the procedure and what they were supposed to do. Rapidly, they pulled out skinning knives and peeled back half of the hide.

Will pushed past Barnes. He slammed the Winchester back into the scabbard and, in seconds, had his lariat in hand. With Bart Russell, his foreman, on one side of the bull, and himself on the other, they hooked onto two legs and dragged the dead animal to the fireline, leaving Barnes in the dust from their horses' hooves.

The heat nearly suffocated them as they dragged the bull along the edge of the fire at the fastest pace the horses could travel. They turned and traded sides to keep the horses' hooves from charring. Other riders came in to trade them off. Back and forth they rode, but the fireline only crawled outward. Soon it was circling wide of them by half a mile on either side, reaching out to envelop the lonely ranch that had become its apparent target.

Will saw the other men look at the fire with hopeless, tired eyes. For hours, they'd fought this one; for a total of weeks, they'd fought others. Some they conquered, some conquered them. The orange flames' reflection flickered in Will's blue eyes. If they didn't get out soon, they could very easily be trapped in the center. There was no hope. The fire was out of control.

Will pulled his hat off, waved it above his head, and let out a war whoop that carried down the line to the other men. The men returned the signal, dropped the smoke-charred lariat, and raced their horses back to the ranch. As they slowed down in the yard, Will pulled up beside Barnes again.

"Get out, Barnes! We can't stop it."

Barnes looked at the fire and swore. He put a hand on his wife's shoulder. "Come on, Grace. Get in the wagon with the children."

Grace hesitated. "But my furniture, Parley. Our bed belonged to my mother. We should have gotten it out. Maybe we still could..."

"No, dear," he replied in a surprisingly patient tone. "It'll take too long to dismantle it, but we got everything else out that the wagon would hold."

The children's eyes darted fearfully toward the fire, then to their mother in a silent plea for her to hurry. Suddenly, Grace Barnes turned on Will. "It's your fault," she shouted. "You just didn't try hard enough. You think this place is nothing compared to that big fancy house of yours. We've had to work hard for everything we have; maybe this place isn't ours, but it's all we have. You wouldn't know what it's like to have to work and sweat and struggle just to put food on the table. You're just a kid who's had it easy all his life. Everything you own was handed to you by your pa. Handed! I hope it all burns. Your fancy house and all your land!"

Barnes finally took her by the arm and dragged her to the wagon. By the time he climbed up beside her and headed north, the fire was starting on the outer corrals. Will followed Barnes out as far as the creek, then let the others go on ahead while he directed his horse down to the cool stream. Behind them, the fire blazed high into the blue Colorado sky and reached outward for the simple cabin.

He watched it consume the dry wood and thought about what Grace Barnes had said. Then he studied his hands, probably for the first time in his life.

The fingers were long and lean. There were places where threadlike scars stood raised and white against skin that was a deep brown. Most of the scars he had received before he was fourteen, before he could find gloves that his hands could fill out properly. One deep one ran the length of his left hand; it had had to be sewn together after a new barbed-wire fence had snapped and opened his palm to the bone.

Slowly, a drop of sweat trickled from beneath his hat and into his eye, burning it more than it already burned from the smoke. He removed the hat, wiped the perspiration away with his shirt-sleeve, and watched the fire inching onward. He pulled the hat back down tight onto his forehead and nudged his tired horse up the muddy creek to catch up with the others.

Yes, he had been handed the CM ranch—in a manner of speaking.

Chapter 1

The afternoon sun moved toward the ragged tips of the Rocky Mountains, lending a reddish glow to the August sky; a sky that had not seen a cloud for months. Outside the Denver Cattlemen's Club, seventeen-year-old Kate Diering waited restlessly in her father's black-topped buggy while he completed business inside. In harness, the proud, high-stepping mare stood listless too, occasionally tossing her head against the leather straps that bound her in place while the fiery hand of the sun burned her raven coat.

Losing patience with the heat and her father's tardiness, Kate picked up the reins and turned the buggy around in the middle of the street, putting her square-shouldered back to the afternoon sun. The little shade the new position provided did not help ease the discomfort caused by the unbearably hot wind that tugged at her chestnut hair, trying to pull the coarse, thick strands from the confining bonnet. It lifted the hem of her green cotton dress, threatening to reveal the petticoats beneath. In vain, she tried to keep the skirt down with a slim hand, but she finally tucked the yards of calico beneath her legs as best she could. The effort brought more beads of perspiration to her

7

forehead until they slowly began to trickle down the sides of her face. Unable to tolerate it, she removed her bonnet and dabbed at the moisture with a handkerchief.

Kate swore between clenched teeth, knowing her father would not approve of her colorful language—but an hour had passed since she was supposed to meet him. And he was still inside the pretentious brick building where he had been since noon. She was shriveling up in the same slow fashion as the tall prairie grass. She dared not leave, though, for if she wasn't there when he appeared, he would chastise her for "dawdling" with her shopping and making *him* wait.

From the eastern horizon, a demon tongue licked at the sky, signaling yet another prairie fire. Hardly a week passed, it seemed, without a fire breaking out somewhere between the high mountain meadows and the distant flatlands. This past month, the surrounding country had frequently been choked in a haze of smoke from the great fires. Dust and cinders sometimes floated through the air, covering everything and drifting inside the dwellings whose doors and windows remained flung open night and day to catch the faintest breeze.

At least today the wind had cleared the town of the haze, but it also fanned the distant fire that scattered the cattle who fought for a mouthful of grass on the sun-scorched range.

Kate glanced up and down the length of the street. The town was quiet in the afternoon hours. She eyed a small restaurant, knowing a cold drink would help her parched throat. If she were allowed inside the club, she could simply tell her father she would be waiting for him at the restaurant. But the only women allowed in were those of a sporting nature, and even those women entered through the back door. She supposed she could just send him a message, but she hesitated, deciding to give her father a few more minutes.

She looked at the upper-story windows of the club, wondering if it was more than business that detained her father. But she knew he would have no reason to find a harlot now that he'd married the young and lovely Cordelia Kincaid.

The slow syncopation of plodding hooves drew her attention from her thoughts and her discomfort. Preceded by a cloud of dust, a band of riders moved down the street in her direction. Their horses were unwilling or unable to hold their heads up and dragged their feet in tired effort. The men drooped in their saddles, their wide-brimmed, tall-crowned hats pulled low against the afternoon sun. She recognized only one, although she hadn't seen him in four years.

There was no trace of a slump to Will Chanson's broad shoulders, and from a distance it appeared he hadn't changed much during her stay in England, except for possibly becoming more handsome.

But there was more to Will Chanson than simple good looks. She had always been fascinated by that spellbinding quality about him, that perfect combination of charm and reckless spirit. But he'd never seemed to notice her at all. Her heartbeat quickened.

By their blackened appearances, Will and the other riders had apparently been fighting the fire to the east. As they passed, they politely touched the brims of their soiled, battered hats in a silent gesture of respect. She nodded her acknowledgment and watched them file by on their way to a saloon. To her surprise, Will Chanson reined his horse in, while the others proceeded on. She met his curious blue eyes and blushed.

"You're a strong one, Kate." Both his smile and his tone were warm and welcoming. "This heat would kill some of those Eastern and European imports we've been getting around here." With only a slight hesitation he added, "Are you back in Denver to stay?"

His easy greeting and friendly smile caused something inside her to fall and then rise sharply. She took a deep breath. "Yes, I suppose I've been educated beyond what's customary for a female."

Will smiled at the unglossed sarcasm in her voice and studied her fully, allowing himself the pleasure of her beauty. "How was England?"

She laughed, a lilting sound. "Green." Her heavily lashed gray-green eyes sparkled up at him, meeting his bold gaze with her own.

"It was a bad time to come back home. I think we're about to burn up and blow away," he said, gesturing at the soot that covered his clothes.

He made no excuses for his appearance, offered no apologies. Kate found his self-assurance very appealing. It was as though he expected everyone to accept him as he was, or not at all. His laughing sapphire eyes were made more brilliant by the black smudges circling them. But he could not completely conceal the weariness in his strong features as he pushed the smoke-darkened hat back from his forehead. From beneath it, a strand of dark brown hair slipped down onto his forehead and curled there boyishly, contradicting the air of maturity he effortlessly carried on his six-foot frame. She knew he was twenty-eight, but he'd taken control of the CM ranch at the age of eighteen. She supposed he'd had no choice but to become a man at an early age, and it was written very plainly on every part of his tall, sinewy body. He was a man who could turn any woman's head, and a man who could hold his ground against any other man.

"Did you get the fire under control?" Unable to meet his eyes any longer, she looked eastward, toward the orange horizon.

Will followed her gaze. The fires were gradually eating the precious grassland acre by acre. He and everyone else hoped this wasn't going to be a repeat of '85 and '86. In those two years, the cattle industry was crippled by droughts and blizzards, and many ranchers were brought to their knees. Many others, including the huge Eastern and British cattle companies, fell into bankruptcy.

There had simply been too many people, too many cattle, and most of all, too many rich "investors" moving in to pocket all the money they could from the booming cattle industry. Many men had said that those two years had been God's way of teaching them all a lesson—a lesson it had taken him five years to recover from. It seemed the only people who had come out ahead were the parasites—people like Clayton Kincaid, the millionaire banker of Denver City.

Will hid his brooding thoughts from Kate. "No," he finally replied. "We didn't do much good, and now the wind is pushing it another way. There's

11

no telling how much grass this one is going to chew up before the wind stops."

"It usually quits in the evening," she said, then added wistfully, "I so look forward to the evenings. If the moon is up, I like to get out of the house and go riding. It seems the only reprieve."

"And where do you ride all alone at night, Kate?" Will asked, a new and provocative tone in his voice. "Isn't it a bit dangerous? You could meet some renegade night rider."

Yes, it was dangerous, but not in the way his deeply probing eyes were suggesting. Was he hinting that he might be such a rider? The idea that she might meet him some night sent her head spinning and made her feel strangely reckless. "No," she responded impulsively, telling him with her eyes that she read very plainly his unspoken implication. "I never see anyone."

"Perhaps you will."

"I'm not concerned. I stick to the old wagon road to the deserted Lander place. It's quiet out there, and the road is good and solid, but a little dusty!" She laughed. "And I don't worry about my horse falling into badger holes."

Will stored the information away. "Are you waiting for your father?" he asked, nodding in the direction of the Cattlemen's Club.

Kate was both relieved and disappointed to turn the conversation away from nighttime rides. "Yes. He had business to discuss with Mr. Kincaid."

Will tensed at the mention of the man who had so recently been occupying his thoughts. He and Kincaid, the president of the Cattlemen's Club, had never gotten along. It was something that had started as soon as Will's father, Tyler, had turned the ranch over to him ten years ago.

The CM ranch was a source of power and wealth that Kincaid dearly wanted to control. But Will refused to do business with him, choosing instead to go to a rival banking firm.

"How long have you been sitting here in the sun?" he asked. "From the flush on your cheeks, I'd say you're close to having sunstroke."

Her color deepened, but she inwardly breathed relief that he had mistaken it for the heat, or at least had been courteous enough to pretend that he didn't know it was caused in part by his presence. "About an hour, I guess."

Will nudged his tired horse a few feet away from the buggy and then stepped to the ground on a long, leanly muscled leg. "Let's go inside and tell your father you're waiting. I have some business in there myself with *Mister* Kincaid."

The disregard he had for Kincaid was evident, and for a fleeting moment Kate wondered about it, but then all thoughts fled her mind as he held out his hand to help her down. She knew instinctively that his touch would burn her flesh even though he was miles away from the heat of the fire.

"What's the matter, Kate?" he asked, his lips curving into a lopsided grin, as if he had read her thoughts.

She collected herself and tried to appear a vision of poised womanhood. "Nothing. Don't you know I can't go into the Cattlemen's Club? Women aren't allowed—except...well, you know..."

He laughed, still holding her hand. "I'm a member of the club, and you're my guest. I would hate

13

to see you faint from the heat, and if you have no more shopping to do, then it's only sensible to tell your father you're waiting."

"Could you tell him for me?"

"Any woman who rides alone beneath the moonlight on a deserted road surely can't be afraid of a building and a few old men. Come on, Kate. Where's your sense of adventure?"

Her sense of adventure was intact, but so was her sense of her father's disapproval. She wasn't afraid of a few old men but she was respectful of her father's instructions. She'd spent all her life obeying him; it wasn't easy to stop now.

Will's smile softened as though he understood some of her dilemma, but the mischievousness in his eyes deepened. "Let's break the rules and see what happens."

Such a glint of humor lurked in his eyes that Kate was enchanted. Something inside her yearned to leap the fences of her proper upbringing. Her heart pounded harder; she could not refuse his dare.

She stood up, and with both hands, he snared her small waist and whirled her to the street with easy grace. When her feet were on solid ground, his hands lingered for a long, breathless moment. Then, with an insistent grip on her elbow, he directed her toward the door of the Cattlemen's Club.

"Don't worry, Kate." He chuckled. "You won't see any men running around in their underwear. They lounge around, smoke Havana cigars, read the *Breeder's Gazette,* and conjecture about what the cattle prices will be come fall. They hire managers to run their 'spreads' and never leave their mansions in the city. But there aren't too many

14

left now. The Great Blizzard thinned out everything that was weak—both cattle and men."

Kate knew he spoke of men like Kincaid, men who had survived the Great Blizzard, not from physical strength but from financial strength. And Kincaid had been here when her father had arrived, destitute. Kincaid had given him the money to start the ranch. He had been there when Tom Diering was desperate. Kate supposed, though, that her father had always been desperate. God knows she loved him, but he was a dreamer, a man who always sought the next hill, the next green valley, a man who had always been so wrapped up in those dreams that he had never had time for her. But with Kincaid's help, Tom Diering had finally achieved his goal and was now a rich man.

She stepped into the semilit foyer, and her feet sank into a deep, thick rug. She halted at the pressure of Will's hand on her arm. As her eyes adjusted to the dimness of the interior, she searched out the room inquisitively, trying to absorb it all before she was tossed out.

They looked into the Great Room, huge, yet comfortable in a male sort of way, with heavy leather-and-horsehair sofas and chairs. The three men present glanced at her with surprise but showed no sign of reproof. After saying their hello's to Will, they went back to their business. The room smelled strongly of tobacco—a purely masculine smell and one Kate didn't mind at all. The gleaming wood-paneled walls were obviously polished and oiled several times a week to keep the dust down, and hanging from the panels were fine paintings by well-known artists.

It was indeed a cosmopolitan place—"exclusive," her father had said proudly when Kincaid had insisted that he join. "I'm one of them now, Kate. I can stand alongside the best of them." But Kate wondered, as she looked at the finery, if he truly did fit in here. Perhaps she knew her father too well, perhaps it was all in his mind, but she knew he could never be happy, not even if he had it all. There would be something, somewhere, that he had to have, something just over the next rise, and that would make him miserable, make him feel as though he were a failure. There was nothing anyone could do to change his incurable despair.

Will's hand rested on the small of her back, erasing her thoughts and forcing her to focus instead on the warmth of his fingers and the pleasant tingling his touch and his nearness aroused inside her.

"I have some business with Kincaid," he continued. "Please, after you, Kate."

Clayton Kincaid held his glass of Scotch in a slim hand that showed no traces of work. The other hand held his cigar. He remained seated in his high-backed leather chair, his legs crossed, and had no intention of rising despite the word from Harper, the English servant, that a Mr. Will Chanson and a Miss Kate Diering were in the Great Room waiting to see him and Mr. Diering.

"Tell him I'm busy," Kincaid said.

"I don't believe he will take no for an answer, sir," Harper replied in his precise English accent. "He is a disreputable sight. Apparently, he's been fighting the prairie fires, and he's making a bloody ruin of the carpet. Soot and dirt are falling everywhere, sir."

Tom Diering listened to the exchange and moved restlessly in his chair. He'd had about all the discussion he cared to have with Clayton. All the man was doing now was driving his point home. Clayton had agreed to lend him the money; that was all he cared about. He didn't want lectures on how he was going to pay it back. Clayton was his father-in-law. He wasn't worried that the man would actually foreclose on him. He was only concerned that Kate—and especially Cordelia—didn't discover he was in debt and going in further. He knew much of the problem was due to his wife's extravagance, but he didn't have the heart to deny her anything. He might lose her if he did, and he could never bear that. So she mustn't know of their financial distress. Things would recover; they always did.

What was unsettling at the moment was Clayton's sudden interest in having Kate as a wife. "She's grown into a lovely woman, Tom," he had said. "She'd be perfect standing beside me on the campaign trail for senator. Why don't you see what you can do to turn her head in my direction."

Tom looked nervously at the banker. It was not so much Kincaid's desire for Kate that worried him, as the hinted ramifications of what he would do if he didn't get her. It was another form of subtle blackmail—something Kincaid was very good at.

Kincaid's crystal-blue eyes could shatter glass as well as people, and when they met his, Tom dropped his gaze. He fought to keep his strength against the domineering man and quickly said,

"Kate's probably done with her shopping. It's time I left."

"Although I admire her spirit, she knows better than to come in here, Tom. I wouldn't want her doing something that might hurt her reputation just now. Maybe you should have a little talk with her."

"I will, Clayton. I'm sure she had a good reason. Kate is a levelheaded girl." At least he thought she was. She had always been quiet and reserved.

Arrogance flirted on Kincaid's perfect features. "I'm sure she is, if she's anything like you, Tom. No doubt it was that Chanson kid who put her up to it—don't leave just yet." He turned to Harper. "I may as well see what he wants. Send them in."

As Will stepped into the doorway behind Kate, Kincaid clenched his jaw. How dare Chanson come into this club looking like a tramp from the alleys. But the CM ranch was one of the biggest in the state. At this point, Kincaid knew he couldn't toss Chanson out of here on his ear, no matter how he yearned to do it.

Kincaid scrutinized the two, and it struck him that they looked as though they belonged together. They were both young and impetuous, disobeying society's rules. The thought irritated him. He didn't need Chanson disrupting his plans for Kate. He had enough trouble from Chanson as it was.

"What brings you to the club in such a hurry, Will, that you couldn't even clean up?" Kincaid said. "I hope you can afford to replace the carpet Harper says you've ruined."

"I can"—Will's eyes glittered with satisfied delight behind the grimy mask—"but it'll clean."

Kincaid set his short glass of liquor on a nearby table and repositioned his cigar in the other hand. He had expected such a refusal from Chanson, so he ignored it, tucking it away on the long list of abrasives already beneath Will's name.

He turned to Kate, observing her young, nicely developed form. Since she left for England, she had developed into a beautiful woman, yet he felt no immediate rush of desire to his loins. He had learned long ago that women were much too easily captured and much too hard to rid oneself of later. Somehow the challenge of possessing their bodies had been replaced by the more lusty temptation of possessing land, money, and the souls of men. The latter was the most satisfying victory.

And, of course, if a woman could stand quietly beside him and aid that ultimate goal, then he could find a use for her. People liked stability. A married man had a better chance at public office. And if a candidate's wife was young and beautiful, many men would vote for him simply because they were enchanted with her.

He quelled the surge of adrenaline at the excitement over his new plans, but then he saw Will watching him. In those smoke-circled eyes was evidence that the younger man could almost read his mind. Clayton's gaze slid to Will's hand as it rested so casually on the small of Kate's back. She didn't seem to mind, and Clayton's agitation increased; he smiled, even though he didn't feel like it.

Will was the one man who wouldn't give in to him. Clayton had thought it would be easy to take over the CM ranch when Tyler Chanson had gone back to Texas, leaving it to Will, but it had been ten years now, and he was seeing that the younger Chanson was every bit as formidable as his father. At every turn he was in Clayton's way, and now he was stepping in and drawing Kate's attention.

Will stepped forward, disrupting Kincaid's musings. He was seating Kate, something Clayton realized he should have done himself. Perturbed at the oversight, Kincaid tapped a small bell on the desk. Harper appeared in the doorway. "Bring the young lady some lemonade," he said, then added, as if it were an afterthought, "and a glass for Chanson, too."

Will sat down in the chair opposite Kincaid. "Harper, bring me whisky instead. The smoke from the fires can't be washed away with lemonade." His eyes met Kincaid's; he knew the man had purposely ordered the mild drink to make him look the child in Kate's eyes.

"I have Scotch here in my office. Will that do?" Kincaid's cool eyes leveled on Will. The challenge was always there between them, icy and growing.

"You know it won't, Clayton, so why do you always ask?"

"Just hoping to polish your edges, I suppose. With your parents permanently in Texas now, someone needs to put you on the right path."

Tom Diering, feeling the tension, stood up slowly, straightening his body as though he were seventy instead of forty-five. "Kate"—his voice was tired—"we should be going now that you're done with your shopping."

Will met her eyes and read disappointment in them, but he also saw a hint of something else— encouragement, he hoped, and to his mind's eye came a picture of her riding beneath the moonlight. Without disobeying her father, she stood up. She was so close to Will, he could feel the folds of her dress on his shoulder. The nearness washed over him with exciting warmth. Yes, he would see her again, very soon.

Tom and Kate moved to the door, but Kincaid halted their departure. "Tom"—his cold eyes rested on Kate thoughtfully and then narrowed on her father—"think about what I proposed. It could benefit all of us."

Tom glanced nervously at Kate, hoping Kincaid would say no more. Then, hastily, he put his hat on, tugging it down tight on his forehead and concealing a glimpse of fear in his expression. "I will, Clayton. Come along, Kate. Cordelia will be wondering what's happened to us."

When Tom Diering and Kate had left the room, Kincaid stood up from his easy chair and sauntered to the door, calling for Harper and then telling him that he and Will weren't to be disturbed. He closed the door and turned to Will.

Will met his steady, assessing gaze, feeling his anger rise. Their every encounter, no matter how slight, turned into a battle of wits.

Kincaid was a fine figure of a man for being in his fifties. His medium build was naturally trim. He wore his gray hair cropped close to his head, and his blue eyes were not only startling but disconcertingly shrewd. He had a strong, handsome face. His cheekbones were high and his chin square and powerful. Will knew there were plenty of women in town who wished they could tie the millionaire down, but Kincaid courted only money and power. Will had to admit that he hadn't liked the way Kincaid had looked at Kate today, although he had been more than aware of her himself. Unexpectedly, he felt protective of her, especially against this man whose every move was planned for a specific gain.

"I see you've been fighting fires. You know we can have you kicked out of this club for doing what you did today. Just because you are the largest cattle company around here doesn't mean you can walk on people. I suggest you pull in the reins, my boy, before somebody else is forced to do it for you."

Will bristled but only leaned deeper into his chair, crossed an ankle over the opposite knee, and swallowed the whisky Harper had brought. Kate's lemonade sat on the small table near his foot, untouched. She should have had a chance to drink it. She was probably suffering more than she would ever let on.

He pulled his thoughts back to Kincaid. He was fully aware of his slovenly appearance, and he wanted nothing more than to go home and wash away the smell of the fire, but he'd come here looking like this intentionally. He would have to pretend it didn't bother him if he was to be the thorn in Kincaid's side that he wanted to be.

"Yes, I've been fighting the fire—been fighting one somewhere all summer. Fighting to keep my cattle—and yours—from starving to death or burning up while you sit here in comfort drinking Scotch and smoking expensive cigars. I'm beginning to think you have an aversion to the security of your holdings. Unless you have so many holdings that ten thousand head of cattle mean nothing to you."

Kincaid's contempt deepened and the crystal

eyes turned colder as he took a step closer to Will. "I have men to do the dirty work for me. I'm not the fool you are."

"If you don't work alongside your men, Clayton, you'll wake up some morning and find them all gone—or worse, find a bullet in your back."

"And your motto is, I suppose, 'Don't ask your cowboys to do anything you wouldn't do yourself.'"

"It comes pretty close to that, but it's not just the men who work for me, it's anybody."

"Ah, integrity. From your actions and your appearance here today, I honestly thought you had abandoned any pretense of being a civilized man. And the way you dragged Kate in here was shameful and embarrassing, not only for her but for Tom as well."

"Maybe, but what is more shameful is the way you treat Tom Diering."

"If he doesn't have any backbone, that's his problem."

"How can he go against his father-in-law and still maintain peace at home? You've got him where it hurts, Kincaid, and you know it. You're the slime of this town."

Clayton Kincaid never took his eyes off Will. "I perform a service here that everyone needs and wants."

"So you left Chicago to grace this fair city with your enlightening presence? I suppose your tactics are admired by the business world. How many men have you lent money to at twenty-four percent and then foreclosed on the following year when they couldn't make the payment? You've acquired a lot of land and cattle that way, haven't you?"

Kincaid shrugged. "What did you come here for, Chanson? If you thought you were going to have me fighting fires out of sympathy for your appearance and your sad stories, the ploy didn't work."

"I should have known you'd never consent to some 'honest' work." Will stood up and slapped at his pants with his dirty hat, succeeding in arousing enough soot to fill the air. He turned to the door and derived some pleasure from seeing Clayton trying to swish the air clean of the floating particles. "I came here to tell you that your manager and his family got burned out today. Just thought you'd like to know."

Kincaid's astute eyes narrowed. So now he'd have to have another cabin built for his manager. It didn't bother him; it wouldn't cost much. There was something more important bothering him at the moment, and although it galled him to do it, he had to ask the younger man's opinion.

He tried to be more congenial as he dug for information. "Wait." He forced a smile to his straight lips as Will turned to face him. "What's this fool talk about everybody selling cattle just because of the drought? Tom owes me money, but I tried to tell him not to panic and sell anything right now. Prices are way down. He couldn't make ·a dime. He'd just be giving them away."

"So you just lent him more money." Will was incredulous, but it appeared he was accurate in his assumption. "That was generous of you. Why didn't you just give him a new rope and tell him to go hang himself?" Will shook his head in disbelief, pulled the door open farther, and covered his dark hair with the grimy hat. "Tom's right, selling is the thing to do right now. Giving away a live cow is easier on a man's conscience than having to watch the buzzards eat a dead one. It's called 'minimizing your losses,' Clayton."

The door closed behind Will, and Kincaid stared at it. He'd gotten his answer, but not exactly in the manner he'd wanted. Damn Chanson. He would smash him someday. He'd find a way.

Chapter 2

Tom Diering wished he could gallop the black mare away from the Cattlemen's Club, but he could not let his desires rule his better judgment. She was a good horse; he didn't want to kill her in the heat. Besides, he knew a man couldn't run from himself, from his pain and his anger and what he was and what he was always destined to be. He honestly believed he could have made it this time if Clayton wasn't holding the purse strings to the ranch. Clayton wouldn't let him make a move, or sell a cow, without his consent first. It was *his* collateral, he said, and Tom supposed that much was true.

Kate sat quietly next to her father, feeling his anxiety as strongly as she felt the cotton dress sticking to her skin. Away from Denver, the buggy skirted the dry prairie, and in the distance an orange flush still draped the horizon. "Didn't your business with Clayton go as expected?" she asked, looking straight ahead at the mare's neck dripping with sweat.

Diering adjusted the flat leather reins in his big, weathered hands. In his hunched position the black suit coat he wore appeared too big, although he was a big-boned, rangy man nearly as tall as

27

Will Chanson but thinner in the chest. Kate dabbed at her brow again and wondered why he didn't remove his coat, why he didn't seem to notice the smothering heat.

"It was an issue involving the Cattlemen's Club," he said in a stern, tight-lipped way. "It had nothing to do with the ranch."

Kate wasn't sure why she doubted the truth of his reply, but perhaps it was because she saw the wrinkles of concern in his forehead that had, in the past, always signified some personal worry. Her father didn't take to women telling him what to do or giving him their opinions when it didn't concern them, especially regarding the ranch. Yet she'd helped him a great deal with the ranch, and she had done it because she enjoyed it. It was better to be outside doing men's work than inside in the company of her stepmother, Cordelia, the twenty-seven-year-old beauty who was eighteen years her father's junior.

Kate sighed. Sometimes her father could be a peculiar man, a man whose motivations escaped her, but yet she held her regard for him because he *was* her father, and she tried to understand him as best she could.

She watched the land slip by. The drought had taken its toll on the grass. Still, many of the ranchers were holding their herds regardless and praying for a mild winter with light snows that wouldn't cover what little remained. Kate knew, though, that God did not answer all prayers.

"Maybe we should sell some of the cattle," Kate said suddenly, her thoughts emerging into words she hadn't intended.

Tom Diering glanced sharply at his daughter.

Surely she couldn't have known why he had really gone to talk to Clayton? He slapped the reins against the mare in a nervous gesture, but the horse ignored them, somehow knowing it wasn't a command. Tom knew the risks of keeping the cattle, and he'd wanted to sell them, but Clayton had scoffed at him. All Clayton saw was the profits to be made in the industry. He conveniently omitted the risks because, for him with his millions, there were no risks. Clayton looked out for his own interests and figured that if Tom sold his cattle now at giveaway prices, he wouldn't be able to pay the full amount of the loan back. What Clayton failed to see was that if he lost a large number of cattle this winter, he wouldn't be able to pay back anything, even interest.

Tom felt trapped. He was getting in deeper and deeper, and although Clayton had been good about financing him for ranch improvements and living expenses, Clayton had hinted today that he would have to start receiving something back. Tom shook his head in frustration; Kincaid didn't understand the way things were out here. He didn't understand it at all. You couldn't simply tuck a cow away somewhere until conditions were to your choosing.

He snapped at Kate, saying words he didn't mean, but he couldn't let her find out about his desperate situation. "I know what I'm doing, girl! I'll sell the cattle when I see fit. I'm not about to give them away."

Kate sat back against the unyielding leather seat and looked away.

Tom clicked to the mare, and she picked up speed for a few paces before slowing once again from the heat. Damn, but Kate had always seen right through him, and he didn't like it when a woman could do that. A man had to have his pride and his secrets, but he'd never been able to hide his weaknesses from her. She watched in silence and saw his very soul.

He glanced at her sidelong. Maybe he should take Clayton's proposal more seriously. With his financial situation the way it was, it might be to his advantage to direct Kate's romantic interests toward Kincaid. As Clayton's wife, Kate would be well taken care of and highly respected for the rest of her life. And, of course, Kincaid had insinuated that there would be security in it for Tom as well. But he wanted Kate to be happy. Above all else, he wanted what was best for her, even though he knew he wasn't good at showing it.

He had always been too busy; he'd never been close to her. She'd gone her way, raised herself. He felt guilty about it, as guilty as he felt for bringing her mother out West in her fragile condition. Meline had never been strong, but Kate wasn't like her at all, except in looks. Kate was as strong and wild as the land.

That, in itself, would make it harder to convince her to marry Clayton, but he didn't like her being with Chanson the way she had been today. He'd like to know how that had come about, but he wasn't going to bring it up and thereby make her more determined to see him.

He had to admit that Will was a worker, and he was smart, but he had what he had because he'd been given it. Tom had never had the kind of breaks and luck that made other men rich. In ten years, Will had changed from a determined kid set out to prove himself to the position of a highly respected cattleman. He had that respect everywhere he went—except maybe with Kincaid. At twenty-eight, Will had it made, and here Tom was forty-five and still struggling.

Kate refrained from saying anything else, and her father retreated into a glum silence. Her thoughts shifted to the moments she'd spent in Will's company. It was easy enough to recall the feel of his hand on her waist, and it was much more pleasant than trying to make conversation with her father. There had been a flirting light in Will's eyes, and she wondered if he looked at all women that way. Her lips curved into a smile at the way he had, in a mere glance, surveyed her from head to foot with obvious approval.

Excitement built inside her again, and she pushed her father's brooding problems from her mind. The sun was nearly down. It would be cooling off soon. There would still be a full moon tonight, easily lighting the road to the old Lander place. As soon as it touched the eastern horizon, she would slip quietly from the house...

Will stepped down from the saddle. His feet burned as if they had been on fire. The last light of day helped him see as he led his horse to the tack room. He'd stayed too long in the saloon with the others, and he'd drunk more whisky than he'd needed, but it still hadn't dulled his senses enough to stop his mind from churning over the day's events.

After turning his horse loose in the corral and putting up his gear, Will walked wearily to the house. The heat inside was oppressive, even though Lorna, Bart's wife and Will's housekeeper, had left the windows open to catch the cooling evening breezes. Since the rains had stopped, the winds blew down from the mountains, spreading the dust, as fine as flour, over everything and into every nook and cranny. But the dust problem soon was made trivial by the hundred-degree heat, and the former was easier to put up with than the latter.

Will climbed the stairs to his room and gratefully collapsed into the chair by the bed. With tired, aching arms, he pulled his boots off. He stripped from his sooty clothes and kicked them into a heap in the corner and out of the way. With one purpose in mind, he found clean clothes and hurried to the bathing room. There, he took a towel from the shelf and wrapped it around his trim middle. On bare feet and with clothes and boots in hand, he hurried to the swimming hole to cool off.

The moon was just rising, washing the countryside with its silver glow. It tipped the trees and struck its light onto the water. The hole, manmade and fed by the creek, faced the big house. All the men used the swimming hole, and Will was surprised to find it empty now.

Reaching the water, he forgot his fatigue, tossed the towel aside, and dove in gracefully, barely making a splash. The cold shocked his heated body, but he struck out for the opposite bank with long, powerful strokes. After he had swum four laps, he languished in a backstroke that served only to keep him afloat while he relaxed.

He closed his eyes and thought of Kate again. There was a feistiness in her and a femininity that blended together to make her a strong woman. Weak women had never appealed to him, and even though Kate was quiet and obeyed her father, Will knew she wasn't weak.

She was a paradox, in a way. As a young girl, she had dressed in a baggy shirt and a leather skirt, riding her horse as though the two of them were intent on beating the wind. Today she wore a dress and seemed all prim and proper, like a lady. He couldn't help but wonder, though, if both sides of her were placed back to back, what kind of woman would be there waiting in the middle.

He glanced at the moon, moving away from the trees now. He stepped from the water and reached for his towel. It was a good night to stay outside, a good night to take a moonlit ride.

There was no color to the land, but the illumination of the moon drew everything into vivid shapes of black and white. It was nearly as light as day, but in the stillness of the night, he heard the hoofbeats of Kate's horse long before he saw the two of them galloping down the curving band of road. From behind her rose the dust from her horse's hooves, lingering in the still air before drifting away across the prairie.

He nudged his horse from the stand of cottonwood trees that lined the small creek. He gauged her speed and her distance and with perfect timing edged his mount into a gallop that soon brought him to her side. He saw her smile as she recognized him, but she only stretched out farther along her horse's neck, forcing it to a greater speed. Sparked by the excitement of a race, Will needed little urging to get his horse to meet the challenge.

The thundering of hooves pounded in Kate's ears, as did the vibrant beating of her heart. Her hat left her head, falling to her back and held there by the string encircling her neck. Her hair fell loose in a thick mass nearly to her waist and was blown in a wild, twisting disarray. Faster and faster she urged the long-legged mare that gladly tried to outdistance the steed at her side. Up ahead, she saw the bulk of the Lander cabin, darker than the night that surrounded it. With one last surge of speed, the mare shot past the stallion by a head, but then, laughing, Kate gradually leaned back in the saddle and drew her mare to a halt.

The horses circled around one another until their owners had quieted them. Kate was alive with the thrill of the race; it was bright in her eyes when she looked at Will. "I won."

There was an intensity between them as their eyes met, and both Will and Kate struggled to regain their breath after the fierce ride. This was the Kate Will remembered as a child—riding like the wind on the range, challenging her father's ranch hands. With her hair loose and windblown, she did not look like the prim and proper lady he'd seen this afternoon, and yet both were equally appealing to him.

Will stepped to the ground and placed a hand on the mare's bridle to stop her prancing. "Let's walk," he said, extending his other hand toward Kate.

Hesitating at first, she finally accepted his offer and easily swung her leg over the cantle of the saddle and to the ground. Hand in hand they began to walk, leading the horses behind.

Now that the sound of running hooves and

laughter had drifted away with the billows of dust, the sounds of the night returned: an owl making his occasional hoot atop a distant tree; the cry of a nightbird from the mountains; the sound of frogs in the water and crickets in the grass.

They walked to a group of trees and, still holding Kate's hand, Will leaned against the trunk of a cottonwood. From beneath the brim of his big hat, he gazed down at Kate. The white light outlined her tall, slender figure and her expression was one of anticipation. Will took a deep breath to steady a sudden breathless sensation, almost as if he had run the race instead of the horse. "I was hoping you would come."

She felt more than a bit nervous, but she too would have been greatly disappointed if he hadn't come. She took a step closer and tilted her head back as she met his gaze. She felt the temptation and the danger that lurked in the unknown and the untried.

With only a slight hesitation, his arm encircled her small waist and carefully, almost as if she were a fragile piece of china, he drew her against him and held her there in the strength of that one arm. Distinctly, he felt her soft body making its lasting impressions on his own, as well as on his mind: the thrust of her breasts against his chest through the thin cotton of her blouse, and the feel of her perfectly curved hips clothed only in the soft, supple leather of her split riding skirt.

He knew he should not be as bold with her as he had been with other women, but he could never remember wanting any other woman the way he wanted her now. He tilted his head down and, drawing his other arm around her, simultaneously lifted her to her tiptoes and into his full embrace. Kate's lips quivered as she tried to refuse his advance, but it was fruitless. Although she knew this wasn't proper, she couldn't fight the desire to know what it would be like to kiss this man. Will had always made her heart beat faster and now his closeness overpowered her.

Kate put her arms around him, feeling the solid muscles beneath her fingers, muscles hidden by his white cotton shirt and snug-fitting black vest that left no guessing as to the width of his chest or the narrowness of his waist. Her breath escaped her, pushed from her as the sturdy wall of his chest pressed into her breasts. His lips took not just one kiss now but toyed with her teasingly. Finally, he drew his head back from hers a few inches and, breathing heavily, looked deeply into her eyes.

He released her, and taking her hand in his once again, started to walk in the dry meadow that surrounded the old Lander homestead.

A new and glorious feeling swelled inside her. The heavy thudding of her heart barely slowed. His nearness was distracting, more so now than ever. Now she knew how his body felt against hers, and she was a little shocked by just how much she longed for his embrace again.

"Did you have a hard time getting away?" he asked.

She shook her head. "You know there's no secrecy on the ranch, with the cowboys roaming everywhere or lounging around in the evenings by the bunkhouse, but no one pays any attention to my night rides anymore. My father balked at first, but Cordelia was more than happy to see me out of the house, and I think she finally convinced him not to worry."

Will stopped and turned to her. "Your father had reason to worry." He lifted a hand and fingered the long chestnut mane of her hair. "This would make a very lovely scalp on an Indian's belt. He overlooked one thing, though."

"And what is that?" She responded in kind to the mischievous gleam in his eyes.

"The Indians have been subdued, but not the cowboys."

Unable to stop himself, Will turned the waist-length mass of hair in his hand, winding it around his fingers. With a gentle movement, he put just enough pressure on it to tip her head back to the angle he desired. He studied the softness of her lips again, their perfect form and fullness, the shape that molded so well to his own. Slowly, he lowered his head and tasted their sweetness again.

He moved his lips to her cheek, and then her throat, finally whispering in her ear, "Are you aware of what you're doing to me, Kate? Do you have any idea at all?"

She opened her eyes, pulling herself from the pleasant intoxication of his touch. Through black, spiky lashes he gazed down at her, still questioning, and for the first time she realized he needed and wanted more than she was ready to give. Yet how could she deny him and still hold him? She was not experienced at the games of love, but she was more than ready to learn.

She touched his arm and held the rich blue gems of his eyes captive with hers. From his arm, her hand lifted to the strong angles of his clean-shaven face and to the black moustache above the firm, generous lips—lips that easily drew up on one side when he smiled, as though he saw through the world and everyone in it. And then, without a word, she stepped away from him and once again began walking.

Immediately, Will moved with her, keeping pace, understanding her answer and accepting it—for now. "Is your father going on roundup soon?"

"Yes, probably within the week. He'll be back for the Cattlemen's Ball, I presume. He doesn't dance—much to Cordelia's chagrin—he simply stands on the sidelines, but Cordelia wouldn't miss it for the world. She'd have Clayton take her before she'd miss an opportunity to flirt with all the—" She caught herself. What she was about to say wasn't polite, and her personal opinions should be kept to herself.

Will smiled. "All the men?" When she nodded, he continued. "It's no secret. You've been gone for four years, but everyone knows about Cordelia. Your father is very tolerant, or very trusting."

"He sees no wrong in her."

Will loved to watch the animation in her face as she talked. Her face had memorable and strong features—defined cheekbones, firm jaw, a perfectly proportioned forehead and straight nose. Her eyes were a perplexing color, and they were her dominant feature. Wide and full of expression, they easily revealed her emotions, even those she might try to hide. He saw strength in the sturdy way she pulled her shoulders back, and even though there was shyness and innocence in those gray-green orbs, they glinted with something deeper, perhaps defiance or determination, and a lust for the unknown.

Kate continued. "I suppose you'll be attending, despite your differences with Clayton?"

Will stopped walking. "I don't know if I will or not. It all depends."

"On what?" she asked, enjoying his closeness. His blue eyes were assessing her thoroughly, so thoroughly that she suddenly felt a bit unnerved.

"It all depends," he continued, "on whether you would consider going with me." Will realized he had never been unsure with any woman before, but now he found himself strangely fearful that she might refuse.

The rapid beat of her heart made her wonder if the pounding could be seen through her blouse. She wasn't sure what it was she was feeling toward Will, but an instinct deep inside ruled her decision, which was nothing more than the simple desire to be with him.

"Of course, Will. I'd love to go with you."

The sparkle in his eyes changed to a smoldering glow; its intensity was focused on her and caused a pleasant shiver to run through her. "I want to see you before that, Kate. That's still a month away. Will you be going with your father this year on roundup like you used to?"

She too didn't want to wait a month to see him. "No, my father thinks it's no place for me anymore. He didn't mind when I was a child, but so much has changed since he married Cordelia. She has tried so hard to make a lady out of me."

"That shouldn't have been difficult."

She chuckled. "Cordelia thinks it's a hopeless job."

"I'm sorry you won't be going on the roundup. I'm leaving day after tomorrow myself. It's a long time until the ball," he said. "Could you meet me here again tomorrow night?"

There was an urgency in his tone as his hand slipped along her shoulder to rest on the heated flesh of her neck. She closed her eyes momentarily against the rush of feeling that overwhelmed her body and her mind. When her eyelids flickered open, his eyes were still on her as he waited for her answer.

"I—I can't, Will. Mr. Kincaid is coming for dinner at seven o'clock."

The pressure of his hand on her neck was enough to throw her off balance until she was pressed against him once again. A kiss found her lips, one not so tentative as those that had gone before, one that silently possessed her as the burning iron of a brand would do.

"Mr. Kincaid," he said bitterly, when he finally released her. "And is he coming to see you? Or is he coming to see Cordelia and your father?"

She was confused by his attitude, by the implication of jealousy. "Why would you think he's coming to see me?"

"Because he's single, and because you're beautiful."

Her lips parted in a smile. "I'll see you in a month," she said, knowing she couldn't trust herself to meet alone with him again.

"A month is too long," he objected in a rough voice, yet he knew there was nothing either of them could do about it.

Kate left his loose embrace reluctantly, caught her breath, and wondered at the tumultuous feeling he had left churning inside her. "I had better go now, Will."

"I'll ride with you."

Alarm lit her eyes. "No! My father—it wouldn't be wise if he knew I had met you out here."

"Why not? He'll know my feelings soon enough."

She stepped away from him, nervously considering the implications of her growing attraction for him. "He doesn't like you, Will."

"I've felt that for a long time, but I've just never known why."

"I doubt he even knows why, but Dad spends so much time with Mr. Kincaid that he is influenced by his way of thinking in most everything."

"I don't care how they feel about me," he said truthfully. "My only concern is that they don't sway you to their way of thinking."

"I do my own thinking."

He breathed a bit easier at the reassurance, but a lot could happen in a month, even a day. With that thought in mind, he reached for the blue bandana at his throat and untied it. He slipped it around her shapely neck and loosely tied it in the front. "Just a little something to remind you of tonight, Kate."

They kissed one last time, and he helped her mount her horse. Will rode with her as long as she would allow, and then he turned his horse south, glancing over his shoulder occasionally at her small departing figure in the glow of the moon. It seemed he'd always known her, seemed he'd just been waiting until she arrived. She had turned his life completely around, and it had happened in a day.

Chapter 3

The next day, as dusk slipped over the land, Will finished preparations for the roundup and then led his horse to the tack room to unsaddle it. He wished he could have gone to see Kate again, but she was in the company of *Mister* Kincaid tonight.

Suddenly, he was startled by footsteps in the soft dirt behind him, and turning around in the evening light, he saw the carefree grin of Dexter Marlow, one-time cowboy turned prospector. It'd been six months since he'd been around. "You shouldn't sneak up on a man like that, Dexter."

"You shouldn't be so jumpy," Dexter responded with a big grin. "Or you shouldn't be so preoccupied."

Will hung the saddle on the bench in the tack room and then led his horse to the corral. Dexter followed along behind. "What brings you down out of the mountains this time?"

Will had never known how old Dexter was, but he guessed him to be around thirty-seven or -eight. Dexter's face looked like it had been chipped from granite by a sculptor who needed more practice with the chisel. He was always nervous and unsure of himself. He picked his words carefully, not wanting to offend anyone, but he loosened up and joked with Will more than he did with most people.

Finally, he said, "Saw some color up behind Pike's Peak, but I had to quit and come down for some grub." He moistened his lips and glanced at Will in hopeful anticipation. He made a motion to tuck in his filthy shirt, which was missing a few buttons and revealed the hairless white skin of his ballooned stomach. He was a big man with massive shoulders and heavy thighs. His arms were bulky, and he was overweight, but his face didn't carry any of it. His face really didn't fit his body at all.

Will pulled the bridle from his horse's head and it gladly walked away from them, circling the dusty corral to find a suitable spot where it then lowered itself to its front knees and finally to its side and back, kicking vigorously to get the sweat and the feel of man and saddle from its back.

Will turned to Dexter and closed the gate behind him. "Need some money?" Dexter always needed money and Will had been grubstaking him now for several years. The man didn't ask for much, and he swore that someday he was going to hit the mother lode. Will knew his kind, the kind who enjoyed the hunt more than the find. Dexter was so honest it hurt. He was a pathetic man who wanted everyone to like him—which they did—but who felt there was no possible way they could.

Licking his chapped lips again, Dexter grinned nervously. "I guess you know me pretty well, don't you?"

Will chuckled as he returned to the tack room

with Dexter on his heels, the man's big feet slapping heavily on the ground behind him. Will hung the bridle on a long nail. "That's the only time you come around," he joked. "How much do you need?"

"Well, I *would* come around more often," Dexter started to apologize, "but I can't be no good here. I get restless just knowing I should be looking for the gold. I know it's there." He stopped abruptly as though he had said way too much. "Oh, twenty-five dollars ought to buy me a pretty good grubstake for a while."

Will led the way to the house. "I'm going to expect a return on my money, you know." It was the same thing he always said, but it made the miner feel like the money wasn't a handout. Actually, Will didn't expect any of it back.

"Oh sure, Will. Sure. You can count on that. I tell you, I found a nugget the size of my fist...in a strange place, too. It's not far from a granite outcropping at the base of a mountain, and I've got a feeling in my bones. I know there's been some salting and a lot of hoaxes over there, but I just got a feeling."

"They say the formations are all wrong over there. Maybe you're wasting your time."

"I don't care what they say. Gold is where you find it."

Will opened the door to the two-story house, and Dexter followed him in. After hanging his hat on the tree near the door, Will strode across the spacious main room, which contained the fireplace, sofa, and chairs, to the safe. The room didn't fit the standard design of a parlor—it was more informal and relaxed—and here everyone met and company was greeted. There hadn't been many changes in the house in twenty-eight years, but Will liked it that way.

With his back to Dexter, Will spun out the combination and pulled open the heavy door. He counted out thirty dollars and handed it to Dexter, whose stubby fingers hesitantly reached for it.

After locking the safe up again, Will straightened to his full height. "Can you stay and have a bite to eat? I imagine Lorna's got something cooked."

Dexter licked his lips and squinted up at Will, a perpetual habit from being outdoors in the sun. Some concern wrinkled his brow. "Ain't you got yourself a wife yet? I thought you'd be married by now."

"You never had the good sense to find a woman to wash your underwear, Dexter," Will teased, "so don't be preaching to me."

The miner fidgeted, embarrassed, and his eyes darted off, taking in everything around him while his face turned a vivid red. "I never got me a wife 'cause I never found a woman who liked to hunt for gold, but you ain't got that excuse. Besides"— a pained expression made him look even more pathetic as he inevitably told the truth, or what he believed to be the truth—"there ain't no woman who would want me."

The conversation wasn't new, and Will knew that deep inside Dexter would love to have a wife. He just considered himself too homely, and his extreme shyness did the rest. And there was some truth in the fact that she'd have to like to look for gold. "Like I said, Dexter, you won't know until you try."

They stepped through the door to the kitchen and the aroma of chicken made Will realize just how hungry he was. He'd be leaving tomorrow on roundup, and this would be his last good meal for a month.

Lorna had her back to them, finishing up the dishes. She was a small woman, classic-featured and pretty, with light brown hair and blue eyes. Her baby daughter was playing on the floor with some wooden blocks one of the cowboys had made for her. She was the image of her mother.

"There's some chicken in the warming oven, Will."

"I hope there's enough for two. I'd like to feed Dexter and get him on down the trail before he worries himself sick over my single state."

Lorna pushed a stray strand of hair from her cheek and, smiling, went back to washing dishes. She understood the banter that went on between them. "Yes, I believe there's plenty."

Will noticed that Lorna looked tired. After he and Dexter had washed and filled their plates, he said, "As soon as you finish, Lorna, go on home. I'll clean up these plates of ours."

After Lorna and her daughter left, Dexter swallowed the large mouthful of food he'd been wallowing around on his bad teeth and said, "You ought to have a bunch of kids yourself, Will. This here is a mighty big house to be spendin' nights in it alone."

No one knew that better than Will. He remembered when his whole family still lived here. It had never been quiet, except when they were all asleep. He had always thought of the house as a queen standing on the hill, for a house was a woman: strong, graceful, always there with warm, open arms. He loved this house in particular because it had been his mother, Roseanne McVey, who had had it built just before his birth when she and three vaqueros had decided to stay in Colorado after her father had been killed on a cattle drive to Texas.

Will's father had told him what had happened all those years ago, not even keeping Will's illegitimate birth a secret. It didn't bother Will to know it; the important thing was that his parents had been deeply in love, and that although they'd been separated for a year, their love had been strong enough to draw them back together again. Will knew that nothing but death could ever separate them again.

He hoped to have a marriage like theirs someday. He smiled to himself, for immediately Kate Diering came to mind.

"What makes you think I spend them all alone?" he said, letting Dexter think he was a free-wheeling bachelor, as most of the boys assumed.

Dexter shrugged and took another bite. "Because I know you wouldn't bring one of those girls from town here in plain sight of your hired hands. You're the boss of this outfit, and you know you got to keep their respect."

"Tell me, Dexter," Will said, changing the subject. "How much of your mother lode are you going to cut me in for?"

Dexter wiped his greasy fingers on his dirty pants and picked up his coffee cup with both hands while he contemplated his answer. After a long gulp of the hot liquid, he said, "Well, I could cut you in for one half." His voice rose on a question, as if he wondered whether that would be acceptable.

"Sounds to me you're pretty sure you won't hit anything," Will joked. "Otherwise, you wouldn't be so generous."

"I didn't state all the conditions." Dexter was loosening up a bit. Will was one of the few people who didn't treat him like he was dumb, and he appreciated that. "If the hole has to be mined, and coming from granite it won't be no placer diggings, you're gonna have to find a big outfit who will mine it."

Will's interest wasn't in Dexter's mining visions, although he tried to keep the conversation going. Instead, he kept thinking of Kate in his arms in the moonlight. She had surely grown into a beauty. He nodded absently to Dexter's last comment. "Sure. It sounds fair enough to me. Mother always said not to put all your eggs in one basket."

"I know you got a lot of baskets, Will, but I'll bet you don't have gold in any of them."

"No," he acknowledged, his mind still on Kate's visage. "I guess that's one thing I don't have."

After Dexter had taken his money and headed toward town for his supplies, Will washed the dishes, turned off the lamps in the kitchen, and turned toward the darkened living room. Without lighting a lamp from the foyer, he moved up the stairs to the room he used to share with his brother, Lee. He'd kept it, although he knew he could use the master suite now. But the master suite wasn't a place for a man alone. It was a place to take a woman, to make love, to make children.

It hadn't been used since the day his parents had left. With them had gone the trusting vaquero, Diego Padilla, and their robust house-keeper, Lolita Alvarez, who'd gone back, as she said, to "die in Texas." And she had, shortly upon their return there. His uncles Rayce and Keane Chanson had spent some time with them on occasion but were now permanently settled on ranches of their own with their families, and they didn't have time to come around much anymore. He even missed the constant chatter and giggling of his baby sister, Rena, who was now a young lady of eighteen.

In the dark, he found the chair that waited for him by the window. He gladly collapsed into its support and pulled his boots off. The thud they made on the hardwood floor emphasized the emptiness of the house. Unexpectedly, an image of Clayton's face appeared in his mind, and he couldn't help but wonder what Kate would be doing while he was gone.

Chapter 4

Kate removed her riding hat and placed it on the foyer table. She caught her reflection in the gold-framed mirror that hung over the small wooden table. Automatically, she straightened the blue bandana around her neck that Will had given her, then tried to smooth the tangled mass of windblown hair.

From the parlor came a rustle of silk, and in seconds, blond Cordelia moved into the room with an elegance that Kate presumed she'd been born with, for it was much too natural to have been learned. Kate had, in the beginning, been intimidated by the woman ten years her senior, and she had felt envious of the flaxen hair, perfect face, and eyes as bright blue as the Colorado sky. Next to Cordelia, Kate felt plain, and whatever she wore came out looking drab. Cordelia's clothes could outdo anything anybody in Denver might have designed. Yet, there was a flaw in Cordelia, and as Kate had gotten to know her true character over the years, she no longer considered her a woman worthy of envy.

As usual, Cordelia swept a critical eye over Kate's attire: a cotton blouse, split riding skirt, and tall boots. "I see you finally made it back. Did you have to fix any fences?"

The question was asked snidely, for Cordelia did not approve of Kate helping in any way on the ranch. Kate enjoyed it and, for the most part, the men didn't mind as long as she didn't try to compete with them or take over their jobs. "It isn't proper for a lady," Cordelia had said time and time again, but Kate shrugged it off.

"Only a couple of stretches needed repairing," Kate replied as she moved to the stairs that would take her to the second story and her room.

"You're late. My father will be here any time for dinner, and Aimée has the meal nearly prepared. As I've told you before, she does not appreciate having to keep it warm or serving it cold. It is hardly a good reflection on her fine talents."

Before Cordelia had married Kate's father, they'd had a cook from town whom Kate enjoyed helping, but Cordelia had been appalled that they didn't have someone more professional. They also did not have a housekeeper, but both were hired immediately when Cordelia moved in.

The cook was Aimée DuBois, a short, skinny woman with a long, skinny face and brown eyes. She was unmarried, middle-aged, and bitter. She had left France for a new life in the United States, but the West simply didn't match up to her expectations of wealth, power, and opportunity. If she hadn't cut all ties in order to leave, she would have returned to Europe. Aimée kept to herself and her dislike for her situation was evident in the meals she prepared. Cordelia, of course, found her exquisite in every way.

On the other hand, their housekeeper-maid,

Minnie Gillespie, was an unpretentious red-headed widow from Denver. She was barely five feet tall and was shaped like a beer keg. She was happy and pleasant and was Kate's only ally in the house.

Kate started up the stairs, hoping to avoid further confrontation with Cordelia. "If the meal is nearly ready, then I need to change."

"You certainly do." Cordelia's full, heart-shaped mouth twisted and thinned, showing her disapproval of the soft leather riding skirt and the blue bandana around her neck, which clashed horribly with the light green blouse she wore. And yet there was something different about Kate, something she'd noticed last night when Kate had come back from her ride. She was smiling, happy; her eyes were bright, and there had been a high flush to her cheeks. The look was still there today. If she didn't know better, she would think it was the look of a woman in love.

Cordelia's eyes narrowed at the thought of it. She took a second look at the blue bandana; it was definitely a man's style. Surely, the girl wasn't sneaking away from the ranch to meet some stupid cowboy? She'd get herself in trouble, and then they'd all have to bear the shame of her sullied reputation.

Cordelia watched Kate take the stairs. "Kate." She turned. "Yes?"

Cordelia was about to question her, then decided against it. She'd discuss it with Tom first. She moved a pale hand along her waist, smoothing material that was stretched tautly over the corset that thinned her figure even more and pushed her already perfect bosom into larger proportions.

"Wear something decent tonight, will you? I don't want you to disgrace me in front of my father."

Kate took a deep breath and started up the stairs again. She'd heard all the remarks before and some that were even worse. Her stepmother chose to be at odds with Kate at every opportunity. Kate had tried to please her at first, but soon found that impossible.

She proceeded to her room once again, not bothering to respond to Cordelia's taunt. She had reached the second-floor landing when the front door opened and her father came in. She turned back and silently watched the exchange. Cordelia smiled charmingly, took her husband's hat, hung it up, kissed him on the cheek, and spoke to him with a kindness that belied her true character.

Her father loved Cordelia in the same desperate way he lived: as if it all might end tomorrow. She could understand why he was so taken with the blonde: She was the epitome of beauty. He'd fallen madly in love with her the moment she'd arrived from Chicago. She too had seemingly fallen in love with him, but Kate always wondered whether Cordelia had enough room in her heart and mind to love anyone but herself.

Diering ran a hand down the length of her arm, but Cordelia pulled away and laughed apologetically. "You're dusty, Tom."

He stepped away from her and toward the parlor, where he kept a few bottles of liquor. Cordelia followed him. There was a lengthy silence below, and all Kate heard was the rustle of silk again and the many petticoats beneath. Then the French doors closed, blocking off any more of their conversation. Guessing the discussion would be about her, Kate moved down the hall to her room.

To her surprise, she found Minnie filling the large tub in the small bath area of the elegant room. The woman smiled warmly as Kate stopped in the doorway. "Mrs. Diering told me to have this ready for you when you came back from riding."

"She does look after me, doesn't she?" Kate's lips twisted sardonically.

Minnie's smile deepened, for she and Kate had found they could share confidences the very day Kate had returned from England. "You know how things have to be when she is expecting company. Spotless. Even you."

"Yes, we must all conform to Cordelia's conceptions of life—not that I didn't *want* to bathe," she hastily added and watched Minnie hesitate on the verge of laughter. "I just didn't think there would be time. I'll get my robe."

From her wardrobe she removed her cotton dressing gown and draped it over a chair near the bath alcove, recessed from the main part of the bedroom and draped in sky-blue curtains from ceiling to floor on all four sides. The front curtains could be drawn for privacy and to keep drafts out. The ostentatious design was "a must" after Cordelia had seen it done in Europe. Most homes were lucky to have a bathing area off the kitchen for everyone to share, but Cordelia had designed one for every bedroom.

When Minnie left, Kate locked the door and quickly stripped off her riding clothes and undergarments, then gratefully sank into the warm water. She knew she mustn't linger, for Clayton Kincaid would be arriving any minute, and Cordelia would not tolerate tardiness. Yet, when Kate was thoroughly scrubbed, she couldn't resist leaning back in the big tub and soaking for just five minutes before getting out, drying, and wrapping herself in the refreshing coolness of the cotton robe.

She brushed her hair until it shone and then, with Minnie's help, coiled and pinned it into a bun, dressing it up with jeweled combs placed on either side. She chose to wear a high-necked white blouse with a bodice that was heavily adorned with wide lace and was fastened up the back with tiny pearl buttons. A dark plum-colored skirt finished the outfit, conforming to her small waist perfectly with no need of a corset.

Kate selected a simple strand of pearls and matching earrings. It was silly, she admitted as she looked at her reflection in the mirror, but she imagined herself dressing for Will and wondered if he would like what he saw.

As she descended the stairs, she heard Kincaid's businesslike voice coming from the parlor. She had hoped her entry would go unnoticed, but the gray-haired banker was facing the doorway and stopped talking as soon as she stepped into the room. Cordelia turned too, her eyes narrowing in harsh scrutiny as she scanned Kate's choice of clothes, no doubt disapproving. She could have dressed like a queen and still Cordelia would not have been pleased.

With all eyes on her, Kate moved uncomfortably toward a chair, wishing she could fade into the gaudy, red-flowered drapes that Cordelia had picked. They matched the velvet on the elaborately carved rosewood chairs and sofa. Before she could find an inconspicuous spot, however, Clayton intercepted her in two easy strides, with movements as graceful and quiet on the thick rug as an elusive mountain lion moving through tall grass.

She had to admit that he *was* a handsome man, one that any woman could be easily charmed by — any woman but herself. She didn't know why she automatically excluded herself, but she had an uneasy feeling about him. *'Something' wasn't good.* Will certainly didn't like him, but he seemed to have tangible reasons, while her own were unfounded.

Clayton's smile was meant to captivate, and it did hold a fascinating quality. She noticed for the first time the details of his face: firm lips, good teeth, an aquiline nose, strong jaw, and very few wrinkles for a man his age. He had a very practiced speaking manner. "There's no need to sit, Kate, we were waiting for you. But," he said, his smile deepening, "it was worth the wait. You are very lovely, indeed. Now"—he held out his suited arm—"please allow me the privilege of escorting you to the dining room."

Clayton Kincaid had never been kind to her before; as a matter of fact, he had hardly noticed her existence. In stunned silence, she politely linked her arm through his as Cordelia and Tom led the way to the dining room. Kate noticed her father did not appear as tired as he had earlier, and he was standing much straighter now, looking his full height of six feet. She guessed that love did that to a person: lifted the burdens from their shoulders.

Kincaid helped Kate to her seat and then took

his own next to her. "It's good to have you back from England, but I must admit I was more than surprised to see you come into the Cattlemen's Club. I believe you know that isn't customary. As a matter of fact, it's quite frowned upon."

How easily he could treat her like a woman one moment and reprimand her like a child the next; it was something she did not appreciate, and it was something she would not forget. "I'm afraid you can blame my appearance on Will Chanson, Mr. Kincaid. He insisted I come inside to get out of the heat. He was afraid I was going to faint."

"Will is a reckless sort. I'm afraid it will get him into trouble one of these days. He doesn't know how close he came to being kicked out of the club altogether after that foolish stunt. Perhaps if you speak to him again, you might mention it to him."

Kate had no intention of relaying Clayton's message to Will, but she kept her thoughts to herself.

Cordelia, in the meantime, glanced first at one then at the other with curiosity. An unfounded jealousy began to gnaw at her. She had always found Will attractive, and it bothered her that he had been with Kate. Once again, she thought of the bandana Kate had worn earlier.

She tried to conceal her true emotions when she spoke. "What did Will do, Father? And what was Kate doing with him?"

Clayton turned to Kate. "I'm afraid Kate will have to tell you that." His cool eyes bit into her in a way she didn't understand, for he had been so polite only moments before.

Finally, Kate picked up her napkin from the

table and placed it over her skirt, not meeting any of her interrogators' eyes. She resented being forced to explain her actions and her whereabouts as though she were still a child of eight. But to maintain peace she replied honestly, telling what had happened the day she'd been in town. Of course, she knew she could never mention the night ride.

"You could have refused to go into the club," Cordelia said. "I'm sure Will didn't force you to break the rules."

Kate thought about Will, and she felt a blush rise to her cheeks at the remembrance of his hungry, urgent kisses and his hot, strong hands lingering on her waist.

Cordelia's sharp eyes spotted the flush. "It would appear there's a bit more to it than our dear Kate is telling." Her eyes narrowed as she watched Kate's blush deepen. "You know, Kate, you must beware of men like Will Chanson. I'd hate to see you get your heart broken. He's a rake, or so I hear. Very handsome and very eligible—one of the most sought-after men in Denver—but he isn't the kind to be content with one woman. His kind never are. He's been with too many women to be happy with one."

Kate was speechless, her words caught in a tangle of anger and humiliation. Cordelia had hit too close to the truth about her feelings toward Will and now put doubt in her heart about his true feelings for her. Was he simply using her? The thought was almost more than she could bear.

Clayton pulled a cigar from his vest pocket and went through the usual maneuvers of lighting it, toying with it for a while first and rolling it in his fingers. He wanted Kate; he just hadn't decided the best way to go about presenting himself. She showed no interest in him. He was so much older he was sure she looked on him as a father figure. He wanted to dispel that idea if she harbored it. But now Chanson had stepped in, making his task more difficult. Clayton didn't like his interference; he would have to find a way to eliminate it as quickly as possible.

He cautioned her, fortifying what Cordelia had said. "It would be wise to listen to Cordelia's advice, Kate. What I know about him is firsthand, and I can assure you, he uses women. It seems to be a game for him."

Luckily, Aimée came with the cart, which held the steaming bowls of food from the stove. As easily as the Kincaids had started the topic of Will, they ended it and went on to other things, but Kate could not dislodge their words of warning. They had said things about Will that she had never heard before from any source, and she couldn't bring herself to believe any of it. She had never seen deception of any kind in his sapphire eyes, and until she did, she would listen to her heart.

Cordelia angrily paced her bedroom floor. Her silk skirt and crinoline petticoats swished in a sound that pleased her, and that she enjoyed despite her frustration. She fanned the air with her hand, trying to cool the flush on her cheeks. There was a time when she would have been the one to catch the eye of men like Will, but not anymore, not since she'd married and "settled down." From the time she was fourteen, she'd had them clamoring for stolen moments, stolen kisses. She truly missed the adventure, excitement, and danger of those times: the secret meetings in dark, forbidden, and hidden places. Now she cursed the boredom of her life, of her bedroom.

Finally, Cordelia changed from her dress into a velvet dressing gown. She leaned back on the yellow-flowered chaise longue to try and force herself to relax. Her room adjoined Tom's, but she went into his only when sexual desire demanded a man for fulfillment. With a stiff-bristled brush in hand, she stroked the blond curls that reached down her back. It was ten o'clock, and finally Tom had come in from his usual night check outside. She could hear him moving around downstairs, in no apparent hurry to come upstairs, which suited her fine. It irritated her that he was more at home in the bunkhouse with the cowboys than he was in the main house where he belonged. It was a flaw of his she had never been able to accept.

She'd come West because of the adventure of it. In Chicago, it sounded romantic to share the bed of a rugged cattleman and ride the plains with him. Now, it was getting hard to write letters back home; there was nothing to say. It had all been an illusion. The romance wasn't real; all that was real was the dust, grime, manure, and work.

Tom had been so handsome when she'd first met him. She'd been attracted to him the way she was to Will Chanson now. But the picture he'd presented had soon faded along with the glamour, for he was just a man, nothing more. He was stubborn, backward, even a bit stupid, she'd decided. He wasn't educated and he wasn't suave. He was just a cowboy who tried to be a baron—a word that no respectable cattleman would call himself or his friends.

So when reality hit, Cordelia decided that Tom could come into her room only at her request. He hadn't been happy about it, but he had accepted it with a closed mouth like everything else she insisted upon.

She waited until she heard his boots hit the floor in the bedroom next to hers. The rustling of clothing ceased, and the bed creaked. When no more sounds came from the adjoining room, she stood up, checked her image in the cheval glass, and readjusted the gown higher over her bosom. She was going into his room only to talk.

She opened his door quietly and waited a moment for her eyes to adjust to the darkness cut only by the faint light from the window.

"Cordelia?" He rolled from his side to face her, looking much older than his years in the silver cast of the moonlight. "What is it?"

His voice was soft, holding that hopeful quality she had come to detest. "Is it so strange for a woman to come into her husband's room?"

He watched as she came forward, closing the door softly behind her. "You haven't for—"

"Yes, I know." Irritation made her tongue sharp. "It's been weeks." She had originally had thoughts of sitting on the edge of his bed, but now she moved to the chair in the corner, hating the pleading in his voice. "I've come to discuss Kate. I'm afraid the girl is heading for trouble."

Tom sat up tiredly and propped himself against the polished wooden headboard of the big double bed. "What do you mean?"

There was no concern in his voice when they

discussed Kate. "I'm so worried about her, Tom," Cordelia began, hoping to keep her true thoughts about the girl concealed. "I think she may be meeting a man — possibly Will Chanson — on these night rides she's been taking."

Tom released a tired breath and frowned. He too was concerned about this sudden development with Kate, but he felt everyone was blowing it out of proportion. True, she had come into the club with him yesterday, but for good reason. Of course, he would take action if he truly thought Kate was becoming involved with Will. He had his reasons for not liking him, but all the talk about Will being a philanderer was hogwash. He was no worse than the next cowboy, and certainly no worse than Tom himself had been before he'd found Meline and settled down. It wasn't Chanson he was worried about right now but Kincaid. Kincaid wanted Kate, and he had a way of getting what he wanted and of making other people do his bidding. Tom was afraid of what would happen to himself if he allowed Kate to marry *anyone* other than Kincaid.

He couldn't tell Cordelia about Clayton's proposal; she might find out about their financial troubles. If she learned he was nearly bankrupt, she would leave him. He would have to lie, and one lie led to two. No, it was just easier to keep his business with Kincaid private for now. "What do you propose?" he asked.

"I know how you dislike Will, so I suggest we keep them apart. We could send her back to England, or actively start looking for a suitable man for her."

Tom considered it only for a moment. He couldn't afford the fare, but he wouldn't tell Cordelia that. "No." He shook his head. "My relatives were good enough to take her in for her schooling, I wouldn't want to burden them again."

"But they said they enjoyed her." Cordelia couldn't understand how that was possible, but she felt desperate to be rid of the girl.

"I wouldn't mind seeing her married," Tom said absently, "but not Chanson. Maybe your second idea was better."

Cordelia tried another angle. "I haven't wanted to complain to you, Tom, but Kate has always treated me cruelly and without respect. I've tried to be her friend, but she refuses any effort I make." Cordelia looked away rather than at her husband; it made the lie easier. "Her presence here is affecting our relationship."

Tom thought about the problems that had been with them ever since he'd married Cordelia. There was a competition between the two of them, as there was between many women, but he saw no way to help them change their attitudes toward one another. The problem had gone away when Kate had been in England. In order to have peace at home, peace with Kincaid, peace of mind—he'd just have to find a way to send her away again, even if it was through marriage this time. "Do you know some men who would be acceptable?"

Cordelia stood up and moved to the door. She would get rid of the girl somehow. She turned her head away from him momentarily so he wouldn't see her pleased smile in the faint light. "No, I don't know anyone, but I'll talk to Daddy. He has connections." She pulled the door open. A shaft of light from the lamp in her room fell across Tom's bed. She saw the longing in his eyes again and quickly turned away. "I know you're tired, dear. I'll see you in the morning. Good night."

The door closed snugly behind her. Tom heard the click of a lock that would secure her safely in her room. He thought about the old times. He missed the carefree life of being nothing but a cowboy. There had been no men to boss, no loans to make and pay off. There had always been somebody else to worry about all that.

More than ever, though, he missed the one woman who had loved him as much as he had loved her. Together they'd made a child: Kate Meline. His wife had given her own life so that the child could live. He knew it was wrong, but deep, deep inside during those early years, he had sometimes wished it had been the child who had died instead.

But now Kate reminded him so much of her mother, and yet she was an entirely different personality. He had a different life now, a new wife— one he could never seem to satisfy, one who hated Meline's daughter. He leaned back in bed and thought of Will, of Clayton's "deals," of Cordelia's demands, and of his own expectations. Finally, he closed his eyes. He just didn't know what to do anymore.

Chapter 5

The CM ranch had not escaped the rash of ranch fires unscathed. The horses in the meadow Will surveyed shuffled through the ashes of the grass. Normally, when an area had burned, it was only a matter of time before new green shoots appeared, but in this high mountain meadow there was nothing to replace the lush grass except a few weeds that could survive without rain.

This season had been so dry that back in June the grass had already withered. Now, what hadn't burned in prairie fires was short and sparse. Will had fenced off some higher pastures next to the mountains to help with winter feed, but it wouldn't be enough to winter twenty-thousand head of cattle.

Ahead of the two riders were about one hundred head of cattle wearing the CM brand. They snorted their dislike of the burned smell their hooves stirred up. They had, no doubt, been close to a fire, and the memory was fresh in their minds.

The sun was setting behind the mountain chains that stretched in dragonlike humps along the western horizon. When the burned area was behind the men and cattle, Will moved his horse to the opposite side of the small herd and pulled him up next to Bart's mount.

"There's a hollow just beyond here. It's a good holding place," Will said. "Let's get them there, and then we'll camp for the night. We can take them home tomorrow."

When darkness had settled over them and the cattle were bedded down, Will took the first turn night herding. From atop his horse, he glanced over at the campfire and saw Bart in the flickering light, trying to settle his slender form in his bedroll. The foreman, two years older than Will, pulled his hat over his face and then, as on other nights, began to sing softly in his melodious voice. The crooning not only helped the cattle relax, but helped Will as well. After a few verses, Bart was silent, and Will figured he had gone to sleep.

Will didn't have to circle the herd, since it was a small group. He positioned himself before them and only occasionally lifted the reins to move on a leisurely stroll in a wide circle around them, to keep himself awake more than anything.

Now, as he circled the dark humps of cattle in the hollow, he was disappointed that they hadn't found more. Normally, many more moved into the tall, lush mountain parks in the fall when the grass on the plains began to dwindle. But he and Bart had found so many dead carcasses that he had soon quit counting. It was a bad omen. He'd only had the CM for ten years and he was still recovering from the blizzard of '86. If he went under now, it would appear to all that he had failed because his dad had gone back to Texas, leaving him in charge.

There seemed to be only one bright spot in the

midst of his problems and that was Kate. She had truly been tempting there in the moonlight. Being with her stirred a new feeling inside him that he'd never felt for a woman before. He had to admit, his mind hadn't been on the roundup this year nearly as much as it had been on her.

Kate fingered the brooch and necklace. It was heavy silver laden with emeralds and diamonds. She'd never worn it because she'd never had a gown elaborate enough to wear it with, and also because the silver had come directly from Clayton Kincaid's silver mine in Leadville. But it would go perfectly with the emerald-green dress she'd had made for the Cattlemen's Ball.

She glanced at the clock sitting on the small table in the corner of her room. Cordelia and her father had already left for town, and Will would be coming soon. She moved to the full-length mirror that stood by the window. With Minnie's help, she had worn a corset, making her waist even smaller and pushing her breasts higher toward the rounded but not plunging neckline. The silk dress was overlaid with rows of wide lace in a lighter shade of green. The neckline, in front and back and over the shoulders, was bordered with lace. The waistline was sleek and tight, as were the sleeves that came to a V at her wrists.

She hadn't told Cordelia or her father that she would be attending the ball, and she wondered what would happen when they saw her there. She hadn't lied about it; they simply hadn't asked. They hadn't expected her to go. She'd had to do some quick thinking when she'd received a written invitation from Clayton just a week ago.

Stunned and a bit frightened at his interest in her, her return message had been evasive and apologetic. She declined, but didn't say why. The entire week she had lived in fear that Clayton would say something to her father, but he hadn't been out to the ranch, and her father and Cordelia hadn't been to Denver.

With nervous fingers, she fumbled with the clasp on the necklace and finally fastened it, straightening it into place just above her cleavage. In her hair, which Minnie had swirled atop her head, she placed diamond-studded combs. Dainty diamond-and-emerald earrings completed the picture of perfection she sought.

Then, in the evening quiet, she heard the sound of horses' hooves, and moving to the window, she saw Will below, driving a team of slender bay carriage horses into the yard. No doubt, they were some of the well-bred stock the Chanson ranch was noted for. With her heart picking up speed, she gathered the lace shawl and matching beaded bag from her bed.

His knock sounded just as she reached the ground floor. She opened the door to find him even more handsome than she remembered. His frame easily filled the small confines of the doorway. The black suit he wore was of the finest cloth and fit precisely across his square shoulders. Beneath it, a black vest hugged his firm chest and sported a gold watch chain draped across the front. Unlike some men who wore their pants quite baggy, his fit snugly over muscular but slender thighs. His dark brown hair shone in the last light of the day; its visible softness contained a natural, thick wave that was a temptation for a woman's fingers.

Kate was unable to resist matching the quiet gaiety of his smile. "It's good to see you again," she said softly. Will had just recently returned from the range and the only contact they had had was the recent exchange of notes regarding the ball.

His eyes drifted over her leisurely, obviously enjoying the trip from head to toe. When he once again met her gaze, there was appreciation in his eyes. "You will most certainly be the most beautiful woman there, Kate."

She murmured a thank-you, pleased by his compliment, and stepped out onto the house's wide veranda, closing the door behind her.

"Have I missed your father and dear stepmother?" He put his hand on the small of her back as they moved away from the house.

"Yes, they left just a few minutes ago."

"What did they say when you told them you were going to the ball with me?"

Kate was silent as Will helped her into the showy, glistening black carriage. When he settled in next to her against the rich leather seats and picked up the reins, she said in a small voice, "I'm afraid I didn't tell them."

Will made a clicking noise inside his mouth and tapped the reins to the team of horses; they moved away from the house on evenly matched strides. "I see," he replied thoughtfully. "Then don't be surprised if our entrance causes a commotion. I didn't come prepared for battle. I wish you had warned me."

"They'll have to keep face—at least Cordelia will. Don't worry, the ax will fall on me after it's all over."

He glanced sidelong at her. "Then perhaps you should come home with me."

She laughed away his flirtation. "Under the circumstances, I think it best to take my chances with Cordelia and Dad."

His voice softened, losing some of the lightness. "Don't you trust me?"

"I've heard a lot about you."

He chuckled. "Some rumors may be partially true, but I'm too busy to develop a real reputation. And if you honestly believed what you heard, you wouldn't be here alone with me—unless you'd like to experience my expertise firsthand."

Kate was surprised when he drew the horses to a stop and transferred both reins to one hand. He slid an arm around her shoulders and pulled her close. "It's been a long month, Kate. I've thought of nothing but that night ride together." His hand slid to her neck and with gentle fingers directed her closer to him. Slowly, he placed his lips over hers once again.

Kate had yearned to feel his lips again, to reassure herself that what had happened before hadn't been a dream, to reassure herself that he *did* care and that what the others had said simply wasn't true. But she had yearned for the feel of his lips again for selfish reasons as well, for the pure physical pleasure his nearness, his touch, his taste could draw from within her. And she was thrilled because there was no disappointment.

When they arrived in town, Will halted the carriage in front of the large building where the dance was being held. The huge grounds were immaculate. Potted flowers had been placed along the boardwalk, and even the lawn was lush and green despite the dryness and lack of water everywhere else. A carriage attendant stepped forward and stood staidly erect until Will stepped down and turned to help Kate to the ground.

As she leaned forward and Will's hands went around her waist, he hesitated and looked up into her face. At the sight of her creamy bosom partly exposed, he held his breath for a moment and then whispered, "I'd better ask now for at least three dances with you before you're swept away by a horde of goggle-eyed suitors who will surely be clamoring for your attention."

Kate laughed. "Which three dances would you like?"

"The first, the last, and one in the middle."

"Then you shall have them."

He easily lifted her clear of the carriage and set her down within the tentative circle of his arms, holding her there for a moment. The carriage attendant stepped past them and climbed into the conveyance, gathered the reins, and turned to Will.

"Your name, sir?"

"Chanson."

"Your horses will be well taken care of, sir. Very fine horses, indeed."

Will waited a moment with a hand at Kate's waist until he could be certain that the young attendant would handle the horses carefully. When he was satisfied that the boy was capable, he turned Kate toward the well-lit building and the music within.

"That day I took you inside the Cattlemen's Club, I said you were adventuresome. Now I know for certain. Just promise me one thing."

"What should I promise you?" she asked, trying to hide her nervousness.

"That if your father ruins my face or puts a bullet in me, you won't turn your back on me as though you didn't know me."

"Never fear," she said, although her own heart was pounding. "I'll be the one to suffer his anger."

Inside, a swirl of color met Kate's eyes. The room was brightly decorated in autumn colors of yellow and orange, but the most vivid decoration was the dresses of the many ladies who, by all appearances, had dressed to outdo each other. It would be hard to say which lady could be considered the most elegant.

As they stepped into the foyer, they were met by a short, stocky man in a black servant's garb. He took Kate's shawl but she kept her small beaded bag on her wrist. There was so much activity and so many groups of people that their entrance was not noticed. Kate glanced over the sea of faces, wondering where her father, Cordelia, and Clayton were, and what they would say or do when they saw her. Will's hand on her lower back urged her farther into the room, toward a man on the wooden platform who was speaking in a loud voice, drawing everyone's attention.

After some brief words of introduction, he said, "The dancing will now begin!"

The orchestra swept into a waltz, and Will leaned down, whispering in Kate's ear so she could hear above the music. His breath tickled her ear, sending a pleasant shiver through her body. "The first dance is mine."

Kate willingly went into his arms, and on light, easy feet, they stepped into the waltz, moving naturally into the circle of people. She liked the feel of his body so straight and firm against hers, bringing forth those sensations she remembered from the night they'd met in the moonlight. She had no difficulty following his lead. Breathless, she looked up into his eyes. No words were spoken; they silently shared the pleasure of the moment.

Cordelia realized she wouldn't have recognized Kate at all if she hadn't first seen Will, who was taller than most of the men. When she glanced to see who he had chosen for his partner, she nearly gasped. As it was, she lost her timing and became momentarily entangled with her partner, a man from the Cattlemen's Club and a friend of her father's. Tom wouldn't dance; she had expected that before they ever left home.

As she whirled about the room, she tried to glimpse the couple. Damn the girl for not telling them she would be here—and with Will, no less! Tom wasn't going to like it any better than she did. Then Cordelia's cornflower-blue eyes narrowed on Will. Damn him for seeing enough in Kate to even bring her. Surely he didn't care for her when there were so many other more desirable women around.

When the dance ended, Cordelia left her partner standing in the middle of the dance floor as she rushed off to find Tom. He was at the punch bowl discussing cattle business with some other ranchers. She contained herself as best she could and interrupted politely, drawing him off to the side. "Look across the dance floor," she instructed in a breathless whisper. "I think there is something you should see."

Tom wanted only to look at her; she was the

most beautiful woman at the ball, and probably the most expensively dressed in her powder-blue dress straight from Paris. It had hurt his bankroll, but he could not deny her anything that would make her happy. "What is it?" He wasn't interested, but did as she asked.

"Will Chanson."

"Yes, I expected he would come."

"No." Exasperation lifted the pitch of her voice. "Don't you even recognize the girl he's with?"

Tom focused on the lovely young woman in the green dress looking up into Will's eyes. It took him a moment to realize it was Kate. To his amazement she looked very much like a woman and very much like her mother. He felt a pain in his chest; he had never realized her full beauty until now. But then sudden anger banished the pain. He watched his daughter with keen eyes. She smiled at something Will said. They looked like young lovers as they exchanged words and glances. They acted as though no one was in the room but them. They had gone behind his back, but worse, Clayton was going to think *he* had allowed it.

He moved back to the punch table and set his small glass cup down. Cordelia was on his heels, her hand clinging to his coat sleeve. "What are you going to do, Tom?" Excitement and uncertainty were mixed in her tone, and her eyes were alight.

Tom didn't answer as he headed straight across the dance floor. Before he reached the other side, however, the music started again. Will pulled Kate into his arms, and with smiling faces, they set off in a breathless swirl.

Despite his anger, Tom didn't want to make a scene, so he got off the dance floor and out of the way of the dancers. He found a spot against the wall, nearly fading into the heavy dark green velvet drapes that graced the long, narrow windows.

Cordelia watched Will as she stood next to Tom. To be in his arms would surely give her more excitement than she had felt in years. "What are you going to do now?" she asked impatiently.

Tom ignored the irritation in her question, not realizing she was disgusted at the way he had handled the situation so far. "I'll wait."

"And if they stop on the other side of the dance floor this time? Are we to go racing back and forth across the floor all evening, trying to catch them?"

At that moment they were interrupted by another friend of Clayton's asking for a dance with Cordelia. She accepted gladly, leaving her husband's side.

Tom waited. When the music ended again the orchestra immediately started another dance. Will and Kate began dancing once more. After their third dance, however, Will pulled Kate to the side and Tom made his move.

Kate's eyes grew large when she saw her father approaching them. When Will saw her stricken expression he turned to face the older man.

Tom stopped an arm's length from Will. "What are you doing here with my daughter?"

"You know the answer to that, Tom."

Diering's anger shifted to Kate. "How dare you come here with him and not tell me. You've gone behind my back, right down to having that dress made. You are still under my roof, Kate Diering, and I will see that you never go out with a man again without my permission."

Will stepped to the left, placing himself partially in front of Kate, as if to protect her. "And what will you do, Tom? Horsewhip her? Lock her in her room?"

"Don't give me ideas, Chanson."

Will's lack of respect for the older man was evident. "I hope you don't do anything so foolish."

"What would you do if I did?" Tom replied, unmoved by Will's warning.

"Please." Kate stepped around Will, placing a hand on his arm and admonishing her father. "Don't ruin the evening. I only want to have a good time. Is there anything wrong with that?"

"No." He looked at Will again. "But I don't approve of you doing it with the likes of him." Tom noticed there were some people listening to their conversation. Suddenly, he turned on his heel and strode away, nearly bumping into Clayton Kincaid.

Clayton turned and watched Tom go back to the punch bowl, then with a smile on his lips joined Will and Kate. "My, my. It appears Tom wasn't expecting to see you here with his daughter."

Neither of them replied, but Clayton wasn't disturbed by their silence. He gazed openly at Kate, noticing the cleavage above the rounded neckline of her dress. "You are indeed lovely tonight, Kate. I'm sorry I didn't get my invitation to you sooner."

Will's hand tightened on Kate's arm. Clayton's compliment made her uneasy. It lacked sincerity and contained a nuance of offensiveness. She managed a polite thank-you and then glanced up at

Will, her eyes begging him to rescue her from the drilling scrutiny of the banker.

Will immediately took her hand to escort her onto the floor again. "If you'll excuse us, Clayton. We're going to dance again."

Clayton stepped in front of them, his smile widening as his eyes looked so deeply into Kate's that she felt as though he were trying to hypnotize her. "I believe it's time you let someone else dance with this lovely creature." His hand encircled her other arm and with a slight tug pulled her an inch or two away from Will. "You don't mind, do you, Will?"

Will's hand was tight around Kate's fingers, and Kate felt his indecision, but finally he released her and courteously stepped back. "Yes, I mind, but I can understand why you would like to dance with her. I'm sure it's been on the mind of every man in this room. I'll humor you this once, Clayton."

Clayton didn't like the way Will always managed to turn the tables on him, making *him* look like the younger and less experienced of the two. He bristled inwardly as he led Kate onto the dance floor. He pulled her into his arms closely, and then looked over her head at Will. With a conquering smile he met the rancher's scathing gaze, and then whisked Kate away.

Kate found herself pressed up against Clayton in an uncomfortable viselike grip, much tighter than Will held her. His movements weren't of the same fluid gracefulness as her former partner either, and she found it difficult to adjust to his awkward way of dancing. She did not feel in motion with him as she had Will. Neither did her body seem to mold to the shape of his.

"I believe you have stirred up a hornet's nest, my dear Kate. Your father didn't look pleased. I know how he feels about Will, and from what I heard of the conversation, I assume he didn't know you would be here with him."

"I'm old enough to decide who I keep company with."

"Ah, yes, and I do believe you made your choice." Inwardly, Clayton's throat was tight with anger and frustration. Again he'd been outmaneuvered by Will. He should have asked Kate sooner, but he had not considered her going with anyone, and Will had been on the roundup the entire month. As for asking any other ladies in town himself, there were none he cared to be with, and if he showed any attention to a woman, he was soon backtracking as she tried to ensnare him in marriage.

Will had apparently asked Kate to the ball before he left on the roundup, and Cordelia's suspicions about the two of them seeing one another secretly had probably been accurate. If they were serious, his plans could go awry, unless Tom put a stop to their courtship. And yet, Clayton was beginning to see something that could perhaps benefit him in a way he hadn't anticipated earlier. Kate could very well be the weakness in Will, and if that were the case, then he had found the perfect tool with which to knock Will to his knees.

Kate was relieved when the song finally ended and Clayton, ever the gentleman, directed her back to Will, who was standing by the punch bowl with cup in hand and an eye on their every move. Clayton released her at Will's side and Will picked up a cup from the table, filled it with the pink punch, and handed it to her. She took it gratefully, realizing she was thirsty from the dancing.

Clayton exchanged a dueling glance with Will and then, with a polite and stiff bow to Kate, moved off into the crowd.

After that, Will found himself on the sidelines quite frequently as more and more men cut in on him, wishing for the pleasure of holding Kate in their arms. He drank glass after glass of punch as he watched the other men whirl her about the room. Each time she smiled up at one of them, a strange pain dug into him in the vicinity of his heart. He was stunned to realize he was jealous.

He set his punch cup down as he heard a song ending. He strode onto the floor, and as her latest partner ended his last three beats, Will was there with a claiming hand on the small of Kate's back. He forced a smile to lips that would have preferred to snarl. He had made his claim again, and this time he would not relinquish it.

Seeing that Kate was out of breath from the nonstop dancing, he escorted her out of the stuffy room, past the open double doors, and onto the wide veranda where the hot autumn day had cooled only slightly with a soft night breeze. A row of trees, branches and leaves limp from lack of rain, bordered the veranda and made it a secluded spot from onlookers both inside and outside the building. Around them were many potted plants, unfortunately looking a bit wilted from the scorching heat.

No sooner had they found a bench to sit on than a butler came by with a tray of drinks. They both gladly accepted one; after the waiter had gone, they drank in silence, listening to the music.

"You look flushed," Will said, watching her sip from the dainty glass. "How are you withstanding dancing in this heat?"

She laughed and ran a hand across her forehead in a tired gesture. "I'm glad you rescued me, quite honestly."

She took another sip of the punch, and Will studied the way her lips fit over the edge of the glass in an unintentionally enticing way. He thought of little else but kissing them again. The urge to satisfy the craving took command, and his tanned hand reached out to touch the smoother skin of her cheek. With a flutter, her lashes came up, revealing large eyes that focused on his lips.

He leaned toward her and gently blotted out the inches that separated them. When his lips touched hers it was with a thrill that flowed throughout his body. Heady, as if the punch had been spiked, he drew back, surprised that a mere kiss had affected him so intensely.

"I thought about you constantly while I was gone, Kate." He took her hand in his.

She wondered at the abruptness of the kiss, but said, "I did the same about you."

"You didn't tell me Kincaid had also asked you to come with him."

"I saw no point in mentioning it."

Will tried to control the extreme jealousy building up inside him. Why must Kincaid be his rival in everything, even love? "Have you been with him before?"

Kate could tell it had been difficult for him to ask the question, and it made her lighthearted, for it was an indication of his true feelings. She smiled and traced the firmness of his cheekbone with her eyes. "No, but I can't imagine what I've done to catch his eye."

"That's simple. You're the most desirable woman here, and Clayton wants everything that is desirable." He placed a light kiss on her lips again. "Now, would you care to dance again?" he asked softly. "With me?"

Kate saw that much of the devilment had gone from his eyes, but it had been replaced with the wanting she was coming to recognize in him and feel in herself. It lay in the depths of his gaze, smoldering like hot ashes ready to burst into fire. Without being told, she knew intuitively that if she were caught inside the flame, she would be consumed in its heat.

"Yes," she replied. A strange feeling had taken over and she knew that whatever their relationship had been before their lips had touched, it had since changed immensely. "Will you allow me to freshen up in the powder room first?"

Will stood up and took her hand, noticing the softness of the skin and the strength of the bones. He helped her to her feet. "Of course, I'll wait here. Just promise me you won't let anyone waylay you between here and there."

She set her empty glass on the bench behind them and looked up into his face. If there was any deception there, she could not see it. It pleased her that there were no soft lines in his face, only distinct angles and planes. Possibly the only soft thing about him was his dark brown hair that enticed her with its gentle curl at his ears and at the collar of his shirt. But although there was no softness, there was tenderness. She had felt it in his kiss. She had seen it in his eyes, although the twinkle of humor was never far away. She hoped no one would detain her when she left his side. She only wanted to return quickly to the hard strength of his body against hers, and to the feeling of belonging in his arms.

"I won't, if I can avoid it."

Will watched her leave and doubted if she was fully aware of the effect she was having on him—and obviously some other men at the dance. He memorized the gentle movement of her slim hips and wondered what she looked like beneath the expensive trappings. He could never remember when a woman had occupied his mind any longer than the time it took to make love to her, but somehow he knew Kate Diering would be different.

From behind him, Will heard the rustle of silk and at the same moment felt a hand on his sleeve. Startled from his reverie, he turned to face the silent intruder. It was Cordelia. Where she had come from, he had no way of knowing, but now he wondered if she had seen him kiss Kate.

With her hand still on his arm, she said, "Why, Will, what are you doing out here all by yourself?" At the same time she raised herself up on tiptoes and looked past his shoulder at Kate. "Has your companion left you alone? That wasn't very smart of her. Surely, she must be aware that there are many eligible females at this ball who are dying to have a dance with you tonight, and who are totally disheartened that you've danced with no one but Kate."

"I wasn't aware that the women were lining up

waiting for me," he said jokingly. "But it wouldn't have mattered. I don't intend to abandon Kate."

"She's certainly been abandoning you! From what I've seen, she's not turning down any dances to save herself for you."

There was a sexual connotation to her words, and the pleasantness she tried to convey came out, instead, heavily steeped in venom. It was easy to see she had little regard for her stepdaughter.

"It's hard for a woman to refuse a man politely," he replied, not wishing to satisfy her by becoming provoked in any way.

"Don't get to thinking she has eyes only for you," Cordelia continued. "Remember, I live with her. She isn't as innocent as she acts or looks. As a matter of fact, she's quite a flirt with the cowboys. I mean," she hurried on, seeing the storm brewing in his expression, "why else would she want to spend so much time with her father? It's surely not because she enjoys chasing cows and fixing fences. It's because she likes to be where the men are. She's gone for long stretches of time by herself—all day sometimes—and she takes night rides." She hesitated, looking up at him and trying to read something in his eyes. When she saw only a veiled expression she continued. "Why, it wouldn't surprise me a bit to find out she's been meeting somebody out in a line shack somewhere."

Will pulled in a silent breath and compressed his lips. He didn't want to hear Cordelia's stinging words; he didn't want to believe them, either. She was putting ideas into his head that would never have gotten there by themselves. A needle of jealousy pricked him, infuriated him.

Cordelia's hand moved up his arm and drew his attention back to her. She looked into his eyes, her gaze sultry and inviting. "How about a dance with me while you're waiting," she suggested. "Kate won't mind. After all, I'm family."

Will politely refused but with a hint of a bow that moved him back just far enough that her hand slipped from his arm. "Thank you, Mrs. Diering, but I promised Kate I would wait here for her."

Cordelia's smile faded but didn't wilt completely. Enough of it remained to belie the sarcasm that spilled out in her words. "And you never break your promises?"

Will tried to maintain his level of composure, suppressing his dislike for her. She was Tom Diering's wife; he wanted no more trouble than he had with him already. "Never, except for things that are beyond my control."

A finely arched, light brown brow rose on her high forehead. "Then, perhaps some other time."

He nodded, his usual smile gone now. "Yes, perhaps."

Cordelia left him, and he glanced in the direction from which Kate would return. She was still not in sight. The orchestra had started another dance. He sat back down on the white bench and waited.

Will stood up when Kate stepped onto the veranda. Relief crossed his face and humor lit his eyes. "I was beginning to think you'd been stolen again, although I didn't see you in the arms of any other beau. Please"—he held out his arm, smiling down at her—"let me have this dance before it's snatched away from me again."

86

They danced three dances without stopping. For Kate, the people around them were nothing but a blur. She became lost in the small world of his arms. When they stopped momentarily, it was a second before she realized Will had been tapped on the shoulder. His look was one of exasperation as he turned to the man, keeping an arm around Kate. Before them stood Clayton and his daughter, Cordelia. Kate didn't care for the smile on either of their faces.

"Will," Clayton began, looking instead at Kate, "the ball will be over soon, and I would love to have another dance with this beautiful young woman. Surely, you won't refuse me."

Cordelia stepped forward at Will's hesitation and slipped a silk-covered arm through his. "We'll exchange partners. After all, that's the fun in coming to dances."

Clayton took Kate's arm and gently but firmly extricated her from Will's grip. Will met Kate's eyes and relaxed, knowing she liked the situation no better than he did. As Kincaid pulled Kate into his arms, she looked over his shoulder and smiled at Will. Will drew Cordelia into the dance position, being careful not to pull her too close, but much to his dismay, she pressed her bosom up against his chest anyway.

Will tried to follow the movements of Clayton and Kate, but the banker quickly swept her out of sight. He listened absently to Cordelia's mindless chatter as he thought about Kate. Finally, the dance ended and he politely took Cordelia's arm and led her to her father, who was now across the room. He didn't know or care where Tom Diering was. He only hoped the man had cooled down

87

about him bringing Kate and about Kate's acceptance.

Kincaid reluctantly released Kate and Will took her arm, immediately zigzagging her through the crowd and to the main door. "Kate." He bent his head and whispered in her ear as they walked. "We're leaving, if you don't object too much."

"What is it, Will?" She glanced up at him with a worried expression as her feet hurried along beneath the many petticoats trying to keep up with his long strides. "Is something wrong?"

"Yes." He chuckled. "I'm tired of trying to keep you away from all the men in here. It's wearing me out physically and mentally."

She laughed. "If only it was against the rules to cut in."

"It wouldn't matter. Out here rules were made to be broken."

When they reached the foyer, the servant stepped forward stiffly. "Are you leaving, Mr. Chanson?"

"Yes. Please get the lady's shawl and my hat."

Once they were outside, while they waited in the warm night air, the carriage attendant brought their vehicle. Will helped Kate inside, handed her the shawl, and then settled into the seat next to her. He urged the horses quickly away from the building but slowed them when they were a block away.

"I hope you're not angry with me for taking you away from the dance early."

Kate leaned back against the firmly upholstered leather seat; the movement put her closer to him. "No, I don't mind at all. I was afraid I would have to suffer through another dance with Clayton."

"And I with Cordelia. But it's early," he added. "Would you like to take a leisurely drive around the city?"

Her eyes lit up beneath the glow of the street lamps, and she nodded with enthusiasm. They set off along the quiet, empty street, enjoying the solitary clip-clopping of the horses' hooves and the occasional small talk.

By the time Will turned the carriage for the country and into the dark of the prairie, lit only by the stars, Kate knew she was falling in love. It had been so simple. Her heart had gone of its own volition.

Will pulled the carriage up in front of her father's huge white frame mansion and Kate hoped they were the first to arrive. Will secured the reins and stepped out, holding his hands out to give Kate assistance. As he had done before, he encircled her tiny waist easily and lifted her lightly to the ground. This time, however, he did not release his hold, nor did she remove her hands from his muscled arms.

Without any particular haste, he drew her against him. His arms tightened about her slim back, spreading over the lace-covered silk and heating her skin beneath. His intent was clear, and Kate welcomed the lips that moved to hers. He pulled her closer as his kiss deepened, drawing from her all the strength she had left in her tired legs.

She savored the feel and the smell of him, knowing she would treasure the memory of this moment until she saw him again—or in case she didn't. She was prepared for disappointment. She had grown up with it.

Her breathing was shallow when Will released her and stepped back, keeping a hand around her waist. In the starlight she saw the serious, rather than the mischievous, gleam in his eyes. "I'll be gone again for a while, Kate. I've got to go back out on roundup—this time to the plains. When I get back, though, I'd like to see you again."

She shouldn't have worried about not seeing him again. She would have to start trusting him more and listen less to the warnings of others. "I'd like that, Will, but from the way my father greeted us tonight, he would forbid it. We'll have to be careful."

A frown creased Will's forehead. "What will he do when he gets home? If you think there will be trouble, I won't leave."

Kate's smile vanished and she looked at the ground. Then, with a prideful tilt of her head, she met his worried gaze again. "No, there won't be trouble," she lied. "Don't worry about it, Will. I'm sure he'll lecture me, but that's all." Her real concern was for Will; she could handle her father.

He took her hands in his. "Kate, maybe it isn't wise to keep going behind his back. I don't want any harm to come to you."

"He would never consent to you seeing me."

What she said was true, and he had always known Diering disliked him. He nodded in acceptance of what they faced.

Then, in the quiet, they heard the sound of horses and carriage wheels. Kate's eyes grew large in alarm, and she hastily pulled her hands free of Will's. "You'd better go. They're returning."

"I won't run from him."

"Please, Will. I don't want you and him getting into a fight."

It wasn't his nature to back down, but there was a fearful pleading in her eyes that greatly troubled him. There was time only to concede to her wishes. He embraced her again. "All right, I'll leave, but only because you want me to. Think of me tonight."

"Will I have a choice?"

"No. None." He hastily kissed her again and then released her. After she had turned to the house, lifting her skirts to go up the front steps, Will got into the carriage and headed for the CM ranch.

In the dark of the house, Kate hurried up the stairs and to her room. Out of breath from fear and excitement, she closed the door and locked it. She still remembered her father's outrage when, as a child, she had asked about her mother. She had never asked again. Now the locked door might not prove beneficial, but it might buy her some time and allow his temper to cool.

She waited in the dark, holding her breath. She heard the sounds as her father and Cordelia came in. She couldn't catch any specific words, only the low pitch of their voices. She braced herself for the worst when she heard her father's footsteps on the stairs and in the hall. They halted at her door then, miraculously, went on by. His door opened and closed. She started breathing again. He probably had a plan to prevent her from seeing Will, but somehow she would.

Chapter 6

The fall roundup wasn't organized in the same tight form as the spring roundup. The ranchers might join together in a given vicinity, but generally each ranch owner sent out his men only to those areas he wished to cover. The fall roundup was to brand any late spring or summer calves and to doctor sick animals. At this time the older steers were sold, as were any cows that were no longer performing their function of producing good calves.

It was a time of living in the saddle, eating from the chuck wagon, and sleeping on the ground. Many men put up tents, but since there had been no rain for months, and since there was none threatening, they all slept in the open to catch any hint of a breeze. Even being rained on at this point would have been a blessed relief.

In early October, Will left his men and headed back to the ranch to check on things there. He was disappointed to see the condition of the cattle. There were years when even the meager grass would have supported them, but this was not one of them. To add to the problem, the government had opened up land to farmers who tilled up the precious grass, only to see their crops shrivel up and die, and the ground crack and turn so hard a plow could barely break it.

A couple of miles away lay the Diering ranch. Will had ridden this way intentionally, hoping for a glimpse of Kate or a chance meeting. The anticipation picked up his spirits and his heartbeat, but as he drew nearer, his nostrils were filled with the acrid smell of burning grass.

In alarm he stopped his horse and looked upward. He'd been so deep in thought he hadn't noticed the haze of smoke moving along the horizon, thinning out into the blue of the sky. The rise of the hill was just in front of him now; he was heading right into a fire. Worse, the Diering ranch was also directly in its path.

He laid his spurs to the horse's flanks and the animal leaped into a gallop. When they crested the ridge, Will reined him to a sliding stop and held him in a firm hand while he danced sideways, eager to be off again.

Below, Will saw flames licking the horizon. Directly in its path was Diering's magnificent, two-story white house, nestled in the distance in the low spot between three knolls. The fire was hot, with very little smoke, and raced along the ground consuming the dry grass. Its momentum was increasing. Now that he was on top of the hill, he could hear the drone that had not yet become a roar. The ranch was quiet; the cowboys were all gone on roundup. That would leave Kate, the servants, and probably Cordelia, but no one was in sight. Had they already gone to safety?

Kate turned over on her bed. Her skin was hot and sticky even though she wore nothing but a thin chemise. Groggily, she pushed the sleep of her afternoon nap from her head and her eyes. She felt worse now than when she had lain down. She would have much preferred going on the roundup, but her father had refused, saying it was no place for an unmarried woman. She guessed, though, that one of the biggest reasons he hadn't allowed her to go was because he didn't want her seeing Will.

There was nothing to do in the house; Cordelia's servants took care of everything. At least staying in her room enabled her to avoid Cordelia. She asked so many prying questions: Why had Kate and Will left the ball early? Where did they go? What did they do?—all the while insinuating that he had bedded her.

She forced herself into a sitting position on the edge of the bed and rubbed the stiffness from the back of her neck. Then, on leaden feet, she stood up and walked to the bureau where a bowl and pitcher sat atop a lace runner. From the china pitcher, she poured tepid water into the bowl and splashed it onto her face.

She reached for the small hand towel nearby. And then she smelled it—something was burning. Her senses came alive. Along with the smell she could now hear a faint rumbling. In sudden fear she raced to the window. A gasp caught in her throat. For a frozen second she could only stare at the orange wall of flames just beyond the yard, reaching upward and leaping over the firebreak that had never been sufficient and then had grown over with weeds in midsummer. Hadn't their foreman reminded her father that it needed to be replowed? Now the weeds were tall, brown, and dry.

She dropped the towel and ran for the door, jerking it open with such force that it hit the wall and then swung back and forth on its hinges as she ran down the hall. On long legs she was at Cordelia's door in seconds, flinging it wide without knocking. The blonde was asleep on the huge bed, the satin cover carefully folded back.

"Cordelia! There's a fire. We've got to get everyone out of the house!"

Her stepmother came awake slowly and sat upright, pushing strands of her tousled blond hair aside. In a stupor she stared at Kate, wondering what was happening. Kate suppressed the panic rising inside her and repeated her order. "We've got to get out of here. There's a fire!"

Cordelia stood on unsteady feet and moved to the window while eyeing Kate with suspicion and doubt. "What are you talking about? Is this some stupid little trick?" At that moment her gaze shifted to the yard below and the moving demon of heat and flames bearing down on them. She screamed, putting a hand to her mouth. With wild eyes she looked at Kate again but her reflexes were paralyzed. Then small frightened sounds started coming from her throat as her eyes darted around the room and over everything that was in it.

She began moving, hurrying from object to object, grabbing up trinkets, jewelry, clothes. Kate hurried into the room and grabbed Cordelia by the arm, causing her to drop everything she had gathered. She started to pull her toward the door. "We've got to get out of here. Come on!"

Cordelia resisted, pulling back and trying to free the grip the younger woman had on her. "Leave me alone! These things are mine. I won't let some damned fire have it all!"

Kate managed to pull Cordelia into the hall. "You can buy more clothes, Cordelia. Now we've got to get Aimée and Minnie out of here."

Cordelia looked back at the expensive furnishings of her room. "Damn you, Kate Diering, you'll pay for this."

"Shut up, Cordelia, or I'll leave you here to burn."

Cordelia saw the seriousness in Kate's eyes, and for an instant didn't doubt it at all. Down the carpeted stairs they raced. When they reached the foyer, Cordelia ran to the front door and pulled it open. "Cordelia!" Kate called after her. "Where are they? Help me find them."

Through the glass in the door Cordelia saw the flames eating closer and closer to the yard and the house. "It's going to burn the house down! My beautiful house."

"Cordelia! The servants." Finally, Kate turned to the kitchen and yelled "Fire" at the top of her lungs. Finally Aimée and Minnie came running to see what the commotion was about. When they joined Cordelia at the door and saw the flames from the window, they ran from the house.

When Kate's bare feet touched the warm wood of the front veranda, she was unexpectedly pushed back by the encroaching heat of the fire. It had advanced very rapidly and was now on the edge of the corrals. The wind blew sparks in her direction.

In the middle of the yard Cordelia was turning

in circles, not knowing what to do or in which direction safety lay. Minnie and Aimée ran to her and tried to get her into motion and away from the fire. Kate knew they could never outrun the fire on foot before exhaustion overcame them.

She ran to the corral where the horses were now squealing and circling the round perimeter as they looked for an escape from the advancing flames. There was no time to halter or bridle them, and although they were gentle, they could bolt and run under these conditions.

Several lariats were draped along the pole corral and Kate retrieved them. In her loose chemise she climbed the pole fence, dropped down into the enclosure, and approached her black mare first. She had to force herself to walk up to it calmly because, in its fear and confusion, it saw her as one more threatening thing.

The black mare continually eluded her, side-stepping, tossing her head and dancing just out of reach, snorting and staring at her with wild eyes and flared nostrils. "Starr, come here!"

At the command of her voice, the black mare twitched her ears forward and looked at Kate through different eyes. Behind her, Kate heard the other women sobbing and telling her to hurry. Finally, Minnie ran toward the corral. Her movement caused the mare to bolt again.

"Stay back, Minnie," Kate warned in frustration, "but be ready when I catch this one and turn it over to you."

Finally, she was able to loop the lariat over the mare's head. She ran the horse to the gate and Minnie opened it just enough to receive the rope.

She pulled the horse through and Kate closed the gate to keep the others inside.

"You and Aimée get on it. Head east to the creek. Then go downstream away from it!"

Kate didn't wait to see how they mounted the horse. She picked up another lariat from the ground and moved to the next horse, one she knew would be easy to catch. Behind her, she heard another scream but ignored it, concentrating only on capturing the horse. Throwing the lariat over the horse's head, she leaped aboard, the chemise slipping up to her thighs. She bent down and pushed the gate with her hand and then her bare foot. She went through and the other horses followed, pushing past her and running as fast as they could to the east.

In their dust, Cordelia stood still in the middle of the yard, watching Aimée and Minnie riding clumsily for safety behind the herd of horses. Kate raced to her side and stretched down a hand as she held the eager horse in check with the single lead of the lariat.

"Come on, Cordelia! Get up behind me. Give me your hand!"

The woman's eyes were huge and scared. The fire had reached the corral. Cordelia clutched Kate's hand and managed to get half on the horse with one leg over the horse's back. Desperately, she tried to get all the way on as the horse circled the yard, snorting in its own frenzy to be away from the fire and the confusion the two half-naked women were causing.

Then Cordelia was up. Kate straightened the horse out and dug her heels into its sides, but suddenly a blow from the side struck her in the head. There was a flash of white. She saw a hand take the lariat from her, the same hand that had pushed her into the air and onto the ground.

Will spurred his horse faster, lying low over its neck as its long, powerful strides consumed the distance from the ridge to the ranch lying below, still half a mile away. Kate was there trying to get the horses from the corral. He knew it had been only a matter of minutes since he'd started his run and since he had seen Kate and the others, small figures in the distance, come from the house, and yet it seemed like an eternity.

Over his horse's head he saw the fire leaping up around the yard, its dry grass perfect tinder. Then he saw—or thought he saw—Cordelia push Kate from the horse. As his horse raced into the yard, Kate rose to her feet. She took one glance at the fire and started running. He hollered to her but she couldn't hear over the increasing low roar of the blaze.

He swerved his horse to the right to come up behind her, slowing its pace as he estimated the distance and the speed before he reached her. The horse skidded to a near stop when it was practically on top of her. Will reached down, enclosing her waist with a strong arm. He pulled her up against him, released the tension of the rein, and the horse was running again.

When they were farther from the flames and the drifting sparks, Will pulled his horse to a stop. Kate wriggled herself up behind him, not knowing where he had come from but very thankful for his appearance. They both glanced back as the horse whirled in circles in its effort to flee again. The fire had started on the house.

Will leaned forward. Kate's arm tightened around him. The horse knew the signal and gladly sprang into a gallop away from the suffocating hell of the blaze. Will directed them toward the creek. He knew his horse was getting tired and would be slowed considerably now with two aboard. If they were lucky, maybe the fire wouldn't jump the high, water-eroded dirt banks and the strips of green grass that lined the creek bottom on either side of the water.

The horse's neck was lathered with sweat when it hit the sloping dirt bank. It skidded down the embankment and lunged into the water. Will hoped that they could stay in the water and get out of the burning path before his horse gave out completely.

Suddenly, the horse went down on its knees and let out a shrill scream. Both Kate and Will leaped off to keep from being pinned beneath it. The horse struggled to get upright but cried out in pain; its right front leg dangled oddly. Without speaking, Will jerked his rifle from the scabbard and thrust it at Kate. In seconds he had the saddle off and flung it up onto the opposite bank, away from the encroaching fire that moved on the wind at an incredible speed. When he looked at Kate again, their eyes locked in silent understanding of the situation.

Kate's mind churned with disbelief as she stared at the animal and at Will's own pained expression. In water to her knees, Kate flung the rifle back to Will with a thrusting, angry motion. He caught it in midair.

"Do it!" she cried, her eyes dry but with tears in her voice. Then she turned and pushed her small frame into the weak current, the water tugging at her bare feet and legs. She kept on walking, trying not to think of the fire or the skinny strip of green that was their only protection. When she'd gone twenty feet the report of the Winchester brought her to an abrupt halt. Her shoulders sagged. She heard water sloshing behind her and then felt Will's hand on her arm.

"Come on, Kate."

His voice was flat and lifeless. She knew it hadn't been easy for him to kill his horse. She looked up and saw the flames closing in on them. She turned to Will and he looked over her head at the wall of flames, only a few hundred feet away now and advancing fast.

Will looked down the length of the small creek in the direction of the fire and noticed that flames were skirting along the edge of the high dirt embankment just above their heads. "It hasn't jumped the water yet. Maybe it won't."

They watched as the blaze drew closer. They couldn't outrun it and they knew it. Their only hope was the water. As it came along the edge of the sloped bank, they turned their faces from its heat. Then Will tossed his gun onto the opposite bank and pulled Kate down into the water with him. On their backs they kept only their faces above the water. Kate closed her eyes to the red heat that felt as though it were singeing her eyelashes.

Despite the heat surrounding them, the water was cold, and in their narrow, wet bed Kate was highly aware of Will's body next to hers, touching her intimately through the thin wet chemise. She focused on the nearness of Will instead of the fire roaring along the high banks above them. Gradually, the heat on her face cooled and she opened her eyes.

Will got up and helped her stand.

The fire raged off to the northeast, and to the southwest lay a strip of black, smoldering land. Now that the danger had passed, tears of relief blurred Kate's eyes and spilled down onto her cheeks. Immediately, Will's arms came around her and he pulled her into the haven of his body's protection and stroked her wet hair.

She was angry with herself for displaying weakness and giving in to fear. She wiped at her eyes. "I'm sorry," she apologized, not wanting to look at him. "I'm just relieved."

"I know."

The gentle understanding in his voice drew her head up. She had almost expected him to be irritated with her, the way her father would have been, but his blue eyes were on her, bright with an arresting glow. Suddenly, she realized that her clinging chemise was leaving nothing to his imagination.

In haste and embarrassment she turned her back to him and folded her hands across her bosom, only to realize with a growing blush that she was now presenting her barely concealed backside to him. She looked back over her shoulder at him with pathetic, helpless eyes, noticing that his own attire was fitting his body quite closely as well.

Will hadn't meant to stare, but he had been more than aware of every curve of her body as they lay together in the water. Now, what he had felt was being presented to him in explicit detail, and he could not find the strength or the will to turn away. He took a step toward her, drew her back against his chest, and once again into his embrace. He felt the releasing of his own tension as his lips touched her wet hair in light kisses, increasing in intensity as they moved along the side of her face, reaching over her shoulder to find her forehead, eyelids, cheeks, and neck.

Beneath his hands was the softness of her stomach, barely covered by the skimpy white undergarment. His caress slid upward to her firm, round breasts that molded so perfectly in the cup of his hand. She sucked in a sharp breath, but her attempt to pull away was easily squelched as his arms turned her to face him and tightened on her once again, holding her captive while he found her tender wet lips.

His kiss took away her resistance and Kate leaned against him, knowing she should pull away from the heat of his caress, and yet unwilling to stop the surging pleasure that he had ignited in her body. One of his hands left her breast, leaving it cool to the air, and slid downward to her inner thigh. She knew he must stop, and with her hand she caught his.

"Will...please...don't."

A sound of frustration rose in his throat, but he obeyed and moved his hand to her waist, gripping it in a tightness that seemed born of a deep, inner pain. Kate felt the hardness of his manhood pressed against her. She felt the short puffs of breath escape his parted lips as they moved over her face. Beneath her hand, his heart was thudding heavily, rapidly. The hand on her breast slid around to her back and up to her head, cupping it and holding her upright to receive a kiss as fiery as the blaze that had nearly consumed them. Only now she saw that this blaze was much more dangerous.

His mouth moved over hers, more demanding than his other kisses, almost as if there were some point he must reach or die trying. Kate didn't understand. She only knew that a desire inside herself urged her closer to his male hardness, instinctively seeking his body for the answer to the need. Her lips parted, her tongue twining with his in a way that seemed natural to the growing urgency of some primitive call she was yet to learn about.

Unexpectedly, his kiss ended, and the hand that had held her head slipped to her knees as he bent and easily lifted her to his chest and out of the water. He stepped to the grassy border of the creek and laid her down, stretching out next to her. She cradled his face in her hands, and in seconds his lips were on hers again, stirring a need that made her feel purely wanton.

Again his hands caressed her body, more freely now, touching in a tantalizing way as they descended downward, coming to rest on her pelvic bones and easily drawing her hips closer to his. As his muscular thigh slid between her legs, an electrifying signal flashed to her brain, and finally she turned her head away from him. With her hands on his shoulders, she whispered in uneven breaths that were agonizing because her body did not agree with her words. "No, Will...stop... I shouldn't..."

A moan rose in his throat, and he ground out

his frustration between clenched teeth. "For God's sake, Kate. I'm a man. How long do you think your kisses can satisfy me?"

A new kind of fear surged inside her. She didn't know or understand the sexual act fully. His urgency, his anger at her, and the straining of his body against hers frightened her more than the fire, and she pushed harder at him until he finally cursed and rolled from her. He took a sitting position next to her on the grass, drawing his knees up and loosely draping his arms over them as his breathing slowed.

She hadn't wanted to fight him; she was just so confused. It had happened too fast. Their relationship had evolved too quickly, and doubt rose inside her. Could it be that he did only want her for sexual fulfillment? Well, she wouldn't give herself to a man just to keep him. She sat up, then stood up, looking down at him now in anger that she didn't fully understand—anger that protected her from hurt.

"If that's all you want, Will Chanson, you can go to those ladies in town who...who sell it." Her voice shook, and her words weren't quite as forceful as she'd intended.

He stood up and the sparks lit his eyes. He leaned toward her in an angry stance. "Then that's *exactly* what I'll do. I made a mistake by thinking you were more of a woman than you are." He hated himself for saying that, but he was too proud to retract the heated words.

When she started to move away from him, down the creek bank, he cursed beneath his breath but went after her, caught her arm and jerked her around. "You can't go anywhere looking like that."

She pulled her arm free of his, moved farther away from him, and tipped her head back belligerently. "I don't see as I have a choice."

He compressed his lips and fought the desire still raging inside him to take her here and now. The fragile, wet cloth of her chemise clung to the full upthrust of her bosom. He forced himself to look at anything but her body as he hastily undid his wet shirt and stripped it off. He tossed it at her, and she caught it with one hand. "Put it on," he commanded.

Kate took a deep breath to steady her indignation. How dare he be mad at her because she hadn't given in to him. He had no right to think she was that kind of a woman. She jerked at the wet shirt, finally getting it on. The long tails hung down past her thighs.

When she had it buttoned she lifted her eyes to him again, determined not to let him see any weakness. It took steely willpower to stand her ground. Then her eyes strayed to his broad chest and the mat of black, coarse hair that angled down to his trim stomach and disappeared into his jeans.

Staying far enough apart that their bodies didn't touch, they walked down the creek until they found a gentle slope they could use to get out of the creek bed. Will dug his booted heels into the bank and assisted Kate—despite her insistence that she didn't need any help. They climbed the short incline to the opposite side.

"What about the horse?" Kate asked, but she couldn't bring herself to look back at the animal that had saved their lives.

Will found his Winchester and saddlebags. His reply was sober. "I'll come back and pull it up out of the water and get my saddle. Come on. We've got to beat the sun home."

They headed southward for Chanson range but had only gone a few yards when they heard shouting behind them. They turned and saw Minnie and Aimée aboard Kate's horse and Cordelia bringing up the rear on the other. In their anger at one another they had forgotten about the other three women. Cordelia seemed reluctant to approach. Kate's cool gaze centered on her. Will too stared icily at her.

When she stopped her horse in front of them, Cordelia lifted her chin defensively. "I know it looked like I pushed you off the horse, Kate, but I really didn't." Her eyes darted to Will as if to gauge his belief of her story. "It was purely an accident."

Will noticed Cordelia was dressed as scantily as Kate. They must have both been taking an afternoon nap. Her blond tresses were dirty and wet, hanging limply and dripping water down the side of her face and into her cleavage. Like Kate, there was little of her figure left to the imagination because of the thin soaked material of her undergarment, but although she was an attractive woman, there was nothing about her that appealed to him.

"If that was the case, Mrs. Diering, why didn't you stop and help Kate back on? You knew there was no way for her to escape the fire on foot."

Cordelia stammered, possibly one of the first times she had ever been at a loss for words. "I only reached around Kate because I thought she was having trouble with the horse. When she lost her balance and fell, the horse just went crazy and took off. All I could do was hold on. I'm not going to beg you to believe me. It's her word against mine anyway." Her gaze examined Will's bare chest more thoroughly and she missed the cold stab of Kate's gray-green eyes. Her voice softened as she continued, tilting her lips into a smile made just for him. "Besides, all ended well, didn't it? You came along and rescued her."

Kate felt that she had definitely been pushed, but arguing over it would change nothing. She turned on her bare heel and continued walking south. Will looked at Cordelia with contempt. He called to Kate. "Come on back here." She stopped and looked over her shoulder at him. He knew she wasn't going to like what he was about to suggest. "I want you to ride behind Cordelia to the ranch and send someone with a horse for me."

Kate's expression darkened as she looked at Cordelia. "I'd rather walk. Just have Cordelia send back two horses."

Cordelia was instantly filled with benevolence as she sensed the hostility between Kate and Will. She nudged the horse closer to Will and spoke in a nicer tone, wondering what could possibly have happened to put them at odds with one another. "Kate, why don't you ride on to the Chanson ranch. I can stay here and walk with Will." Without waiting for a response, she slid to the ground, aware that her chemise slid up nearly to her shapely buttocks in the process, and also aware that Will had seen it. "I mean, after the misunderstanding about the horse," she continued, "it's the least I can do to make amends." She handed the reins to Kate, but the younger woman merely clenched her fists at her sides and refused to take orders from her stepmother.

Will saw the blonde's ploy, and he took the reins and turned to Cordelia. With a hand on her bare arm he turned her around to face the horse again and then bent down and gripped her ankle. "I'll help you back on, Mrs. Diering." He glanced over at Kate and his jaw set again in a stern line. "If you two can't get along, then one of the other ladies can ride behind Cordelia, and I'll put Kate on the other horse."

Kate was furious that he would be giving her orders, but under the circumstances it would be better to be away from him. She returned his glare and didn't reply.

The feel of Will's hand on Cordelia's leg filled her with a tingling that brought back the many tantalizing memories of her single days and made her wish that just once she could throw aside the bonds of her marriage and relive those days with Will. She placed a hand on his naked shoulder, delighting in the strength beneath her fingers. "Very well, Will. I'm sure that's best." She leaned her upper leg against his chest as he boosted her aboard. Her chemise slid up to her thigh again, but she made no move to cover herself. His eyes drifted up her leg before resting on her face, but she could read none of his thoughts.

Will helped rearrange the other women on the two horses, and then put them in motion, standing still as he watched Kate until she disappeared from view. Not happy at the prospect of the long walk ahead, he set out with the sun blazing down on his bare back and chest.

The sun was moving toward the evening sky,

his feet hurt, his skin was burnt, and his throat was parched by the time he saw one of his hired hands top the crest of a low hill, leading a spare horse. Will mounted without so much as a greeting and headed once again into the sun. The cowboy wanted to ask questions about the fire. Will was hot, tired, and laconic. He thought the long walk would enable him to cool off where Kate was concerned, but if anything, he was worse than before and baffled by the entire situation.

By the time they saw the CM nestled in the valley, the sun was gone and dusk had settled over the land. As they rode toward the two-story house, not as big or as grand as Tom Diering's mansion, Will was glad that it still stood.

He had expected the women to still be at his ranch when he got there, but he found that they had gotten a hired hand to take them to Cordelia's father's mansion, and he couldn't help but wonder if Kate had wanted to go there rather than see him again. No matter what had happened between them, it disturbed him to know she would be living under Kincaid's roof until the house was rebuilt.

He clenched his fists, wanting to punch something. He was being thwarted at every turn. Perhaps Kate would prefer the "gentlemanly" charm of Clayton Kincaid.

Chapter 7

Tom Diering was devastated. He had ridden off by himself after he'd seen the ranch in ashes, and then sat in the heat of the sun nearly all day, contemplating his financial ruin and wondering what he was going to do. When he could find no solution, he had put his head in his hands and cried. Then he had cursed. He had raised his fist to heaven and cursed. But there had been no response, save a hot breeze that had dried the wetness on his face and made him feel like a fool.

Now, sitting in his usual chair in Clayton Kincaid's office at the Cattlemen's Club, he wondered if God were related to the banker, because Clayton always made him feel like a fool, too.

"I can certainly see your dilemma, Tom." Clayton leaned back in his chair and propped his snakeskin boots on the corner of the desk. He took a puff on his cigar and studied Tom openly, twitching his lips as his mind rolled. "However," he continued, "you are in debt to me extensively as it is, and the way I see it, you could sell every last cow that you own and you would still owe me money. I just don't know, Tom. The amount of money it would take to build a new house like the one you lost would be tremendous."

Kincaid seemed to like to make him crawl, and this time Tom knew he had no choice. He couldn't tell Cordelia that he was penniless, except for the cattle and the land, and that selling them *would* leave him absolutely destitute. As far as his wife was concerned, all he had to do was go to the bank and draw out enough money for the house and call up contractors to start work immediately. Already she was charging clothes and house furnishings all over town on his account.

He looked at his scuffed cowboy boots, the ones he'd been wearing on roundup. "I can't tell Cordelia. You know that. She might leave me, Clayton."

"Perhaps it would be better for both of you if she knew that you're not the man of wealth she thought you were when she married you. How can you live with the deception, Tom?"

"I'm surprised you didn't tell her the truth long ago."

"I could have, but she was in love with the notion of marrying a rich cowboy. I didn't discourage her because I thought that with the right financial help you could become a respectable cattleman. I've never thought it hurt to indulge Cordelia. I always figured she could divorce you any time she grew up and saw the foolishness of her 'romantic' dreams. But she's stayed with you much longer than I ever anticipated. I suppose my money has kept her in the manner to which she was accustomed. I suppose if Cordelia has money for clothes and parties, she could even put up with a broken-down cowboy."

Tom wanted to get up and save what pride he had left. It would please him to tell Kincaid to go straight to hell, but he knew he couldn't lose Cordelia. She was the only thing in his life that truly mattered. He had never thought he could win someone as beautiful and as sophisticated as she, and now all he hoped to do was keep her. He'd lost one wife; he couldn't lose another. He may as well be dead if that happened.

When Tom didn't say any more, Clayton removed the cigar from his mouth and took a drink of Scotch from the small glass that was ever present in his hand. He wasn't sure why, but it was at moments like these, when men came in and sat across from him, asking for money, that he was reminded of his true wealth and position in the world. He owned them all, really.

"Very well, Tom. I can't put my daughter out in the street, now can I? And I surely don't want the two of you living under my roof indefinitely. Therefore, you may have whatever it takes to replace the house, but do try to curtail Cordelia's extravagances. I won't pay for anything that you didn't already have. It will be up to you to explain *that* much to her. You'll be the one to listen to her tirades." Clayton smiled and took another puff on his cigar and then blew the smoke in Tom's direction. "But I'm sure you won't mind, will you? Being in love the way you are."

Tom stood up. He still wore the same sweaty clothes he'd had on during the roundup. Kincaid twitched his nose in disgust. "And why don't you go to the store and get yourself some new clothes too, Tom. In case you hadn't noticed, I have several bathrooms at the mansion. I know you've only just gotten back from the roundup, but feel free to use any of them anytime."

Tom nodded. His heart picked up speed as he tried to get up the courage to thank Clayton, but the words stuck in his throat and he could only stare at his benefactor.

Kincaid smiled; he read Diering's mind. "Don't bother to thank me. You know I'd do anything to keep my son-in-law out of trouble." He hesitated and a deeper gleam appeared in his eyes. "I know you'll come to my aid when I need help."

Tom braced himself, wondering what Clayton would want in return for his generosity.

"You'll be staying with me until your house is rebuilt. I see it as a very good opportunity for me to court your daughter. Before this happened, I had invited some friends from Chicago to come out and visit for a while. We're having a dinner party this weekend at my estate. Of course you and Cordelia will be expected to be there, as well as Kate." He took another puff on the cigar and blew the smoke toward the ceiling. "I want to be Kate's escort. I'll expect you to inform her of the arrangements."

Tom tried to temper his anger. Why couldn't Clayton do his own courting? Was he afraid she'd refuse? Well, if she had a lick of sense, she would. But he couldn't allow her to, because he knew Clayton could very well decide not to give him the money to rebuild. God, how he hated crawling, begging.

He swallowed hard and stuck his battered hat down on his head. "I'll see that she accepts."

Kate was more than happy when the dinner party came to a close. After Clayton had excused her, she hurried up the carpeted stairs and breathed easier when the door to her room was closed behind her and locked. She had resented having to appear with Clayton, but her father had insisted.

"He is letting us stay here, Kate," he had said. "He's doing this for you only because he doesn't want you to appear at the party unescorted. Try to enjoy yourself. You may find you enjoy his company." He seemed to have a hard time saying the words, as though he himself did not believe them.

He had also told her he didn't want her seeing Will again. "If you do, and I discover it, I swear, Kate, I'll shoot him. I don't want my daughter getting tangled up and hurt by a man like him."

In the dark she undressed, all the while hoping that the double crew of carpenters would get her father's house rebuilt quickly so she could leave this stifling atmosphere and Clayton's constant scrutiny. She sat at the small vanity and slowly pulled the pins from her hair, letting it tumble into heavy waves past her shoulders. The soft hairbrush felt good on her scalp and she brushed for a long time, finding relaxation in it.

Her thoughts strayed to Will again, as they had so many times over the last two weeks. He hadn't tried to contact her, hadn't tried to make amends for their argument the day of the fire. Was it possible he had only wanted to seduce her, and when he found he wouldn't so easily, had lost interest in her? If that was the case, then it was plain to see he had no deep feelings for her, and she should accept it and forget him.

But she wanted to hear it from his lips. She wanted to see him again. But how, after her father's threats? She had already gone behind his back in order to go to the ball with Will. She knew she would be asking for trouble if she tried again. She could not risk Will getting hurt. If only there were a way to make amends with him, to tell him how she felt. Maybe they could work something out. And maybe she could convince her father...

Finally, she went to the large four-poster bed and climbed onto it and under the luxurious covers, but sleep wouldn't come. She lay awake for an indeterminate amount of time in the dark, listening to the sounds of the house and the occasional noises drifting up to her wing of the huge mansion.

Outside, she heard the rattle of carriage wheels over the cobbled entrance road. She rose and walked to the double glass doors that led out onto a small balcony. Pulling back the heavy velvet drapes a sliver, she was able to see into the frosty courtyard below and watch the carriages moving along the street.

The heat of October had finally been replaced by the deep chill of November. The cold air seeping through the window forced Kate to the warmth of her bed. She nestled deeply into the bed and closed her eyes for sleep, wondering if she would be able to stop her mind's rambling. Suddenly, she was startled into an upright position by a noise just outside her bedroom door. There was a tap. She chose not to answer it, hoping that whoever it was would go away. But it sounded again, and again, more insistently.

She tossed the covers back, slipped her dressing gown back on over her nightgown, and tying it securely about her waist, went to the door and whispered, "Who is it?"

"Clayton. I want to talk with you."

Her heart leaped to her throat and began to thump. What could he possibly want with her? "It's late. I'm in . . . my nightclothes."

"That's perfectly all right, Kate. I'm here only to talk with you."

It was strange how no one refused Clayton Kincaid's desires, except perhaps Will. Kate opened the door a crack, but Clayton pushed it back with persuasive insistence, forcing Kate to step back.

She instinctively drew her robe closer about herself, and Clayton was very much aware of the action. She turned away from him and walked several feet away to the vanity. "What is it, Mr. Kincaid?"

He smiled condescendingly. "Can't you call me Clayton in private as well as in public?"

"I'm sorry. It's a habit."

He saw the hint of defiance in her eyes and the tilt of her chin. Why was she the one woman who didn't desire him? The others would gladly accept his money and the prestige that would come with being his wife, but Kate was different. She seemed to care nothing for either. Maybe that was why she interested him so much. He enjoyed conquering a woman who tested his wit.

"Your father tells me you haven't seen Will since the day he rescued you from the fire."

She assessed her predator. Stealthily, he went about manipulating people, controlling them, slicing them down to a size that better suited his purposes. "That's correct."

"I think you should be aware that in the time you've been here, I've seen Will several times over at Mae's—you do know about that establishment, don't you?"

Kate tensed, felt the strength go from her body, but she remained very straight and still in front of him. "Yes, I know about it. Why are you telling me this?"

"Because I think you should know what you're up against if you think you're going to change him, or win him. Even if you did, I doubt he would be loyal to you. His sort never are. It's quite simple, Kate. None of us wants to see you hurt, especially me.

"Look around you, Kate. Think about what it would be like to live here permanently"—he hesitated and his eyes intensified on her—*"as my wife*. You would get much more security than you ever would with him."

The air went out of her; she fought to remain standing when she only wished to find a chair to steady her against this unexpected...shock. Her tongue was dry but she forced it to move. "And what of love, Clayton?"

"Love is a state of mind, dear Kate. Two people only have to make up their minds to love each other, and they will."

He quietly left then, closing the door behind him. She turned to the bed. *Will at Mae's.* Why should that upset her? He had probably been there plenty of times before. But it hadn't mattered then. Now it hurt that he would turn to other women for what she had denied him. And yet maybe it merely proved that he had simply wanted from her what he could get from those ladies at the bordello. If he thought no more of her than that, then everyone was right about him.

She walked to the bed, removed her dressing gown, and once again crawled under the covers. She stared at the dark ceiling and tried to blink away the burning in her eyes. A tear slid out and down the sides of her face and into her hair. Shortly, it was followed by another.

Will stopped his new mount, a young buckskin, at the brick-pillared entrance to Kincaid's mansion. Across the three-acre manicured yard, the house rose to three stories in a Victorian style, abundant with turrets and towers. The estate itself encompassed some thirty acres and it obviously took a large crew in summer to plant and care for the trees, shrubberies, lawn, and flowers. A large three-tiered fountain, graced with nude figures sprawled in the bend of the curved drive that was lined with gas lamps to light the way at night. Painted white and adorned with intricate, wrought-iron detailing the same color, the ugly structure reminded him more of a wedding cake than a place to live.

Will nudged his horse through the entranceway and up the graveled drive. He dismounted and wrapped his reins around an iron hitching rail that had the carved figures of horses at either end. Then he made his way up the curving walkway to the ornately carved double doors.

Kate was inside and he had some things to say to her. He had to try and make her understand the way he felt and why he had acted as he had the day of the fire. He had examined his actions for two weeks, and he knew he'd been in the wrong. He would not let her slip away.

He pounded the door knocker three times before

Aimée, Tom's French cook, finally opened it. She too must be living here now, earning her keep by answering the door. Judging from the scowl on her face, she found her situation far from pleasing.

"Is Kate here?"

Aimée's heavy-lidded eyes half closed and her thin lips smirked. "No, she went into town today with her stepmother, and they haven't returned. Mr. Diering isn't here, either."

He was disheartened, to say the least. He had come here to see Kate even if it meant doing battle with her father, but apparently Tom had already gone to the cattlemen's meeting.

"I want to leave a message. Do you have some paper I could write on?"

Without replying, or asking him in, Aimée left the door standing open and went back inside. In a few minutes she returned with a piece of paper and a pencil. Will wrote a hasty note telling Kate he would like to talk to her and asking her to send word to the ranch when she would be available.

He folded the paper in quarters, wishing he had an envelope to seal it from the curious eyes of the French woman and whoever else might choose to read it. He handed it back to her. "Will you see that Kate gets it as soon as she returns?"

Aimée took it and nodded. Then, without comment, she closed the door snugly in Will's face. Gritting his teeth at her rudeness, Will turned and rode for the cattlemen's meeting.

Will straightened his gray Stetson, and with his hand felt to make sure the pinch down the center was right. Then he placed a hand on the cold doorknob of the association's meeting house, guessing that the temperature was already below zero.

The other members were inside the starkly furnished room, dressed in wool suits and white shirts, but most hadn't taken off their overcoats and were huddled around the small wood stove in the center of the room. The cold seeped in through the thin wooden walls, making the roaring blaze impotent. These definitely weren't the posh surroundings of the Cattlemen's Club.

The Cattle Growers' Association was a separate entity. The Cattlemen's Club had been established for the sole purpose of the cattlemen's entertainment. It was the Cattle Growers' Association that actually tried to make policy and get laws passed that would aid the ranchers.

Will pulled up a chair and joined the others, who tried to make some room so he could warm his hands by the fire.

Clayton Kincaid stepped forward from behind the others, looking out of place in his expensive wool coat and derby hat. Next to him stood Tom Diering, looking uncomfortable in new, stiff clothes. At least at these meetings Kincaid was not the president; Will was. And even though Clayton sat there in smug observation, he usually kept his mouth shut.

Will called the meeting to order. He listened to the business with only half an ear while his mind remained on Kate and the need to see her again soon. The meeting was adjourned with all in agreement to hire an agent to look into some cattle rustling.

Will buttoned his coat and followed the others into the frigid, starry night. Some went toward the saloon to get something warm inside before starting home; others headed for the nearest hotel, deciding it wasn't wise to try and ride miles, risking frostbite of their fingers and toes.

Will pulled his thick elkskin gloves over cotton liners and decided he'd head home. He took a step in the direction of the livery when Clayton stepped beside him.

"You were pointing your finger at Vaughn in there, accusing him of cattle rustling. You'd better lay off him or you'll find yourself dry-gulched one of these days."

Will started walking again toward the livery and Clayton fell into step, his paces falling short of Will's long-legged strides. "He's got no business being a member of the association when it's pretty damned obvious what he's been doing to keep his herd count up."

"You don't have proof."

"You only need proof for convictions. I can't pull him in on my hunches, but I know he's guilty just the same."

At the livery Tom Diering was saddling his horse. He looked up at them, but then went back to his business with an air of indifference. Will had been wanting to speak to him all night. It wasn't right that he couldn't see Kate just because Tom didn't like him. It was time they talked.

Will walked to his horse's stall, started saddling him, and got right to the point. "Tom, you said you wouldn't let Kate see me again without permission. Well, I'm asking for it now."

Tom straightened his back. His shoulders were

a bit stooped, but he held his head up militantly. Will saw him glance past him at Kincaid, a cautious look in his eye. "It won't do you any good to ask. You won't be seeing Kate anymore. If I so much as hear you've touched her again, I'll blast a hole in you the size of your fist."

Will stopped what he was doing and looked over the horse's back at Tom's determined expression. "What exactly is it you've got against me, Tom? Whatever it is you've got stuck in your craw, I wish to hell you'd cough it out."

Diering pulled himself into the saddle. His nervous glance kept straying to Kincaid, who stood nearby, listening. "I don't need to explain anything to you, but just remember one thing—stay away from Kate, or I'll kill you. You've been warned."

Clayton drew his own horse from the stall to prepare it for the short ride across town. In the shadows of the livery he watched the exchange between Diering and Chanson, seeing the trouble brewing, and seeing his position in the middle of it. Kate was definitely the weak link in Will Chanson, but then a woman usually was a man's downfall. He'd planned to have Kate as his wife, but suddenly he was seeing that she could be useful to him in another way. If he could capture her—like a pawn—it would then be a simple matter to capture the CM ranch.

He watched as Will mounted his horse and forced it out into the cold night. Then he too stepped into the stirrup. Will went south and he turned north, but from over his shoulder he glanced at the broad back of the man who was instinctively his rival.

Clayton smiled, although the cold nearly cracked his lips. Will wanted Kate, and she just might be the straw that could break him.

Chapter 8

Will took off his gloves and rubbed his numb fingers. He tried breathing on them, but his breath was so icy that it nearly turned crystalline as it drifted upward into the November blue of the afternoon sky. He draped the reins over his arm and started walking, hoping he could get some feeling back into his feet. The leather shotgun chaps protected his legs a bit, but he wished he'd worn his woolly chaps instead. At least the heavy leather coat was a blessing.

There was going to be a big freeze tonight; he could sense it. He'd come out to check the fence line, but it had been pure misery trying to fix the breaks in the extreme cold.

He stopped to open a wire gate and felt a cold breeze push at his back. A strange medley of notes danced on the cold wires as the wind touched them, like fingers on the strings of a musical instrument. He paused and listened, and looked down the length of the four ice-crusted silver strands.

When the wire had first been brought into Colorado, his father had walked away from the general store and the high-pressure salesman. Tyler Chanson had worn a sadness that made him look older than he was. "It's the end of the open range, Will. It's the end of a lot of things."

"We have to change with the times, Dad," Will had replied, secretly fascinated by the shiny metal with the cruel, sharp barbs. But now the wire stretched to the horizons as far as he could see, and he understood his father more clearly.

He wished he understood what to do about that mule-headed Tom Diering. He'd thought about it ever since the association meeting, but hadn't come up with any good ideas. Nor had he heard from Kate; she hadn't responded to the message he'd left with Aimée. But he knew one thing for sure: He wasn't going to be frightened away by Diering's threats.

The wind picked up speed and whistled through the thin metal threads again. He shivered and gathered up the reins, slumping deeper into his coat, and wondering what kind of country it was that could smother a man with heat in October and freeze him to death four weeks later.

He thought of the summer just past and the grass scorched by the heat and the fires. He thought of Kate Diering's inexperienced yet fiery kiss. He had never been preoccupied with any woman before, and he had never sought any other since that day of the fire.

His feet were cold, but a shot of whisky might warm him up. It was only a few miles to Denver. He glanced at the sky from over his shoulder. There were no clouds in any direction, but it was the ominous silence alternating with the occasional rush of the wind that made him feel as though some danger lurked just beyond view.

Then a rider emerged from the stark south-western horizon, and Will knew instinctively that the man had nothing to do with this odd omen hanging over the cold land. He kept his buckskin in check, its back hunched up beneath the saddle as it tried to draw all its parts closely together in a futile effort to keep warm.

The rider lifted a hand in greeting as the horse, looking small beneath the man's bulk, trotted closer. Will soon recognized Dexter Marlow and his cold lips attempted a smile. His hot breath drifted upward and mingled with the heavy vapor from his horse, shaggy with a heavy winter coat of hair. But Dexter rode with an urgency and the expression on his face showed it. Will sensed something was wrong and before Dexter even drew his horse to a halt next to Will's he hollered across the distance between them.

"Will, I been lookin' all over for you. There's somethin' I've got to show you. It's the mine, Will. It's the mine."

Will tucked a gloved hand beneath the buckskin's black mane, hoping for a little warmth from the heat of the animal. "What's the problem, Dexter?"

Dexter's horse danced next to Will, seemingly sensing his rider's excitement. "Just come on with me. You've got to see it." Dexter reined his horse back in the direction he'd come.

Will put his own into motion to catch up. "Hold on. I'm not about to ride up to Cripple Creek in this weather. Besides, I think a storm's brewing."

Dexter shook his big head, covered tightly with a cap and encircled with a wool scarf tied beneath his chin. "Would you believe me if I said it wasn't?" It amazed Will how the man could know things like that, but he did, not even questioning his unique ability.

Will nodded and looked at the clear sky above the peaks of the Rockies. He'd never known Dexter to be wrong, and he didn't have anything better to do anyway. "Okay, but let me stop at the ranch. I'll need a few things, and I'll have to tell the boys where I'm going."

"Scoff if you want to, Will, but you saw the samples. The assayer says they're rich, some of the richest he's ever seen." Dexter Marlow circled his horse around a granite outcropping on the side of a hill and stopped. He removed his hat and wiped the sweat off his brow with his dirty coat sleeve. Despite the cold, he was sweating.

"Did you tell the assayer where you got it?" Will asked, following close behind.

"Hell, no. I hedged. I don't want no run on this place."

Dexter stepped down from his horse. The mine overlooked a wide mountain meadow and was prime summer grazing ground for cattle and horses. He stood on the edge of a hole he'd dug back into the side of the hill. It was one of many he had dug and abandoned over the years. There was a lot of brush and rock around the hole, some of which he'd placed for concealment, but from below, the spot wasn't noticeably visible.

Will dismounted next to him. His boots crunched on traces of the season's first snow. It was hard to believe that after all of Dexter's years of wandering and searching he may have finally found his mother lode.

"Are you sure that assayer knew what he was

talking about?" Will asked as he peered down into the worthless-looking hole.

Dexter ignored Will's skeptical question. "I know it doesn't look right. The hills are all wrong. There're no ravines for likely sites, not much of a quartz indicator—in some places, absolutely none."

"Maybe what you found was some of that salting from Mount Pisgah a few years back."

"Don't be so damned optimistic," Dexter replied sarcastically. "It's here sure as you and I are. Now, come on and I'll show you."

Dexter had dug into the hill a good distance, but it was barely more than a crawling space. With a lantern he reached the end of the "cave" and held the light up to the rock wall. "There's the vein right there. It's a good one, too. My guess is that it'll get better the deeper it goes."

"Or vanish altogether."

Dexter ran his hand over the rough wall of rock in a gentle caress, not letting Will's skepticism discourage him. "It's part yours, Will. That's part of the grubstake agreement. There's only one problem at this point. We're going to have to dig this thing deeper and brace it up to make a regular shaft out of it. That's going to take money, work, and men."

Will ran a hand over the vein and followed its golden course as far as the light shone, which was almost to the end of the wall. "And if you do that you bring in everybody from California to Maine."

"I'm not the first one who's been nosin' around up here. It's going to happen sooner or later. This place has been crawling with people this summer. A lot of them have found gold, too. The word's been out for years. It's just going to take one legitimate claim and the rush will be on. I say we get this claimed legally and maybe some other holes around here. Where there's one vein, there's sometimes others connecting with it."

Will was familiar with mining from the aspect of investment, but owning a gold mine was different. As he looked at the vein in the rock, he was beginning to understand the fevers men got when they saw the ore.

Finally, he backed out of the small mine and straightened his shoulders. Before them the quiet pastureland stretched to the west, white with snow and glistening beneath the afternoon sun. The high mountain meadow was terminated abruptly, though, by the bands of mountains that lay one behind the other until they faded into the blue haze on the horizon.

Dexter's nervous energy was obvious as the big man shifted weight constantly from one foot to the other, waiting for Will's decision. Will wasn't interested in amassing fortunes and owning the entire state the way Kincaid was, but he wouldn't disappoint his friend.

"Come on, we'd better stake our claim."

The words were barely out of his mouth when Dexter jerked his hat off his head, tossed it into the air, and let out a whoop that echoed out across the wide, empty meadow below them. "You won't regret it, Will. I swear you won't. There's going to be some good things come from this mine, you'll see. What are you going to name her?"

Will picked up his horse's trailing reins. "I'll give you the honors since you discovered it."

"No, no." Dexter's eyes sparkled with excitement as he hurried to collect his own horse. "I don't know no pretty ladies to name it after. I can't think of nothin' fancy." He pulled his heavy body into the saddle. "Names don't mean much to me."

With one hand Will easily swung aboard and led the way back down the rocky ledge to level ground. "All right," he said with certainty. "We'll call it the Kate Meline."

Dexter chuckled and kicked his horse up next to Will's. "We're going to be the richest men in Denver—maybe even the whole state of Colorado—when we get all the gold out of the Kate Meline."

The streets were still white with snow from the recent storm. The temperature had dropped below zero, and the town was moving stiffly, if at all. The extreme cold hurt Kate's throat and stung her lungs as she stepped out onto the wooden veranda of Clayton's mansion. She pulled her fur collar up over her face and put her hands in the blue fox fur muff, thankful for the warmth. Clayton stepped up behind her, but she moved out of his reach, not wanting to feel his touch and consequently have him see the telltale signs of repulsion in her eyes.

She went to her father's six-passenger sleigh that would take them home to the new house. She had always loved riding in the sleigh when she was younger, loved the emerald-green color and the matching green plush cushions, the swollen sides and swan's head that gracefully arched in the front. But today, with the unwanted assistance of Clayton, she found a seat in the middle and watched while the baggage was crammed into the rear seat. She was unable to conjure up any of those remembered feelings.

Her father helped Cordelia onto the front seat with him and she snuggled next to him, linking an arm with his, more lovable toward him than usual.

Clayton stood at the side of the conveyance. "I'll be seeing you soon, Kate."

There was a tone in his voice that made it sound almost like a command. Kate merely nodded in response as her father put the horses into motion. She didn't look back at Clayton, glad to be away from him, realizing that he had never uttered a word of sincere emotion despite the fact that he wanted her to be his wife. She wondered if he ever had deep feelings for anyone, or had ever spoken any words of love, true or false. He treated the marriage proposal as just another deal, another business matter. He was as cold as the frigid December day.

The horses chose the path of least resistance to the Diering ranch while the narrow silver cutters on the sleigh slit the snow with hardly a sound. Kate heard her father and Cordelia talking about the new house, but she let her mind wander, catching only words and occasional phrases.

Instead, she dwelled on her own thoughts and her own life, wondering what was to become of it. She would be eighteen soon. Most girls were married by that age, or at least engaged. For her, there appeared to be no future. What she had experienced with Will now seemed only a dream, and she had no intention of even considering Clayton in the same capacity.

The ranch came into view, and Kate craned her

neck to look. Covered with snow the yard showed no sign of the fire. The house had been rebuilt to duplicate the grand splendor of its first life; it was almost impossible to tell that it was not the same tall structure. The house was painted white, with black shutters and a dark roof that contrasted with the snow.

Even the sky was white with low clouds, silently and heavily threatening more snow. It was a calm day, so if snow came, it would pile up without the usual wind to push it into drifts. It could be hazardous if the snow became too deep and the grass was buried. The cattle would go hungry.

Tom stopped the sleigh in front of the house and immediately two cowboys hastily pulling on their coats emerged from the bunkhouse to help carry the bags. Kate accepted help from one of the cowboys and then went into the house ahead of the others.

Although everything about the house, even the furniture and the floor and wall coverings had been replaced with duplicates whenever possible, Kate didn't feel as though she had come home. It was, in essence, Cordelia's house. It always had been.

She was halfway up the stairs when her father and Cordelia came in. "Kate!" her father called in a voice that was gruffer than usual. "Aren't you going to have dinner with us?"

She turned to look at the two of them. They didn't fit together; her father was a plain man at heart—even fancy clothes didn't change him. She met Cordelia's petulant and spiteful gaze. No, Kate just wanted to be alone; she was tired from the thoughts that never seemed to rest, tired of the pressure she had felt at Clayton's. "If you will excuse me this once, I'd rather go to bed. Please enjoy yourselves. I'll see you in the morning."

When Kate's door closed behind her, Cordelia turned to Tom. "Why do you let her get away with such insolence?"

Tom was still looking upward at the spot where Kate had stood. For an instant she had reminded him again of Meline. "Perhaps it's just as well that we dine alone, we haven't for so long now. But you're wrong about Kate. She wasn't being insolent."

Surprise flared in Cordelia's eyes, and Tom realized he rarely disagreed with her openly. He held out his arm, hastily making amends. Having freed herself of her ermine coat, Cordelia tucked her arm inside his. He led her to the dining room where the table was prepared and waiting for their return.

"The house is splendid, Tom. It's amazing. I don't feel as though it ever burned. It feels exactly the same."

Tom seated her and moved to the other side of the table across from her. Cordelia adjusted the full skirt of her new dress while Tom silently cursed the starch of his new white shirt as it rubbed on his neck with every move. Dressing for dinner was a custom he'd never liked, and he'd had to stay dressed that way practically the entire time they had been at Clayton's. Sometimes he longed for his casual cowboy days, but back then he had longed for wealth and prosperity, and for a woman like Cordelia.

Meline had never wanted more than a small white frame house, but she had understood his dreams and had stood by them, right down to coming to Colorado when her fragile condition was worsening. Even then, as he'd sat across the table from her, he had wished she was more elegant...

A surge of guilt flooded over him. It was odd how sometimes reality didn't match up to a man's dreams.

Cordelia shook out her napkin and then spoke in a low, but distressed voice. For the first time she was able to air her feelings about the latest development. "I can't believe my father has taken a liking to Kate." She realized how that had sounded. Sometimes she tended to forget that Kate was still Tom's child. She hastened on to explain. "I mean, she's so young. He's almost forty years older than she is."

Tom couldn't tell Cordelia that he didn't approve of the match either; he couldn't tell her that if Kate didn't marry Clayton, the man could very easily pull the rug out from under him; couldn't tell her how close he was to bankruptcy. He had no choice but to encourage Kate to accept Clayton. He could only hope that Clayton would move swiftly as her suitor and sweep her off her feet. That way, he wouldn't have to interfere.

"You must admit, dear, it's better than her being with Chanson."

Cordelia felt a helpless desperation. She didn't know if she agreed this time. She had been betrayed by her own father. How *could* he be interested in Kate? What did Kate have that attracted the men so? Now the richest man in Colorado was courting her. Kate would be living the social life Cordelia yearned for and was accustomed to, while she was stuck out here on this damned ranch for the rest of her life with nothing to put excitement in her days or nights.

It wasn't fair that Kate could be so fortunate, and she didn't seem to even appreciate Clayton Kincaid. If Cordelia could persuade her father to give up this foolishness she would, but she knew he did as he pleased. She hated Kate in a way she never had before, but these were thoughts she had to keep to herself. There was no one here she could talk to.

"It seems she causes us problems at every turn. Maybe we should simply send her back to England. It would end my father's foolishness, and Will Chanson's as well."

"I'm afraid Will would find a way to see her regardless," Tom replied glumly. "As for your father, I'm beginning to believe he would make her a good husband, despite the age difference."

Cordelia sucked in a sharp breath, halting the wineglass so suddenly in midair that she spilled a few drops onto the skirt of her new dress. She cursed beneath her breath at the accident and at Tom's idiotic attitude as she wiped at the liquid, managing only to force it farther into the threads of the fabric. Then she gave up, shrugging her shoulders. What did it matter? It had served its purpose. She could throw it away and get another.

Her eyes strayed to Tom. She smiled suddenly. It was a wicked thought, but she realized she could do the same with him.

Chapter 9

Cordelia was standing at the window when Kate came down the stairs. Kate had spent the better part of a week in her room thinking about Will.

Her stepmother turned at the sound of her footsteps. Anxiety creased her usually smooth face. "Kate, I'm so glad you came down. I'm terribly worried about your father."

Kate acknowledged to herself that Cordelia did look genuinely concerned. "Why? What's wrong?"

Cordelia twisted her pale hands together and moved nervously about the foyer in a small square, stopping occasionally to glance out the window. "Your father left early this morning and said he'd only be out an hour or so to check the cattle, and then he was going to return to take me to town. It's not like him to keep me waiting. I'm afraid he might be hurt."

Kate knew it wasn't unusual for her father to become so involved in his work that he forgot to eat, but he wouldn't break a promise to Cordelia. "Where did he say he was going?"

"I'm not sure." Cordelia waved her hand impatiently. "I never listen to all their ranch talk, you know that. I saw him go south with a hired hand. That's all I know."

139

Kate had never seen Cordelia so upset. She eyed the woman dubiously, wondering if something else was bothering her. She tried to calm her down. "He's probably checking the fences and driving the cattle to a place where the feed is easier to get. The heavy snowfall this year has caused a lot of problems."

"I know. I know." Cordelia's patience was wearing very thin. "But I'm worried, Kate. What should we do?"

Kate reached for her coat near the door. "I'll have one of the men go out and try to find him."

Cordelia grabbed her arm. "No! I mean, the men are all busy with their own jobs and Tom would probably be furious if we took one of them away from his work. You're not doing anything. Why don't you go look for him? Please."

Kate didn't share her stepmother's concern but decided she would pacify the woman. "Very well, I'll go change my clothes."

"Oh, you don't need to do that. Just put on a coat and some boots. For heaven's sake, Kate. It's a calm day."

"It may look nice, Cordelia, but it's very cold — below zero, as a matter of fact. I'll get on some warm clothes and then I'll go."

In her room, Kate found her wool underwear and a pair of wool pants she'd bought long before she'd ever gone to England. It made riding in the winter much warmer and easier. She had to struggle to get them over both the bulky underwear and her hips. They had been too big for her four years ago, but conformed to her shape almost *too* perfectly now. She then layered her top half with underwear, a flannel shirt, and a wool sweater.

From her wardrobe she pulled a heavy man's coat and a pair of woolly chaps. A scarf and a cowboy hat, and several pairs of socks beneath her riding boots completed her garb.

She looked at herself in the mirror. Her attire wasn't attractive in the least, but she knew all too well how cold she could get sitting on a horse.

Kate left her room and joined Cordelia again in the foyer.

"It took you long enough," Cordelia snapped. "Do you think all that was necessary?"

"Perhaps *you'd* like to go, Cordelia." When Kate saw the stricken look on the blonde's face, she nodded and pulled the door open. "I thought so."

It was every bit as cold outside as she had suspected. Immediately, she felt the sting of it on her face as she walked to the corral to get her horse. As she led the mare to the tack room she looked north and then let her gaze follow the front range of the Rockies southward. The sun was hidden behind a solid sheet of unmoving leaden clouds that covered the entire sky and reached down toward the circle of the horizon in all directions. With an uneasy feeling she saddled and bridled the horse. Then she pulled herself into the saddle.

She pointed the mare south and it seemed more than eager to go in that direction. There was no sign of any life. Kate found herself continually looking over her shoulder, but there was nothing there.

There were no tracks to follow although Kate used the usual trail. It could be that Cordelia was mistaken about where her father had gone. She rode until she saw the barbed-wire barrier that marked the Chanson property.

She started to turn her mare north but a longing to see Will tugged at her. She could ride over to his place and ask if he'd seen her father, and then perhaps she could get answers to some of the nagging questions about their relationship. She reined the horse south and stepped down and opened the wire gate that separated the properties. When her horse had stepped through to the other side, she struggled with the three-stranded wire blockade. Though she cursed the bulky gloves that prevented dexterity, she knew that if she removed them the frosty wire would freeze instantly to her skin. Finally, she succeeded in closing the gate and once again straddled her horse, bending over its neck in a crouch as the cold began to find its way through the layers of wool clothing.

As the Chanson ranch came into view the qualms welled up inside her with incredible size and quantity. She stopped her horse at the hitching rail in front of the house and stepped down, absently wrapping the reins around the horizontal pole. With her boots crunching in the snow she walked up the path to the house and, at the door, removed her hat and scarf, letting her long hair fall freely. Maybe that, at least, would make her look like the woman she wanted Will to see.

She lifted her hand to knock when a man's voice behind her sent a pleasant chill down her spine and made her almost whirl on her heel to face him.

"Kate. What brings you this way on such a cold day?"

He stood at the foot of the porch steps, and from her position, she had to look down at him. "Will ...I was just about to ...knock." His disarming sapphire eyes were more brilliant with the snow as a background, but they did not contain their customary twinkle. She saw a coldness in them that she guessed was not caused by the weather. She tried to guess what he thought of her unannounced visit, but she could gauge nothing from the stony set of his jawline. Her heart fell. What had she hoped for? Open arms?

"I'm looking for my father. Have you seen him?"

He propped a foot on the lowest step and placed his forearm on his knee, leaning his body forward. "No. This is not a place he generally likes to visit." Instantly, he was angry with himself for being so harsh toward her. She hadn't answered his message, which obviously meant she wasn't interested in a reconciliation, but he would have to accept the fact that she had politely terminated their brief relationship.

Kate filled the silence with an explanation taken without a breath. "Cordelia said he had come this way and was supposed to be home within an hour, but he hasn't returned and she's worried."

Will was more interested in Kate and how pretty she was than in Tom Diering. He fought the urge to feel the loose, silken tresses of hair beneath his fingers, and fought to keep from pulling her into his arms.

"He could easily have changed direction," he heard himself say. "You know what it's like when you're looking for cows."

"I know, but Cordelia was worried."

"Are *you* worried about him, Kate?"

The sound of her name from his tongue always sent little goose bumps popping out all over her. "Well, no. Not really. I've always believed he could

143

take care of himself. Cordelia stays at the house so much she doesn't understand what goes on beyond it."

Feeling foolish for coming here and wondering if Will could see inside her to the real reason for her visit, Kate moved toward the steps. Surely, Will knew he was blocking her way, but instead of stepping aside, he merely straightened up, filling the space even more with broad shoulders made wider by the heavy wool coat he wore.

"Excuse me," she said, trying to shoulder her way past him. "If you haven't seen him, then I'd better be going."

He moved aside slowly and watched her as she twisted her long hair up onto her head and then expertly drew the scarf over the top of it, covering both with the wide-brimmed cowboy hat. It wasn't stylish, but she was beautiful anyway.

She walked past him and to her horse, but suddenly he moved so fast it surprised them both. In two long strides he was at her side and caught her arm just as she was lifting a foot to the stirrup. "Why would your father have reason to come on my range, Kate? Do you know something I don't?"

Kate stared up at him, shocked by his hasty action and the implication of his words. He may just as well have slapped her face. "My father isn't rustling your damn cattle, Will Chanson—or anyone else's. Now, I'd better be going or Cordelia will be worrying about me, too."

Will's smile had a sardonic curve to it. Nevertheless, it had the power to make her heart skip a beat.

"Do you really think Cordelia cares what happens to you? From what you've told me, I would surely doubt it."

Kate shook her arm free of his hand and quickly got into the safety of the saddle. She pulled her horse away from the railing and away from Will. The animal reluctantly obeyed, preferring to stay in the shelter of the house. Kate's heart ached from his harsh words and cold behavior. "No, I doubt she does. It seems to be the consensus."

She kicked the mare into a lope until they were out of the yard. Finally, she slowed to a walk because of the slick footing. She pulled her hat down against the burning bite of the cold air on her face. She drew her collar up higher and breathed into it to avoid inhaling the air directly into her lungs.

She pushed her horse hard until she reached the property-line fence and was once again on Diering land. For the first time she noticed large, fat snowflakes drifting onto her horse's mane, their delicate forms in vivid contrast to the coarse black hair.

Then from the east she heard shouting and looked to her right to see two cowboys pushing a small herd of cattle toward the west. One of the men was her father. She pulled rein and, when they were closer, moved out of the way and to the back of the herd to join them.

Her father's expression darkened with anger and she soon found that it was meant for her. "What in the hell are you doing out here, girl? This ain't no time to be joyriding. Can't you see there's a storm coming?"

Kate had ridden with her head down for protection but also because she was deep in thought.

Now she looked north and saw that the previously heavy gray sky was white. A curtain of snow fell from it, its perimeters so definite that the lines of demarcation could have been drawn with a pencil. It moved on a piercing wind that preceded it and suddenly blasted them with its stinging force, snatching at Kate's breath and pushing her farther back into her saddle. As the snow drew nearer, it widened out, reaching to enclose the horizon in all directions.

She called out over the sudden roar of the wind, answering her father's previous question. "I came looking for you."

"What the hell for?" He waved his arms and cussed at the small herd of cattle as they tried to turn away from the encroaching storm.

Kate now had to yell to be heard above the noise of the wind and bawling cows. "Because Cordelia was worried!"

Tom's expression softened for an instant but then turned hard again. The lines on his face deepened, becoming brittle in the cold. "We're trying to get as many of the cattle as we can to some sort of shelter. You'd better get on home now before you go and get yourself lost. Tell Cordelia I'll be there when I can."

The snow had reached them now in a sweeping rush, instantly matting on the backs of the cattle and the riders' coats. Kate looked northward toward where the house lay, still some miles off, and she was reluctant to set out across the open plains. The visibility was shrinking. The mare fought her tight hold on the bridle reins as it circled, wanting to turn its back to the cold wind and stinging snow. Kate watched her father and the hired hand, Riley, set out again away from her. In an instant the distant horizon completely vanished from sight.

The cattle turned their heads from the furious blast and huddled in a tight circle to get protection from each other's bodies. Kate's father and Riley tried in vain to break them apart, but it seemed a losing battle. Kate advanced to try and help them. The snow had now completely blanketed the animals. Her father shouted at her to go home. She tried to turn her horse north, but it refused.

A steer from the group of cattle moved away from the shouting men and, faltering, left the herd, putting his back to the wind and the snow. Hesitantly, and then more willingly, the others followed. In seconds they were gone, drifting with the storm, despite the efforts of the men to stop them.

Tom Diering cursed and set out after them again. Kate followed this time, feeling safer in the company of the men. The snow was becoming so heavy and the wind increasing with such ferocity that to ride into it was nearly impossible. It slashed at Kate's face, numbing it and making it difficult to keep her eyes open. The curtain of white fell directly in front of her; she couldn't see beyond Starr's ears.

Again her father and Riley tried to circle the cattle and push them westward again, but the cattle bent their heads, refusing the commands. The white closed in around them all. Kate could hear shouting, and even the occasional striking of hoof on hoof, but she could see nothing unless it was nearly touching her.

Then she heard a frightened call. "Tom, where

are you! I can't see you. God! I can't see anything. I can't—"

"Stop your horse, Riley," came her father's answering shout above the howling wind. The words were brief as the wind whisked them away with the snow. "We'll get a rope and secure ourselves together so we won't be separated. Riley, call out!"

Riley answered, but his reply in the whistling wind seemed to shift and his location evaded them. Then a mightier surge pummeled Kate in the back, nearly toppling her from the saddle, and with it came an even heavier blast of snow, sucking at her breath and burning her numb face with a new degree of pain. She clutched at her hat, pulling it so low that it was nearly in her eyes, to keep the wind from picking it up and carrying it away.

The temperature had been below zero when she set out on her quest, but now with the wind blowing, it dipped even lower. Knowing it would be impossible to turn the herd now, Kate looked to her father to encourage him to give up and let the cattle fend for themselves, but she no longer saw the dark, snow-matted form. There was nothing there but a solid wall of driving snow.

She pulled Starr to a stop, suppressing the sudden panic growing inside her. She searched in all directions, shielding her eyes with her gloved hand. "Daddy!" she screamed. "Daddy!"

But the only sound she heard was the wail of the wind. Kate knew she was approximately a few hundred feet from the Chanson's fence. She could try to find the gate again and make her way back to the CM ranch, which was closer than home, but she would still have to cross open ground without the aid of landmarks. Under these conditions, she knew she could ride within twenty feet of the yard and never see it.

Kate called for her father again, but there was no answer. She let her horse have the rein and its instinct. With heads down, they moved southward again and away from the pelting fury of the storm. The horse picked up speed and Kate let her go until she found some of the cattle. She could hear the sound of their hooves, their occasional bellows, and could feel the bumping of their snow-covered backs against her legs.

Being in their midst gave her a sense of security and she was reluctant to leave them. She wondered if her father had stayed with them, or if he had headed straight into the storm for home.

She called out every few minutes but received no reply. Finally, she stopped her horse again and looked about in rising fear and panic. The urge to cry surfaced, as well as the hot sting of tears in her eyes, but she knew she could not give in to it or there would be absolutely no hope of survival. But she could not see a thing! The feeling of helplessness was so overpowering that she found herself losing the ability to think. What was she going to do? Which direction should she take?

Kate called out again, the desperation tightening her chest painfully, but the wind's scream was louder than her best effort. She turned in the saddle in one last attempt to sight her father, but the snow lashed at her like a whip with its fine, sandy, bitterly cold texture.

She felt the body of an animal brush against her and then disappear, lost to the white, frightening world that enveloped her. There was not a sign of a landmark anywhere. With a sinking heart, she hunched her shoulders against the wind, acutely aware of the cold settling into her fingers and toes, wondering what it was going to be like to freeze to death.

Will saddled his horse, not liking the color of the sky to the north or the deathly calm. It looked like a blizzard setting down on them and Kate was headed right into it. Will leaped into the saddle and urged the buckskin out of the yard as fast as he dared force him on the snowy ground. From across the plains he could see the cattle moving restlessly, circling, not grazing, and occasionally looking northward. Will had seen those signs before and he knew exactly what they meant.

As he drove his horse into the oncoming weather, the cattle turned tail and headed south, forming long lines. Occasionally, he saw Kate in the far distance but she was too far away to hear his call. He wished he had not let her go, but afterthoughts were useless now. He was just thankful he had been home. Just last night he and Dexter had returned from Cripple Creek. Dexter had intuitively known a blizzard was coming.

A mile before he reached the division fence the air had turned noticeably colder. He saw the storm coming in a solid wall of white and then, in an instant, it whirled down upon him in slanting fury.

He had to find Kate and get her to safety. She would never make it across the open range to the Diering place in this blinding blizzard. He forced his horse onward. It lowered its young head nearly to the ground to try and get away from the freezing gale. Will could gauge his direction only by the direction of the wind blowing the snow. Frozen pellets of ice formed on his face from his warm breath meeting the cold air. He couldn't see beyond the length of his arm and he knew his horse couldn't either. He pulled his collar up higher around his face, barely feeling the rough cloth against his numb skin.

Then he heard noises coming to him on the wind. He halted his horse and listened harder, trying to catch anything above the demonic howl assaulting him. Then again he heard a sound, like a shout, but it was weaker, higher pitched, and to the southeast. He lifted his reins and signaled his horse to move, but it took only a few steps before he stopped. In front of them was the wire of the division fence.

Again he heard the sound coming from farther down the fence to the east. He moved his horse closer to the sound that sighed on the wind. Then he saw movement, a dark form with its upper portion completely matted with snow. With it was a few head of cattle, following the fence to the east, keeping their backs to the wind as much as possible.

Hope surged inside him, as well as fear that what he had seen may very well not have been Kate. Will shouted into the wind, hoping it would carry in the rider's direction. "Kate! Kate!"

He waited, listened. There was no answering reply. He pulled his Colt revolver from his hip holster and pointed it upward. With cold fingers he found the trigger and fired one bullet into the sky. He knew Kate didn't have a gun to give an answering reply, but if she heard the sound she might be able to find him.

He continued to fire, waiting after each shot for an answer of some sort, but there was none, not even the earlier sound of shouting he thought he had heard. Then he saw movement again and his heart leaped with hope. He edged closer to the fence to look to the other side. To his disappointment, it was only another small group of cattle filing eastward.

With hopelessness settling over him, Will tried to look into the storm again. Its fierceness had increased to a degree he could easily compare with the Great Blizzard of '86, but he had to keep on; he had to find her. He couldn't leave her alone out here. He looked to the east, although he saw nothing there, but instinct took hold of him and he went in that direction. He had seen the rider; it was all he had to go on. He could only hope it had been Kate. He tried to guess what she might do, and wondered if she had thought about the Chanson line shack a couple of miles away, just off the division fence.

With renewed hope he let his horse move southward along the fence. He pulled his collar up and his hat down, wishing he'd put on more clothes. But he'd left in such haste...

Kate thought she had heard a gunshot over the scream of the wind, but she couldn't be sure of its location because the wind carried the sound away. She didn't know if her father had a gun with him, but she dared not set out after the sound until she could better locate it. But while she waited and listened, it did not sound again.

It must have been only her imagination. The cold had burrowed itself to her skin now and was extremely painful. She wondered if she would know the moment of death or if it would sneak upon her as a silent ghost, unseen. She followed the cattle. With eyes closed to narrow slits, she became highly aware of the swaying movement of the horse, almost as if she were being rocked in her sleep. The world around her disappeared in the unrelenting howl of the wind. She knew the Chanson line shack was ahead, if only she could reach it in time; and if only she would know when she was there.

With that thought in mind, she focused her mind away from the visual world she had been used to and tried to go by the feel of the land, the gentle ups and down. The Chanson line shack was just off a steep incline and in a protected cover of scrub trees and brush on a small stream. But the stream would be buried by snow, and if she veered from the fence too soon, or too late, she would miss it.

She tried to forget the cold that was stealing her senses and mobility, thinking that if she ignored it, it could not overcome her. She had no way of knowing how much time had passed. She only knew the snow was piling up in drifts along the fence that caused her horse extra effort.

With no warning, the ground went out from under her horse. Starr floundered, lunged, and then sank back helplessly in snow up to her neck. Without footing, she couldn't get herself out of the snow that hadn't hardened yet. Still in the saddle, Kate realized that the snow had drifted over the steep, rocky incline that marked the protective cove of the line shack. She felt a surge of exhilaration; she knew exactly where she was.

She slid from the saddle and into the snow, going

in up to her waist. Only a tight grip on the saddle horn kept her from going deeper. The wind wailed over the bluff and dropped snow onto her with amazing, and frightening swiftness. She struggled to get out, fearful that she may be buried alive.

The urge to cry nearly incapacitated her ability to think straight, but she fought the panic. She pulled, kicked, and struggled along with Starr as both tried to get out of the soft, deep snow. Her lungs were soon burning from exhaustion and from inhaling the subzero air. Her heart even felt as though it might burst.

Leaning her head against the saddle, she released the tears that had been threatening, but they froze almost instantly into crystalline spears on her numb face. The cold spread throughout her body. She knew she might not make it to the line shack. It had been below zero, and with the wind blowing, the temperature would be pushed to somewhere around sixty below. It was almost warm inside the snow, she realized.

The thought of giving up and staying where she was crossed her mind. But knowing she had to get to shelter, she forced her legs to move. With arms outstretched to keep her balance, she struggled downhill, grabbing the horse's reins and trying to force Starr forward. Cussing and yelling at the horse in her desperation, she kept on moving.

Will followed the fence, knowing he would hit the steep drop-off that led the way down to the line shack. He knew it was a bad place for drifting. The snow usually buried the fence as it sloped downward, so with a gloved hand, he began to feel for the posts to his left. His horse moved into deeper snow and he proceeded cautiously. Will sensed the drop-off, for he had been over it many times in his life and had spent many hours fixing the broken wire on the steep slope. Instinctively, he turned away from the fence, due south, and began a wide swing to a more gentle ascent.

The wind brought the sound of a shout and hope welled inside him. It was indeed a person, and that person was close. No doubt it was the rider he had seen earlier. He pulled his revolver from his holster again and with stiff fingers that were nearly frozen into the position in which they'd held the reins, he managed to pull the trigger. The shout went up again. This time he knew it was close. It sounded just under the cornice.

"Here! Oh . . . here! . . . the fence!" He caught only part of the words, but it was enough. He turned his horse away from the steep, drifted slope and in his mind tried to estimate the distance to a more gradual descent. Then he took his chances and plunged the horse over the bluff. It went into snow up to its chest but it lunged on powerful legs upward, taking another leap and then another until it found firm footing on more solid ground. Will doubled back toward the fence and into the direct onslaught of the northerly wind. He leaned over the horse's neck and together they pushed forward until the wire fence once again marked their position.

He got off his horse but kept a rein in hand, and started moving up the slope, the snow getting deeper and deeper on him until he could barely get one leg out and another in. At least the hill was not long, perhaps a hundred feet from top to bottom. He squinted through the white, nearly blinded by it. He took two more steps and saw the dark, snow-covered horse and rider. They were both nearly buried by the snow blowing over the top of the ridge.

Will floundered across the four feet that separated them. He cupped the person's face with his hands, peering at its snow-covered features and easily recognizing the delicate structure. His heart quickened with relief, and he thanked God that he had found Kate, but then fear took the place of relief as he began to worry that he might not be able to save her.

He brushed her face clean while pushing aside the strands of wet hair that had fallen from the protective cover of her scarf and hat. He wondered if she had the energy to get out. One glance at her horse told him the mare had given up.

"I'm going to get you out!" he shouted. She nodded, but there was no smile on her face, only pain.

He pushed his way back through the soft snow to the buckskin and worked at the leather saddle ties that held his lariat. He cursed his frozen, clumsy hands as time ticked by, realizing the dangers of Kate's condition—and even his own.

At last, he had the rope free and keeping a restraining hand on his horse's reins he made his way back up the slope to Kate. He took the lariat's loop and placed it over the black mare's head and then he moved to Kate. He took her arms, which were stretched out onto the snow, and helped her turn until she could reach the saddle horn. He placed her hands over it.

"Kate!" he hollered close to her ear, trying to make his mouth work in the frozen condition of his face. He felt paralyzed. There was no feeling in his lips to help form the words, and he knew they were distorted to a degree, as though he were drunk. "Hold on to the horn. I'll get my horse and pull you both out."

She moved her head in the pretense of a nod. He moved two feet away and could barely see her for a fresh flurry of snow that had taken the space he had vacated, but what he could see was not encouraging. Her face was translucent in the cold, her eyelashes heavy with matted snow that also clung to her face, forming crystals from her breath. He knew his own was the same. They didn't have much time left.

He awkwardly climbed back into the saddle, each movement a torturous effort. He made a dally around the saddle horn and pulled back on the reins. The buckskin's muscles tightened and he bowed his head nearly to the ground. The rope grew taut. The buckskin dug in as he backed up. Through the flurry the black mare struggled forward at the tightening rope around her neck. She lunged and with the pulling force of the other horse was able to keep moving until she got her legs, once again, beneath her.

The rope slackened and Will got down as quickly as his frozen limbs would allow. Kate clung to the saddle horn, her body leaning against the horse's side. She looked at him, but her eyes appeared glassy. He released her hands from the horn and drew her against him, but her body was stiff and unpliable.

He lifted her onto her saddle. She nodded as he handed her the reins. Her lips tried to move but couldn't. He reached a hand to her cheek. "It's all right, Kate. You're with me now."

Chapter 10

At the bottom of the slope Will turned the buck-skin due south, gauging the direction again by the wind at his back and the fierce angle of the snow. He knew the line shack was only a short distance from the fence. It was cradled in the basin of two low-running hills that stretched out north and south. On the eastern side of the creek that divided the basin, the cabin huddled in some bushes for protection from the wind that hurdled the snow over the opposite western slope and piled it up into a cliff bank like the one Kate had stumbled into.

Will tried to follow the creek bed, but it was already filling up with snow. The water beneath was frozen and then only existed in isolated pockets. Finally, he was halted by the corral poles that stretched across a wide, shallow pool in the small stream, allowing animals from the corral to get water.

He circled the horses around the corner to the open gate and into the corral. In the far corner of the corral was the small barn, constructed especially for horses, storing grass hay, or sheltering any sick animals that needed temporary care.

With renewed energy and determination he

pulled the barn door open and quickly led the horses inside. Out of the force of the wind, he was finally able to straighten his body. His chest burned from the exertion, but he had no time to dwell on the pain of it. He drew in a cold breath against the hammering of his heart, and pulled Kate from the saddle.

Trying to get his mouth to form words was a task in itself, and again they came out in a slow, slurred condition. "Kate, start walking... in here. I'll unsaddle the horses... and give them some hay. Keep moving."

She stared straight ahead, unblinking, almost as though her eyelids were frozen open. He took her arm and started her moving in a small eight-foot circle. Her shoulders were hunched from the extreme cold and he knew all she wanted to do was curl up and try to get warm; he wanted to, too. But, guessing by the leaden way her booted feet were touching the earthen floor of the barn, there was less feeling in her feet and legs than in his.

When Will was done with his task, he circled Kate's shoulders with his arm. Together, leaning on one another, they left the barn. Kate waited in her tight, hunched stance while Will fumbled with the barn door latch and finally closed it with his frozen fingers.

The cabin was just on the other side of the pole corral, rubbing backs with it. It was a squat one-room log structure that possibly measured twenty by twenty.

Each step was agonizing, but finally they reached the crudely made cabin door. Pushing it open with his shoulder, Will immediately moved

Kate to the bed and pulled off a large buffalo robe that covered it. After placing her down he wrapped the robe around her tightly, trying to roll her up in it from head to foot. She closed her eyes and let him do what he would, not having the ability to do for herself.

"Kate."

She forced her eyes open and looked into his snow-covered face. There were parts of her that had no feeling left, not even pain. Her mind was one of those parts.

"Don't go to sleep, Kate." His lips could barely mold around the words, and she felt pity for him, knowing that the cold was hurting him the way it was her. "I'll...I'll build a fire."

He moved to the small cookstove and in slow, jerking movement began the process of building a fire. She must help him. She pushed the robe aside and tried to stand up. Her legs nearly crumpled beneath her but she shuffled across the small room toward him.

"Get under the robe," he managed, and she saw the spark of anger in his glazed sapphire eyes.

"No." For the first time she tried to talk and realized how nearly impossible it was. "I'll help."

She handed him the sticks of wood from the box while he laid them expertly inside the firebox. Then, as he glanced at the cupboard next to her, she saw the box of matches and handed them to him. She moved to better see the warming flame flicker on the fine bark tinder until it reached upward with snaring fingers and enclosed the larger wood. They both stared at the life-giving blaze until it was burning freely on its own. Will replaced the round iron stove lids but left the damper open. Then he led Kate back to the bed.

Together they sat on the edge and wrapped the buffalo robe around them, slowly building the heat in their bodies and drawing out the cold. Kate looked around them at the semidark room, whose only fraction of light came from one very tiny window. It was still terribly cold in the cabin, but out of the force of the wind, it felt much warmer than what they had both endured.

Slowly, feeling began to emerge, not only in her body but in her brain. Along with it came a fierce pain as the thawing process began. She clenched her teeth as the feeling of needles began to jab her feet and hands. She started kneading her hands together in an effort to alleviate the pain.

In alarm, Will's arm moved to encircle her shoulders. "Don't rub your hands, Kate. If they're frostbitten, you'll do more damage."

He stood up and pulled her to her feet, and the pain was even more intense as she stepped down on them. Will pulled the wool covers back from the small bed that would barely fit two people. "Let's get our boots and outer clothing off."

Kate sat on a small wooden chair next to the bed and tried to pull the frozen, stiff leather boots off. Will immediately came to her aid and gently but firmly pulled them off and then helped her remove her snow-covered coat and gloves. She hesitated when it came to her pants, but she knew it would be foolish and useless to get in the bed with them on.

She looked up at him and then down at her hands that were flushed and beginning to sting with a painful heat. He was impatient and said, "It's no time for modesty, Kate."

At that, he turned his back to her and returned to the stove, checking it again for wood. She realized his action was intended to give her a moment of privacy, and while his back was turned, she undid the buttons with fingers that moved in agonizing pain and wiggled out of the pants. As quickly as her numb body would allow, she got into the cold bed, hoping it would warm up soon.

Will eventually turned around and walked to the bed, stooped, picked up the heavy buffalo robe and stretched it across the bed. "It's old," he commented, "but it'll keep us warm."

She noticed his face was red, and from the way his long fingers curved around the buttons on his coat, she knew they hurt as badly as her own. When he started to undo his belt, she turned to her side, keeping her back to him. She listened to the movements, feeling a strange new warmth flowing from the center of her body. When he pulled back the covers she kept her eyes on something other than him, even though he still wore his shirt and long underwear.

"I'll take the wall," he said in explanation as he slid down on the other side of her, facing her. "You'll be warmer on that side, closer to the stove."

She moved back closer to the edge of the bed, but he put his arm over her and drew her back up to his length. "Don't be afraid of me, Kate. We need to thaw out and the best way to do that in our situation is to let our bodies warm each other. The fire is going good now. We're safe."

"It doesn't feel any warmer in here."

"It'll take a while."

He pulled the covers up higher on their shoulders and, with a hand that already felt warm against her cold skin, drew her head against his chest. She felt his lips on the top of her head and his warm breath on her hair.

"Why were you out in the storm, Will?" She asked the question that had been on her mind since he had miraculously appeared to rescue her, just as he had that first time, the day of the fire.

His hand slipped from the covers to glide along her cheek and then rest softly on her face. The cold throughout her body scurried away on the new heat that his touch and his nearness created.

"Because I knew you would never make it home when I saw the storm coming."

"You were right," she murmured. "I wouldn't have." And she wondered if he would have done it for anybody, or if he had risked his life because of special feelings for her.

His hand caressing her cheek titillated her senses. She did not draw away from his lips as he lowered his head and touched her mouth with a light, gentle kiss. His kiss deepened, his tongue slipping between her lips, and she quickly fell victim to the pleasant sensations that he created.

Finally, Will pulled away and buried his face in her neck and the sweet-smelling strands of her rumpled hair. He felt so relieved to have her safely in his arms. A tremendous fear had stricken him out there in the blinding storm, a fear that he wouldn't find her, a fear that she would die. Her nearness and his thankfulness for her life pulled a need from so deep within him that he was startled by the intense awareness of it and the overpowering urge to satisfy it.

Instead, he drew her head to his chest again. "It'll be all right. Go to sleep now, Kate."

She was extremely tired, and the increasing warmth beneath the covers was adding to an uncontrollable drowsiness. There was still the stinging sensation in her body, especially her hands and feet, but then her eyes popped open and she tilted her head back to look into Will's eyes. "I wonder if my dad made it home or to shelter."

Will's expression was extremely grim, but he tried to encourage her. "He may have made it to another line shack. He may have even made it home."

Kate put her head back on his chest, listening to the beat of his heart, thankful for his nearness, thankful that he had cared enough to come after her. She was no fool where her father's chances were concerned. Will had another line shack on the western end of the property fence, but somehow she doubted her father would ever go there, because of his stubborn pride. He was on his own, and she knew it. As sleep settled over her tired mind and body, she couldn't help but wonder if her father had made an effort to find her.

Tom Diering stumbled up the snow-covered steps half on his feet and half on his hands. He banged on the door; his hands were too frozen to turn the doorknob. It was wrenched open by Cordelia. She stared at him for a moment as though she didn't recognize him. His face was stiff with small icicles and his eyelashes were caked with snow. His color was completely gone.

Cordelia gasped and her hand flew over her mouth as she simultaneously backed away from

165

him. On hands and knees he crawled inside the doorway and Cordelia started for the kitchen on a run.

"Aimée! Minnie! Hurry! Come quick. My God, it's Tom!"

The two female servants appeared in the arched doorway of the kitchen. Upon seeing Tom, Minnie shrieked but leaped forward, grabbing his arm while trying to help him to his feet. With the other hand she threw the door shut, blocking out the shrieking wind and excruciating cold. Aimée stood by with a sour expression on her face, not moving from her spot near the kitchen.

"My Lord," Minnie exclaimed. "He's stiff as a tree branch. Aimée, don't just stand there, get some warm water. Cordelia, help me get him inside. We need to work rapidly if we're going to save him."

Cordelia advanced hesitantly, afraid to touch him. But at last she circled his other rigid arm with her own, feeling the cold from his body immediately seep into hers. She shivered, despite the heavy shawl she wore to ward off the intensive cold filtering into the house. With the last of his strength and their helping hands, they got him into the parlor and in front of the fireplace. They stretched him out on the rug.

"Not too close to the fire," Minnie warned. "We're gonna have to thaw him slowly."

It was a task, but they finally got his outerwear off, covered him with several wool blankets, and put a pillow beneath his head. The icicles on his face started to melt and the glassiness of his eyes began to disappear. Minnie brought some warm tea that Aimée had fixed, as Cordelia stood over Tom, her lovely face reflecting her shock.

Minnie dropped down to her knees next to him and lifted his head. His face was still unpliable and most of the liquid spilled onto his chin. He tried to speak, but it was an incoherent effort. Aimée came in with a pot of warm water.

"Cordelia," Minnie said, "get some towels and we'll wrap his hands and feet in the warm water." While she spoke, she gently turned the extremities over in her hands and examined them.

Cordelia still stared dubiously at the pot of water. Finally she gave words to her thoughts. "Minnie, can't we do this somewhere else besides in here? I mean, I would hate to ruin this rug..."

Minnie's eyes were sharp on her, but she curbed the words she longed to say. "I'll get some blankets to put under him."

She hurried away and returned quickly. With Cordelia's help they spread the blankets out over the rug and rolled him onto them.

Minnie dipped the towels into the water and wrapped his feet. He objected as the pain of the thawing process began. "He's very lucky to be alive. I just hope the damage isn't extensive."

"What do you mean? He'll be okay. He's just cold."

Minnie was astounded at Cordelia's stupidity, but she tried to keep any tone of authority or superiority out of her voice. "Sometimes a person just gets so cold that he never warms up again. I'll work with him, ma'am. Why don't you go up and tell Kate to come down. She'll want to help with her father."

Cordelia put her hand to her mouth again. "My

God, Minnie. I was so worried about Tom that I completely forgot about Kate going out to look for him before the storm. She hasn't come back."

Minnie stared in disbelief and felt that the look of concern on Cordelia's face was not genuine. She knew how Cordelia felt about her stepdaughter; it would probably suit her just fine if Kate never came back. The thought of the girl out there made her shudder as a different kind of cold overcame her. She looked down at Tom Diering, closer to death than Cordelia realized. He had found his way home in the nick of time; it was easy to see that there would be no hope for a mere slip of a girl.

Tom's glazed eyes were on her. His face had thawed a bit more now, and his words were more intelligible. "I . . . saw her . . . we got . . . separated."

Minnie looked at Tom's feet again, but her thoughts were momentarily on Kate. A tear slipped from her eye, but she turned her face to the fire and let it fall soundlessly to the carpet. Cordelia left to get some dry clothing, and Aimée returned with more warm water. The three faces were blank, devoid of emotion. Didn't anyone care about that poor girl?

Will woke with a start and looked at the stove. The glow slipping from around the iron stove lids had diminished, an indication the fire needed more wood. He withdrew an arm from under the blankets and noticed that the small cabin was warm enough now to go without a coat, although there was still a chill in the air.

The line shack had been made from thick logs,

dragged down from the mountains and then mud-chinked to make them tight. Will was thankful now that it had been his father's policy to give priority to the comfort of the hired hands. "There may be a time you'll have to change boots with them," Tyler Chanson had always said, and now Will knew it wasn't just talk.

He had no way of knowing what time it was, but it was far from morning. And the howling wind told him the storm had not abated in the least.

Kate was still cradled against him. Carefully, he pulled his arm from beneath her head, allowing the pillow to cradle her instead. He propped himself up on one elbow, instantly feeling the chill of the room on his shoulder, but he granted himself a moment to study her in the faint red glow that slipped from around the stove lids. He didn't touch her, although the desire was strong. It was time to let her sleep; she had been through an ordeal.

Reluctantly, he admitted the fire needed wood, and quietly he swung a long leg over Kate and winced when his foot touched the plank floor. The pressure on his toes brought painful reminders of the cold and he hoped that neither one of them had experienced anything but superficial frost-bite.

Quickly, but as quietly as he could, he went to the stove door and piled more wood inside. Then he hurried back to bed and once again over Kate to his side against the wall. He closed his eyes, but sleep wouldn't return. He lay on his back and his shoulders filled the space, pressing firmly against Kate, making it hard for him to ignore her.

He could see her delicate profile and the lips that were soft and inviting. Then, as if his thoughts had penetrated her sleep, the heavily lashed eyelids fluttered and opened, staring over at him sleepily. For a second the gray-green eyes widened in surprise, but then she remembered where she was.

"I hope I didn't wake you," he said softly. "I had to put more wood on the fire."

"I didn't think I would ever get warm again."

"How do you feel? Any more pain in your feet or hands?"

"A little stinging sensation."

"Yes, I think we're going to live."

"Unless we starve to death. My stomach's empty."

He smiled lazily and rolled to his side, facing her, propping himself up on one elbow. "So is mine, but we always keep some staples on hand in the line shacks. I think we can rustle up something until this storm passes over."

"What time is it?"

"I hope you're not wanting to eat now?" His eyes danced with the light of the fire reflecting in them. "I think it's the middle of the night."

"I think I can survive until morning. It's so warm now. I don't think I ever want to get out from under these covers." She nestled down deeper and closed her eyes again, highly aware of his proximity but liking the feel of his body and the return of that exciting physical craving she had experienced only with him.

But it was more than the companionship of another human being. She knew her predicament would have been highly unpleasant indeed if she'd had to share a bed with anyone else. Will was different. She felt as though she belonged with him, as though being in the same bed was normal. At the same time it excited feelings in her that she had never had before, feelings that she knew came from the deep and natural instinct to make love to this man she desired.

She opened her eyes and saw that he was still watching her. "Maybe the storm will end soon," she offered hopefully, admitting to herself that she didn't care now if it did.

"Mmm, maybe." Will's thinking wasn't about the storm, either, only about the woman so near him. He slid a finger along her cheek. Her skin was warm now. "I'm glad I found you, Kate."

"So am I. Otherwise, you'd be burying me come spring."

"Kate?" He started to speak and then stopped, wondering if this was the appropriate time to bring up the fears that had eaten away at him for nearly two months. She looked over at him, her long hair sliding on the pillow, glowing in the dim red flickering light and tightening the urge that was increasing in his loins. He curled the long strands of hair around his hand and rubbed the softness of it between his fingers. Why was everything about her so enticing when he could have the same from any other woman?

"Yes, Will?"

Her soft voice urged him on. "Kate," he began again. "Why didn't you answer my message?"

She stared blankly at him. "I received no message. When did you send it?"

A glimmer of hope surfaced inside him. He told her about everything. "I thought your reply would be waiting when I got back. When there was nothing, I figured you'd washed your hands of me."

Happiness enveloped her, lifting the pain from her heart. "Aimée didn't give me a message. I would have answered you if she had."

"I didn't know if you would, not after our argument."

"I wondered why you hadn't contacted me. I thought—"

His fingers fell on her lips, silencing her doubts. He leaned toward her until his head was only inches from hers. "Kate, I've missed you." His hand slid to her neck, igniting sensitive nerves that brought her entire body to life. His gaze shifted to her lips and then he claimed them with an ardent kiss that grew in familiarity and possession.

He slipped an arm over her and drew her against him. Easily, he enveloped her in his arms, the same way the small cabin enveloped them in its dark warmth. His hand slid up her back to rest beneath the heavy mane of her hair. Automatically, she tipped her head back to look into his eyes glowing with the reflection of the fire, burning with their own lambent flame.

His lips hesitated inches from hers. His whisper barely reached beyond his breath. "If you want me to stop, tell me now, Kate, while I still can."

Beneath her hands, she felt the steely muscles of his body pressed the length of hers. She felt no danger, only the curiosity and the need inside her that made her want to meet, and match, the desire in his eyes. Her hand slid tentatively up from his chest and stopped along the curve of his jawline, where his beard was a day old. But it did not detract from his handsomeness. With a slight pressure she drew his head the few remaining inches until his lips touched hers in an encompassing heat she had longed for, dreamed of. Her fears were gone. She knew she was ready to know him completely.

Chapter 11

Like a cinder leaping to life, Will's lips sought hers in urgency: roaming and searching, tasting, giving and taking satisfaction and desire. His arm kept her pressed firmly against him as his masterful kisses consumed her.

For a moment he broke away from her, ran a hand along her face into the thick tresses of her hair, and searched her eyes with a longing she felt herself. She knew that if she was ever to draw away from him, it should be now. But the sound of his name slipping softly from her lips told him of her consent.

He lifted himself over her, the muscles in his shoulders straining the cloth that covered them. Kate moved her hand along the strength of the tightened muscles. Her fingers found the pulse point in his neck, and she felt the strange yet exalting sensation of being a part of the very life of him.

His breathing was shallow, as though he were holding it, waiting. She moved her hand to his lips, memorizing by touch the firm shape of them. They formed a kiss on her highly sensitized skin. Then, balancing himself on one arm, Will took her hand from his lips and turned it over, kissing it thoroughly from palm to back, from fingertip to wrist.

Will noticed that her eyes were smoky in the dusky light of the cabin, and they watched him intently but trustingly. He ran a hand along her face and trailed the fingers to her collar. Purposefully, he pulled the flannel cloth aside and slowly lowered his head until his lips were on the warm, vulnerable skin of her neck. The pure female scent of her flooded his nostrils and washed over his entire body.

His need for her was quickly becoming more powerful than any he had ever known. He tried to control it, wanting to make love to Kate with care and caution. He did not want to lose the trust that was in her eyes. He wanted her to enjoy it as much as he was going to. It was important that he push his own needs to the back of his mind to concentrate on her pleasure.

Kate drew in a sharp breath that caught momentarily in her throat as his deft fingers easily released the buttons that held the oversized shirt together. His hand brushed her bosom as he pushed the cloth aside and from there easily removed all garments that had concealed her body from him.

Her lips moved with his, toyed with his, made love to his in sweet abandonment, parting and coming together, straying to other areas close by. His kisses moved from her face downward, gliding along her shoulders and arms. She lay with closed eyes as his hands slid over her exposed abdomen, pulled taut in a natural reflex of the feelings he was drawing from deep within her. She could not suppress the sudden intake of air as his lips found her breast in a tender caress, but she immediately gave in to the pleasure he inspired.

Kate's instincts took over as her hands worked to unbutton his shirt and slide it off his shoulders. He rose to his knees and quickly shed the rest of his clothes, tossing them carelessly onto the floor. For the first time she looked at the heated flesh of his manhood, then at the hardness of his entire body. It was what she had always expected in a man, and there were no flaws to disappoint her dreams. In like manner, he relished her naked female form, and then, as she lifted her arms, he melted into her embrace.

Kate was surprised at her own lack of shyness. It did not bother her at all for him to see her completely nude. It felt right with him. When he covered her body with his, he reached behind him and drew up the covers, enveloping them in a private cocoon and closing out the cold world of the blizzard that raged just beyond the log walls.

Will rolled to her side, next to her. His kisses and caressing teased her until she pressed her body to his, reaching for the fulfillment he wanted to give her. His kisses took in her every curve. She moved restlessly beside him, and he heard her cry his name.

His lips never left her body as he turned her to her back and rose above her. Her legs entwined about him. Their arms encircled one another tightly, and Will drew her against him in the powerful need he could no longer suppress.

In minutes they became lost in their own blind world where nothing existed beyond the small space of their entwined bodies. On powerful wings, they soared beyond the fierce and wild wind into a dizzying calm where they halted, hung suspended, and then drifted from the height like a single snowflake to a soft place once again on earth.

Will gradually became aware of the soft play of her hands on his skin. He lifted himself slightly from her, and kissed her neck. Then rose a bit more to look into her eyes. He saw what he wanted to see in her contented smile, and he relaxed next to her, his lips again finding the sweet taste of her skin. Between his kisses, words from a deep well of feeling inside him emerged into the night on a whisper. "I need you, Kate. I have always needed you—forever it would seem. Now I have you, and I won't let you go." His lips moved over hers, while his hands roamed her body in a desperate sort of wandering, as if he were afraid he *may* lose her. "I want to marry you, Kate. I love you."

The soft words touched her heart. In this world of snow and isolation it was easy to dream, to respond to his love. Nothing existed beyond this small room, and tomorrow was very far away. Her lips touched his shoulder and moved along his collarbone, up his neck to a point so sensitive she felt his shudder of pleasure and the low moan of satisfaction in his throat. "And I love you. Yes, I'll be your wife."

He enveloped her tighter in his embrace; she felt the hard thudding of his heart. "We'll never be apart again, Kate."

"Never."

He smoothed back the strands of tangled hair from her face and shoulders. He kissed her again and rolled to his side, drawing her to her side too and cradling her slender, soft form against his own hard, lean one. She laid her cheek against the coarse, black hair on his chest and slid her arm over him. She closed her eyes and sighed, knowing she had never felt so happy and contented in her life.

Even naked, she was warm next to him, but they drew up the covers that had been pushed aside and discarded during their passion. Will found a comfortable place for his chin just above her head and his hot breath tickled her hair. Outside, the continual whine of the wind beat at the cabin, but strangely enough, it was almost a comforting sound to Kate now. She was warm and safe and in the arms of the man she loved.

As she closed her eyes and listened to Will's steady, even breathing, she began to drift off to sleep, too. In a gossamer vision she thought of Clayton's proposal and her father's hatred for Will, but they would both simply have to accept her decision to become Mrs. Will Chanson. There was nothing either one of them could do about it.

At eleven o'clock, Bart bundled up and fought his way to the bunkhouse, holding on to corral poles to keep his direction. He didn't want to get lost a few feet from his house and freeze to death in his own front yard. Despite the gloves he'd put on, his fingers were tingling from the cold by the time he flung the bunkhouse door open. All the men inside sat huddled around the stove in the center of the room, cradling hot cups of coffee to help chase away the chill.

He managed to get the door closed against the force of the wind and then stared down at the snow that had piled up on the floor in just seconds. When he looked up, all the faces watching him were anxious and expectant.

"He's not back yet."

The cowboys were silent. There weren't very many of them left this time of year. It was a slow time. The only ones that Will had kept on during the winter were the ones that had been with the ranch for years. The seasonal drifters had left after the fall roundup.

There was a shifting of chairs and bodies while some of the men stared off at nothing and others looked into the murky contents of their coffee. One said, "Maybe we should have gone out looking for him before it got dark."

"Maybe," Bart replied, "but you can't see your hand in front of your face out there. Will wouldn't want none of you risking your lives for him."

The silence deepened among them and, as if on cue, the wind hit the bunkhouse with a new punch that rattled the cups on the small cupboard. A loose shingle snapped and banged over the top of the roof before flying off into the gale. The men looked, wondering if any more of the roof was going to go. They accepted the truth, but felt no better about their helplessness. Will wasn't just the man who gave them a job; he was their friend.

A lanky cowboy stood up so suddenly his chair tipped over backward. He set his cup down on the table and spilled half the contents. Then he started pacing the floor. "I'd just like to know why in the hell Will took off the way he did anyway. He headed right into that storm. He saw it comin' plain as day."

"No one knew it was gonna be this bad."

"Will knew it. He's seen those northers move in plenty of times in his life."

"Must have been a damn good reason."

"Reason enough to die for." The lanky cowboy stopped his pacing and hung his head, resting his hands on his skinny hips in a despairing stance.

"Listen," Bart said, trying to get the hopeless feelings out of his head as well as theirs. "You're all talking like he's dead. For hell's sake, give Will some credit. Maybe he's holed up somewhere."

"You said yourself you can't see your hand in front of your face. How is he going to *see* to hole up?"

Bart wanted to punch something, but instead he turned to the door and jerked it open. The gust of wind nearly threw him backward as it rushed inside, picked up the cowboys' hair, tossed it around wildly and then dotted them with fine, powdery snow. Bart put his full weight into the wind and, thanks to someone on the inside of the bunkhouse, pulled the door closed behind him and made his way back home.

Tom woke up in a cold sweat. Kate had been calling for his help and he had ridden away. He hadn't actually. He had just lost her in the storm. There had been no way to find her.

As the guilt receded, he felt the pain in his feet. He pulled his leg out from under the cover and looked at his toes beneath the glow of the oil lamp. They had a strange, pale glossiness to them. Large blisters were forming, almost like burns, and the skin was cold, hard, and insensitive. He didn't have to be told that it was frostbite. Nor did he have to be told that if the damage was bad enough, gangrene could set in.

He thought of the cattle, knowing they would be drifting with the storm by the thousands. They'd head southward to keep the wind at their backs, hoping in their animal way that they could escape it. They would pile up at the fences, stand motionless and huddle together in an effort to get warm, and then they would freeze to death as the snow drifted over them.

He had nearly been ruined five years ago by the Great Blizzard as many ranchers had been. He had hung on only because of Kincaid's help. Kincaid's cattle company had taken a beating back then too, but he had other investments that had bailed him out and enabled him to make "loans" to the less fortunate. But this time he might not be so generous. With Kate dead, there was no bargaining tool, no pawn to entice Clayton.

Tom rolled over and covered his head with the pillow to try and block out the sound of the screaming gale outside his two-story window. He tried to block out the idea that Kate was dead. He felt terribly alone. She was his last link with the past and his happy days. It was odd, but sometimes the pleasure was more in the dreaming of the dream, than the living of it.

God, how he needed someone to talk to, and even some comforting arms. If only Cordelia would come in...

As Kate's eyes adjusted to the white light of the morning coming in through the small window, she remembered where she was. For a moment, she simply reveled in the nearness of Will and listened to the wind circling the corners of the cabin. Even though it still howled, she felt safe now. She was in no hurry to return to the tensions of her "home."

She stretched beneath the covers, finding she was sore in places she hadn't been before. She smelled the pungent scent of burning wood and heard the crackling of the fire, as though the damper had been thrown open. Then she caught the tantalizing aroma of fresh coffee, enticing her taste buds and her empty stomach. She glanced at the stove and saw the tin pot steaming on the stove plates.

She turned to Will. He was still asleep, but she knew he had risen early to make the fire. Softly, she kissed his cheek and he opened his black-lashed lids, turning his head in her direction. Immediately his hand moved beneath the covers and found hers, holding it now in open familiarity that had no restraints.

"The coffee smells good," she said.

"I made a full pot." Will closed his eyes momentarily, but then he turned to his side and forced himself awake. He didn't want the storm to end. The longer it lasted the longer he could stay here with Kate.

He pulled Kate into his arms, wanting to hold her. He ran a hand over her velvet skin. Although she had agreed to marry him, he was still afraid her father might cause trouble. He pulled the wool blankets and heavy robe up higher on their shoulders and forced himself to relax. The warmth of her body felt even better than the heat of the fire and he gladly curled himself around her, content in the simple comfort of their shelter, and thankful that she was alive and in his arms.

After a while, he left the bed and quickly slipped his pants on. Kate laughed at his antics as he balanced on one leg and then the other, hopping up and down as he tried to keep from setting his feet down fully on the cold floor. While he buttoned his jeans, he hurried to the cupboard and filled two cups with the coffee.

Kate began to rise, reaching for her clothes by the bed, but the colder temperature of the room outside the buffalo robe made her want to retreat into its warmth. "Stay in bed," Will ordered and then returned to her side and sat on the edge of the mattress. Putting the coffee cups on the floor, he gently eased the flannel shirt from her as she tried to untangle the sleeves and put it on, shivering from the cold now assaulting her. He straightened out the shirt and draped it over her shoulders, relieving the goosebumps that had broken out all over her body.

"I opened the draft. It should warm up in here pretty soon," he said, handing her one of the cups of coffee. "The storm sounds as bad today as it did yesterday."

Kate gladly sipped at the coffee, feeling the rush of its heat spread over her cold body. "I heard some shots after I got separated yesterday from my father," she said. "I wonder if he ever made it home."

Will debated whether to tell her that it was he who had fired the shots. He supposed it was possible that Diering had done the same thing, but something told him that the man hadn't.

"They may have been my shots," he said quietly. "Don't let your mind dwell on what may have happened to him, Kate. We made it. There's a good chance he did, too. I'm sure they're all thinking we're dead, too. I just hope none of my men have gone out trying to find me."

She chuckled. "I doubt they would be so foolish as to do that. They can always find another boss."

Unable to resist her tousled, beautiful appearance, and the desire to relive last night, Will leaned toward her and put an arm around her shoulders. With his kisses, he heated the graceful curve of her neck. "You can be a cold woman, Kate Diering."

She steadied her hands on the coffee cup as his fingers moved aside the collar of the shirt to make more flesh available to his caress. Then she placed a kiss in the hollow of his neck, silently delighting in the feel of him beneath her lips. "I can also be very warm."

"I can't dispute that." Her hand moved over his body in a tender caress that easily pushed the outside world to the back of his mind.

"Well," she said, smiling, "if you're not too busy and have nothing pending—no places to go, no people to see..."

He leaned closer to her. "For one so young and inexperienced, you learn quickly."

"Learn what?" She feigned ignorance, but had a knowing glint in her eye.

"How to possess a man—body and soul."

"And heart?" Her own heart clipped rapidly, waiting anxiously for his response, for even though he'd spoken words of love once, she wanted to hear them again.

He kissed her lips tenderly. "You had my heart from the very beginning."

He took the cup from her and set it on the floor near the wall next to his. With the light of the day, Kate watched unabashedly as he stood beside the bed and removed his pants in an unhurried moment now, but one bright with the aura of anticipation. He pulled back the covers and slid in next to her, laying her back on the feather pillows and mattress and stretching his body the full length next to hers.

"I just realized I'm very hungry," she whispered, waiting for his kiss. "I could eat a cow this morning. And I wonder if my clothes are dry." She bantered, happy that his nearness and his touch was making the necessity for both seem inconsequential.

"I'll feed and clothe you later." His voice was husky with the desire she easily recognized now.

She smiled and drew him into her embrace. His lips found hers and easily they fell, once again, into the passions of love.

Some time later, when the hunger of their passion was satisfied, they rose to answer the hunger of their stomachs. Kate slid from beneath the warm covers and dressed quickly; Will's eyes never left her as he donned his own clothes. He observed the gently, but provocatively, rounded curve of her hips and derriere in the soft wool pants. To see a woman in such attire was a rarity; most wore split riding skirts while others still clung to the old tradition of cumbersome riding habits. He had to admit, though, that the pants offered an interesting view of a woman's physical attributes, and he didn't mind at all.

Kate opened the cupboard doors and took an inventory of what was there. All the canned goods had burst from the cold. All that remained were the staple items in tight-lidded tin containers with labels: beans, rice, coffee, flour, sugar, salt, baking powder, and lard. It was a Godsend that Will insisted that his line shacks be fully stocked, not only for cowboys taking temporary shelter from a storm, but for those assigned to some winter duty on the fence line in the area.

"What I'd give for some bacon and eggs this morning," she said as she removed the containers. "But I know I should be thankful for flapjacks."

Will finished hooking his belt, idly watching her, noticing the flannel shirt that fell softly over her full breasts, enticing his imagination. He moved to the stove to check the fire. "Did your father always preach to you about being happy with what you had the way my folks always did?"

"Yes," Kate responded. "He would get mad at me for wishing for things that were unreasonably out of my reach. He even does it now that he has money. Of course, it seems to be all right for Cordelia to make wishes, because there's nothing she doesn't get if she wants it."

"Things could be changing after this storm."

Kate moved to the table, picking up a comb she'd found in the cupboard drawer. She watched him as she smoothed the tangled strands of her hair.

The realities of the world beyond them moved to the front of Will's mind and suddenly he felt defeated and grim. "There are going to be some heavy losses when the snow melts away," he finally said. "So many of us are still trying to recover from the last bad winter; this could be the last straw if it doesn't end soon."

Kate knew what Will said was true, but she

187

didn't want the storm to end. She wanted to stay here with him forever; away from the problems that she knew would be facing her when she returned. She had eagerly agreed to marry him, but what if her father was serious? What if he really would harm Will?

He said no more and, with concern in her eyes, Kate watched as he dressed to go outside and tend to the horses. He put a hand on the door latch and looked back at her. She tried to smile, not letting him see her fear.

"I'll be back shortly."

She nodded. "I'll have breakfast ready."

While he was gone, she looked about the cabin, trying to distract herself from the loneliness she suddenly felt. The room was roughly twenty by twenty. Three beams held up the roof, one on either side of a center one that formed a peak in the middle, allowing for more headroom. A couple of tattered rugs—one by the door and one by the bed—helped to conceal the wooden planking of the floor. The door was heavy wood with the cracks battened and cross-braced in the shape of a Z making it even sturdier. It was painted a terrible green, probably some cowboy's idea of decorating. And, in the old wood, scores of initials had been carved in random locations.

The walls were decorated with old calendars and nails that were hooks for everything from clothes to bridles. There was a shelf or two that added some space to the cupboard by holding medicines, both for man and animal. But the most distracting thing about the cabin was its disturbing silence, strangely increased by the mournful and monotonous cry of the wind.

After what seemed a terribly long time, the door flew open with force, and Will stood in the doorway. Kate let out the breath she had been unconsciously holding and smiled in relief at the sight of him. In one arm he carried another load of wood, which he deposited in the box by the stove.

"I think the storm's worse today," he said as his lungs took in air. With cold fingers he removed his hat and began undoing his buttons, brushing some of the snow away to make the task easier. "I doubt we'll even be leaving tomorrow."

Kate went back to the meal, checking the pan to see if it was hot enough to cook the flapjacks. She relaxed—at least for now.

Chapter 12

For days the storm raged and the drifts increased. Will needed to spend more time shoveling his way to open the barn door in order to feed the horses, and Kate found it increasingly unpleasant to step out in the savage force of the wind in order to fill pans with snow to melt for water. Even occasional trips to the outhouse, following the rope that Will had strung between the two structures, was a dangerous and tiring undertaking. The only pleasurable hours they experienced were those spent beneath the warmth of the buffalo robe in each other's arms, making love or talking, and planning their future together.

Will taught her how to play poker with some old, grimy, dog-eared cards they found in the cupboard. They used matches for money. Will's nimble fingers shuffled and distributed them with obvious experience, but Kate took all the winnings. Will said it was nothing but beginner's luck.

As they lay in bed on the fifth morning, exchanging private things about one another, both past and present, Kate heard Will's stomach grumble its complaint of hunger.

"I think we'd better eat," she said, chuckling.

He nodded, still reluctant to leave her side.

As Kate dressed, she eyed the small wooden tub Will had brought in on the second day. It had been nailed to the cabin's exterior wall but had apparently not had much use; cowboys weren't keen on taking baths when they didn't have to. But she was going to take another, and she was looking forward to it. She had filled every pot and pan last night with snow and this morning the water was hot and ready for her bath.

For breakfast she made baking powder biscuits, and although they were both tired of their diet, they ate in silence, appreciating what they had.

"I don't know how much longer the food will last, Will," Kate noted with a worried frown.

"The storm will end soon," he said. "I've never known one to last much longer than this. And even if it should go on for weeks," he said with a teasing smile, "there's plenty of cattle around the barn and corral now, looking for protection from the storm. I'll kill one if I have to. Don't worry, we won't starve."

He pushed himself away from the table to go out once again into the storm and tend to the horses. He wished he had enough hay in the barn to feed the hungry cattle bellowing at the door, but what little was there had to be kept for the horses.

He didn't want to go out in the blizzard; he preferred the warmth of the mud-chinked log cabin and the sweet thrill of Kate's kisses. "Perhaps you could wait for your bath until I get back." His eyes ran over her intimately as he put his outerwear on. "I'd like another one myself. We could share this time."

"The tub isn't big enough," she said, knowing

he certainly knew it, but had something else in mind.

"Then we'll take turns. I'll scrub your back and then you can scrub mine."

"I could go out and help you," she offered. "It would go faster."

"No, it's too miserable out there." He cupped her chin in his hand and kissed her lips again. Then he forced himself back to the door and pulled it open. "I'll hurry."

Kate cleaned up the dishes, washed them, refilled the kettle with snow and then swept the floor and made the bed. The cabin was beginning to feel like home. She rummaged through the cupboard and found another clean but thin towel. She pushed the tub as close to the stove as was safe, and then, to make a warm bathing area, took one of the wool blankets from the bed. With some ingenuity she tacked it to the ceiling behind the tub. It would hold the heat better in the small space and protect against drafts.

With nothing left to do, she sat in the chair by the fire to wait.

When Will opened the door the wind helped to push him through the low-framed entrance. Will tried to unclasp the buttons on his coat but his hands wouldn't function. Kate saw his struggle and immediately stepped forward to help him.

The snow that had built up on his coat froze her fingers with an iciness that burned. After she had the last button free, she reached up with her hands and slid the bulky cloth over his broad shoulders and down off his arms. Gratefully he moved to the stove while she hung his coat up.

Will eyed the arrangement Kate had made to

help hold heat in around the tub. When his hands were sufficiently warmed, he poured the contents of all the pots and pans into the tub. When the last container was empty he placed it on the table with the others and turned to Kate. "The water's just right."

She realized that, in its own way, this event was as intimate as the ones they had already shared in the small bed.

Will took the first step. Slowly he removed his shirt and then his pants. Although she had felt every inch of his body against hers and beneath her caressing hand, she still watched with fascination as he stood before her. He looked the way she had always thought a man should look, possibly the way God had intended for man to look, but the way so few men did.

He placed a hand on the loose flannel of her shirt, and gently drew her closer. With his eyes never leaving hers, he undid the buttons and slipped the shirt from her skin. His hands slid along her shoulders and down her arms and then aided her in removing the soft wool pants hugging her hips. When she was completely naked, he gazed at her with the desire she recognized and felt within herself. And then, tenderly, he pulled her into his arms, kissing her lips, face, neck, shoulders, breasts. As his manhood rose to announce his need, he turned Kate toward the tub.

"You go first."

She was able to sit Indian fashion in the small tub, and soon found herself relaxing completely with eyes closed as Will soaped her body in gentle, circular movements. His touch, even with callused hands, was soothing and quickened her heartbeat, making her wonder how something as simple as touching could pull such feelings from deep within. After he rinsed her off, he dried her and helped her from the tub. He took a blanket from the bed and draped it around her to keep her from getting chilled.

The tub was nearly too small for Will but he fit into it with his long legs draped over the side. Kate took up the bar of soap and lathered it in smooth motions over the muscles of his shoulders, arms, and back and then along the iron-hard strength of his legs and arms. He bent his head forward, relaxing under her tender massage.

"I'm a little stiff from shoveling snow," he said. "That feels good, Kate."

She responded to a growing desire to let her hands roam idly over him, not caring that the wool blanket had slipped from her shoulders. She didn't notice any chill in the room. She rinsed him off, and as he stood up she handed him the towel. He quickly dried himself. Without words, they moved to the bed and slipped into a warmth that their bodies soon created.

"I never want this to end, Will," Kate whispered against his lips.

"It won't, Kate. You'll soon be my wife in name as well as heart."

Will's lovemaking satisfied Kate just as it had the first time. She lay awake next to him, listening to the familiar swish of the snow against the cabin and the roaring of the wind that had now become an expected part of their existence here.

She thought of her father, wondering if he were alive. She thought of what he would say when she returned. It was a shameful thought, but for a moment—just an instant—it occurred to her that if he had perished in the storm, he would not be there to prevent her from marrying Will.

Will had believed that they could convince her father of their love. As for Clayton's proposal, it was insignificant. She had never given it serious thought, nor would she now. She would simply have to tell him politely that she was in love with another man. If she were married and gone, Cordelia would be happier, and if Cordelia was happier, Tom would be happier.

She tried to rationalize it all, but none of her ideas sounded very convincing. Her father was who he was, and she knew him much better than Will did. She knew what he could do when he went into a rage. Her only alternative might be to marry Will without her father's blessing. If only she could stop time and stay in the line shack forever.

Will stirred and pulled Kate away from her silent thoughts. At her smile, he drew her into his arms again, enjoying her beauty more each time they made love. He was entranced by the softness of her lips that held him like a willing prisoner, helpless against his need for her.

"Love me again, Kate," he whispered in her ear, and then teased, "unless you'd rather gamble all your matches away."

She responded positively, her answer nothing more than the love in her eyes. With him, Kate was loved and wanted. But, she mused, being with him *was* a form of gambling—win, draw, or lose. Unfortunately, the stakes were much higher than a box of matches.

* * *

The fire was nearly gone, and it hadn't done much to take the chill away. Cordelia didn't want to get out of the warm bed, but she tossed back the covers, pulled on her heavy robe, and fastened it tightly around her waist.

Even the rug was cold, giving her feet little relief from the cold floor. She curled up her toes as she walked across the room. She moved the screen and piled three more logs onto the fire in symmetrical order, then she nearly dove back into the warmth of the down comforters.

She knew she would be warmer if she shared the bed with Tom, but he would misconstrue her needs and she wanted no more from him than a little body heat. She found it increasingly difficult to be intimate with him. He simply did not stir her desires. Sometimes she tried to think of someone else—one of the men she had known long ago in Chicago. But try as she might to remember those days, she was haunted by the recurring picture of Will the way he had looked the day of the fire, bare-chested and lean. None of the men she had known had looked like that.

She closed her eyes. *Kate*. Kate must surely be dead, she thought. Cordelia knew she should feel remorse, worry, or concern, for it was she who had sent her out. But she felt nothing.

She didn't know how Tom was reacting to Kate's fate; he had said very little before they'd taken him to his room to wait for the storm to end so a doctor could be sent for. But, for her, everything would go much smoother without Kate around.

When the gray dawn crept in the window at the end of a week, Kate felt Will stir next to her.

He reached across her, enveloping her with his arm, almost as though he sensed her wakefulness and was preventing her from getting up to face the day.

And then she heard it—a hollow ringing instead of the wind. The absolute silence sounded strange and out of place. She opened her eyes and they were stabbed by a brilliant yellow light, so bright that she closed them again and put her hand up for protection. A shaft of sun filtered in through the glass in the dirty little window. The storm was over.

"Will!" She sat up. The blankets fell away from them both and Will looked about in startled alarm. "Will, the blizzard is over."

An odd sensation flooded over him. He was happy to see the sunlight, but with a twinge of regret his eyes focused on Kate's naked back and the chestnut hair she'd just washed again yesterday. He fingered one of the tendrils, silky and soft, feeling a tightness building in his chest. "Yes, it's over."

Kate waited in the extreme silence, listening, foolishly thinking maybe it was only a lull. Reluctantly they rose and prepared to leave. They didn't exchange their silent thoughts, their worries; they didn't have to, for their concerns were the same. Giving the line shack and the funny green door one last look, Kate preceded Will into the brilliant light of the new day.

Chapter 13

The sun reflected off the snow, nearly blinding them with its brightness. The sky was blue; there were only scattered remnants of the clouds that had carried the blizzard. They rode in silence away from the line shack, taking the easiest way around the drifts. They found some places where the wind had blown the snow completely away only to pile it up farther along in drifts as high as twenty feet deep.

In silence they passed the cattle that were pushed up against the fences, snowbound. In the deep ravines, more cattle were buried in the snow unable to get out. They stopped, and with their lariats, pulled out several, but then Will decided to move on.

"Come on, Kate. I'll send some cowboys out. Right now we need to get you home."

The foreboding feeling he'd had in summer was nothing compared to this. The cattle that hadn't died in the storm would die now from lack of grass. But he had survived the blizzard of '86 when the best and the richest had gone under. Times had been hard, but he could never see quitting to give satisfaction to people like Clayton Kincaid and Grace Barnes who believed his success was inherited and not achieved through his own labor. But the main reason for persevering was his belief that a man simply didn't walk away from something he loved without a damn good fight.

He'd foreseen the trouble that was now upon him, and was glad that he'd dumped the majority of his cattle last fall. But he still had thousands of cattle trapped in the snow-covered range waiting for him to find them and move them to a place where they could find feed. It wasn't going to be easy.

The horses were tired when they reached the rise overlooking the Diering ranch. Kate reined her horse to a stop and looked for sign of her father, but she saw very little activity in the yard. Their breath rose upward against the icy blue sky and Will looked over at her questioningly. She smiled at him, loving the way he looked next to her, the way his body had felt right with hers.

"I can ride on in alone from here, Will. Thank you for coming this far with me."

He frowned and clenched his teeth. "I'll face him with you, Kate."

"We don't know if he's even alive."

"He's too ornery to die."

"You really dislike him, don't you?"

"Has he given me any other choice?"

A deep love for Will surged inside her and she tried to memorize his face. "No, I suppose he hasn't."

Will's agitation increased. "I'd like to face him with you to explain everything and ask for your hand in marriage."

She could not refrain from touching him one last time. She moved her gloved hand along his bearded cheek. "Maybe it would be better if you didn't. Give me a chance to talk to him first, break the news to him, let him digest it. It might be better if he didn't know we had spent the time together." Confusion and anxiety showed on her face.

"And why not? I'm not ashamed of it."

"I need to break it to him gently, Will, maybe not tell him at all. If there are consequences to pay, I want to be the one to pay them."

"Damn it, Kate—"

Her hand on his lips silenced him. She was extremely afraid now, afraid that her father would kill Will. She'd probably have to lie, not mention that she'd spent the time with Will. And then, later, she could tell her father that Will wanted to marry her.

Will encircled her shoulders with his arm and lifted her slightly from the saddle and up against him. His lips quickly warmed the coldness of hers and were reluctant to separate from them. When he sat her back in her saddle, he gathered his reins with both hands. "All right, Kate. I don't like it, but you talk to him alone. I'll be gone for a couple of weeks hunting cattle. When I get back, I'll be by for his answer."

Her heart sank as he rode away. She turned her horse to face the ranch, and it headed eagerly for the buildings that sprawled in the distance. She didn't want to go back to this oppressive world, but she would be seeing Will again and that was all that mattered. She could suffer anything as long as there was that hope.

The yard was empty as she silently approached. She figured the cowboys were probably out trying to gather the cattle to count the live ones, as well as the dead.

Her horse gladly went into the barn. The big door had been left open but the stalls were all empty and so were the corrals. The majority of the horses had been turned loose like the cattle to fend for themselves. Only the minimum number of riding horses were kept and fed during the winter.

Kate led her horse into the stall. After removing the bridle and saddle, she tossed the mare some hay. With her hands in the oversize pockets of the coat, she walked to the house on hesitant feet. Normally she would have enjoyed the sun and the absence of the wind, but today she was tormented by the possibility of her father's death.

The porch steps creaked beneath her weight as the front door opened soundlessly. She stood in the foyer and listened to the quiet of the house. She removed her hat and let her hair fall free, and was taking off her coat when she was frightened by a deafening scream that made her gasp and jerk upright.

Cordelia stood in the entranceway to the parlor with her hand over her mouth. She screamed repeatedly like a woman who had completely lost her senses. Kate started toward her, but Cordelia only screamed louder.

The screams brought Aimée and Minnie. When they saw Kate they too gasped and stopped abruptly in their tracks. Finally Kate understood. She suppressed a sudden urge to laugh. "I'm not dead, if that's what you're worried about."

After the initial shock wore off, Minnie stepped forward and threw her arms around Kate. "My heavens, Kate. How did you survive that blizzard? We all thought you were gone."

When Minnie stepped back from her hug, she kept her hands on Kate's shoulders and looked her over carefully. "You seem to have fared well enough. Tell us what happened."

Cordelia finally found her tongue and spoke now in a voice scratchy from the screaming. "Yes, Kate. Please tell us what happened. Where were you?"

Kate looked beyond her and into the parlor. "Where is my father?"

Cordelia turned sideways, her full satin skirts rustling and the movement stirring up the over-powering fragrance she wore. She pointed up the stairs. "He's in his room, recuperating,"

Cordelia then turned her back to Kate and returned to the parlor. As she started to close the door behind her, she said, "I can't bear to talk about it, Kate. Let Minnie explain."

"You look as though you could use some good hot food. Come into the kitchen."

Kate followed Minnie. "Please, Minnie, tell me about my father!"

After Minnie had settled Kate on a chair and put before her some hot coffee and cake, she sat down across from Kate and began to tell her about Tom.

"Your father made it home from the blizzard, all right, but he got frostbite in his fingers and toes. Gangrene set in. We sent someone to town in the wee hours of the morning, as soon as the storm broke. The doctor came hellin' it out here. He amputated some of his toes and a couple of fingers. He left after your father regained consciousness."

Kate digested the news with brooding silence. "At least he isn't dead."

"No, but he thinks you are. I'm sure he'd like to see you."

Kate wondered if that could be true. She had never felt as though she held any special place in his heart. "I'm not the reason he's ... I mean, did he stay out looking for me?"

Minnie's eyes darted away from Kate's. "I don't know that."

Kate stood up, hesitating, thinking that maybe she understood it all too well. Deep down she'd hoped that maybe he had, but she supposed she had known all along that he wouldn't jeopardize his life for hers. "I'll go upstairs, Minnie. Thank you for your concern."

Kate ascended the curving staircase slowly. On the upper floor she stopped and took a deep breath. She'd thought about what she would say whether her father believed it or not. She walked the few remaining steps to his door and tapped lightly. There was no response from within.

Kate opened the door and stepped inside. She was surprised to see that the room was bright and cheery with the sun streaming in through the windows. But although the room appeared cheery, it also stank of something that reminded her of a dead animal. It nearly gagged her as she stepped in farther, desperately wanting to cover her nose with her hand. She made the motion to do just that when her father spoke, chuckling in a bitter way, and surprising her that he was awake.

"It's my flesh you're smelling, girl. Toes rotted

nearly off before we could get the doctor here. Fingers, too. It's a vile smell, and it's a vile feeling to have something on you that's dead and that you can't get rid of."

He was lying flat in bed, gripping the blanket with one bandaged hand. Next to the bed were several empty bottles of whisky and one that was three-fourths full. His eyes were glazed, obviously from the heavy consumption of alcohol. His bandaged feet stuck out from beneath the covers. The rest of his underwear-clad body was concealed by blankets. He was pale and his hair stuck up every which way as though it hadn't been combed for days. It looked more gray than before.

She shivered from the cold assessment of his eyes as they moved up and down her body. She stepped closer to the warmth of the fireplace. Mindful of her own appearance, she nervously tried to smooth out the wrinkled shirt that she'd washed while at the line shack but had had no way to iron.

"I thought you were dead," he said bluntly and with no particular feeling that she could discern.

She stared at him for a moment, wondering if he was disappointed that she wasn't. "I thought you were, too."

He nodded, but his scrutiny ran so deep that she felt perspiration beneath the flannel shirt. Surely he couldn't see the change in her; couldn't see that she was no longer a virgin? Was it written on her face?

"Where did you go?" he asked, his eyes drilling into her like sharp needles. "I see you fared better than I did."

"I made it to the Chanson line shack," she said.

His gray, bushy brows rose and the glint deepened in his eyes. "And how did you eat? Doesn't appear to me that you went hungry."

"There were some things in the cupboard—flour, sugar, coffee."

"I'm surprised you didn't say canned goods."

Was he trying to catch her in a lie? "No." Her nervousness deepened. "The cans had burst from the cold."

"And Chanson just happened to escort you home? How did he know you were there? Did he just 'happen' to meet you as you were riding home?"

The bitter quality in his words cut into her. She glanced to the window. Apparently, he had seen them from his two-story view. He had probably seen Will kiss her, too. "Yes, he did, as a matter of fact." She tried to look him in the eye.

"I don't believe you. I think you spent the entire time at his place—with him. The kiss he gave you was mighty familiar."

"He kissed me at the ball, too. It doesn't mean anything. He was just glad I found the line shack and was alive."

"I'm not a demented old man." Suddenly he sounded exhausted. "I know what you've done."

She moved backward toward the door, feeling a fear seeping from him that she couldn't understand and couldn't deal with. She wondered if he was drunk or feverish from the gangrene.

"You think if you let him get you with child then he'll have no choice but to marry you. Well, you're wrong. I refuse to let you marry him. I have better plans for you." His eyes brightened with a growing irrationality. "Knowing Chanson, I think he just took your virtue with no intention of marrying you. I'll tell you something else about men like him—he'll just keep on using you, like a whore, until he grows weary of you. And if you ever try to see him again, I swear, Kate, I'll shoot him dead. He's no good for you, Kate. No good, do you hear me?"

Kate ran. She didn't close the door behind her. The hall was blurry in front of her tears, but she groped and found her room. Inside, she closed the door and locked it, leaned against it for a second as if she'd outrun an enemy. Then she went to the bed and fell onto it, face down. Her father had made it sound so sordid, and it hadn't been that way at all.

When Kate finally stopped crying, it was dusk and her eyes were swollen and red. Sitting up, she stared at herself in the mirror.

"You are a fool. A stupid fool for ever thinking *he* would understand someone's love besides his own."

She realized she should have known her father would give them trouble. He *would* kill Will. He'd do it just because he had said he would, just because he couldn't back down from his word. She started to cry again. How could she ever see Will again when it meant risking his life?

A knock sounded at her door. "Who is it?"

"Minnie. I thought you might like me to prepare a bath for you."

Dear Minnie, she was the only friend Kate had in this house. She brushed her tears from her face and reached for the dressing gown that lay across the foot of her bed where she had left it days ago.

She hoped her uncontrollable sobs wouldn't be heard through the door, or at least that Minnie wouldn't guess the real reason she was crying. "Yes," she said falteringly. "It sounds wonderful."

She moved to the mirror, hoping somehow to obliterate the signs of her crying by wiping at her eyes. Of course it didn't help, so she let Minnie in, and while she answered questions about the blizzard, she busied herself at the wardrobe, pretending to consider what she was going to wear.

When Minnie was gone, Kate once again locked the door and gladly discarded the dressing gown to step into the high-backed tub. She closed her eyes as the warm water washed over her. Immediately her thoughts were filled once again with images of Will. She leaned her head back against the tub and looked to the ceiling. Her eyes burned from the tears she had shed. "Why do you hate him so, Daddy? Why...?"

Will reached across the bed for Kate. He sat up, suddenly realizing she wasn't there. Letting out a disappointed sigh, he lay back down and stared at the ceiling, bright with morning light. He'd slept in; he'd been tired after leaving Kate and then going out with the cowhands to locate cattle. Their job was far from finished. They would have to ride miles to the south to rescue cattle and turn them back toward home range. The losses from the storm were dismally high.

He pushed himself up again and draped his legs out over the side of the bed. He needed to get going. He could faintly hear Lorna working in the kitchen below. They'd all been happy to see him ride in. Everyone had believed him to be dead.

They had spent the time worrying about him, while most of his own thoughts there in the line shack had been of Kate. He had been so aware of her presence, her every word and action. Now he wanted to get up and see her across the table from him again. And he would, damn Tom Diering. He'd have Kate for his own. If Diering wouldn't consent, then he'd steal her away in the night. With that decision made, he felt more like facing the day. When he entered the kitchen, Bart was there. While Will ate, they discussed the blizzard and what they would do over the next couple of weeks to get things back to some degree of normality.

Finally, Will swallowed the last of his coffee and stood up. "Thanks, Lorna. It's good to be back home."

"I'll bet you got lonely in that line shack," she said.

Will smiled as his thoughts focused on Kate again. "Yes, but I managed fine. Played a lot of cards and spent quite a bit of time in bed."

"You always manage, don't you?" Lorna laughed.

"I'm not a man to roll over and succumb when the odds are high."

"Well"—Lorna flushed a little from revealing her concern for her employer—"we're all glad to have you back." She hurried on, not used to sentimentality. "Will you be back for dinner?"

"No, just pack us something we can put in our saddlebags. We'll be back by supper, though."

The cowhands split up in twos. Some wore black kerchiefs over their faces with holes cut out for their eyes to forestall snow blindness. Others painted their faces and eye areas with burned matches or lampblack. Will and Bart headed south, their faces smudged with the latter.

They rode in silence, Will hoping for a warm wind that would melt enough of the snow to uncover what was left of the summer's grass. He had reserved pastures on the property that were protected by hills and trees, if only he could get the cattle back there. It had been a cruel year. It was enough to make the strongest man falter, but he knew—had always known—that this occupation was not for the weak of mind or the weak of body, and it was also not for anyone who didn't like to gamble.

For two weeks Will and his men moved southward, gathering cattle and holding them until they got a herd large enough to move back to the ranch. The cattle hadn't been easy to find as they wandered in search of food and shelter in canyons and under rimrocks. By now, because of the deep snow, many of the cattle were almost too weak to move. They were easy prey for the wolves and coyotes who had grown fat and sleek from the abundant carrion feasts.

Will was anxious to see Kate again, so with only a couple of hundred head of cattle, he headed for the ranch alone.

Under a white sky that threatened more snow, Will hurried to the house to bathe and change. It was now late afternoon and it would be dusk before he made it to Diering's, and dark before he got back home. But he had to see her. He'd had nothing else on his mind since he'd left her.

In thirty minutes he was out the door, to the barn, and on a fresh mount. The bitter north wind stung his lungs with each breath of air he took. He decided he'd never hated winter as much as he had the last few weeks. It was said that the men who came north from Texas and stayed were those who had come to an understanding with the climate. They had accepted early on that a man couldn't conquer it, that he could only contend with it. But over the last few weeks, Will was beginning to think that that wasn't true at all. The men who had come here and stayed were pure fools.

As he approached the Diering house his eyes scanned the upper story, wondering which room was Kate's.

It took a while for his knock to be answered. An older woman, probably the Minnie of whom Kate had spoken fondly, stepped back with a smile and held the door open.

Will moved onto the rug in the foyer and removed his dress hat, holding it in his hands. "I'm here to see Kate."

"Is she expecting you?" Some surprise lit the woman's friendly eyes.

"No, I'm afraid I haven't been able to get a message to her."

"I'll have you wait in the parlor by the fireplace, Mr. Chanson. This winter surely beats all, doesn't it?"

She led the way into the room just off the foyer and then left him standing in the middle of it, fingering his hat and glancing around. It was an elaborate house, much more so than his own place, but there was an impersonal showiness to it that he didn't like. He moved to the warmth of the fireplace.

He heard footsteps and turned around with a smile for Kate, but found instead the hateful glare of Tom Diering. He was leaning on a cane, and carrying a Navy Colt revolver. His eyes were dark with hatred and a crazy sort of fear. Will had no doubt that he might use the gun.

"Why are you here, Chanson?"

"I've come to see Kate."

"You've seen enough of my daughter. You took her to the Cattlemen's Ball without asking my permission. You won't see her again—although I have the feeling you have, haven't you?"

"What do you mean?"

"I saw you bring her home after the blizzard. I saw the way you kissed her. She said she wasn't with you the whole time, but she's my daughter and I know when she's lyin'." He took a better grip on the gun and his cane at the same time, bracing his feet against the floor in a battle stance. "Now, I want to know what went on between you two during that blizzard. Were you lovers?"

Diering steadied the Colt and cocked the hammer with his thumb. "For your sake, Chanson, you'd better say no."

212

Chapter 14

Minnie hurried to Kate's room and rapped impatiently. When Kate opened the door the maid's eyes were wide with fear. "Kate, Will is here and your father is downstairs threatening to shoot him. You'd better hurry."

Kate's heart leaped to her throat. She lifted her skirts and raced down the stairs. Just as she reached the parlor door the deafening roar of the gun made her gasp in fear and disbelief. The impact of the bullet knocked Will back against the fireplace. She screamed and pushed past her father, knocking him over and sending the smoking Colt skidding across the floor.

Blood was coming from Will's left shoulder, seeping through the fingers of his right hand that had automatically gone to the wound. She ran to him, trying to help him to a chair, but he forced himself from the slumped position back to his full height. She held on to him, looking up into the face she loved, but his eyes were on her father as he tried to get back onto his feet, too. She had never seen so much venom in Will's expression. Suddenly he looked much older than his years; and a man who had been pushed one step too far.

"Will, I'm so sorry. I—"

"Don't, Kate. This is not your doing."

He took his eyes from her father then and looked down at her. The glow of hatred softened into the look she remembered so well. She wanted to put her arms around him, but she simply held on to him, feeling the increasing weight of his body.

Then she whirled on her father and took a position in front of Will, as if she could protect him. Slowly she stalked toward her father, with fists clenched at her sides and her eyes shooting fire. "You had no reason. How dare you shoot an unarmed man. I should see you to jail myself."

Tom was on his feet now, tottering a bit on unsteady feet that didn't balance well without all ten toes. He gripped his cane in a crippled hand and tried to stand. In retaliation and reflex, Kate pushed Tom hard in the chest with both hands and knocked him backward. He stumbled and collapsed onto the plush red sofa.

A hand on her arm turned her around and she looked up into Will's face. "Don't, Kate. It wasn't like he didn't warn me."

The blood from his arm came out in small spurts and her shock was replaced by major concern for him. "I'll take you to the doctor." She started for the door, but Tom spoke. He had retrieved the gun and once again had it pointed at Will.

"He can get himself to the doctor. If you go another step with him, Kate, I swear I'll put a slug right in his heart."

Kate looked at Will helplessly. He walked to the door, brushing past her close enough to feel her breasts against his wounded arm. In the entryway she opened the door for him. He placed his hat on his head.

"Will—" Her eyes searched his to see if he hated her now, but there was only warmth in his gaze.

"I'll be fine, Kate. Don't worry."

She stood in the doorway and watched him walk to his horse, gather his reins, and step into the saddle. Then he covered his wounded shoulder again with his right hand. When he had his horse pointed toward Denver, she turned on her father who had clumsily made it to the parlor door, gripping his cane in one hand and still holding the Colt in the other.

Emotions welled up inside her: hatred, disbelief, pain, hurt. She had once thought her father a decent man. She had looked up to him as though he were a god who could do no wrong, whose every decision was the right one and not to be doubted. Now she would have run after Will if she wasn't afraid it would jeopardize his life even more.

"How could you hate him so much? He has never done anything to you. You're jealous of him, that's all. I can see it now, although I'm not sure why. What you've done won't change the way I feel about him."

With no warning her father's hand came back and lashed out across her face, striking her with such force that she fell back against the stairs. A startled cry escaped her throat, while her eyes blurred with a white pain in her side.

"He admitted that you cheapened yourself for him just like a whore. How could you do this to me? My own daughter. I ought to kick you out of this house, but you'd run straight to him and I'll see you both dead first."

Kate heard a scuffle and her father's cursing. Clayton Kincaid had appeared from the dining room with Cordelia behind him and was wrestling with her father, easily subduing him.

For the first time in her life she was happy to see the banker. She quickly got to her feet and moved well away from her father.

"Let me go, you son of a bitch!" Tom shouted. "It's none of your affair."

"It is entirely my affair."

With a force Kate wasn't aware Clayton possessed, he released her father with a shove, sending him sprawling on the foyer floor. Clayton reached for her, taking her by the arm and hauling her along with him and up the stairs. She caught a glimpse of Cordelia's hate-filled eyes on her, but she was soon whisked beyond sight.

He kept her moving down the hall until they reached her room. "Pack your things, Kate. I'm taking you out of this house tonight." She stared at him dumbfounded, and he continued, showing more spark than he ever had before. "Your father is dangerous, my dear. He seems to have lost his mind."

A deep pain began to throb in Kate's chest. An uncontrollable sob caused her to gasp and she sat back suddenly on the bed, trying to subdue it with little success. Her father hated her; she knew that now. She rolled to her side, curling up, feeling the hot trail of tears roll onto her face. She wanted Will. She wanted to know if he was going to be all right. She wanted his arms around her. Instead the bed dipped beneath Clayton's weight, and she drew back in alarm. She sat up quickly, staring at him with wide, frightened eyes. But his touch was gentle as his finger removed the last tear and held it like a diamond gem, shimmering crystal clear.

"You're in love with Will." He watched Kate intently as she tried to collect herself. Such a pretty young girl. No wonder Chanson had bedded her; he would himself, but he would make her his wife first. As his wife, she would not only help him become a senator, but she would effectively be the pawn in his game to capture the king—Will Chanson. The moment he had been waiting for had finally come, and he would waste no time in seizing it.

"Are you carrying his child, Kate?"

His blunt question rendered her speechless, and when she finally did find her tongue, she was indignant. "Is that what everyone is worried about? That I might be with child and shame you all? Well, you can quit your worrying. I'm not."

Clayton was relieved. A child would have complicated his plan, although it could have been dealt with. Everything could be dealt with. He stood up then and walked to the wardrobe. He pulled the doors open and began pulling out dresses in a selective manner and tossing them onto the bed next to her.

"Pack these and we'll be gone."

He was moving so hastily it was confusing her. She definitely didn't want to stay here with her father, but she didn't want to go with Clayton either. "No, I can't go with you. I—"

"You want to go to Will. I know." He moved swiftly, found her small trunk and began folding the dresses quickly. "That's not a good idea, Kate. Not yet. Your reputation would be ruined completely if word got out that you were staying with him."

"Will has asked me to marry him," she said defiantly and then waited for his reaction.

He stopped his packing and looked at her with his piercing blue eyes. "If you do, your father will surely kill him. Forget your foolishness, Kate. Think about Will. Isn't his life more important than defying your father?"

"I love him."

"I think we know that all too well, my dear. But does he love you enough to lose his life for you?" At the stunned look on her face he continued. "We need to get you out of this house. Your father is unbalanced." He laid the last dress in the trunk and moved to the door. "You can finish packing while I go downstairs and tell him what I'm going to do. And Kate"—he pulled the door open and stopped to look back at her—"if you truly love Will, you'll tell him good-bye."

Kate stared at the door. Like a whirlwind, he had taken over, leaving her breathless and confused. She wanted nothing more right now than to get out of this house, and if it meant going with Clayton Kincaid, then so be it.

Cordelia met her father at the foot of the stairs. She grabbed his arm to assure he wouldn't get past her. "What are you doing?"

"I'm taking her with me."

Cordelia's lips twisted into a pout. "How could you fall in love with her?"

"Love?" He almost laughed. "I have never loved any woman, not even your mother." She gasped and took a step back, clutching at her heart. He smirked. "Surely you can understand that, my dear? You don't love Tom, either, but you married him for your reasons."

Her eyelids fluttered as the truth of his words hit home. "I want Kate for my wife," he continued. "I don't need to explain it to anybody, Cordelia. Not even you. And I don't want her hurt."

Clayton's eyes dug deep inside his daughter. He knew her all too well. She was jealous of any woman that threatened her beauty, her status, or stole men's attention away from her. In her heart she had never been true to Tom, or any man, but Clayton didn't care, nor did he blame her. He'd never been faithful to one person either.

Cordelia gathered her skirts and turned to the stairs. Kincaid crossed the hall into the smoking room and closed the door behind him.

Tom Diering had found a high-backed leather chair and settled himself into it. He was guzzling whisky. Clayton's disgust overwhelmed him; he had never had much respect for Diering, but he had none now.

He moved to the center of the room. Diering watched him, but was sullenly silent as he continued to drink. His eyes dared Kincaid to reprimand him. Clayton found a bottle of Scotch behind the cabinet door and poured himself some without getting permission. With glass in hand he began to move around the room, glancing out the window for a while, noticing the bright red spots of blood on the snow just outside the window. At least Chanson wouldn't die from the wound. He was the one power here in Denver that stood in Clayton's way, and if Will wouldn't sell the CM, then

219

there were other ways to get it, but only if Chanson remained alive.

Finally, Clayton turned to Tom and noticed the bottle of whisky was down about three inches. "It was a stupid thing you did, Tom. You could have killed him."

Tom's eyes narrowed. His hand on the bottle shook. He'd made a threat and he'd had to abide by it; hurting Will was the only way he could get to Kate, the only way to make her stay away from him, the only way to make her accept Clayton's proposal. He tipped the bottle to his lips again. "I should think you'd be happy. I did it for you. She'd be marrying him instead of you if I didn't put the fear of God into both of them. I'm only trying to stick to my end of the bargain, Clayton."

"Do what you have to do, Tom, just don't kill him. Make Kate believe you will; make Will believe you will. I don't care, but I do suggest you start *seriously* trying to direct her toward the best course for her future. I've asked for your daughter's hand in marriage. Now I want your consent—and your guarantee."

Diering lifted the bottle to his mouth again and drank deeply before answering Kincaid. "You have my consent. I can't give you my guarantee. She's got a mind of her own."

Clayton could wait no longer for things to take their natural course. There was only one language Tom Diering understood. "You know, Tom," Clayton said, "I wouldn't be surprised if Chanson comes back, gunning for you." He waited for Tom's reaction and then relished the pleasure of seeing the man's frightened look. He continued. "On the other hand, if *you* kill *him*—like you almost did today—you'll wind up in jail and then all the money you owe me won't get paid. I'd have to foreclose on you, tell Cordelia..."

Tom sobered as he straightened up in his chair. Clayton wore his usual conniving smile; the one Tom hated. For a split second, he wondered who he hated worse—Kincaid or Chanson.

"I'm taking Kate with me tonight—for her safekeeping." Clayton drained his glass and left it on the small desk next to Tom. He walked to the parlor doors and opened them: "In the meantime you do some thinking about the situation. Then I want to see you in a week at the club. We'll make final arrangements."

The doors closed behind him. Tom stared at them for a long while. Finally he shrugged indifferently, enjoying the dull way the whisky made his body feel. He put the bottle back to his lips. At the moment, he just didn't give a damn what Clayton Kincaid had up his sleeve.

Dr. Benjamin Smith handed Will a cheap bottle of whisky. "Drink it. All of it."

The whisky warmed Will's cold body but it did little to dull his mind even after half a bottle. Dr. Smith busied himself preparing the instruments, occasionally glancing over his shoulder to check Will's progress.

Ben Smith had been the attending physician at Will's birth, and if things had turned out differently, Will would have been raised as his son. He had been in love with Will's mother, the beautiful Roseanne McVey. He would have married her too if Tyler Chanson hadn't suddenly reappeared from the dead all those years ago. Now Dr. Smith had a good wife and his own children, but sometimes at night in the dark he would stare upward at nothing but a memory, and wonder what life would have been like.

Suddenly, he grabbed the bottle away from Will. "You drink so damn much I can see you're immune to the stuff. Let me start digging and you'll pass out."

Will was surprised at the doctor's harshness. He was usually quite amiable. "With an attitude like that, maybe you ought to just put another bullet in me and end it."

Will's sarcasm cooled Dr. Smith off. He wasn't a cruel man; it was just the memories. He rubbed a hand over his face and apologized. "I'm sorry, Will. You know, I remember when you were just a six-month-old baby and you got shot—grazed on the leg. Your mother took the next bullet that was meant for you and she nearly died."

"I know. I've heard the story before, from you and from them."

"How'd you get yourself shot, anyway? I'm beginning to think you're following in your father's footsteps." His voice turned cold and hard again as he cut the cloth away from Will's shoulder. "He had a knack for getting shot just about every turn he took."

Will watched and winced as Dr. Smith washed the blood away from the wound. When they'd both decided it wasn't very bad, he said, "Why do you hate my dad so bad? What did he ever do to you— outside of keep you in business?"

Dr. Smith glanced at Will sharply, not realizing his feelings had come out so blatantly. He saw too much of Roseanne in Will's eyes, but there was also too much of Tyler there, too. He looked back at the wound. "I don't hate your father. Whatever gave you that idea?"

"You did."

Dr. Smith picked up the tweezers and gripped Will's arm. "Now, this is going to hurt." The pain shot up Will's arm and to his head. Everything went white.

Benjamin Smith studied the face that had suddenly gone pale in unconsciousness. "It always is quicker than whisky," he muttered.

When Will regained consciousness, he immediately felt the pain in his arm and with his good arm he reached out and touched the bandage. At the movement, Dr. Smith got up from his small desk, laying a pencil on a record book. He rolled his white shirtsleeves down and took his coat from the coat tree. "You can stay here all night. You probably have a little fever, so you shouldn't go out. I'll be next door in my house. If you need me, throw something at the wall or holler."

Dr. Smith turned the lamp off and headed for the door, leaving Will alone in the dark room. He lay back down and then, with his good arm, pulled the wool blanket up higher on his chest.

Tom Diering's face appeared before him, and then the gun. He felt the impact of the bullet again and the smell of the smoke burned his nostrils. He knew what to expect from Diering now. Next time he would go prepared. Diering may have thought he would give up, but Will had never given up on anything he wanted. He had experienced something unlike anything he had had before. It made him uncommonly alone without it. He knew now that no bed would be warm without the presence of the woman he loved.

Kate placed her gloved hand in Clayton's waiting grip and allowed him to help her to the snowy ground. He turned to the driver. "Take the horses to the stable and then have Miss Diering's things brought to the house."

Without words they took the shoveled path to the mansion, its dark course dimly lit by gas lamps. Kate hung back at the ornate double doors, then reluctantly gave in to her situation. In the house's great hall, the chandelier was unable to chase away the interior darkness. To her right the gleaming, curving stairway led to the open hallway above. The hall was balustraded for a distance and then disappeared behind the walls that hid the upper chambers. She knew it all well. A cold depression settled over her.

The butler appeared and helped Kate with her coat, brushing the fur collar down with a fond hand before taking it to the closet to hang.

"You'll be using the room you were in before," Clayton said. "Oliver will escort you there and carry your bags. If there's anything you would like, please let me know. Now, if you'll excuse me, I have some business to attend to in my office."

Kate was glad to be alone. Oliver, the English butler, led the way to the guest room on the second floor. The room was large and decorated with dark furniture and accessories, definitely a man's choice. The heavy velvet drapes were drawn, making it extremely gloomy.

Feeling very tired, Kate sat on the edge of the

bed unable to keep her shoulders from sagging. It seemed she had no home. She was angry and nervous because she knew Clayton's desire was something she could not agree to. But what choice did she have? She couldn't go out on her own at this point, penniless and unprepared. She could no longer stay with her father and Cordelia, and her chances of ever being with Will were too dangerous to consider. She knew she mustn't think like a prisoner, or she would find herself one, but at that moment she did feel very much like a prisoner. She wondered if Will was all right. She felt a responsibility for the pain he was surely suffering. Oh, how she wanted to see him, comfort him, but would he want to see her after what had happened? Would he think her worth risking his life for? But an even bigger question was, did she love him enough to tell him good-bye?

Clayton remained at the house for a week, as though he had appointed himself her guard. Consequently, Kate spent most of the time in her room and suffered through meals with either Clayton watching her from the end of the table, or listening with half an ear while he entertained guests. As each day passed, she felt more and more like a bird in a cage waiting for the moment when the master would forget to latch the door.

The day finally came when Clayton prepared to go into town; she had seen his driver take the city brougham from the carriage house and direct it to the front of the mansion. She quickly changed into a blouse, riding skirt, and boots, and hurried to the stables out the back entrance. The attendant saddled her a horse on request, although he did it painstakingly slowly. With reluctance he turned it over to her and revealed his apprehension.

"This is a fine, blooded animal, Miss Diering. It must be handled with the utmost care. Mr. Kincaid didn't give me permission to let you take it, but if you *say* he did..."

She took the reins and prepared to mount. "Don't worry." She hoisted herself easily onto the sidesaddle with no assistance. "I'll take extreme caution."

She was adjusting the reins when she suddenly heard a voice behind her. She turned her upper torso and stared down into Kincaid's penetrating eyes.

"Where are you off to, Kate dear?"

"I was going for a ride. I'm not used to staying inside."

"What a coincidence. I had no sooner left the drive when I got to thinking about that very thing, so I returned to see if you would like to come into town with me today. You could do some shopping."

Kate's heart pummeled her chest, but she stood her ground. "I'm afraid that's impossible. You see, I don't have any money."

He acknowledged his oversight with a nod of his head. "Of course, but I'll give you whatever you are accustomed to."

"That won't be necessary. I don't need anything. I prefer just to go for a ride. It's a beautiful day."

"Kate." The tone of his voice increased the caution she felt already. "If you're going to see how Will is doing, I can assure you he is doing better." He hesitated, obviously considering his words, and then continued as though he didn't want to say what he was about to.

"You know I want you for my wife; I had hoped you would give it some serious consideration. Naturally, I don't want you to marry Will. You can understand that." He looked into her eyes. "Your father is very serious about you not seeing Will again; he has threatened to kill him. Think about what you would be doing to Will if you went to him."

Kate clenched her teeth to keep her lip from quivering and fought against the tears that threatened to flow. She gathered the reins and nudged the horse toward the gate.

Clayton reached up swiftly, surprised by her unexpected action, and stopped the horse by a hand on the bridle.

"You're not still going out there, are you?"

"Please leave me alone, Clayton." She tried to pull the horse away from his detaining hand as she felt her control rapidly vanishing.

"Your father is very serious, Kate. You saw what he has already done."

A painful sound that was a mixture of a laugh and a sob escaped her lips. "Perhaps I'm foolish, but not that much so. No one needs to worry. I won't jeopardize Will's life by seeing him again. Now please, Clayton, I'd like to be alone."

"Of course. That's understandable."

Clayton released the horse and Kate rode away. Clayton walked back to the brougham, stepped inside, and headed it, once again, toward town. Satisfaction flowed within him. She had finally broken. Now he had only one more step to take and his plan would be complete. He glanced at the blue sky and felt the warmth of the sun on his back. It was a good day; they might get a January thaw.

Chapter 15

Clayton looked across the desk at Tom. "You owe me all the money from having to rebuild the house last fall, not to mention the thousands for operating the ranch. Some of the biggest ranch owners in the entire West have called it quits and gone bankrupt. And here you continue on by my good grace but can't repay me a dime. All you can do is ask for more money." Kincaid was visibly amused. "I think it's about time you accepted the fact that you're no rancher. True, this blizzard wasn't your doing, but you were in over your head before any of this happened. To put it bluntly, Tom, I can't keep carrying you."

Tom's hand, looking odd now with the ends of three fingers missing, circled around and around his hat nervously. Panic overwhelmed him. He found it hard to breathe in the stuffy, smoke-filled room. For a moment he saw his father so many years ago cursing, as usual, asking him why he couldn't do anything right.

"There's one way we might be able to help each other, though."

Kincaid's words drifted into Diering's troubled thoughts. "If you'll remember—unless you were too drunk—I said I wanted to see you today to discuss some final arrangements about Kate's marrying me. As I was saying, Tom, there is one way I could help you out one more time, but this will be the last time. If you fail to keep your head above water, I won't keep your financial problems a secret from Cordelia any longer."

"What is it, Clayton?" Tom tried not to sound too desperate. "I'm willing to listen."

Listen? Clayton nearly laughed. Diering was in no position to listen or even bargain. He had no choices. He was where Clayton liked men to be. In a position where they would sell their souls for the sake of the money he could dangle in front of them. He could own all of Denver, thanks to this blizzard. It had actually been quite a windfall. Now he could grab up even more mortgages. True, his own cattle investments didn't look good, either, but he had plenty of mortgages to collect on. This panic would pass. In a short while more fools would come out here, carrying their dreams and their hopes in tattered bags, and he would be their salvation. He would answer all their prayers.

"I'll give you the money you need to get back on your feet, Tom—and in exchange I want Kate's hand in marriage."

Tom's heart lurched. The clock had stopped. Kincaid was no longer giving him a choice, no longer going to be patient. "But I can't force her to marry you, Clayton. I've threatened to kill Will, thereby keeping her away from him so you would have no interference, but the rest is up to you. You'll have to win her heart."

Kincaid wasn't amused. "I don't woo women. I want her for my wife and I know she won't consent on her own just now. I'm quite sure she won't see

230

Will again, but I can't take that chance, nor can I wait until she's ready to start looking for a husband again. I want to announce my candidacy for the Senate soon. And I want her on my arm on the campaign trail this summer, as my fiancée. We'll be married just before the election. Therefore, it will be up to you—if you want me to continue carrying you—to go to her now and 'convince' her to be my wife."

Tom had nothing against it, he never had, although he wondered why Kincaid would want Kate for a wife when he could have any woman in Denver—and probably had. "Why don't you want to marry her right away, Clayton?" Tom's suspicions rose. "Wouldn't it look better if she were your wife while you campaigned?"

Clayton smiled. "You know so little, don't you, Tom? Can't you see that a young single woman will attract more attention than a married one? A single woman is not yet taken. Men look at her and have dreams of having her, even winning her away from me. They will see her traveling with me and they will get all sorts of wild ideas about her, about us. They will wonder why she stays with me, a man nearly forty years older than she. We'll make a handsome couple. We'll create rumors, sensation. Our names will be everywhere, on every lip, in every newspaper. She will draw the attention, the votes—not me."

Tom considered it and figured Clayton was right, but he also realized that his name would be connected with hers. People would want to know if she was his daughter. The idea sounded better and better.

Of course Kate wouldn't be happy with the arrangement, but eventually she would realize her good fortune and be happy for the position that any woman in Denver would like to hold. She would be well taken care of. She would never want for anything, and he probably wouldn't, either, because he could always go to her if he needed money from Kincaid. It would be the best thing for everybody. But how could he ever get her to consent?

"Do you love her?" Tom asked suddenly; it would ease his conscience if Kincaid said yes.

Kincaid drained his glass. "I'm sure you don't care about that, Tom. All you need concern yourself with is saving your ranch and your marriage—and convincing Kate to be my wife."

Kate faced her father and drew her shoulders back squarely, preparing for battle. Behind her the doors to Clayton's overfurnished reading room were closed tightly against the curious eyes of the servants. This was her father's first visit to her since she'd been here. She didn't have to be told it wasn't a social call.

His face was gaunt and the worry lines around his eyes had deepened. She knew all about the devastation of the blizzard, and she knew he was probably in a financial bind the way every other rancher in the state was, and although she felt sorry for him, there were some things she couldn't forgive, so she looked at him with cold eyes. "Why have you come here?"

Diering helped himself to a chair since she didn't offer him one. "How do you like it here, Kate?" he asked, ignoring her curt remark.

She didn't move from her spot. Her feet were

planted solidly and her arms were folded across her chest. "I don't like it here, but I'm sure you don't care about my feelings."

He swallowed hard. He had tried to care about her since she was a baby, but there had always been something else to occupy his mind. "Of course I care about you. It's your welfare that concerns me. Why else do you think I've tried to keep you away from Chanson? He's no good for you, and someday you'll see that."

Why had she hoped he had come here with an apology for hitting her and hurting Will? "You didn't have to shoot him."

"I warned you I would. Besides, Kate, do you think he came callin' that day to ask for your hand in marriage? No, he just wanted to get you alone somewhere so he could use you again. I'm sure he knows a foolish female when he finds one."

She faced him again, showing the full extent of her own anger and pain. "I know he wasn't coming to ask for my hand in marriage." Her gray-green eyes flashed at him. "He had *already* asked, and I had accepted. He came to ask your permission."

The revelation stunned him. He had never thought that Will might already be serious enough to marry her. His plan had been to stop them from getting to that point.

"Then you're in love with him."

The coldness inside her warmed at the memory of those glorious times Will and she had spent together. She lifted her head proudly. "Yes, I love him. And he loves me."

Diering remembered love and how it was in the beginning. It had always changed for him; faded,

altered. But he hadn't come here to talk about
Chanson; he had his own life to worry about. "I
didn't come here to talk about your lover. I came
here to talk about Clayton. Despite the fact that
you've tarnished your reputation with Chanson
and lost your virginity, Clayton still wants to
marry you. I want to know if you have given any
more thought to his proposal?"

"Why should I when it's Will I want to marry?"

Tom snorted in exasperation. "Forget Chanson!
I told you I'd kill him if you didn't stay away from
him. I thought that first bullet would be enough
to convince you I'm not bluffing."

Kate studied him thoroughly. She remembered
all too well the way he could become when pushed
to the breaking point. "No, I don't think you're
bluffing. But I can't marry Clayton Kincaid. It's
absurd. I detest him."

"You could learn to care for him." Tom stood
up. "Look at what he has. He can provide a good
living for you. You can have anything you want.
The rest of us are in near-bankruptcy from the
blizzard, but Clayton is that much richer."

Kate stared at him, trying to understand why
he was in favor of granting Kincaid what he
wanted.

He continued. "There is no need to live like a
pauper or marry a pauper when you could be living grandly and respectably as Clayton Kincaid's
wife. You should be honored that he has asked for
your hand; you are the only woman he has wanted
to marry. You are still under my custody and I say
you will marry him."

"I will not."

Diering grabbed her shoulders. His glaring eyes

truly frightened Kate and made her wonder if he had indeed lost his mind. He spoke very slowly and precisely. "You will marry Clayton Kincaid, Kate, or I will kill Will Chanson. It's as simple as that."

There was no doubt in her mind that he meant it. He had already proved that he would not back down. She fumbled for the nearest chair and, finding it, sank deep into its support, holding its arms for strength. She stared up at him, already feeling the chill of death, the end of her future the way she had planned it. "I promise I won't see Will again, Daddy. Just please don't make me marry Clayton."

He straightened his willowy form, feeling more confident now. "Do you expect me to believe that? You'd run to him at the first opportunity."

She fought back tears. "Why do you want me to do this? I'll go away. I'll go back to England— anything! Just don't make me marry him."

"I have my reasons, Kate. I want you to marry Clayton for your own good. Someday, you'll see that I'm right."

She didn't know how long she sat staring at the books lining the walls of the room, but she saw none of them. Instead she saw the line shack and the bed with the buffalo robe thrown over it. She could feel the heat of the fire, feel the fire of Will's touch, and see the flame in his eyes that did not go away. She knew she could never live without him, never live if he were to die because of her.

If only she had more time to think. More time to work something out. "You give me little choice," she heard herself say, "but at least allow me one thing—allow me an engagement period."

Diering remembered what Kincaid had said about not wanting to get married until just before the election. Maybe if he didn't say anything about that, he would make Kate think he was not being so cruel after all. "What did you have in mind?"

She rubbed her head, trying to think, trying to buy time. "Later. Maybe this summer..."

"Very well, Kate. I'll talk to him."

She let out a breath and sank deeper into the chair. She had been granted a reprieve.

Tom moved to the door, hesitating with his hand on the knob. "It'll be in the newspaper tomorrow morning. And remember one thing, Kate"—he put the gruffness back in his voice—"don't go back on your word. You can run away, but Chanson will still be here, and so will I."

Will shoved his Winchester into the saddle scabbard and readjusted the Colt revolver on his hip. Then, even though his left arm was still in a sling, he easily stepped aboard his buckskin without the use of it. Despite Diering's threat, he had some unfinished business to attend to, and it wouldn't wait any longer.

He pointed the buckskin north. The path was not any easier than it had been ten days ago. When the Diering place came into view he pulled the rifle from the scabbard and balanced it in front of him. He waited for some confrontation as he moved into the yard. The buckskin picked its steps carefully over the trampled snow in the yard, lifting its ears to the surroundings as it sensed its rider's caution.

Will drew rein in front of the house, and with the rifle in his right hand, swung easily to the ground. He turned to the steps without tying the horse, knowing the buckskin would stay. His longing for Kate pushed the danger to the rear of his mind; the need for her urged him up the stairs, but he did not let go of his caution.

His knock on the door was met with silence from within. He knocked again, louder. Nothing. There was no activity in the yard. The cowboys were all out working. Then to his left he saw the lace curtain in the nearby window rise; in a matter of seconds the door was flung open by the red-headed housemaid.

"Mr. Chanson," Minnie said nervously.

"Is Kate here?"

Minnie tried to glance around him, her eyes darting apprehensively. "No. She's—she's in town. You shouldn't be here, Mr. Chanson." She looked at his shoulder and regret filled her kind eyes. "I was so upset at what Mr. Diering did to you."

"I need to talk to Kate. When will she be back?"

Minnie swallowed hard then tilted her head back to better meet the gaze of the tall man before her. "I doubt she'll be back. She's gone to stay with Mr. Kincaid." Hastily she added, "It's safer there for her. Her father was—"

Will's eyes narrowed as concern for Kate took precedence in his mind. "What did he do to her?"

Minnie looked away and her eyes became moist. "He—he hit her, Mr. Chanson." Her expression showed her distress. "But for your sake, you'd best not come here again." She stepped back toward the door, but then something in the yard caught her attention. She gasped. "It's him."

Will turned around and saw Tom riding into the yard alone. His grip tightened on the Winchester. "Go back inside, ma'am." She did without any argument. He heard the door close softly behind her.

Tom saw him and kicked his horse into a trot, pulling him to a rough halt at the foot of the steps. He hadn't expected Chanson to have the gall to come here again. He saw the Winchester in his hand and the Colt strapped to his hip. He reached for his own rifle in the saddle scabbard but the cocking of the lever on the Winchester halted his hand in midair.

"Don't." The one word was a deadly threat. "I don't need much of an excuse to blow you right out of that saddle."

"You get off my property, Chanson."

"I came to get Kate."

"She's gone."

"I'll find her."

"I'm warnin' you, Chanson. I'll kill you the next time."

Will held the gun on Tom and moved down the stairs and stopped by Diering's horse. "No you won't, Tom. You'll never get the drop on me again." With his slinged arm he pulled Diering's rifle from the scabbard, despite the pain the movement caused in his shoulder. He pushed it into his own saddle scabbard. Then, shifting his Winchester to the curve of his wounded arm, he gathered his reins and stepped into the saddle.

Diering glanced at his rifle now in Will's possession. "I'll turn you in for stealin', Chanson."

"I'll drop it off out by the barn." Will rode away, turning in the saddle to keep his gun pointed at Diering until he was at the edge of the yard. Then, as promised, he took Diering's rifle from his scabbard and leaned it up against the barn. With increased determination now, he headed for Kincaid's.

Will still held his Winchester in his hand although he didn't anticipate problems from anyone at the Kincaid mansion. When the ornate double doors swung open at his knock, the black-suited butler ran disapproving eyes over his rough appearance and the two guns he had on his person.

"Is there something I can do for you . . . sir?"

"I'm here to see Kate Diering."

"May I tell her who is calling?"

"Will Chanson."

The butler stepped aside and allowed Will through the door, led him to the parlor, then left him alone. Will set his rifle aside and, nervous and anxious to see Kate, began moving around the room. It was a cold place in appearance with its high ceiling and rococo furniture covered in an icy blue damask. Even the sun could lend little warmth as it tried to get through the heavily draped window dressings to splash its warmth and yellow rays onto the pale blue carpet.

He sensed her presence, turned and saw her in the doorway. The light in her eyes that had been there during their days at the line shack was still there. But then, as if the sun had passed behind a cloud, the brightness faded. She turned and closed the door behind her.

He walked across the room to her. For a moment they merely looked at one another, and then with his good arm he pulled her against him, seeking out her lips and the sweet taste and smell of her that heightened his senses to their full awareness.

She tipped her head back, receiving his kiss and giving back her own, before a moan of denial rose to her throat and she pushed herself away from him. She turned her back to him and hastily walked as far away from him as the confines of the blue parlor would allow.

He noticed then the hourglass form of her body, remembering all too well what it looked like beneath the dress of pale peach silk. Combined with the upsweep of her hair she looked older, very beautiful and desirable, but she stood so erect, and looked so very untouchable. A strange feeling washed over him, the feeling that maybe he had never made love to this woman, that she was not the same Kate who had shared his bed for well over a week.

"Kate." It was but a whisper from his lips, and one that held the inflection of a confused question.

"You shouldn't have come here, Will."

"I thought you'd be happy to see me."

He took a step toward her, but stopped, watching instead the way her chin lowered and then lifted as if with an effort. When she finally turned back to him she had her back and neck very stiff, and her composure once more in place.

"You can't come here anymore, Will. We can no longer see one another. What happened between us was...is...is over. You must understand that and accept it. It was simply something that happened because of the blizzard."

Kate could not bear to look at his stunned expression. She turned again to the window and took a deep breath. She fought the pain digging into her body and the tears surfacing into pools in her eyes. She knew the only way she could save his life was to send him away forever, make him think she no longer loved him so he would quit trying to see her. She felt him standing silently behind her, unmoving, unspeaking.

Her heart was pounding so loudly that she didn't hear him move. Unexpectedly, she was jerked around and drawn roughly up against him again. She saw the pain and disbelief in his eyes and the determination that marked his character. "I don't believe a damn word of it, Kate Diering." His words were low and rough, meant only for her ears. "Now, what is going on here? What have they done to you? What have they made you say? Minnie said your father hit you."

Will pressed Kate closer against him, annihilating any physical strength she had left to use against him or any emotional strength to fight her love for him. The tears finally overflowed and trickled down her cheeks. But she couldn't give in to her need for him. For his sake, she mustn't.

With renewed strength, she wrenched herself free of his one-armed grip and took a stance well away from him. Her breathing was hard, rocking her as she met his eyes. She wondered if he could tell she was lying. She must convince him. She rushed to the small table near the sofa and pulled out the single drawer in the center of it. From inside she retrieved the article that had come out about the engagement in the newspaper. "Clayton has asked me to marry him—" Suddenly, she broke, her words cracking. She thrust the paper at him as she raced past, out of the parlor and up the stairs to her room. She was going to tell him she didn't love him, but that was one thing she simply could not lie about.

Bewildered, he watched her run away. Then he looked at the headline of the newspaper in his hand. He stared at it in dismay. Every ounce of strength in his body vanished. He felt as though his knees might buckle. He reached for the chair next to him and sat down hard, staring at her name in print there linked with Clayton Kincaid's. It couldn't be true. He read the headline over and over until the words rolled through his mind from memory. At last, he looked away from the newsprint and stood up, dazed. He picked up his rifle and left the house.

Two miles out of Denver he pulled his horse up under a cottonwood tree whose head dipped down into a small creek. There he dismounted and, with eyes that stung, looked down at the newspaper article still in his hand. He wadded it up and threw it on the ground, kicked it with his boot, and watched it land on the very edge of the water.

Gradually, the shock cleared away and his mind began to function. How could he have lost her to Clayton? What had happened? He knew he hadn't been wrong about their love, but there was more to this than Tom Diering trying to keep him and Kate apart. Diering wanted her to marry Kincaid; wanted it so badly that he'd kill to see it accomplished. That disturbed him, but it didn't frighten him enough to give up on the woman he loved. He did realize that forcing any confrontation between himself and Diering would end up with one of them dead. He could not be responsible for killing Kate's father. This would surely drive a wedge between them. He'd have to find another way to get Kate. And he would.

Chapter 16

Bart rode silently next to Will. He'd never seen his boss so silent. Will sat stoically atop his buckskin, his hardened gaze on the devastation left behind by the blizzard. The swollen streams raged in muddy spring torrents and were filled with huge, grinding ice cakes that rolled over each other, upending and tearing at everything in their way as they proceeded on their course. Along with the ice in the water were countless dead cattle, sometimes with their heads up, sometimes with their feet up, as they bobbed up and down in the deafening roar that could be heard long before it could be seen.

Will and Bart rode for days taking in the spectacle, watching the grim procession at every flooded waterway. They also found cattle piled up along fence lines like cords of wood. In other places the coulees were filled with cattle that had sought shelter, or had become trapped, and had been buried alive. Now, with the snow nearly gone, the misery they had endured could be fully understood. It didn't take long to realize the full extent of the blizzard. There was only one bright spot; the losses were high, but not as high as those from the winters of '86 and '87.

Finally, the two men turned toward home with those cattle that had survived. En route they were joined by other ranchers who herded their own pathetic herds. All ranchers who had found cattle belonging to other ranchers saw to it that the rightful owners were contacted.

The spring branding was a solemn affair. But the new grass came up and the survivors were turned loose once again. When the last animal was released back to the range, Will pushed his hat to the back of his head and stared up at the sun that was already hot for so early in the year. He swallowed the bitterness he was feeling and stalked toward the cowboys who were standing around the branding fire. There hadn't been any joking or laughing this spring, hardly any talking. They saw him approach and stood up a bit straighter.

He stopped in front of them. Most of them had been regulars of his before the drought and before the blizzard. He knew they needed and wanted work. It made his task a lot harder. "I guess you know I don't have any more work for you. Come back this fall. Maybe I'll have something then. Go on over to the ranch and collect your pay."

He saw no anger in their faces, only silent resignation. Most had been in the business long enough to expect this. They gathered their gloves and ropes and then rode away on the horses they'd come in on. Will turned to Bart and the other men he'd kept on during the winter. "You can stay on as long as I have something for you to do."

They too boarded their horses and rode back to the ranch to do the other jobs they knew were waiting, or the ones that would be delegated to them later. Will turned to Bart. "I'm going to town. Pay the boys, will you? Then tell Lorna not to fix any supper for me."

"You don't need to take this personal, Will. There wasn't much you could do to stop it from happening."

"No, I guess not. Look, Bart, you and the others can have the day off. I'm going into town to get some supplies to take to Cripple Creek with me. We're starting work on the mine."

"What about the ranch, Will?"

Will looked around, still feeling low at the heavy losses. "There isn't much to do now, Bart. I'm going to leave you in charge for a while. You can always get word to me if you need me."

In town the streets were crowded, but there was an unusual electric feeling to the air and the townspeople talked and shouted and laughed with an excitement that couldn't be accredited entirely to spring. As Will rode past the Cattlemen's Club he noticed a long line of horses tied out front and he wondered if there was a meeting inside that he hadn't been told about. He'd been gone a lot lately and hadn't received word of a gathering, but Kincaid had had a habit of excluding him from the notices since December.

The Great Room was filled with ranch owners and buzzing with talk. There weren't too many solemn expressions, odd considering that most of them had just lost half their herds. When they saw him, one rancher named Nelson lifted a hand and motioned him to join the group, hollering across the room. "Won't do you any good to come asking Kincaid for a loan from his bank. Says he went belly-up, too."

Will didn't believe that for a second. Kincaid might lose his ranch investments, but he had enough other investments to keep him safe for the rest of his life. "I didn't come for money," he said as he joined them.

"Well, what are you going to do? We've all been thinking that this is just a damn good time to quit the business."

A man called Campbell chimed in. "I don't think I'll have a choice. You can't operate when your busted and can't get money. I'm bankrupt. It's all over for me. Anybody want to buy what's left of my place—the price is dirt cheap."

Nelson turned to Will again. "We're all thinking about headin' into the mountains and minin' for gold. Guess they hit some big bonanzas up at Cripple Creek."

So the news was out. Both Will and Dexter knew the rush would be on when they got a mining company in there to start working. "I guess right now it's the only thing that's paying," he said.

Vaughn eyed Will with contempt; he'd like to get even with him for accusing him of rustling in front of everybody. Because of that he'd been watched by some damn agent ever since. "Word is out that you've got some interests over there, too. You're as bad as Kincaid for having your damn fingers in every pie around these parts."

Will walked to the bar and poured himself a shot of whisky. "Just call it foresight, Vaughn."

"Guess you're gonna quit ranchin' now that you've got some high-payin' gold mine."

Quitting the ranch had never crossed Will's

mind. He didn't figure there was anything that would make him give up the CM. It was his life, and he couldn't imagine going from day to day without it being there.

"No, I won't be quitting the ranch."

Vaughn sidled up to him, smiling in that sneering way of his. "Hear tell you've got a mine over in Cripple Creek and that you've named it the Kate Meline. Somebody tells me that's the name of Kincaid's fiancée. Somebody also tells me that old Tom Diering shot you because of her." He started to laugh and looked over his shoulder at the others. "Sounds like to me old Clayton could be gettin' *used* merchandise. I wonder if he knows."

Like a bolt of lightning Will's arm went back and then came forward, his fist hitting Vaughn square in the nose with a punch that could rival the kick of a mule. The rancher fell over backward, and groveled for a minute, trying to get up. Blood was spurting out his nose and mouth. Will took a step closer to him. His knuckles were bleeding where the skin had split from the force, but he had his fist clenched and ready for another. He grabbed Vaughn by the collar, lifted him up off the floor, and then smashed him in the face again. Finally, Campbell and Nelson stepped in and pulled Will off. Clayton's office door opened, and the president of the club entered.

"What's going on in here?" he demanded, but immediately saw that the fracas was between Will and Vaughn. He turned back to his office. "Come in here, Will. We've got some more business to discuss."

Will met the banker's impervious gaze, then,

with whisky glass in hand, followed him into his office.

He went to Clayton's personal liquor stock and refilled the glass, knowing Clayton didn't approve. He turned to stand over the man who had seated himself at his immense desk, the picture of authority and power—the ruler of the kingdom.

"I suppose you're going to kick me out of the club?" He tossed the liquor down his throat and poured himself another.

Clayton smiled and sipped at his Scotch while he studied Will, trying to see if his and Kate's engagement had had the devastating effect he'd hoped. "No, but what was the fight about?"

"The usual."

Clayton's eyes slitted in contemplation. Vaughn had such a loud voice that it had carried through the door. Will had defended Kate; it was a good sign that he still wanted her, that he would still try to get her. As for Kate, she had not been receptive at all. She was going along like a sheep on its way to slaughter. He only hoped he could force her to smile on the campaign trail.

"Actually, Will, I wanted to ask you if you're ready to sell the CM now?"

Will smiled and shook his head slowly as he considered Clayton's audacity. "I've lost a few thousand head of cattle, but I'm not ready to buckle."

"You sold half your herd last fall. Then you lost half of what's left to the blizzard. I figure you've got about five thousand head left, but I suppose you can bring it back into shape with your mining investments and some help from your dad."

Will's insides turned cold at the mention of his

father coming to his rescue. It was probably what most of them thought. Would he never gain credit for standing on his own two feet? He took a sip of the whisky, refusing to let Clayton get the best of him.

Clayton continued. "You must like ranching a great deal to keep operating a business that has to be supported by another."

"If you honestly believed that, Clayton, then why would you want the CM so badly?"

"The land is the investment. I'm not interested in the cattle. They're no longer of any value."

"The land is no good without the cattle."

"Ah, but you're wrong. The land can be broken up and farmed."

"It can, but anybody who tries will go broke in a few years. You can't farm this prairie ground the way you can the soil back East."

"You and I know that, Will, but those poor fools coming out here wanting homesteads don't know it."

Will wasn't surprised at the man's lack of integrity. "Selling these 'farms' over and over, each time for a larger amount, must make for a pretty good profit."

"Of course, and the CM is the finest land around here. It's only natural for people to want it. If I didn't, there would be someone else."

"The roundup showed your losses to be as heavy as anybody's. Maybe you'll be willing to sell out to *me* at the same price you're offering those men out there for their spreads."

Kincaid smiled, knowing Will wasn't serious. "It's not my sole livelihood, nor my first love the way it is yours. Oh, correction, I suppose your first love is still Kate. How is your shoulder anyway?"

Will tried to check his temper. It seemed everyone knew about it.

Clayton continued when Will didn't respond. "Tom's a poor shot, or maybe just a soft heart. Anyway, the incident at least led her on the right path. We're leaving soon to start campaigning."

Will's jealousy consumed him and shot out in the killing flash of his eyes, the clenched jaw, and flared nostrils. Slowly, he stood up. With preciseness he set his whisky glass down on some foreclosure papers, leaving a water ring that ran the ink. He stalked to the door.

"Don't be so hasty, Will. And don't be such a poor loser."

The words stopped Will cold. He turned to face his adversary again. "Did you want something else?"

Clayton propped his feet up on the corner of his desk. "Yes, as a matter of fact. I'd like to buy stock in your new mine—the Kate Meline."

"I'm sure you'll try when it becomes available."

"You know, Will, we may be able to strike up some sort of deal. Make some trades here and there and both of us come out with what we want."

Will's lips twisted, showing his disrespect for Kincaid. "You've only got one thing I want, Kincaid, but I won't bargain with you to get it. I have my own ways." Without a backward glance he left the room.

Clayton moved to the window with cigar in one hand and the glass of Scotch in the other. He watched Will mount his buckskin and ride down the street. He'd given Clayton the answer he needed; he'd made it clear he still wanted Kate; made it clear that he might even try to get her back, but not by means of any "bargains." Well, that much waited to be seen.

He watched until Will had disappeared from view, then he went to the liquor cabinet where the bottle of Scotch was perched. He drank what was in his glass then refilled it. He savored the flavor he had so come to love, the same way he was going to savor breaking Will once and for all. It had been a long time coming, but it was going to be worth every minute.

Kate looked in the mirror at the gown Madeline Franck had created for her. "It's very lovely," she said, trying to show enthusiasm. "It will be just right for the campaign trip."

"I'm sure Clayton will like it," Madeline said, with a nuance in her tone that indicated she knew Clayton very well.

Kate went back into the dressing room and removed the dress. Madeline was right there to help her. "Then you want me to finish the others?"

"Yes. Have them done in two weeks."

Kate put her own dress back on and gathered her hat and purse, pinning her hat on as she moved to the door. "I'll be back in a week for the other fittings."

Madeline nodded. Kate had done all the proper things; said all the right words. She had even managed to conceal her true feelings about Clayton in front of the curious women in the shop. With relief she stepped out into the street.

Kate pulled on a glove and looked up into the sun, thankful for the warmth of spring, even though there was still a bite to the air. She turned to her left and collided full force with the solid structure of a man. "Please forgive me, I—" She looked up into his face and her words vanished from her head. A jumble of emotions took their place.

Will stood before her, his hands on her shoulders steadying her and then moving her from the center of the sidewalk and out of the way of the noisy crowd jostling them. She realized her hand was on his chest. Self-conscious now, she removed it, although slowly and reluctantly.

"What a coincidence to—to bump into you," she managed, nearly smiling because it had been the one thing that had been constantly on her mind during the waking hours and in her dreams at night. For a carefree moment she almost forgot her father's warning.

Will tried to pretend that he hadn't been waiting for her for two hours ever since he'd seen her go inside the shop. "Yes. It's been a while."

His heart looked for signs of hope, signs that she still wanted him. He drew her to a vacant bench on the boardwalk. The pressure of his hand on her arm forced her to sit down next to him. The bench was small and he sat close to her. Casually but purposefully, he leaned back and put an arm over her shoulder, oblivious to the people passing by them.

Kate was nervous under his scrutiny and fearful that she would reveal her true emotions to him, thereby encouraging him. "Was there something you wished to say?" She hoped she sounded indifferent, though inside her heart was crying.

He leaned closer to her, pressing his chest into

her shoulder. "You didn't give me the opportunity to congratulate you on your engagement. I hear you're also preparing to go with your *fiancé* on his campaign tour."

His eyes bored into her, pressing her for an answer, an explanation. She looked away at the flock of people hurrying back and forth in front of them. "Yes, that's true."

"And you've been living with him."

She looked at him beseechingly. "Please, Will. It's not like that at all. It's—"

"It's not like it was with us?"

She stood up, hurt and helpless. He encircled her arm with his hand and pulled her back down next to him. "You didn't answer me, Kate. Is your room the same as his?"

"No!" Indignant, her eyes sparked. "His room is in the wing opposite from mine! Quit making me sound like that, Will Chanson. I am not that sort of woman."

"You are when you're with me."

"Damn you," she said through clenched teeth. "Why are you doing this? Why can't you leave me alone and accept the fact that I don't love you. That I never did. That—"

"You're lying," he interrupted again. He put his hand on her chin and turned her head to a better angle in which to see into her eyes. "I know you much better than you think I do, and I don't believe that you don't love me. I want you, and rest assured, Kate, I am not a man to walk away from something I want."

He released her then and stood up. He held out his hand and helped her to her feet and into the mainstream of people, where he stood for a moment, once again searching her face. Suddenly he smiled, that old mischievous smile that had captured her heart from the beginning. "Until we meet again, Kate." He touched the brim of his hat in a respectful gesture, but the glow in his eyes went much deeper, thrilling her with the daring suggestion that they would, indeed, meet again.

Chapter 17

Kate relaxed in her bath, letting it soothe her tired body and refresh her weary mind. She'd sat through another boring dinner with Clayton, his business associates, and some people involved with his campaign. She'd tried to play the part of a hostess, at Clayton's request, for he was coaching her in the things she would have to know when she became his wife.

She closed her eyes and leaned her head back against the high, rounded back of the marble tub. It was easy to place herself in a happier time, easy to dream that Will would find a way to rescue her, and easy to forget the promise she'd made to her father.

She was awakened from her dreams by the chill of the water. She found the soap and scrubbed her body, hurrying now against the increasing cold. She rinsed, stepped from the tub onto the thick rug, and rubbed at her goosebumps with the heavy bath towel. Still shivering, she reached for her bathrobe and quickly pulled it on, securing it tightly around her waist.

She left the bathing area of her suite and went to sit on the edge of the bed. Its softness didn't interest her tonight. She could think only of the hard little bed in the line shack and the solid frame of the man whose body had curved so naturally to hers.

She paced the floor nervously and stared out the French doors that opened out onto the small balcony of her room. She pulled the doors aside and stepped into the crisp spring air of the night. She folded her arms around her to help ward off the chill of a breeze that moved through the many trees in the backyard. Hidden in the dark branches, the trill of a nightbird challenged her to find its secret place, but it was safe in the darkness.

There was no moon; only the twinkling of stars lit the huge yard, giving form to its objects. She realized with a sadness then that as long as she lived here, she would never be able to gallop again at full speed beneath the moonlight on the dirt road to the old Lander place. There would be no excitement here, no challenges. Life was structured, orderly, tame. Her only obligation would be to look beautiful, to be another of Clayton's showpieces.

Saddened at the thought and troubled by her circumstances, she went back inside, closing the doors behind her. She slipped from the robe and reached for the nightgown on a chair nearby. Then, not caring if tomorrow came, she extended a slender arm to extinguish the pale light of the lamp, plunging the room into welcome blackness.

In the dream she saw the red light from the fire flickering from around the stove lids. The wind raged, a mournful yet comforting sound. His lips on hers were light yet demanding, letting his desire for her be known, even though it was in the middle of the night. She turned to him and responded, felt the kiss deepen, arousing her to the height of awareness. She could recognize the heady male scent of him even in the dark. It enticed her senses, pulled from her the raw desires she had known once. She put her arms around him...

Suddenly, she awoke. A cry of fear rose in her throat but was halted by the masculine lips on hers, overpowering her, consuming her. She struggled forcing her eyes open to the total blackness of the room. Pushing against the man's shoulders she started to force him away, but the familiarity of the form beneath her fingers caused her to relax.

When her struggles ceased, he lifted his head. Her eyes had now adjusted to the pale light that found its way in through the paned-glass doors. She recognized with pleasure the glint of mischievousness in those sapphire eyes she loved so much.

"What are you doing here?" she whispered.

"Aren't you going to ask me how I got in?"

"That, too."

He lowered his head, letting his kisses roam over her face again. He spoke brokenly between caresses, trying to concentrate on what he was saying and not be overpowered by the pure joy of being with her again. "I wanted to prove to you that you love me."

"Will..." She started to protest, but another kiss silenced her.

"Listen to me; listen to your heart."

The bed sagged and then rose as he got up. She could barely see his outline in the dark, but the picture of his body and his face were etched vividly in her mind. "Are you leaving, Will?"

"If you want me to leave, I will."

He stood by the side of the bed. She felt his gaze more than saw it. With a rustle of satin, she pulled back the bedcovers. There was a long silence in the still darkness while he waited. "No," she whispered. "Don't go."

She watched him undress, was willing when he took her arm and pulled her to a standing position next to him, stood very still in anticipation as his strong, callused hands removed her silk nightgown, letting it slide soundlessly to the carpet. He picked her up easily, cradling her in his arms against his sinewy upper torso. Her sense of touch was keen as the softness of her breasts were pressed into the hardness of his chest, and titillated further by the mat of coarse black hair brushing against them.

He laid her back onto the covers and stretched out alongside her. He enveloped her again in his arms and his hard kiss took her breath away. He laid a bare leg over her, as if to keep her there, but at the contact with his hard male shape, she began to tremble, remembering the way he could easily take away her strength, replacing it with ecstasy.

She clung to him, her lips wantonly parting to take the pleasure of his. His touch was sure as his hand moved on a wayward course over her body, taking in every inch of it in a tender, yet exhilarating touch. Her hands slid into the dark thickness of his hair as his lips followed the path of his hands, leaving burning kisses over her entire body. Her hands slid around his neck and onto the muscles of his back as her increasing need for him urged her to draw him closer.

His hand caressed her breast, then his lips took its place and she stifled a moan as a new wave of searing sensations flooded her body and mind. His kisses explored intimately the perfection of her body, while his hands wandered over her quivering, taut stomach.

She moved against him, clung to his strong shoulders, scattered helpless kisses over his face, arms, and shoulders. The tension grew inside her until her movements became restless and her hands on his shoulders were no longer gentle.

He moved his entire body upward, stretching fully over her and taking her face in the palm of one hand while balancing his strength on the other arm. His perfectly defined mouth covered her soft full lips while his body finally offered her relief. She accepted him in the smooth embrace of her legs. His hands moved to her hips, expertly guiding her. At his thrusting entry she hesitated in a moment of glorious relief, only to be swept away on an increasing fury that took her higher and higher until finally the destination was reached and, like the bursting of stars, she was spun into a silver radiance of unequaled splendor.

She felt his passions meet hers, lifting hers again momentarily, and then letting them down once again slowly. She felt the last faint tremors of his pleasure shudder through him and then the full extent of his weight. The sound of his panting as he gasped for air, the solidness of his head buried in the curve of her neck, and his lips touching the tangled mass of her hair made her smile with full physical and mental satisfaction. She held him now in a desperate, deep embrace of need and love.

Her hands slid over his shoulders, her fingertips halting at the ragged feel of raised flesh. She realized it was where her father's bullet had entered his body and threatened his life. A new emotion welled inside her and she clasped him tighter to her while silent tears slid from her eyes and fell soundlessly into her hair.

Will's lips brushed her face and then a fingertip traced the contour and felt the moisture. He lifted himself from her to lie next to her. He propped his head up with one hand and looked down at her face in the dark, seeing now the silvery wetness that shone in the faint light of the stars filtering in through the glass doors. This time his finger took the wetness away and his lips laid a light kiss on hers.

"What is it, Kate?"

She heard the concern, but also a note of apprehension. She hurried to ease any doubts the tears may have put in his mind. She turned her head on the pillow to look up at him. He was leaning on his right shoulder, exposing again the raw scar to the moonlight. She touched it gently. "He may try to kill you if he ever finds out I've seen you again."

Will smiled. "I won't tell him, if you won't," he bantered.

"I'm serious, Will."

"Don't worry so much about death, Kate. It will keep you from enjoying life."

He stretched out again next to her, pulling her into his embrace. She cradled her head on the smooth, hard muscles of his uninjured shoulder and felt the firmness of his chest against her cheek. The steady rhythm of his heartbeat lulled her into a state of peacefulness. For now, everything was all right.

When Kate was breathing evenly in sleep, Will remained awake, thinking. He smoothed a strand of the chestnut hair from her face and studied her profile. He could have her temporarily, like this, but could he have her forever? Could he fight the hold Kincaid had on her father? He'd heard that Tom Diering owed Kincaid a fortune. It was obvious Kate had no idea how in debt her father was—and Will was not about to be the one to expose Tom Diering's shame. Obviously, Kate was the price Diering was paying.

Carefully, Will extricated himself from her. Once she called out his name and he lay back down next to her, whispering, "I'm here, Kate." Then when she had fallen into a deep sleep again, he dressed in the dark and, like a thief, slid back down the trellis that had gained him access to her balcony. On quiet, moccasined feet he left the estate, found his horse where he had tied him in the street, and headed south as the first gray of dawn touched the sky.

Kate waited with anticipation as each night came and went. After seven days had passed, she came to realize that he wouldn't come again. She even wondered if perhaps he had not been there at all, except in her dreams. And the passing of time put a cloudy finish on the memory, making it more dreamlike.

The day came for her to pack to prepare for the campaign trip. She did so in a haze, unable to forget the words that echoed over and over in her mind. *Listen to your heart. Listen to your heart.*

The trip began with banners and a party of well-wishers seeing them off. She did her part, waving and smiling as best she could. Once away from the small crowd, she settled back to her thoughts, unmindful of the man across the seat from her. She stared out the window of the covered private coach. It was the most regal vehicle Clayton owned, enameled in dark blue with gold stripes, lined with pale blue satin, and rich leather. It was drawn by four matching black horses. Behind them, in another carriage, less fancy, were the servants and campaign helpers who would be with them the entire time.

"We'll be staying at a lovely hotel in Colorado Springs tonight," Clayton said, cutting into her thoughts. "I'm sure you'll like it. Have you ever been there?"

She shook her head no, although she had. She simply didn't want to talk about it.

He continued. "It's quite a resort town, you know. People from all over the States—even the world—go there for health reasons. The mineral waters at Manitou Springs have become famous for their healing powers. We'll go there, if you'd like."

"That would be nice." She could muster only the barest of answers.

"You'll like it. It's very modern and elaborate."

Kate thought of the line shack. It was small and dark and plain. She'd even had to duck her head to get through the funny green door, but she'd found love inside its walls. It didn't matter where she and Will might make their bed, even inside Kincaid's mansion—the coldest place in Denver—there would be love in it.

She closed her eyes, remembering. What a trick Will had pulled, making love to her right under Clayton's nose. A smile creased her lips and simultaneously she opened her eyes to look at Clayton. As usual he was watching her, but at her smile a strange suspicion crept into his conniving eyes.

"Did you have a pleasant thought, Kate?"

She nodded, refraining from laughing. "Yes, Clayton. Very pleasant, indeed."

The iron-framed elevator cage lurched and began its rapid descent into the mine shaft. As it darted downward Will caught glimpses of the other "caves" and saw men standing around with candles or lanterns in their hands, while others worked at digging holes deeper into the earth, following veins of gold that snaked into the very core of the earth. He remembered all the times he'd rounded up cattle in this basin and slept under the stars. It looked so normal from the surface. Even men like Dexter could not have fully guessed at the wealth that lay hidden.

The Kate Meline was in full operation. Dexter stood next to him in the iron cage, dancing from foot to foot, his eyes aglow in the light of the lanterns they held in their hands. "You're never going to believe this, Will. I can't wait until you see it."

Will remained reserved, unable to feel much enthusiasm. He had never adjusted to being down in the mines. He didn't like the closed-in feeling, the stifling air, and the dampness from subterranean water that had to be pumped out constantly in some places. He thought he'd get used to it after having spent so much of the last two months underground, but he was always anxious to get to the surface as quickly as possible. He didn't envy the men who labored all day in the mines, but they accepted it. Most were old hands at it, having come to Cripple Creek from somewhere else.

The elevator came to a thudding stop and they braced themselves against the jar. They stepped out of the cage into a long tunnel whose length could not be seen beyond where the circle of their light fell. It was a silent place. There were no men on this level. All Will could hear was the dripping of water somewhere, and the drone, probably from the level above, of a mighty hoisting machine taking the precious ore to sunlight.

"All right, Dexter," Will said as he held his lantern up higher. "What is it you've got to show me? And why aren't we working this tunnel?"

"I've got it temporarily closed off—since yesterday." He led the way down the tunnel. Up ahead Will saw two men standing in the glow of two lamps. They were holding rifles and they stepped forward when they heard footsteps. When they recognized the intruders they relaxed.

Dexter grinned. "I came to show my partner what we fell into last night. Step aside, boys."

Will lifted his lantern again and stepped through the semioval opening. He was standing in a cavity that was about twenty feet square and forty feet high. He stared in awe, realizing why Dexter had sent all the workers away and placed armed guards at the entrance. He was surrounded by a dreamland of solid gold. The walls were dazzling with millions of gold crystals and flakes. Even the floor was strewn with piles of white quartzlike spun glass. It was the fairy-tale wealth that drove all miners on their quest, but he was sure that not even Dexter had been prepared for this.

Dexter waited for his reaction, but Will was dumbfounded. Dexter chuckled and began moving around, running his rough hand over the walls, peeling off a flake here or there. "Can you believe the likes of this, Will?" He didn't expect an answer and didn't get one. "What are we going to do with it?"

"Maybe we ought to just leave it here."

"You're crazy, man. It's our obligation to take it out."

"I suppose it is," Will said, suddenly wishing he could bring Kate here to see it, to share it with him.

He ran his eyes over the golden walls again and then moved to the entrance. "We'll get it out, Dexter, but let's get an ironworker and have him install a vault door. I don't want to mine it just yet. There's somebody I want to show it to first."

Dexter chuckled knowingly. "And who might that be?"

"The lady I named the mine after."

Dexter eyed Will seriously, temporarily forgetting about the gold. "I was beginning to think she was a figment of your imagination."

There were times he'd wondered the same thing, but the newspapers had kept talking about her and Kincaid and his successful campaign during the summer. They were now back in Denver, but they still had a few more places to visit. The last town on the roster for the illustrious couple to visit was Cripple Creek. It wasn't much of a town yet, but there were a lot of people here, a lot of voting men. They'd be here in a month, and he wasn't going to miss it.

They left the cavity and the guards moved back into their positions outside the opening. At the shaft Dexter said, "You go on up and get that ironworker. I'm going down to level three and see how the boys are doing down there. Then I'll be going over to my other mining site and see if I can find another one of these." He pointed behind him at the room made of solid gold.

"You've hit nothing over there, Dexter. It's just a damn hole in the ground."

Dexter grinned. "You said the same thing about this one."

Will laughed as he got into the elevator cage that would take him to the surface. Dexter got into the one beside it that would take him down to level three. After Will had stepped out into the shaft house, he headed for the main door.

Suddenly, he heard yelling from the shaft he had just ascended. In a few seconds came the sound of breaking timbers, a grinding rumble, followed by a rush of air and dirt that struck him full in the face. Then there was nothing but a deathly silence. He leaped back into the elevator cage and shouted to the hoistman, "There's been a cave-in! Lower me back down!"

Chapter 18

Will stood by the window of the simple cabin that had been Dexter's and looked out over the brightly lit street of Cripple Creek. From the commotion and the swinging lanterns, he knew the midnight stage had just arrived. Meeting the stage with a fanfare was a ritual here that was never missed. He sipped at the whisky in his shot glass and listened to his lawyer, Rory James, talking about Dexter's death and the will the man had written.

"I did that checking you wanted me to do," Rory said. "So far I haven't found anybody back in Ohio who would claim the man. I'm sure some distant uncle would if he knew about the mine, but he had no immediate family. He was an only child and both of his parents are dead." The thick-chested lawyer ran a hand through his wavy, sandy-colored hair. "Besides, Will, he had the will written giving his share of the Kate Meline and all his other claims to you. I don't see why you don't want to take it."

For three weeks they'd dug into the tunnel on the lower level, but when they'd finally reached the men, they were all dead. They'd been killed instantly from the cave-in. The only consolation was that they hadn't had to suffer for days.

"I just feel that if he had some family, they've got a right to what he had." Tired, Will rubbed a hand over his face and through his hair.

"Dexter wanted you to have it; that should tell you something. Don't be so damned charitable. You'll be fighting tooth and nail to keep it as it is. Somebody will try to shyster you out of it."

"That's what I have you for."

Will stared out the window again at the swinging lanterns and the people disembarking from the stage. He figured he was probably the only true friend Dexter had ever had; everyone else had shunned him as though he were a half-wit, but, beneath the shyness that sometimes took on the appearance of stupidity, Dexter Marlow had been a very smart man.

"I don't like profiting from his death, Rory,"

"Yes." Rory sighed, glancing down at the papers again. "And that brings us to the second point of this meeting. I drew up these papers you wanted for transferring the ownership, but I just can't figure you out. Why are you so damned determined to dump this mine on someone else? Are you sure you want to do this? Why—in the name of God—do you want to give the mine to Clayton Kincaid's fiancée? Of all the stupid notions..."

Will's mind drifted in and out of the whisky glaze that clung to it tonight. "Because it was named for her."

"That's not a sound reason, Will."

Will heard the lawyer's impatience. He knew it was late and Rory probably wanted to go to bed.

"Because she's going to be my wife pretty soon. It's going to be a wedding gift."

Rory snorted exasperation. "Yeah, and she's going to be mine, too. Do you know how many men have taken one look at her and had fantasies about exactly the same thing? She's going to marry Kincaid. Christ, I think you're drunk."

"Just do as I say, Rory. I want to give the mine to her."

"Yeah, but if she marries Kincaid, you'll just be giving it to him, essentially." He tried to control his annoyance at Will.

"No." He smiled wryly. "If she marries Kincaid, then you'll have some more paperwork to do, changing it back to my name. I just want to know if you set it up the way I asked."

"Yes. She won't know about it until you present it to her, and you'll continue handling the operation until then, or until she takes matters into her own hands." Rory shook his head, plainly not understanding the thinking of his friend, whose affairs he'd been handling for ten years.

"It didn't bother him to go down there," Will said, suddenly changing the subject back to Dexter. "He liked to touch gold, feel the excitement of finding it, but he didn't give a hoot about spending it. It was always on to another piece of ground or another creek somewhere to try and find another lode."

The lawyer leaned back in his chair and watched his friend. "Don't let it eat at you, Will."

Will drained the liquor into his mouth then fingered the empty glass. "He was always dependable in that you knew you couldn't get anything out of him but what *he* wanted to do, and that was looking for gold. I don't like this mining business, Rory." His thoughts shifted again. "I need to be getting back to the ranch."

"Is that what's really eating you? I was beginning to wonder what had gotten into you. You're working yourself to the bone. Haven't had a decent night's sleep in months. You don't take time to eat half the time, and you're keeping that damned whisky glass in your hand too much."

Will straightened his shoulders a bit. He was a little drunk, but he could handle it. "A man has to have something to warm himself up with at night."

Rory shook his head and smiled back at Will as he pulled the heavy wooden door aside. "Maybe you should try a woman. Good night."

Will looked at the closed door for a minute. Then he picked up the whisky bottle and went to the bed, where he stretched out, leaning his back up against the homemade headboard. He poured himself another shot. He moved the glass a bit and watched the amber liquid cling to the sides in a film.

"Try a woman." He chuckled at Rory's advice. "That's exactly what I intend to do."

Kate sat opposite Clayton in the coach, as she had the entire time of the campaign trip. A warm summer wind blew outside but Clayton would not allow the windows to be opened because of the heavy dust on the rough road to Cripple Creek. Despite his fussiness, the dust seeped in elsewhere, rose up between them and hung stagnant in the air. Kate could barely breathe. She could taste it, smell it, and see it settle over her in a fine film. Her only consolation was that it was settling over Clayton as well.

The driver seemed to be going at a reckless pace but she knew they were experiencing extreme jostling because the road was narrow, curvy, and precipitous. At times they went downhill much too swiftly, while other times she felt the horses lunging as they tried to make grades. Occasionally, the coach came to a near standstill and sat at such an angle that she knew it would careen backward at a killing speed if released from the team that struggled to take it over the mountain.

As she clung to the seat for balance, she closed her eyes momentarily and listened to the wailing wheels as they slipped into ruts and over stones. Only the uneven thud of the horses' hooves cut into the creaking and whining of the lurching coach. She listened to Clayton curse the condition of the road. She knew they should have taken the sturdier Concord stage, but Clayton had wanted to arrive at the gold town in style, make a good impression. It didn't matter, she supposed, if the fancy coach got torn up; he could always buy another.

Kate came awake with a start; the coach had ceased its incessant bobbing. Clayton was straightening his derby hat. "We're here?" she asked, peering out the windows at the crowded streets and lights from hundreds of lanterns.

Clayton nodded and waited for his driver to step down and open the door. Surely the town must never rest. Even at this late hour she heard yowling dogs, fighting, pistol shots, and saw mine lights shimmering on the hills high above the town like stars in the sky. Occasionally, she noticed the faint

271

yellow flicker of a candle in a cabin window. She made out clusters of nondescript shacks and tents with people out in front swinging lanterns.

They had stopped at the stage depot and their coach was being greeted with the same enthusiasm as the regular ones. Of course, Clayton had sent word ahead that he would be arriving, so there was quite a group of supporters in the crowd, waving banners and shouting their encouragement.

The door opened and the driver helped her out first, leaving the grand entrance to Clayton. He was immediately mobbed by his friends and supporters and she stepped back out of the way, taking the opportunity to look around. There was a nervous excitement in the air that was contagious. She felt more alive than she had for months.

A young boy helped the driver remove the baggage, tossing it over the heads of the people milling around, luckily hitting no one. After he had collected his money from their driver, he edged his way from the crowd and stepped up to her, nervously holding his cap in his hand. The crowd pushed them back closer and closer to the station entrance, but Kate only laughed, feeling light-hearted at the activity.

"I live here," the boy said. "I hear tell one of our mines is named after you."

Kate smiled. "Yes, that's true."

The boy, satisfied that he'd gotten to speak to her, kicked a foot shyly in the dirt and said, "It was nice meetin' you, ma'am." Then he turned and ran away, his hooting blending in with the other noise.

She smiled, watching him go. She could say one

thing for this campaign trip; she had met some interesting people.

"I see you have your second admirer in Cripple Creek."

The voice from the night, behind her, caused a shiver to run over her. Slowly, she turned as both apprehension and anticipation overwhelmed her. He leaned casually against the wall of the station house, the glow from a lantern over the door lighting his familiar profile.

She was only six feet away from him. "And who might the first be?" she asked, hoping his answer would be what she wanted to hear. Despite the noise, she heard him easily, for she had blocked out the world and focused all her senses on him alone.

He pushed away from the wall to stand within arm's length of her. "Your first admirer is the owner of the Kate Meline. I hope that while you're here you'll engage him to take you for a tour of it. If you were to play your cards right, you could just be a part owner of it someday."

A rush of heat enveloped her. All the little innuendoes in his tone revealed the intimacy and the moments they had shared. He said so much while seeming to say nothing at all. She was hypnotized by his gaze, and she let him fall into hers as well. "I'm very good at cards—poker," she said, her lips curving into a smile. "I had an excellent teacher."

"Where will you be staying?" he asked. "I can't imagine Clayton stretching out in a tent."

Kate chuckled. It was so true. "The best place in town, of course."

"I hope he won't be disappointed."

Will looked past her at the campaign rally that was breaking up. Kincaid looked up and saw him, and quickly but politely left his group and joined them on the boardwalk. He put a possessive arm around Kate's waist, but it pleased Will to see that she stepped away.

Clayton's face reddened momentarily as he glared at her, but he quickly composed himself. "You never stop trying, do you, Chanson? Well, you'll have to in a few months when she's officially my wife."

Will pushed his hat to the back of his head and, towering over the banker, looked down on him with an indifferent air of supremacy. "What makes you think I'll stop then, Clayton?" He turned to Kate, and with a nod of his head said, "I'll be seeing you at the mine. Enjoy your stay in Cripple Creek."

Clayton watched the tall cattleman depart and then turned to Kate, taking her arm. "I suppose you want to see his mine first thing tomorrow?"

"It *was* named after me." She was beginning to enjoy pointing out her previous relationship with Will. It annoyed him a great deal.

"I'd like to see it myself," Clayton said, surprising her. "I'm always looking for potential investments."

They followed their servants to the hotel, where Clayton had reserved rooms. It looked more like a large house than a hotel. The outside was still in the process of being painted, and it smelled strongly but freshly of just-cut lumber. It was a young town and the accommodations weren't excellent, but it was clean, and Kate was happy to be alone again in her own room.

When the door was safely locked, she undressed for bed and climbed beneath the covers. Morning was only a few hours away. She lay on her back in the simple wooden double bed and stared at the dark ceiling. Through the wall she heard wheezing and snoring and the shuffle of heavy boots. From far away came the scratchy sound of a gramophone—a woman singing in a nasal voice. There was raucous laughter below in the street and then the screeching whistle of the mines from the distant hills as the men came from the bowels of the earth and changed places with another crew.

One of those mines was the Kate Meline. Like the people in the street tonight, Kate was exhilarated by being involved with the excitement that the gold produced. Her father's threat on Will's life seemed so far away now. It was easy to forget, and Cripple Creek was a long ride from the Diering ranch. She wanted to see Will again; and her father need never know.

The sun was high in the sky when Kate awoke. She was surprised she had slept so well in a strange place, but she credited it to the tiring ride over the mountains in the coach. She looked at the golden rays filtering in through the lacy curtains and tried to gauge the time. She guessed it was around ten. Immediately, she remembered Will's invitation to visit the Kate Meline mine. With more vigor she put her legs over the side of the bed to begin the day.

Several small, sharp taps sounded on her door and she recognized them as Clayton's, for it was the way he always demanded entry into her bedroom. She hastily pulled her dressing gown on over her nightgown. When it was snugly secured she opened the door.

He was impeccably dressed, as usual, as though he had been up for hours to achieve the image he always presented to the world. In the time she'd known him she'd never seen any other side of him.

"I'm sorry to wake you, but we'd better be going if we're to accomplish everything."

In the smoky haze that drifted into her eyes from his cigar, she saw that he wasn't sorry about waking her at all. He walked to the paned window and lifted the white curtains to better see the activity of the busy, noisy street.

"You haven't seen Cripple Creek, my dear. We'll drive around, as well as tour a few mines. If things go as I plan, this town will make me very rich."

Kate walked back to her bed and opened the bag she hadn't unpacked the night before. "You're already very rich, Clayton," she said as she removed the contents and laid them on the bed. "How much money does one man need?"

"It's not the money, my dear. It's the pleasure of making it."

"Don't you mean the excitement of *taking* it?"

"You make it sound as though I rob people." He turned to watch her as she found her hairbrush at the bottom of the bag and lifted it to brush the glistening length of her hair. The thick, heavy mane was most becoming as the sun lit the strands and drew out their reddish highlights. She had matured into a beautiful woman. She could help him win the election, and possibly some other things. Then, if and when he chose, he could dispose of her.

Kate did not respond, no doubt believing that

robbing was exactly what he did, but he didn't mind. "We'll go to *your* mine first," he continued, "and go down the shaft. You've never been inside the earth, have you, dear? It's an experience we should all have before we're put there permanently."

"What of the recent cave-in?"

"Don't worry. That was in new diggings."

She resumed her brushing. "I'll only go if Will says it's all right."

Sometimes she could be very enjoyable to be around. She had a lot of fire beneath her unimposing veneer. It was no wonder Will had fallen in love with her. But love was not for all men. "You still think about him, don't you?"

The changing inflection in his voice piqued her curiosity, and her suspicion. It was a game of his to dangle tidbits in front of her, so she complied and gave the expected response. "It's only natural, Clayton. We both know why I consented to marry you. It was to prevent a confrontation between my father and Will. Of course I still love him."

Mild surprise surfaced on his face as she spoke, but quickly a veil was dropped over it, successfully hiding all his emotions, thoughts. Kate continued brushing her hair, and he turned his back to her, looking out the window instead.

So Tom hadn't told her the truth? She had consented to marry him simply because Diering had threatened to kill Will if she didn't. She had no idea her father was on the verge of bankruptcy. But perhaps Diering had known her best. Perhaps Diering had known she wouldn't consent to help him keep his head above water. It was fine, Clayton decided. It only gave more credence to his belief that the two young lovers would still want each other after the marriage. The marriage was his ace card, for then he would have Kate as his bargaining tool to get control over the CM. And yet, he had been thinking lately, why settle for just the CM? Why not have the Kate Meline mine *and* Kate herself as his wife? Why not have it all?

Clayton moved from the window to the dressing table and leaned against the wall, staring down at her through eyes squinting against the wisp of smoke from his cigar. "He must love you very much. I hear the Kate Meline is already outproducing any mine here."

Kate kept the brush moving through her hair with the same steady strokes. When she didn't reply, Clayton encircled both her hand and the hairbrush with his large hand. The smile still played on his lips. "Just remember one thing, my dear. You are engaged to me. If you should do anything foolish, such as seeing Will, I'll be forced to tell your father."

The contempt for him showed in her eyes full strength. "I would do anything for Will—even marry you." She jerked her hand free of his. "Now, if you'll leave, I'll dress."

They hired an open carriage to better enjoy the warmth of the day, rather than expose the expensive coach to any more mountain trails. As the road taking them to the mine steepened, Kate looked behind her at the conglomerations of buildings that ranged from the frame hotel they'd stayed in to tents and tar-papered shacks. Now, along with the dwellings, the meadow and hills were scarred by tunnels, shafts, trenches, and open cuts. Winding trails and roads ran everywhere, crisscrossing over one another. The mines were located mainly above the town where the land began to slope upward.

Finally, the carriage came to a halt, and the hired driver called over his shoulder, "This is it, Mr. Kincaid. One of the owners, Dexter Marlow, died here not long ago in a cave-in, but part of it is back in production now."

"Yes, I remember reading about it."

Kate recalled Will talking about Dexter while they were stranded in the line shack during the blizzard. He was a miner forever in search of the mother lode. Will had grubstaked him as a friendly gesture but with no thought that he would ever gain anything from it himself—but he had. For an instant, when Kate looked at Clayton now, she saw renewed greed in his eyes. It was one more thing for the two men to be rivals over. She wondered what Clayton really had up his sleeve by coming to Cripple Creek

"Would you like me to wait for you, sir," the driver said, "or should I come back later?"

"You can wait for us. You'll be paid for your time."

Clayton stepped to the ground and offered a hand to Kate. His attention on her this morning reminded her of a hawk preying on a small field mouse scurrying below in the grass. The incessant smile of derision stayed on his lips to infuriate her, but she kept her feelings cloaked.

The large building covering the shaft head and hoisting works resembled a factory. The area around it was dirty and rocky from waste-rock residue. The interior consisted of an enormous room with several square openings in the floor that were surrounded by beamed framework. Through these openings, or shafts, workers and visitors ascended and descended to the diggings on a platform drawn by treacherous-looking pulleys attached to thick cables.

As Clayton pushed her farther inside, Kate knew instantly this wasn't Will's sort of place. He belonged to the open spaces where the sun's rays could brown his skin and catch on the mischievous twinkle in his eyes, not here inside these dreary, brown walls where a depression clung, despite the gold buried beneath.

The rattling elevator moved too slowly through the dimly lit shaft on its way to the surface. Will balanced himself on the unsteady surface and wiped at the sweat dripping down his face. As he rose higher, the air noticeably improved, but the deeper one went into the shaft, the more difficult the breathing became, almost as if hell could be expected at the next level down. It was definitely no place for a man—if he was still alive.

They had finally gotten all the men out of the cave-in, but the tunnels needed more work. The foreman had pointed everything out to him, but even a novice could see that things had been done haphazardly and in a hurry. Dexter hadn't been one for safety precautions and Will could see that things were going to have to change if the mine was to be safe.

He was glad when the elevator cage stopped in the dim light of the shaft house. He let the foreman step out first. From across the room he noticed a woman's shapely back, clad in a dark blue traveling suit. His heart picked up speed. It was

Kate and she was reading the various notices that had been tacked on the wall; shift changes, men's names. The foreman hurried to her side to assist her.

Then she turned. "Will." His name slid from her tongue before the foreman could reach her. She seemed to be more beautiful each time he saw her. Her expression was guarded, but he thought he saw a bit of that glow that had been there when he'd held her in his arms, making love to her.

"I see you've come to inspect your mine."

Kate's heart pounded against her chest, threatening to break the fragile wall that contained it. Will's shoulders nearly filled the expanse of the elevator cage from which he had just stepped. His eyes glinted with challenging mischievousness that made her carefree and happy, momentarily forgetting about Clayton. She took a step toward him with a smile on her lips, but was halted by reality.

"Yes." Clayton stepped up behind Will, startling both Will and the foreman. He walked past Will and took a position by Kate, placing an arm around her small waist. "We came to see the richest mine in Cripple Creek. Could you arrange a tour for us?" Clayton looked down at Kate with a feigned smile of love.

She bristled and stepped from his clutches. "I told you I won't go down there unless Will goes, too."

Will's attention lingered on Kate. The tension between her and Clayton was obvious, which pleased him. Kate walked away from Clayton, pretending to be interested in something in the room. 'This is all I care to see, except perhaps for some of Will's samples."

She wondered if her eyes told Will she was not interested in samples either, but only in the feel of his arms and the heat of his kiss. Once she had loved him with every ounce of herself. She was willing to do it again just at the signal from him.

Will would show her the cavity, but not when Clayton was around. He made an excuse. "I'm not taking visitors down right now because of the recent cave-in. But I do have a sample." He reached into the pocket of his shirt and pulled out a rock that was heavy enough to strain the seams of the cotton material. He walked up to her. He forgot about Clayton watching them; for a moment the world contained only the two of them. He held the rock out to her.

"From twelve hundred feet—solid gold."

Kate reached for it hesitantly, but only because she was afraid of some invisible power that might magically thrust her into his arms. Her fingers encircled the gold and touched the warmth of his hand. For a second they both held it, and then Kate was given its full weight. She rolled it around in her hands, fascinated by the gleam of the gold that had been imprisoned for so long beneath the earth.

The sudden excitement of touching the gold helped her to comprehend the fever that beset those who fell victim to its lure. Reluctantly, she handed it back to him, wanting to keep it, not for the wealth of it but because it was his.

"It's yours, Kate." Will curled her fingers back around it, refusing to take it back. "Just promise me you won't let Clayton take it away from you. He has plenty of his own gold."

The remark automatically made both of them look up at Clayton, who was watching them with intense interest. But Will also noticed there was no jealousy in his eyes. Was he so sure of Kate's devotion for him that he didn't worry about her old lover stealing her back?

Clayton chuckled. "I see you're still very abrasive, Will. Time hasn't changed you much—except to make you richer."

"That's the name of the game, isn't it, Clayton?" He looked at Kate again. "It would appear that the need for material wealth eventually strikes even the most innocent and pure."

Kate was hurt that he implicated her. Surely he didn't believe she felt the way Clayton did about money?

A cough and the clearing of a throat drew their attention to the mine foreman. "Excuse me, Will, but if you'll sign this equipment order, I'll take it over to Biddulph's."

Will stepped around Kate, brushing close enough to smell the faint perfume of her. The foreman placed the paper on a board and handed it to Will, who hastily scrawled his signature across the bottom and handed it back.

He turned to the two of them. "I suggest we have dinner together tonight if you can spare the time from your campaign itinerary. There's a good restaurant next to the hotel where you're staying."

Clayton stepped up to Kate and took her by the arm, drawing her tightly up next to him. "I think we would enjoy that, wouldn't we, Kate? Will could tell us about the mine."

Kate returned Will's waiting gaze, meant just for her. "I think that would be fine."

Will thought about being in his bed alone last night, thinking of Kate, knowing she was so close. Now he saw in her eyes what he recognized as silent urging. It was all he needed. He knew he would not spend tonight alone, if he could help it. "I'll meet you at seven." He removed his coat from a rack near the door, thinking Clayton was being too accommodating, playing right into his hands. "I'm going into town myself now. I'll ride along with you." He glanced at Kate again; he wanted the opportunity to stay with her.

To his surprise, Clayton was agreeable again. "You can ride with us. Tie your horse behind."

The banker strode ahead of them, leaving them to walk together. He climbed into the carriage, positioning himself in the center of one of the seats. When Will and Kate arrived some paces behind, Will wondered why Clayton had ignored his pretty fiancée, leaving her in the custody of the man he hated the most. It gave Will pleasure to have Kate's company, but he much preferred it without the steely blue eyes smiling at both of them. Clayton's devious mind was at work again, and Will put his guard up.

Will decided that if Clayton wished to throw them together, he would gladly oblige. When he climbed into the carriage, Kate moved over, but he settled himself as close to her as he could and met Clayton's mocking eyes with his own.

The driver slapped the reins and the carriage moved toward town. Kate sat quietly while Clayton discussed the mining, the expected arrival of stockbrokers, the trading of mines and claims on street corners, and of course the necessity of building a railroad to Cripple Creek.

"When news reaches the district about a railroad coming, the stocks will go up," Clayton said, gauging Will's reaction.

Will leaned back farther in the seat, crossed his ankle over the opposite knee, and casually extended an arm around the back of the seat over Kate's shoulders. "Is this railroad proposal definite or just in the promotion stage?"

Clayton was disappointed that Will didn't appear to care one way or the other. Surely the man realized how wealthy he could become. "It's going to happen, but there will be some competition by several railroads. The one who gets here first will also get the monopoly on Cripple Creek's shipping and traffic business."

"A new venture you're sinking your teeth into, no doubt?"

"I should think you'd be interested in the railroad. I hear the Kate Meline is the richest mine here."

"It is, until somebody discovers one richer." At that, Will turned his attention to Kate. "I take it this is your first trip to Cripple Creek, Kate?"

Kate was pleased that Will had purposefully shut Clayton out. Even though he seemed more solemn now, she saw that the lightheartedness she loved was still there. It was something she never experienced with Clayton, who always remained serious.

The mischievous glint in Will's eyes made her

automatically smile. "I was here before it became a mining town. I came here once with my dad to round up cattle. I believe I prefer it the way it was back then."

"I agree with you, but I suppose this was bound to happen sooner or later."

For a moment Kate forgot the invisible bars of her self-made prison as she looked at the full line of his lips. The longing to be in his arms again was growing fierce. It was all she could do to keep her feelings from showing on her face. Even then she wasn't sure she was successful.

Suddenly, she wanted to laugh. For the first time today she noticed the bright blue of the summer sky. It was strange how love could devastate you one minute and lift you to the heights of glory the next.

Then she caught Will's gaze again. The mischievous glint was gone. The world turned frosty and hot at the same time, like a fire burning in the snow, the wood ablaze on an icy bed. She wasn't sure what the look was that she'd seen in the sapphire depths: Pain? Anguish? Love?

The happy moment passed. Will straightened up. Clayton's attention was still riveted on them. He started to talk about the railroad again as though he didn't know anything had happened.

The carriage turned down Bennett Street and made its way to the hotel. When it came to a stop, Will stepped down and turned to help Kate. She searched his face for that ambivalent look she'd seen earlier, but couldn't find it now. Her heart was heavy again. The dream was erased by the reality of her situation. She laid her hand in his. She was struck again by the warmth of it, the firmness of it, and memories flashed through her mind of when his hands had roamed her body and brought her to a pleasure she could not have imagined.

As she stood at the carriage door he released her hand long enough to allow both of his to encircle her waist and lift her to the ground. As her feet found the sturdiness of the ground, her breasts brushed against the sturdiness of his chest. She stepped away but possibly not quickly enough. Clayton stepped out behind her and his knowing eyes told her he missed nothing that went on between her and Will.

"We'll see you at seven," Clayton said as he took Kate's arm and pulled her gently away from Will and to his side.

Will's senses were shocked deeply at the brush of her breasts against his chest. He had drawn her against him intentionally and he wondered why he was causing his own suffering. He didn't like to give up hope, but he wondered if he would ever get her back. He knew Clayton was watching him but still Will could not stop staring at her. "Yes—seven."

He left the two of them and untied his horse from the rear of the carriage. Once mounted, he nudged the animal up next to the driver and extracted another large gold nugget from his shirt pocket. He tossed it to the man, who caught it in a forward-palm catch. "That ought to be enough to pay Kincaid's fare."

The driver grinned as he pocketed the gold nugget. When the carriage had passed, Will turned to Kate and bid her farewell. Then he turned into the maze of the busy street, forcing himself not to look back. He would see her tonight, but he didn't want Clayton to suspect. He wanted no interference.

Chapter 19

Clayton left Kate at the hotel entrance, saying he had some things he wanted to do around town — mainly some socializing in advance of his campaign speech tomorrow. She hurried to her room, looking forward to seeing Will again. She glanced at the clock on the stand near the bed. She had several hours before dinner.

It was a rough town, and even though Clayton had found the best hotel, it still lacked the amenities she had grown accustomed to. She ordered a bath brought to her room, not wishing to use a communal one.

She easily chose between the two evening dresses she had brought. She would wear the green; it made her gray-green eyes more distinct. In front of the small mirror, she tried to calm a shaky hand as she put on jade earrings and a matching necklace.

She smoothed a nervous hand over the dress. It was a favorite and she felt good in it. The neck was rounded, riding just above the fullness of her bosom. The draped bodice was flounced abundantly and then pulled in tightly at the waist. The skirt fell to the floor in three separate tiers of gossamer fabric over silk, each tier edged with a ruffle of the same filmy fabric as the bodice flounce. The entire skirt then was drawn up in the back and gathered to draw attention to the hips. The sleeves were mere strips of lace, dropped off her shoulders. It was not a favorite of Clayton's, but she was not dressing for him tonight.

A knock sounded at the door. The clock indicated exactly seven. It would be Clayton. Kate gathered her small matching handbag and went to the door. They did not exchange greetings. Kate stepped out into the hall, closed her door behind her, then led the way down the hall. In minutes they were next door at the restaurant.

It was not an elaborately decorated place, but it obviously strived to offer some elegance to the gold town. Kate easily spotted Will in the crowded room, not only because of his handsomeness and his imposing figure in the perfectly cut suit and vest, but because his eyes were on her like a magnet, drawing her awareness to him alone. A host greeted them and led the way to Will's table. He stood when they arrived. A small candle helped light the dark corner of the room. It cast a golden bronze glow on his sculpted features and enhanced his smile intended only for her. Kate shivered as his hand slid casually and personally against her shoulder as he drew out a chair for her to be seated.

Clayton ordered Scotch and Will called for a bottle of champagne for himself and Kate. The men discussed the mine and the things that were going on back in Denver. Clayton tried to pump Will for information about the wealth of the Kate Meline, but Will offered no definite figures, or even guesses. Kate could tell Clayton was disgruntled; he was apparently trying to find a way to cash in himself if the mine proved worthy of investment.

As they finished the meal Will poured both himself and Kate another glass of champagne. As he was putting the bottle back in the ice bucket, his face lit up and focused on something across the room. Both Kate and Clayton turned to see a big man with sandy-colored hair weaving his way through the tables. Before he got to their table he held out his hand to prepare for a handshake, and Will stood up, slapping his hand inside the big man's grip.

"Rory! Good to see you in Cripple Creek again." The two men shook hands vigorously and then Will turned him to the other two and made introductions. Rory James's eyes rested on Kate and remained there for a silent moment.

"Miss Diering, I've heard so much about you. With you by his side, I don't see how Kincaid can lose the Senate race."

Kate murmured a thank you, and Will reached over to the next table where there was a vacant chair and swung it over to their table. "Join us, Rory. Have you eaten?"

The big man patted his stomach. "Don't think I will tonight; need to lose some of this lard. I *will* have a drink."

Rory immediately turned to Clayton and struck up a conversation. Within minutes they were carrying on a lively exchange. Thirty minutes passed and Kate and Will hardly said anything. Kate noticed that Will was not bothered at all by Rory's interruption and didn't try to intervene.

Finally, Rory slapped Clayton on the back and said, "If you're looking to get in on the ground floor of some investments—maybe even buy an entire mine for a cheap price—then you've got to come with me." Rory stood up and took Clayton by the arm, literally pulling him out of his chair. His large frame dwarfed the banker, and the latter was no match for the big man's bull strength. Rory pushed Clayton ahead of him between the tables and called back over his shoulder to Will, "We won't be long."

After the two had exited the restaurant, Kate looked over at Will with amazement on her face at the way Rory James had swooped in, taken over, and swooped out. With forearms resting on the table, Will wore an amused smile and his eyes were twinkling more than usual.

"What was that all about?" Kate asked, perplexed.

Will stood up and hurriedly pulled some coins from his vest and tossed them askew on the linen tablecloth for a tip. Then, almost as Rory James had done, he took Kate's arm and pulled her to her feet. "Rory is my lawyer; he's also a friend in need."

He moved her toward the door and escorted her out into the night and back over to the hotel. "Shouldn't we have waited for them?" Kate asked. "They said they'd only be gone a little while."

Will navigated her up the stairs of the hotel with a hand on the small of her back. "His instructions were to keep him all night and get him so soused he'd have to be carried back to his room."

"His instructions?"

They were now in the hall and Will took a key from his pocket and opened a door, nudging Kate inside. "Yes," he said as he closed the door behind him and relocked it. "I told Rory I'd give him a nugget if he'd get Clayton out of the picture for a while."

"Wha—"

But Kate's stunned protest was halted abruptly as Will put an arm about her waist and pulled her against him. His lips silenced all questions or protests. Her arms slid around his neck and she pressed closer to him, longing once again for the satisfaction they could give one another.

In the dark he went to the bed where a lamp sat, and after pulling a match from his vest pocket, lit the wick, bringing a warm golden glow to the room. Next he went to the window and pulled the blind, then the curtains.

From across the small room he looked at her, beckoned her with eyes awash with desire. Kate's heart went out to him and in a few steps she was once again in his arms. "Our love will never end, Kate. Not if you don't let it."

Hungrily his mouth roamed over her face, hair, and then to her neck, even onto the creamy fullness of her exposed bosom. She tilted her head back from the thrill of his touch, unable to restrain the sound of pleasure and wanting that escaped through her parted lips.

She could not resist closing her eyes and absorbing fully the touch of his hands and the way his nearness and his prowess could bring her body to life.

Will slid his fingers behind her head, uncaring that the action was causing some of the chestnut strands to come loose from the pins holding it so neatly in place. With her head tilted back he studied the curve of her graceful neck and followed his admiration with a touch of his lips to the sensitive area. She shivered beneath his kiss, and her heavily lashed lids closed, savoring their togetherness.

He moved his kiss to the corner of her lips. She turned to meet it, gratifying him with the sweetness that he held in his dreams, both waking and asleep. Unable to contain his long suppressed desires for this woman, he kissed her mouth a bit too roughly, but she met his need with equal urgency.

He pulled her tighter against him, the kiss deepening to claim her completely. Finally, he pulled his lips from hers just enough to whisper against the sweet smell of her skin, "I love you, Kate."

She yearned for his lovemaking, but her response came to his ears on a whisper. "And I love you—always, forever."

Easily, he picked her up and carried her to the bed. He placed her gently on the cotton bedcover and stretched out beside her. His gaze took in her face, roaming over it as though touching each part. His lips closed over hers once again.

Kate lifted her arms around his neck and drew him closer. His hot breath teased the sensitive flesh along her neck. A joy leaped inside her as she felt his heart thudding hard against her own. She ran her hands along the strong muscles in his back, wanting to feel beyond the coarse material of his suit coat to his skin. His lips continued their course along her neck while a hand tried to move the silk and lace of her dress aside to reach the more intimate swell of her breasts. The cloth conformed to her too perfectly and didn't allow him freedom.

He lifted his head; her eyes fluttered open questioningly to meet his. "Did I tell you this dress is beautiful and that you are very beautiful in it?" he asked.

"No, you didn't," she responded, vaguely annoyed that he should stop his caresses just to compliment her dress.

"The color is very good on you. I like it much better than the pants you wore at the line shack. Now—would you please take it off?"

Kate laughed. He made her feel happy and alive again, made her forget the months of loneliness.

"You know, Kate"—he ran a finger along the curve of the dress's scoop neck—"you are even more beautiful when you laugh. If you were my wife, I would hope the sadness in your eyes would disappear."

His comment stole her smile as she considered his words, but he didn't wait for a response from her. He stood up and helped her sit up, then helped her remove the confining garment. He took it from her and laid it carefully over the chair next to the bed. When her last garment fell to the floor, he began to remove his own clothing. To his pleasure she gently pushed his hands to the side and reciprocated by undressing him.

Will pulled her against the heat of his naked body, enveloping her slender figure in his embrace. Slowly, he reached down with one hand and pulled back the bed cover. In a fluid motion, they slipped beneath it together and deeper into each other's arms.

Kate had not imagined being with him could

have been any better, but at this moment she was experiencing all the old sensations as well as new ones. They were emotions that went even deeper; emotions born of love and not simply passion. All sounds outside the window faded away as they joined together on a golden ray that took them high into the sky on its fiery beam. Then, like an eagle that soars to its limit and halts on the wind, the wings of their passion dipped and tilted against the sun. At last they drifted together downward, rocking, floating, until finally, like the great bird, they settled back into the defined perimeter of earth.

Will held her in his arms for long, silent moments until he wondered if she had fallen asleep. He saw the contented smile on her lips and he kissed it. He tried to get closer to her, liking the way her body curved naturally to his.

"I want you to stay with me, Kate. Tonight and forever. End this engagement with Clayton."

Kate shivered and Will pulled the covers higher on her shoulder, but she wasn't cold. She was afraid; Clayton was formidable, but her father could be deadly. It was obvious to her now that Will wasn't going to stay away from her simply because she told him to, or simply because she was engaged. She doubted he would even if she married. It pleased her deeply that he loved her enough to be so determined. Of course, even though she'd tried, she'd been no good at concealing her love for him.

She slid her head back farther on the pillow to see him better. A smile crossed his serious expression and he kissed the top of her head and smoothed the hair that had fallen from the pins.

Then, with searching fingers, his hand moved up the back of her head and pulled the remaining pins out. He collected them all in his palm until her hair was free and flowing across the pillow. He reached over her, pressing her beneath him, and laid them on the stand next to the bed.

When he had stretched out next to her again, she said, "I can't leave him because I promised my father I would marry him." She looked away, her eyes blurring on the golden light of the kerosene lamp. "He said if I didn't, he would kill you. I can't be responsible for that, Will. I simply couldn't bear to live if you were dead and I was the reason."

His answer came slowly, and while she waited she watched the play of emotions cross his face in the shadowed room. Finally, he spoke. "So you would marry a man you don't love?"

"Yes."

Suddenly, sparks flashed in his eyes and his voice was angry. He rolled to his back and stared at the ceiling. "Damn it, Kate. I can take care of myself." He changed positions, again turning to his side and propping himself on one arm to look into her face. "Think about it, Kate. I could die tomorrow in that damned mine. There are no promises that life will go on to a certain point. We can only live each day to the fullest, hoping we can live out our lives."

Her own frustration and anger burst. She sat up, refusing to look at him for it made it harder to think. "You simply don't understand, do you? My father will try to *gun you down*." She turned to him beseechingly. "Don't you see? I couldn't bear to have you or him dead simply because I gave in to my desires. My God, Will, I love you too much to hurt you."

He reached out a hand to lay it on the tangled strands of hair that fell to her waist. Gently, he pushed the mane aside and ran his hand over her hot bare skin. His desire for her, so long held inside, took precedence as he bent slightly forward and placed his lips on the satiny texture of her back, running kisses over the entire surface.

"You didn't say anything," she managed as his ardent lovemaking once again tried to push all other matters aside.

"All I can tell you is that I love you and that I want you for my wife, and I believe you want to be my wife. I'll find a way to have you, Kate. If you must know the truth, I would rather be dead than see you married to another man."

The burden on her shoulders was heavy. As his kisses tantalized, the tears slid from her eyes, slowly at first and then gathering speed until her sobs became audible to Will. He sat up completely and took her into his arms and tried to kiss the tears away. He held her until they had stopped and then he laid her back against the pillows.

"Just love me, Kate. Don't think beyond this moment."

In only minutes he had succeeded in obliterating everything from her mind but the need for his love and the need for their bodies to join again. Kate's hands slid to his narrow hips, over his firm buttocks, and up the muscular hardness of his back. "We'll be like this town tonight," she whispered. "We won't sleep until it does."

* * *

The sun found them much too quickly, but when Will came awake, he gently disengaged himself from Kate, who was still asleep. He hastily put on his clothes and left the room quietly. In ten minutes he was back. He undressed again and joined her beneath the covers. She stirred; he kissed her sleepy eyes, then her lips. After he had her fully awake, he fought off his longings to make love to her again. The knock sounded at the door with perfect timing.

Startled, with a look of fear, Kate sat up. The blankets fell away and exposed her bare breasts. "Who can that be?"

Will got out of bed and pulled on his pants. He smiled at her. "Whoever it is, I suggest you cover yourself."

"Will." Worry grabbed her voice as she absently obeyed his command and drew the cover up. "Could it be Clayton?"

"I doubt it. If Rory and his friends did their job, he's stone-cold drunk." He walked to the door and spoke against it. "Who is it?"

"Your breakfast, sir."

Will winked at Kate. "See, nothing to worry about." He opened the door and pulled in a cart laden with platters and smelling delectably of breakfast.

Will gave the young man waiting outside the door a healthy tip, thanked him for bringing the food all the way from the restaurant, and closed the door behind him. After locking it, he pushed the cart over next to the bed. "Breakfast is served, madam."

"Will, when did you order this?"

"While you were sleeping. It's amazing what

people will do for gold—and if you own the Kate Meline."

Kate sat up in bed, Indian style, and tried to make room for the platters in the center of the covers, but she had to hold the blanket to her breasts, feeling very uncomfortable about eating nude. Will saw her dilemma and took his shirt from the bedpost and handed it to her. "I don't mind you eating in the raw, but if you prefer to be clothed, slip this on."

She took it gladly and pulled it on, feeling an immediate relief from the early-morning chill of the room. After buttoning some of the center buttons, she helped Will spread the remaining platters across the bed. He then took his pants off again and climbed in next to her.

Kate removed the lids and was delighted to see a combination of morning foods: bacon, ham, eggs, pancakes, fresh butter, and a variety of syrups. A separate server contained coffee and next to it were a small creamer and sugar bowl. She picked up her plate and heaped it with food. "I'm ravenous. I don't remember ever being so hungry."

Will waited, enjoying her animation. She had matured in the year he'd known her, but he was glad to see she hadn't changed. "It's all the exercise."

His wicked grin made her laugh, something she hadn't done much of lately either. Together they settled into eating, making only small talk. The meal was excellent for its simplicity and perhaps because of it. When they were finished, Will removed the platters to the tray and once again pulled Kate down onto the pillows and into his arms. The happiness was evident in the lights of her gray-green eyes. There was even new color in her face that Will had noticed had been lacking there just yesterday.

"It was delicious, Will." Kate sighed with contentment. "I don't believe I've ever had breakfast in bed."

"Then we'll do it more often." He kissed her quickly, knowing that he could too easily succumb to her charms and her responsive touch. He slid from the covers and stood up, taking her by the hand and pulling her out next to him onto the fringed edges of the rug. "We need to get dressed. I'm taking you home with me—to the CM. You're going with me, and if Clayton wants you back he'll have to come and discuss it with me. If your father wants to kill me, he'll have to come and discuss that, too."

The smile and happiness faded from Kate's face. He recognized the look and knew he had lost again.

"I can't go with you, Will."

He moved away from her, his actions having lost their vivacity. He picked up his pants and pulled them on in a tired sort of way. Next he shrugged into his shirt. "You can't fault a man for trying, now can you?"

Oh, how she wished she could make him understand. She wished she could even understand it herself. Wished she could change it all—mainly her father's way of thinking. Silently, she began to put her clothes on. When Will was dressed he walked to the door and hesitated with his hand on the knob. "Your father's threat has no substance, Kate."

"But he shot you once. Why can't you believe that he will again?"

Will studied her and thought about it. "I don't know. I just feel that your father is a desperate man, but it isn't entirely because he doesn't want his daughter marrying me." He looked her over more carefully. "Maybe where the truth lies, is that his daughter really doesn't *want* to marry me. Maybe she just likes some adventurous nights, but prefers a husband with more social status." He put his hat on, and while Kate stared at him dumbfounded, he left the room.

Rory James did his job well and Clayton didn't stir until he questioned how Kate had spent the evening, and accepted her story of going off to her room soon after he'd left. He went through his campaign speech without the usual finesse and didn't get the response he had hoped for. When it was over Kate found a rickety wooden bench on the boardwalk outside the hotel where she could sit until the coach came from the livery.

Kate adjusted the small hat on her head and looked eastward toward the assay office, from there to the road that wound up through the trees to Kate Meline. She doubted now she would ever have another opportunity to visit it. Finally, she saw the blue enameled coach, cleaned and polished for the journey home, only to be caked with dust one mile down the road. But Clayton would step into it in style. It was all part of the image he wanted to present. She knew now that she too was part of the image.

As the coach wound its way through the many horses, pedestrians, and wagons on the busy street, she stood up and waited. In a few moments Clayton came from the hotel where he'd been waiting inside out of the sun. Exchanging no words, they stepped inside.

Kate drew the shade to shield them from the curious eyes in the street. And then, leaning her head back against the plush leather seat, she closed her eyes against the tears.

Chapter 20

The new dress lying across the bed was beautiful. Instead of putting it on, though, Kate slipped her hands into the pockets of her velvet dressing gown and walked to the window. Below was the familiar sight of the estate grounds with its surrounding trees whose leaves were changing color to another autumn.

She had spent the last few weeks in the house, in her room, hiding and thinking and crying. She thought she might run out of tears, but she saw no end in sight. She had stayed away from town, hoping to avoid Will, knowing it would only increase the pain to look into his eyes and remind her too vividly of the way she had fallen in love, and then the way things had turned out. She had tortured herself with the memories, but there was little else to do here at Clayton's. She had hoped Will wouldn't sneak in again, and yet she had been disappointed when he hadn't. Despite it all, she longed to see him. And now she would.

Clayton was insisting, with some demented delight, that they attend the fall roundup as spectators, something many people from town did each year. His own hired men would be there, of course, rounding up his "investments," but she felt his real reason for going was to inflict more pain on her by forcing her and Will together. She couldn't understand why he would want to do that, but the feeling was there nevertheless.

She had lived on memories and knew it wasn't healthy, but it was all that made her life here bearable. Sometimes she could fall into the past quite easily and stay there until someone came to the door to disrupt her. She could push all the ugly things aside, like her father's threat and Clayton's constant reminder.

She had come to many realizations. Will had done her no injustice, and yet she had done him a huge one. All he had ever wanted was to love her. She had denied him, and now he was gone.

A knock sounded at the door. It would be Clayton. She still wondered at times why Clayton had wanted her for his wife. He didn't love her. He certainly never approached her with any overtures of affection.

After she told him to come in, he pushed the door open and then ran disapproving eyes over her. "You're not dressed." The chastisement was there in the tone of voice, as always.

She didn't move from the window. "I don't want to go."

"I know you don't want to speak to your father, but it's something you will eventually have to face so it might as well be now."

That much was true, but the real reason she didn't want to go was because she was afraid of seeing Will again. Afraid to be rejected, afraid of the emotions he could so easily draw from her, afraid of living the last few weeks of heartache over again with renewed ferocity. If she had to break ties with him, it would be better to break them completely and never see him again.

"Your father is putting on a big feast at his place for all the cowboys and tourists," Clayton continued. "I suppose it's an attempt to get back the old days before the blizzard of '86 when things were better in the industry.

She knew it was her obligation as his fiancée, part of their little "deal," that she attend all functions he requested of her. Still, she felt she was no longer a child who had to answer to everyone who was older. She had aged a lot in the last year; it was evident even in the mirror.

She cocked her head slightly to the side and studied his handsome, deceiving face. He was a very secretive man. It was no wonder he never allowed a woman too close to him. "Why do you keep me, Clayton, when you could find a woman who would serve you better?"

Clayton's expression showed his surprise at the unrelated question. "I don't know why you think you haven't pleased me, Kate. You've done all I've asked."

He moved back to the door and opened it. "Now get dressed. I'd like to be there before lunch."

Beneath the starlight and moonlight, a string band of musically inclined cowboys struck up a loud and lively number to begin the dancing for Diering's roundup party. The day had been a good one. The cowboys had gone out at first light and had returned with cattle in the afternoon. Now was the time for relaxing. Around the large wooden platform especially constructed for danc-

ing were long tables set with white cloths, silver
and china, and laden with delicacies that Cordelia
had ordered from the East and Europe. Tom had
insisted on the local favorites as well, along with
the staples of barbecued beef, gallons of brandy,
barrels of whisky, and kegs of lager beer.

As the liquor brought courage, the younger, unmarried cowboys found the nerve to cross the line
and ask the single girls for a dance, joining the
married couples who were already on the saw-
dusted floor.

Tom watched the festivities, thankful for the
first time for his amputated toes that gave him
an excuse for not dancing. The spirit of the party
rapidly heightened as more people arrived and
everyone relaxed. Cordelia danced with numerous
partners beneath the lanterns that lit the floor.
She had dressed down considerably for the occasion, but she was still the most richly dressed and
most beautiful woman present. Of course, he had
always thought that, right from the moment he
had first laid eyes on her.

He hadn't wanted to give the party at first, but
after listening to Cordelia's tirade, he had finally
consented. He could deny her nothing that would
make her happy. He knew life here wasn't as exciting for her as what she had grown up with in
Chicago. He had thought things would be better
between them with Kate gone, but Cordelia had
decided to go to Chicago during the hottest part
of the summer, and since her return she had still
avoided him, except once a couple of weeks ago.
She hadn't been feeling well since her return, but
insisted on having the party, saying it broke the
boredom of her isolated ranch life.

He took his eyes from his wife and turned to help himself to some punch. He had tried to keep an eye on the large bowl on the center table. It was for the women and children, but there were no guarantees that some fun-loving cowboy wouldn't spike it with vodka or gin as they most assuredly did the others.

To his surprise he saw Will standing there with a glass of beer in his hand. His eyes were on the dance floor, watching the gaiety intently with a narrowed, hard look in his eyes. Tom followed the direction of Will's gaze; it was centered on Kate and Clayton. Tom also watched them for a moment as they whirled. There were no smiles on their faces for one another. It was easy to see that Kate was thinner than she had been, but quickly he brushed aside an encroaching guilt and turned back to Will.

With rising fury he limped toward the young rancher. Will saw him coming and pushed his coat aside, revealing a shiny Colt revolver strapped to his hip. Seeing the gun and the threatening gleam in Will's eyes, Tom slowed his pace voluntarily. When he was within five feet of Will, he stopped. "What are you doing here, Chanson. You weren't invited."

"This party is supposed to be for everyone involved in the roundup, including the spectators." He stood firm. He had no fear of Diering, only an increasing disrespect. "Besides, I did have an invitation. A *personal* invitation from your father-in-law."

"It's not his place to be invitin' anybody, but even so, I didn't figure you'd ever have the gall to show your face on my place again."

"Why not? Kate's promised you she'd marry Kincaid."

"You bet. I made damn sure of tha—" Diering nearly bit his tongue, but the words were already out.

Will's eyes narrowed on the gangly man. His temper was rising, but it remained visibly in check. Coolly, he challenged his antagonist. "You keep threatening to kill me, Tom. What do you say we have a showdown and get it over with once and for all. That is, unless you've only got the guts to shoot down *unarmed* men."

Diering stood his ground for a full minute, clenching his jaw as he considered his action. He had no fight with Chanson, not really. The whole damn thing had gotten out of hand; he'd made a threat, then he'd had to stand by it. Now he had to keep up the charade. He gritted his teeth. "Just get the hell out of here before I have you thrown out, Chanson."

"There's something I'd like to know," Will said, ignoring Tom. "I'm wondering if Kate knows all the details of this arranged marriage you and Kincaid have agreed on. I get the feeling there's more to it than the simple fact that you don't want her marrying me. Am I right, Diering?"

Diering hesitated for a minute, fearful of disclosing the truth to Will. "She agreed, of course. She's no fool. She could see that you had only used her. Could be she just used you, too. Now, how would you feel about that? I'll bet no woman has ever done that. Your type—you just get to thinking that anything in a skirt is going to bend and bow to you and take whatever you dish out and on whatever platter you might wish to serve it.

Well, my Kate is smarter than that." Feeling smug, he added, "Now, why don't you leave and quit ogling her, before I have some of my men toss you out. She isn't interested in the likes of you anymore."

Will set his beer glass down and looked over Diering's head toward the dance floor. The music ended and the couples moved back to the sidelines. "No, I'm going to dance. Don't try to stop me, Tom. You may not live to regret it."

"You're not going to dance with Kate." Diering reached for Will's arm, but Will easily shook him off.

"Would you like me to ruin your wife's fancy party? If she was to get upset, I suspect you'd have hell to pay. Either that, or you'd see her turn to another man."

"Chanson." Diering's command was low and gruff but reached Will's ears as he started to stalk off.

He pivoted and turned halfway around. He eyed Diering sardonically. "Were you wanting to say more?"

"Why did you say that about Cordelia?"

"Too close to the truth? I imagine every man at this party knows more about your wife than you do. I'm afraid it's common knowledge that you don't always keep her happy."

Tom was silent, thinking about her time away in Chicago, her strange erratic sickness since she'd come back. Then he looked at Will, pain evident in his eyes. "Not with you—?"

Will waited, expecting a battle. He'd sat still as long as he was going to. The woman he loved was not more than fifty feet away and he would have her in his arms again. Nobody would stop him tonight. He was enjoying hurting Diering; just this once let it be someone besides himself. In a way, it paid for the bullet old Doc Smith had dug from his shoulder.

"She's tried," he said. "Maybe I'll accept if she offers again."

Will turned to the dancers, half expecting to feel the punch of a bullet in his back, but he didn't think Diering had been carrying a gun. The cowboys were tuning their instruments before striking up a waltz. Will was grateful for their selection. He could hold Kate, at least for a little while.

He walked purposefully to the couple who had their backs to him. Clayton was busy talking to one of his friends from town. The banker didn't fit in at a barn dance, but at least he'd worn a more casual suit than usual. Will figured he was probably here to see how many more ranchers he could foreclose on this fall, and how many others he could buy out for dirt-cheap prices. He would be doing some last-minute campaigning too, no doubt.

As Will stepped up behind them, he touched Kate on the shoulder. When her gaze fell on him, her eyes grew large and surprised. At the same time Clayton turned, holding his head straight and stiffly, as if there was too much starch in his collar, but he wore a smile and a look of expectation.

"You're here to dance with my lovely fiancée, no doubt."

Will noticed, however, that when the man spoke the endearing words, his eyes didn't stray to enjoy the beauty of Kate, nor did his hand rest on her lovingly. This was something that disturbed Will. If a man truly loved a woman, it would show in his eyes. He thought of the comment Tom had made. It nagged at him. Was Clayton's interest in her simply another power play?

Everything inside Will softened as he looked at Kate, a lovely vision in a simple but appropriate white dress. She was even more beautiful than he remembered. "Of course," he replied. "It would be a shame for her to spend her entire evening dancing with an old man."

Clayton let Will's comment wash over him with good humor. "I'm sure Kate would love to dance with you. I don't deny she's young and much more energetic than I." He moved an arm and gave her a little nudge toward Will. "Go ahead, dear. I won't mind."

Kate felt Will's hand on the small of her back, and as pleasure surged inside her the memories of their few precious times together came back to her. When he pulled her into his arms she tried to remain aloof and stare only at the collar of his brown jacket. She was shaking and knew he could probably feel it.

He pulled her closer. The breath escaped her. The feel of his body brushing hers, the rough texture of his jacket beneath her hand, the scent that was distinctly his, all combined to invade her senses. In her mind, she saw them together in their intimacy and she yearned for that again.

Anger built inside her at her helplessness, her inability to change things. She tried to conquer the heartache surfacing anew; if she was not mistaken, it hurt worse than ever. "Why did you ask me to dance, Will?" She looked up at him then,

313

suppressing the need to touch the line of his firm, clean-shaven jaw. "You're only making my situation harder." Helplessly, she sank deeper into her pit of hopeless love as his blue eyes met hers.

He touched her with his gaze, making her feel special, the way he always had. "It was never my intention to make it easy for you to walk away from me and marry a man you don't love. And besides, Kate, if I wasn't already in love with you, I soon would be. You're the most beautiful woman here."

She smiled, knowing he truly believed it. "I thought that honor would go to my stepmother."

"Her beauty is only superficial. Doesn't everyone know that?"

Kate couldn't help but smile. She was pleased that Will, at least, wasn't fooled by Cordelia's false veneer. "I didn't think men were wise enough to see that. My father surely isn't."

"Your father is blinded by love." Will could understand it better now. He realized his own vision had weakened, too.

"He is blinded by many things, as we all are."

Will pondered the bitterness in her reply, and from his intense need of her, pulled her closer. The heat of his desire grew inside until he knew it could soon become too unbearable to stand. The top of her hair touched his chin. The fresh-washed scent of it drifted to his nostrils to entice him. Even her perfume tantalized him with its subtlety.

"I love you, Kate," he whispered against her ear. "Stop the wedding."

She found it hard to speak, to think, with his lips so close to touching hers. Then the music ended. The yard seemed hushed although it still buzzed with the sound of voices as the dancers left the platform or changed partners. She didn't say what was on her mind for fear it might be heard.

Clayton was watching them, too. The look on his face was not one of jealousy, though. Again she felt that he had wanted to see her and Will together again, to prove some point, to hurt her further, to stab Will with his victory. Whatever the reason might be, he was garnering a great deal of satisfaction from something.

Clayton stepped forward just as Will put a hand on her back again and whispered in her ear, "Thank you for the dance. Will you consent to another later?"

She was unable to answer because Clayton stepped up to them and took her arm, gently drawing her back to his side. He spoke to her, but looked at Will. "Go to the punch bowl, Kate. I'll join you in a moment."

Kate nodded and left. Clayton waited until she was at the table before speaking to Will. "I see you still want her." The musicians started a loud, fast song and he had to speak louder. "You can try to get her back. I don't mind, but your efforts won't work. She's quite devoted to me, and besides, the wedding is only two weeks away."

Will took a step to Clayton's side so he could better see Kate filling two glasses with punch. "You make it sound like a game, Clayton. Was she the prize that I didn't know about? Is that why you wanted to marry her—because you knew I did, too?"

Clayton chuckled and took a puff on the cigar

that was in his hand. "That's a very clever assumption."

"Does she know the reason you wanted to marry her?"

"Perhaps not entirely," Clayton replied, not wanting to give away everything to Will, either. The time would come for that. "But she consented willingly. There are some women who have needs and desires that some men cannot fill. Hers was for respect in the community and to know she would never have to worry about being supported. She wanted a social life with important and intelligent people, a beautiful home and fine clothes. I suppose that, after having stayed with me for a while, she saw that she could never have those things or that life as the wife of a common cattleman."

Will thought the description sounded more like Cordelia, but it was not for him to argue the point. He knew none of that was true of Kate. Besides, he had the Kate Meline now. He was richer than Clayton ever hoped to be. There was only one other thing that he needed to know. "Do you love her, Clayton?"

The banker took a deep puff on the cigar, and then with his simpering little smile said, "Of course I do, Will."

Will didn't believe it; he knew the banker was very good at looking a man in the face and lying without batting an eye. "You're not married to her yet, Clayton. Don't count coup too soon."

A peculiar apprehension flitted across Clayton's stark blue eyes. "Don't try to do anything foolish."

"What could I do?" Will feigned innocence and

ignorance. "Like you said, Kate is devoted to you, and the wedding is only two weeks away."

Clayton felt the perspiration break out beneath his suit. They both knew what Will had said was only half true. His lips drew together as doubt entered his head for the first time. But, keeping his composure, he slowly turned and walked away. He felt an unfamiliar form of fear rise inside him; he had been working on this plan too long for it to go awry now. If it failed this time, he knew he would never get such a prime opportunity to obtain the CM ranch and the Kate Meline mine both. Clearly, he would have to do something to obliterate the threat, and still win the prize. He'd have to make sure Will wouldn't have the chance to stop his wedding.

Will looked over the tops of the dancers' heads. Clayton stopped at the punch bowl beside Kate, then took her by the arm and led her away from the dance.

"Why are we leaving so early, Clayton?" Kate asked as he escorted her toward their large phaeton. She had wanted to dance with Will again.

He reached up and jabbed a finger into the driver sleeping on the seat who quickly came awake. "Let's just say I've accomplished my business here," Clayton replied.

He helped her into the canopy-topped vehicle that looked out of place in the midst of the farm wagons, saddle horses, and common black-topped buggies. While the driver hastened to prepare the team, Clayton settled himself on the seat opposite her. She pulled her fringed shawl more snugly around her shoulders. The evening air was cool

now that she wasn't dancing. She wished she had
something warmer, but Clayton would never offer
her his jacket; he wouldn't want to be made uncomfortable. And to have the warmth of his body,
as she would have had if he had been Will, was
completely out of the question. She would rather
freeze.

"Are you cold?" He seemed perturbed, but not
at her.

"You didn't answer my question—honestly, that
is," she said. "Our leaving had something to do
with Will, didn't it?"

"Our wedding is in two weeks, Kate, and yet
you don't make any attempt to conceal your desire
for him. I believe it was quite obvious to anyone
looking."

At first she wondered if he was jealous, but
there was only anger in his eyes. "I thought you
knew what you would be in for when you married
me, Clayton. I never did promise to love you."

"You won't make me into a clown in front of
the entire community."

"And how could you stop me if I threatened the
perfect order of your life? Refuse to marry me?
Divorce me later? What do you want me for, Clayton?" Now her tone and eyes were pleading. "What
is in this for you?"

He studied her for a long moment, making her
wish she had never opened her mouth. Finally, he
said, "Did it ever occur to you that I may care for
you?" He looked her directly in the eye. "What
more must I say?"

He didn't expect her to answer his question, but
she felt his suppressed smile, once again concealing those startling glimpses of emotions. Her time

was swiftly running out and no miracles had happened. No clocks had stopped. She knew, as she always had, that no one but she could stop the marriage. And yet, if she did, would she be sending Will to his death?

Chapter 21

Tom Diering sat in the buggy and watched the sorry herd of cattle heading for market and the few that would be turned back on the range for the winter. The debt he owed Kincaid was due with interest, and he knew that once more he could not meet it. But Kincaid would cover him. He had agreed the day Kate consented to be his wife.

And yet Tom felt an increasing hopelessness. Would he ever get back on his feet? Would he ever be in a position where he no longer owed Clayton Kincaid a dime? He ran a tired hand over his face. He was getting so tired of the burden to pay, as well as the burden to shoulder it alone, keeping it a secret from Cordelia. There were times when he just didn't care anymore, and he wondered if what he was trying to hold on to was worth the effort.

He was getting old. The struggle to accomplish something was slowly losing its appeal. The cattle, the house, the prestige he tried to obtain, the lovely wife—in the end, he could take none of it with him.

Weary from worry and thought, he turned the buggy toward town. With frustration and urgency born of inexplicable fear, he suddenly lashed the long whip out across the black mare's back. She clipped into a trot and held the pace until they were on the outskirts of Denver. He finally slowed her to a stop on the busy street in front of Kincaid's bank. He alighted from the buggy awkwardly, still having difficulty walking without all ten toes.

Inside, he stood for a moment near the doorway to allow his eyes to adjust to the dim light. When he saw that Kincaid was not at his desk, he walked to a teller cage window and spoke to the puny man behind the bars. "I'm lookin' for Clayton."

"I'm sorry, Mr. Diering, but he said he wouldn't be in this morning since tomorrow is his wedding. He left word that he'd be at his estate if anybody needed to talk to him."

Of course. Tom had been so wrapped up in his thoughts he'd nearly forgotten his own daughter's wedding. Feeling ashamed, he nodded and walked back into the sunlight. In ten minutes he was at the huge white mansion, dropping the heavy metal knocker impatiently against the door, while the tightening pain in his chest dug deeper and a tremendous guilt overwhelmed him. He was forcing her to marry Clayton simply for his own gain. And yet, here he was, right back on the banker's doorstep having to ask for more money.

The butler opened the door. His knowing English eyes infuriated Tom. He was only a servant, yet he knew why Tom was here and seemed to smirk at him.

"Is Clayton in?" he asked gruffly.

"Yes, I'll tell him you're here."

"That won't be necessary." He pushed past the

man and headed to Clayton's office. "I know where to find him."

The door to Clayton's office was open. He sat behind his big desk gazing out the window that overlooked the immaculate grounds. He swiveled his chair as Tom's footsteps sounded on the hardwood floor. "I was wondering when I could expect to see you again, Tom. No doubt the roundup is over."

Tom's anger mounted as he laid the blame for his plight on Kincaid. He hated him for knowing about his downfall, hated him for silently gloating, hated him for keeping him dangling all these years, hated him for enjoying it all.

"I suppose you're here to tell me that you can't pay me anything on the note again. It's been years since I've had any money from you, Tom. I agreed that if you convinced Kate to marry me, I would carry you for a while. Unfortunately, I haven't seen any of what you owe me."

"It was another bad winter and you know it."

"Yes, but what about the four that preceded it? They weren't bad."

"I spent those years recovering from the Great Blizzard. Now, just when I've recovered, we have another bad one."

"You seem to be the only one affected, and it seems to take you longer to 'recover' than anyone else. I suppose you're going to blame it all on my spendthrift daughter again."

"It is her fault. She thinks my money is limitless."

Clayton dropped his feet from the corner of the desk to the gleaming hardwood floor. He stood up slowly, and half sat on the corner of the desk. He dropped some of the ash from his cigar into the gold ashtray and looked up at Tom with his usual smile. *"My* money is limitless, Tom, and that's what she's been living on."

It came to Tom then that he didn't have to beg anymore. Two could play the game Clayton thought he had a monopoly on. Even though his tongue was dry from facing this adversary that so intimidated him, Tom felt growing satisfaction from the power he now held over Kincaid. "You have no choice but to carry me, and for as long as I desire. If you don't, I'll go to Kate tonight and tell her to go ahead and marry Will. Tell her that I never would have killed him."

Clayton's eyes narrowed. He couldn't lose Kate right now, not until he was through with Chanson. He had enough problems wondering if Will was going to interfere tomorrow. He came slowly to his feet and, with a fierceness that belied his calm action, grabbed Tom by the shirt collar, nearly jerking him up to his tiptoes. "How dare you try to blackmail me. Let me tell you something you've overlooked. I can always find another wife if you go back on our deal, but you'll most certainly lose your ranch *and* Cordelia. I sincerely doubt you could handle her loss as well as I could handle the loss of your daughter. I'm not marrying Kate because I love her. You just remember that."

He lowered Tom back to his heels, stepped away from him and back around to his desk. He settled himself into his chair as though nothing had ruffled him. He looked up at Tom with a new steeliness in his eyes. "You owe me a lot of money, Tom. Now, how do you propose to pay it?"

So the crafty Kincaid had won again. Tom's

stomach fell and didn't rise. His knees began to tremble and he reached for the chair he had declined to take earlier. For the first time he saw the ledgers lying open on Clayton's desk. They had his name neatly handwritten with a flourish across the top.

Clayton saw what he was looking at and he silently thrilled to the prospect of wrapping up more assets. He could easily foreclose on Tom after he had obtained Will's properties. Although he'd like to keep Kate for his wife, he would no longer need her. For now, though, he would have to have some patience until all the pieces of the puzzle fit perfectly.

He nodded toward the ledgers. "I was just looking at your sheet. You can go over it to verify what I've written. What it amounts to is too many years of supporting you. I want some money, Tom. Perhaps you could borrow some from another bank. Maybe you could sell some cattle and give the money to *me*. Ten thousand dollars would do for a starter, and it would keep your secret a little bit longer. You have my permission to liquidate some livestock."

Tom left the chair as quickly as he'd reached for it. With confusion and anxiety muddling his thinking, he pulled the door open. Ten thousand would be almost as impossible to come up with as a million. Surely Clayton knew that.

"Don't leave so hastily, Tom," Clayton said, suppressing his triumph. "Have a drink. Think about it before you go back to Cordelia."

Tom halted in the open doorway. He shook his head in response and in an effort to clear away the panic blurring his vision. "No . . . no."

Clayton smiled as Tom stumbled from the room. He watched from the window until the buggy careened out of the driveway under Diering's angry whip. He turned back to his desk and stared down at the ledger. He would lose money on Diering, but he would make up for it when he was done with Chanson. Then he would own the CM ranch and the Kate Meline mine.

Tom tore away from town, not mindful of the lather building up on the black mare's neck. His ears were closed to her labored breathing. Beyond the town, on the undulating hills of the prairie, his rage overcame him. He cursed as the wind beat at his face. With fury he stood up and leaned over the front of the swaying buggy and lashed the whip harder and harder across the mare's back. In his mind he imagined Clayton Kincaid taking the brutal sting of his wrath.

When the mare turned into the yard, the buggy went up on one wheel, nearly knocking Tom over the side. He lashed at the horse one last time and then held back on the reins, pulling cruelly on the bit. The horse stumbled and nearly went to her knees. Tom leaped down and stormed to the house, past the curious eyes of the hired hands, the servants, and Cordelia.

Inside his small office, he locked the door and found three bottles of whisky. He took them all from the cabinet and lined them up along the top of his rolltop desk, noticing acrimoniously that it wasn't the fancy mahogany of Kincaid's. He looked around the room. He had wanted to be like his father-in-law. He had tried to make something of his life and himself, but at heart he knew he was still just a broken-down cowboy with dreams that could never be attained.

He popped the cork on the first bottle of whisky and stretched out in his chair. With one slug he poured a third of the bottle down his throat. He ignored the pounding on the door and the questioning voice of Cordelia. His predicament was her fault. Hers and Clayton's.

He pulled a revolver from the drawer and aimed it at the door. He had half a notion to put a bullet through it and into her — then do the same to Kincaid. But as he stared at the amber liquid in the bottle he knew, deep inside, that there was only one way to escape what faced him . . . and only one person to blame.

Will straightened the tie at his neck and then carefully put on his vest and suit coat. With a quick glance in the mirror he left his room and walked down the hall in long strides. There was no smile on his face, only a clenched jaw that gave a look of absolute determination. His jog down the stairs was purposeful; his course set. At the foyer table he took his hat from the rack and positioned it on his head in a precise manner. Then he removed the holster and Colt revolver from another hook and strapped it around his slender hips. He tied it down to his thigh and then, tucking his coattail behind the handle, he left the house.

On long strides he went to Bart's house and rapped on the door. Lorna answered it; she was still in her dressing gown. "I just wanted to tell you that I'm leaving."

Lorna tried to conceal the pain in her eyes that she felt for him, but he saw it anyway. He didn't want their sympathy; he didn't want anybody's. She looked over her shoulder at Bart, who stepped into view, shrugging into his suit coat. "Will's here."

She left then and Bart came to the door. The two men stepped out onto the porch of the small ranch house. Will looked at the Rocky Mountains. "I'll see you at the church."

"You're going kinda early, aren't you?"

"I wouldn't want to miss it," he replied sarcastically.

Bart took note of the Colt at his boss's hip. "Since when do you need a gun at a wedding, Will? You're not thinking of doing something stupid, are you?"

"Just protecting myself from old man Diering in case he takes another notion to shoot me."

Bart studied the hurt in Will's strong face. "Well, I'll tell you one thing, my friend, if you love that woman as much as I think you do, then you're a damned fool not to do something to stop her."

Will turned to Bart with his eyes narrowing on the other man. "I won't guarantee that I won't."

Bart lifted a hand and placed it on Will's shoulder, gripping it in a friendly and understanding way. "Go on, Will. We'll see you there."

Kate allowed the other women to dress her, only doing what she had to do to get into the white satin dress heavily adorned with lace. Cordelia stood in a corner and sulked, still not pleased about her father marrying her stepdaughter. The others tried to show enthusiasm, but Kate's depression was apparent to all, and the bridesmaids went away whispering and speculating about why the new bride-to-be wasn't happier.

Kate had hoped this moment would never come; it had seemed so far away back in January when she had given in to her father's threat. All she could think of was whether Will would come. Ambivalent, she both wanted him near and prayed he wouldn't show. He had said he would rather die by her father's bullet than see her married to another man. She understood it fully; she would feel the same if the tables were turned. He loved her. God, how she was hurting him.

"It's nearly time to go downstairs," Minnie said with a scowl on her face, but staying by Kate after the others had gone. "Let's get your veil on."

Kate let the widow's fingers work it into her hair and pin it, having no choice but to listen to the woman's comments. "You make a mighty pretty bride, Kate. My only regret is that you're not happier about it. There aren't too many high points in a person's life, and sometimes you don't see what they were until they're over. Getting married is one of them. It can be the happiest moment you'll ever have, but if you marry the wrong man, it'll be a day that will ruin the rest of your life. Think about it, Kate. You're only eighteen. You've got a lot of life ahead of you."

Kate felt ill. Her legs were weak, like jelly. She didn't know if they would hold her up. She turned to the door. Minnie opened it and she walked through.

Tom pressed his fingers into his head, cursing the pain and heaviness caused from all the whisky he'd drunk. It hadn't helped him. He had fallen into a depression so deep that he seriously doubted if he could climb out this time. He saw no bright spot at the end of the tunnel, only darkness, only despair. He dreaded having to give Kate away. He could see now what a damned mistake he'd made. What a mess he'd made of his entire life. But he hadn't been content with ruining his own life; he'd had to go and ruin his mother's life and now hers. He only wanted to crawl off where it was dark and where nothing existed, not even his mind. And there he would stay wrapped up in peaceful blackness forever.

"Tom!" Cordelia's voice jarred him from his reverie. "Get up and comb your hair. The wedding will be starting soon." Suddenly, she put her hand to her mouth and raced for her private bath.

He sat back deeper in his chair and waited until she had appeared again at the door that connected their two rooms. She was pale, she'd lost weight, she couldn't keep anything down. She wouldn't see a doctor. Oh, he was no fool. He'd seen the signs before. The first three months of Meline's pregnancy were so bad, he thought she was going to die of starvation, so adversely affected by the child in her womb that nothing, not even water, would stay down.

He'd often wished he and Cordelia would have a child, but he knew without asking that the child she carried wasn't his. She didn't know he knew, but her cheating on him in Chicago was a realization that stung bitterly and hurt more deeply than perhaps even his financial troubles. He had loved her—no, he had worshiped her. And she had given him nothing in return.

He stood up, feeling ill himself. It was his mind; it hurt, it ached for relief from the problems that had plagued him for so long and that seemed not

330

to have an end in sight. Automatically, he combed his hair and looked at himself in the mirror. He'd been handsome once; he wasn't anymore.

She was waiting. He turned to her. "Go on downstairs. I'll be but a minute."

In a trance, Kate was helped from the carriage that had brought her from Clayton's. She was taken to a private room to wait until the ceremony began. She waited there alone, standing in the middle of the floor. She was numb. Her hands were clammy, and finally she placed them on the lacy skirt of the wedding dress, letting it absorb some of the moisture.

Kate heard the people gathering and their noisy chatter. This was one of the biggest events Denver had seen. It was the wedding day of Clayton Kincaid, the eligible widower who was finally going back to the altar. Talk was that he would win the Senate race for sure. He was popular, he was well known, and tidbits about his engagement to Kate had appeared frequently in the society column, winning him more notoriety.

He would get everything he wanted, she realized with an increased bitterness flowing through her. But then, Clayton Kincaid always got everything he wanted.

Minnie stepped into the room. "It'll be about twenty minutes, Kate. Here's your bouquet."

On an easy lope, Will's buckskin took the low hill and dropped down into a long hollow. With no warning he dove right into the center of six armed men, all wearing bandanas over their faces and with every rifle pointed at him. The thoughts of

Kate that had occupied his mind vanished instantly as he wheeled his horse away from the group and reached for the Colt at his side. In seconds he sent a slug in their direction. In another instant he was racing for town, just a mile away. Surprised at his sudden and unexpected action, the men were slow to respond, but too soon he heard the report of the rifle and the bullet that was much too close.

The buckskin stretched out and ran at top speed down the hollow and up the other side. Denver was just over the next rise. Another bullet cracked and he returned it with one of his own, but then an incredible force struck him in the back, ripped through the meaty flesh of his side, and nearly knocked him from the saddle. Almost instantaneously the buckskin's front legs crumpled and he flipped over frontward, somersaulting Will into the air.

He hit the ground rolling, but before he could collect his wits the riders were upon him, dismounting, and swarming around him. One kicked his gun from his hand and another sent a searing bolt of pain into his side with a well-placed blow from a fist. He was grabbed on either side by two of the men and held tight while one of the burly men knotted his gloved fist and rammed it into Will's stomach, forcing the air from his lungs.

Helpless against their assault and the ferocious pain of the bullet wound in his side, Will lost strength even to brace himself against the man's fists that hit again and again until finally something cracked inside him. A shot of white flashed through his head from the excruciating pain, and then everything went black.

* * *

"Where's my father?" Kate asked, trying to pull herself out of the numbness that was keeping her from thinking and feeling.

"I don't know." Minnie was still sullen. "He and Cordelia haven't arrived. All I know is what I was told. Mr. Kincaid is losing patience and won't wait another minute. He's standing up at the altar and the crowd is beginning to buzz. He wants someone to stand in for your father. He says his lawyer will act in that capacity."

Kate was flustered; her mind wasn't working at all. *God, I don't care.* She closed her eyes. Just get it over with. That's all that matters. "Very well." It was her own voice she heard, although it sounded so remote. "Go tell them."

Minnie gave her one last admonishing look and then left the room. In minutes she had returned. The muffled sound of the music began to play, and now, moving only on instinct, she opened the door and walked down a short hall and was met by Clayton's lawyer. She put her hand on his arm and together they stepped into the chapel.

The church was jammed with people. Probably everybody in Denver had come to see the millionaire marry. She tasted the bitterness again. It was strong. She passed the pews of spectators in a blur. She saw no one, nothing was distinct. She thought of Will. She looked to the end of the aisle and saw Clayton standing there in a light gray suit and white shirt. Everything about him was gray: his hair, his clothes, her future with him.

The lawyer left her at the altar next to Clayton. Clayton took her hand and placed it on his arm. She thought she saw a smile on his face, but there was still no love, no genuine caring. She felt so light-headed, as though she might faint, and she clung tighter to him but only out of desperation. All his friends were here. It was a big day for him. Damn him, damn her father for not even showing up.

"Kate Diering, do you take this man..."

The words came to her from someplace far away and were slow in registering. Clayton's grip on her arm tightened. Her panic was rampant. *I love you, Kate. Stop the marriage. Don't worry so much about death that you ruin life... It'll be a day that will ruin the rest of your life.*

"No—" It was a moan from her lips. Suddenly, hot tears burned her face and blurred her vision. Her shoulders slumped and she fought to keep her body upright against racking sobs that soon made themselves evident in the shaking of her slender body.

Clayton's words bit into her mind, threatening her. "Don't you dare humiliate me in front of everybody."

The preacher repeated the question. Clayton's fingers were hurting her so badly, it nearly blocked all else from her mind.

"No." It was louder and more forceful. "I—I—can't!"

She wrenched herself free of his hold, grabbed up the voluminous yards of her dress, and, before his stunned eyes and the entire town of Denver, she ran.

Chapter 22

The aisle was long. She was painfully aware of the hundreds of people rising to their feet with startled gasps and frowning faces. Then they all became a blur. She reached the church doors and fled down the steps and into the street, not knowing or caring where she was going. She ran, finally feeling the exhilarating breath of freedom. The harder she ran the more power she felt in her lungs to take her even farther. She dodged pedestrians, horses, buggies, all the while keeping her long white skirts high. Gradually, she began to feel a burning in her chest and a tightening pain in her legs that signaled she had nearly pushed herself to the limit. Then, over the hammering sound in her ears, she heard a shout.

"Kate! Kate! Stop!"

She pressed on, feeling the pain now that threatened to stop her escape. She saw an alley. She darted into it. Without warning her legs crumbled and she fell headlong, trying to catch the fall with her hands. Out of breath and knowing she could go no farther, she heard running feet behind her. She pushed herself up on her hands and knees. When the male hands grabbed her shoulders she struggled, knowing she had to get away.

"Leave me alone! I won't marry him. I won't."

"Kate." The gentle male voice flowed past the drumming in her ears. "I won't send you back."

The hands lifted her to her feet, but her legs were weak now and quivering and would barely hold her up. She felt his hands pressing into her shoulders. She opened her eyes. It was Bart Russell.

"Kate." His voice changed in tone now and she felt a cold chill run over her. There was something in the one word and in his eyes that warned her of bad news to come. She braced herself and yet her body had no more strength than her legs. His grip on her tightened as he tried to help her stand.

Bart looked into her frightened eyes. Damn it, where was Will? She needed him now more than ever. "Kate, I'm taking you over to Doc Smith's."

She protested, and feebly tried to get out of his hold. "No, I don't need a doctor. Just take me away from here, Bart. And warn Will. Daddy will probably try to kill him now. I—I went back on my word."

Bart shook her slightly to make her quit rattling. "Listen to me. Your father is at Doc Smith's, Kate." Her eyes widened in alarm as all kinds of thoughts rushed to her mind.

"Did he and Will...have a gunfight?"

Bart's voice barely reached her ears but there was a great sadness in it. "No, Kate. Your father has tried to kill himself."

"No..." The word barely slipped through her lips but was strong with denial. Then the last of her strength failed her. Bart caught her up and hauled her into his arms. He started back out the alley and toward the doctor's office.

Lorna was coming toward him. "Is she all right?"

"Yes."

"People are coming from the church, Bart."

"Where's Will?"

"I don't see him."

"Damn it, he left before we did. I wonder where in the hell he is."

Lorna carried the baby and hurried along beside her husband, trying to keep up with his long strides and glancing behind her at the people coming from the church. At least Clayton was nowhere in sight. No doubt he wasn't in a mood to face anyone in Denver at the moment.

They reached the doctor's office. As they stepped through the door, Cordelia leaped from a chair and stared at them with a wide-eyed look. Bart pushed past her and carefully laid Kate down on a sofa next to the wall. Diering was apparently in the inner office and Bart's eyes strayed that way.

"How is he?"

Cordelia was indignant. "I don't know." She turned her attention to Kate, her eyes narrowing to mere needle points of hatred. "What is she doing here? What's the matter with her?"

Kate was getting her strength and her senses back. She forced herself straighter on the sofa as her mind felt the burden of her thoughts, but Cordelia's criticism of her immediately drew her up. Before Bart could respond, Kate was on her feet, feeling the weakness in her legs, but forcing herself to step up to Cordelia and face her. "Nothing is the matter with me, Cordelia. I'm fine now. How is my father?" She was troubled by her father's desperate action, but understood that there would be no answers for a while and then only if he lived.

There was moisture in Cordelia's eyes, indicating the possibility of tears. "I don't know how he is." Then she broke. She turned her back to them and her shoulders began to shake as sobs racked her body. "Do you have any idea what this will do to me? The humiliation. Everyone will look at me as though *I'm* to blame. As though I wasn't a good enough wife and couldn't keep him happy."

Kate grabbed her by the shoulders and pulled her around roughly. "Don't you care that he may die! All you care about is your reputation."

"I hope he does die." Her words were low and vicious. "It's what he wanted. Otherwise, he wouldn't have put a gun to his head on *your* wedding day." Then she looked around in confusion as she had another thought. A gloating look slowly appeared on her face. "Well, well. It looks as though Tom stopped the wedding, didn't he?"

"No," Kate said. "I stopped the wedding. I'm not going to marry your father."

Cordelia stared at her in disbelief for a moment and then tossed her head back and laughed. "Well, good. I hoped he might come to his senses, but at least you did."

The door burst open then. In its opening stood Clayton, a rage so deep in his eyes that Kate shuddered. He looked for her, then came into the room and slammed the door behind him. Bart left Lorna's side and stepped next to Kate.

Kincaid saw him and knew he'd have to take on the cowboy to get to Kate. He forced himself to restrain his temper. A hatred emanated from him and focused on Kate. She shivered from the coldness of it, but she also noticed a wild look in his eye that had never been there before; a sort of fear out of character for the invincible millionaire.

"You've humiliated me in front of the entire town. You'll pay for it—one way or another."

"Accept it like a man, Kincaid," Bart said.

Kincaid turned back to the door and jerked it open. His eyes remained on Kate. "I see your lover isn't here with you. If you left me for him, it may be one of the biggest mistakes you ever made."

He started to leave. Cordelia ran after him. "Wait for me, Daddy. I can't stay here."

When the door was closed behind the Kincaids, Lorna, Bart, and Kate sat down in the small room to wait for the doctor. Ten minutes later Dr. Smith emerged from his inner room wearing a glum expression. Kate came to her feet, not liking the look on the doctor's face. Inside, she felt small and frightened but tried not to show it. "How is he?"

Smith looked at them. "He's going to live; but can anybody tell me why a man would do what he just did?" Kate sat back down. Nobody replied. Dr. Smith continued. "The head wound isn't bad. Apparently, he had intentions of putting a bullet in his brain but then chickened out at the last second. He jerked just enough when he pulled the trigger that the bullet missed, leaving a deep graze and powder burns. He's in a mild state of shock. You can see him when he comes out of it." He walked to his desk and sat down, picking up a pencil to jot down some notes. Then, as an afterthought, he looked back at Kate. "I'm sorry it disrupted your wedding, Miss Diering."

Bart moved to the door, pulling back the thin curtains to look out. Finally, he opened the door and spoke to Lorna. "I'm going to see if I can find Will."

A more intense chill settled over Kate. Could Will's disappearance have anything to do with this violent action of her father's? Had her father shot Will, and then himself? She was almost afraid to ask any questions, but she needed answers. "Bart, do you know if Will was going to come to ... the wedding?"

Bart knew now that she loved Will as much as he loved her, and the foreboding feeling nipping at him was made more intense by the knowledge. "Yes, Kate. He left before we did." Bart looked away from her and studied the hat in his hands for a moment. "He was going to try and stop you from marrying Kincaid."

The true extent of Will's love for her washed over her anew. Tears gushed from her eyes. She had been such a fool. "I was only trying to save his life," she said. "My father said he'd kill him if I didn't marry Clayton."

Bart and Lorna exchanged surprised glances; Will had said nothing to them. "I'm going to go look for him, Kate. Why don't you come with me?"

Her tear-stained face lifted with hope. Then she glanced at the door of the room where her father lay. Dr. Smith turned as though he hadn't heard the airing of the family problems. "Go ahead, Kate. Your father is going to be fine. It'll do him good to rest for a while. If he wakes, I'll tell him you'll be back."

With new purpose, Kate followed Bart and Lorna out of the office. She crowded into their buggy with them and they drove around town. Bart stopped at a few of Will's favorite saloons, but no one had seen Will. With increasing concern, they headed back toward the CM ranch. Their ride was silent, each wondering what could possibly have happened to this man they all loved. Bart thought maybe he had just gone off somewhere by himself and gotten drunk, unable to face Kate's marrying another man. And yet, he couldn't convince himself. He knew Will too well. Will backed down to nothing. If he set out to do something, he did it. Bart didn't relay his suspicions to the women, but he was afraid something serious had happened to Will.

As he pulled the buggy to a stop at the ranch, the cowboys came out to meet them. Bart stepped out of the buggy and then helped Lorna and Kate down. The men ran questioning eyes over Kate in her wedding gown, the expensive fabric now ruined by her fall in the alley, and torn by her running feet.

One of the cowboys coughed, clearing his throat. "Have you seen Will?" he asked Bart, then glanced over his shoulder, nodding his head in the direction of the corral. "His horse came back without him." There was a pregnant pause. He obviously didn't want to alarm anyone, and yet fear was in the eyes of all of them. "There was blood all over the saddle."

Kate reeled and felt Lorna's steadying arm go around her. She didn't know how much more she could take in one day. If Will was dead...how would she ever go on living? She forced the morbid idea from her mind, and clenched her jaw. She had to be strong. She had to find him. If he was wounded, time could be crucial. They would have to find him right away. She took a step away from Lorna and steadied herself. Then, with the others watching her, she gathered her trailing skirts and headed off toward the corral, where the saddle hung over the top pole. She opened the gate and stood there for a moment, looking at the buckskin. He was limping on one front leg; one of the cowboys had put a bandage around it.

"He apparently fell, ma'am." She heard a voice behind her.

She walked up to the horse slowly. It eyed her inquisitively, but allowed her to approach, and then sniffed at the tentative hand she held to his nose. She got a hand on the halter and then moved closer, working her way along his side, running her hand along his neck, withers, and back. When her hand reached his hip it stopped. *Blood.* She swallowed hard and forced the panic from her mind. She whirled and stalked toward the others. As she closed the gate behind her, she moved with renewed strength and determination. "Bart, we've got to find him."

"We'll start a search between here to Denver," he said, and then turned to the cowboys. "Get saddled up, boys."

They took off running, one hollering over his shoulder, "We already are!"

"I want to go," Kate said. "Do you have a horse I can ride?"

Bart looked her over, unable to conceal his surprise, but realized he could not deny her this. He knew it was better to be taking action than sitting around waiting, wondering. "I'll get you one."

Kate turned to Lorna. "Do you have something I could wear?"

"Yes." Lorna turned towards the house, carrying the baby. Kate was right on her heels. Inside the small but homey ranch house, Lorna set the baby down and went to her wardrobe, pulling out a split riding skirt, blouse, and tall laced boots similar to the ones Kate had always worn. With swift fingers Lorna rapidly undid the tiny pearl buttons at the back of the wedding gown and helped Kate out of the cumbersome attire and all the confining undergarments. In ten minutes Kate was dressed. Lorna handed her a hat as she went out the door.

"Kate," she called, stopping the younger woman. There was understanding in her eyes; she knew how the love for a man could be consuming, knew how much Kate was hurting and worrying. She wished she could go too, but there was the baby to be tended and pots of coffee and food to be made for the searchers when they returned. "Good luck. We love him, too."

Kate choked back tears. She nodded and hurried to the horse Bart had saddled and waiting. The other cowboys had gone on ahead, and Bart and Kate set out on a gallop to catch up with them.

They went in groups of twos and fanned out over the area where they thought Will might have ridden. Bart knew that oftentimes the men on horseback didn't follow the winding wagon trail whose course detoured rough terrain. A man on horseback might instead take a more direct course to town, one that was considerably shorter. A mile from Denver, Bart and Kate dropped down into a long hollow. Immediately, they pulled rein. The grass was trampled and cut by horses' hooves, as though some battle had taken place here.

They circled the area, looking for signs. Both got off their horses and walked. They found spent cartridges from rifles and a revolver. Bart picked them up and put them in his pocket. They found an area of grass that was particularly smashed down. Resembling bright balls of red fluff, darkening spots of blood stood out in the light of the sun.

Kate's shoulders slumped. She looked around the wide expanse of land helplessly. There was no sign of him. He'd been hurt, badly, and yet he was gone. "Bart, what's happened here? What are we going to do?"

"Somebody ambushed him and there was a fight. I suspect whoever did it has hauled him off somewhere, otherwise I think we'd have found him, or his horse would have stayed with him."

"But who? And why? I doubt it would be road agents this close to town and in broad daylight."

"No, you wouldn't think so. Come on, we've got to keep looking."

With no answers to their questions, they got back on their horses and rode reluctantly away from the scene, both wishing they could find a clue. As dusk slipped down on them, ending the search, they went back to the CM, tired and defeated. Kate could only nibble at the food Lorna had fixed. The others were silent, watching her as if they were trying to guess her next action.

Finally, she spoke. "We'll start again at daybreak. We better get some sleep."

The men pushed their chairs back. The scraping sound was hollow and empty to everyone's ears. They found their hats, and on shuffling feet left the long table in Lorna's kitchen. They said their good-nights quietly. When the door closed behind them, Bart turned to Kate.

"We'd like you to stay here with us, Kate."

The problems of the day had overwhelmed her. She realized then that she'd been so worried about Will, she hadn't gone back to see her father. Her gratitude was evident in her eyes. She stood up, feeling as though she didn't have the strength in her body to make another move. "Thank you, but I really should go into town and see my father. Perhaps you'd lend me a horse?"

"It's late, Kate," Bart said. "Why don't you go tomorrow? We'll need to go in and get the sheriff to help us with Will's disappearance."

She didn't say anything, but wondered if tomorrow would be too late for Will. She nodded, knowing his suggestion was best. She went to work gathering up plates and cups to have something to do. Bart went outside while the women cleaned up. Kate and Lorna said very little. When they were finished, Lorna got the baby ready for bed and Kate watched, quelling the new feelings of pain surfacing in her.

She'd wanted a child. Will's child. She'd wanted a life like Bart and Lorna had. Now she had nothing. No home, no family. She couldn't think of Will possibly being dead. And she realized that if he was, then the suffering she had put them both through to try and save his life had been in vain. They could have been together all these months. They could have had some happiness as man and wife, even if only for a little while.

Feeling the threat of tears, Kate hastily made

an apology to Lorna and left the ranch house. She stumbled through the dark searching for a place to be alone, to think. Her feet took her to the front porch of Will's house. The need for his presence beckoned her inside. She opened the door and stepped into the foyer. She stood for several minutes in the dark, waiting, listening, as the thought came to her that he might have returned home while they were out searching and he was now here in the house.

As the new idea gave her hope, she reached for the dark shape of the hurricane lamp sitting on the foyer table. She groped near its glass base and found a container with matches inside. She lit one using her belt buckle as a striking place. The flame reached up and illuminated the night. She removed the lamp's chimney, laid the match to the oil-soaked wick, and then blew out the flame. Replacing the chimney to protect the lamp from the draft, she picked up the lamp and moved into the large living room.

From there she searched every corner of the lower floor. Then, feeling like an intruder, she made her way up the stairs. Taking a deep breath, she checked each bedroom. All three were vacant. One looked more lived in than the others—some of Will's clothes were tossed carelessly on a chair. She stepped into the room. Hesitantly, she reached out and touched the jacket lying on the chair. Then, her last hope vanishing, she set the lamp on the night table and sat wearily on the edge of the bed.

The tears she had stopped earlier came freely now. With no one around she didn't try to stop them. She laid her tired head back into the softness of his pillow, thinking she would get some comfort from knowing he had slept on it just last night. But being near his things and in his house only intensified her love for him and the terrible loss she was feeling at not knowing where he was or if he was alive. She was stunned and hurt by her father's attempted suicide, wondering what could have driven him to make such an irrevocable decision, but at the moment she could fully understand despair.

She felt caught in a terrible web she couldn't get out of. She closed her eyes and still the tears came. Finally, as the hours of the night passed, sleep found her troubled mind. And, at least for a time, it washed away her pain.

After three hours, when Kate had not returned, Bart went looking for her. A light in Will's room led him directly to her. He stood in the open doorway for a moment. In the circle of light from the lamp, she had fallen asleep on Will's bed. His heart went out to her. Her exhaustion was a Godsend, but he wondered how many of the cowboys would sleep tonight, including himself. The sign hadn't looked encouraging. But what puzzled him the most was the fact that the entire thing looked as though it had been planned. It looked as though Bart had been kidnapped intentionally. They just had to find out why.

On booted feet, muffled by the big braided rug, Bart crossed the room to the bed and turned the wick down low on the lamp, leaving just enough light in case she woke up in the night wondering where she was. At the moment she reminded him of a small, helpless child. Then, carefully, he lifted the cover and blankets from the empty side of the bed and drew them over her. She didn't stir. Releasing his breath, he turned and quietly left the room.

Will opened his eyes. He saw only a deep blackness surrounding him, its substance unbroken by light from any source. The pain torturing his body drew him to full consciousness. He remembered now what had happened to him, but he had passed out when he'd felt his rib break. He couldn't remember anything after that. He didn't know where he was.

Kate. Suddenly, he felt very sick; the illness took precedence over the pain. Kate was married now. He hadn't made it there to stop her. He tried to move; the pain shot through him with increased intensity, nearly sending him back into unconsciousness. He moved his hand down along his side and felt the warm stickiness that he knew was his blood. His shirt was soaked around the area of the wound, but the wound didn't appear to be bleeding profusely.

He turned his head to the side and tried to see through the thick blackness, wondering if he was blind. Because of his inability to see, his other senses came to the fore. With one hand he felt the area he was lying on. It was cold and damp and hard: rock. He put both arms out and reached as far as he could in either direction, but felt nothing around him, just the granite beneath his fingers. And yet, even in the inky blackness, he felt confined, surrounded.

There was a stillness about the place that was heavy. He listened and isolated only two sounds. The ticking of his pocket watch, which now seemed loud, and the more distant, yet steady, sound of water dripping. Almost simultaneously the sense of water brought a damp smell to his nose. The place was closed in, musty, a place where little outside air could penetrate. Instantly, he put all the sounds and smells together. It was a place he recognized now. He was inside the earth—a cave, or a mine.

As the realization dawned, it was not the fear of his wounds taking his life that bothered him, but not knowing exactly *where* he was or how to get out. He wondered who had brought him here and if they would return. And, under the circumstances, it was obvious no one who could help him would know where he was.

But there had to be a way out. Despite the pain, he forced himself up on his hands and knees. He began to move slowly, inching along, knowing that if he were in a mine tunnel, there would probably be an opening in the side of a mountain. But if he were in a tunnel off a shaft, he could fall to his death at its opening. He had only gone a short distance when the pain overcame him again.

He lay back down on the cold ground, feeling small rocks beneath his back now. His hand feeling along his side found that the bleeding had started again. Despite the pain, he pressed his fingers into the wound to try and put enough pressure on it to staunch the flow of blood. He knew now he would have to lie still if he was to stay alive. And yet, if he stayed here too long, he would die anyway. He closed his eyes and considered his choices. Unfortunately, this was one of those times when none of them were to his liking.

Chapter 23

The next morning Kate approached the doctor's office with apprehension. Would her father be there waiting for her, or some person she didn't know? What could she say to him after he'd tried to end his life? The door opened just as she was reaching her hand for the knob. Cordelia was on the other side of the threshold, glaring at her. "It's about time you had the decency to come and see your father."

Kate stepped through the narrow doorway, past Cordelia, without commenting. Dr. Smith was there at his desk. Kate's eyes silently asked what she should do. He nodded toward the door, telling her without words that it was all right to enter the adjoining room.

Inside, the shades were drawn. Kate noticed it and thought how her father had always liked to be able to see out when he was indoors. He was in bed, lying back on the pillows with white bandages wrapped around his head. His eyes slowly opened and were drawn to her, but there was nothing inside them; no spark of love or hate. No glow of life.

She moved to the edge of the bed.

Diering knew what was going on in her mind,

or at least he could guess. It was in everyone's mind. He was a yellow-bellied coward for jerking the gun away at the last minute. He was a coward for having thought he should do it in the first place. His head ached from the deep graze along his scalp. The doctor had shaved his hair away and stitched the gap back up, but it ached until he thought his head was going to explode. It had been a stupid move. He could see that now.

His eyes hurt when he moved them, but he slid his gaze toward Kate. She looked sad and tired, but also very pretty. Pride swelled inside him. She had had the courage to run away from that damned Kincaid. He should have done the same thing years ago. He'd been wrong to try to prevent her from marrying Will. He had been selfish, concerned only with his own foolish desires.

His mouth was thick and cottony. He ran his tongue around the inside and over his lips to moisten them. At last, he spoke, but it sounded like a croak. "I didn't think you'd come."

Her heart went out to him, but she couldn't help wondering if he had something to do with Will's disappearance. "How are you?" Somehow the question sounded as though she didn't care, but she did. It was just that he had hurt her so badly. She didn't know if she could forget and forgive, or even if she should. It was wrong—she knew it—but right now she felt he had to prove himself to her. Prove his innocence, prove his love, prove that he wouldn't do it all over again.

A gurgle rumbled inside his throat that represented a chuckle. "Alive," he responded to her question.

Kate saw a spark of life in his eyes before he

looked away from her in what she recognized as prideful shame. She felt the need to touch him, yet she knew the division between them might never be fully mended. She was afraid too that if she put her arms around him, he would push her away. "Why did you do this, Daddy?"

Diering glanced up but saw no reproof in her eyes. He admitted now that he never had. All that had ever been in her eyes was a yearning, and he had always turned his back on it. He had expected to see Will with her, since she'd broken off with Kincaid. He wondered if his violent threats had separated them forever. He'd been wrong about Will. Will had simply tried to be a good neighbor after his father had gone back to Texas. He'd filled Tyler Chanson's shoes in fine form and Tom knew now that his own distorted notions had made Will seem like an enemy.

He remembered her question and answered it. "Kincaid's going to take the ranch away from me if I don't come up with ten thousand dollars."

She had never guessed her father was in debt to Kincaid. He had kept it a very good secret, and yet, it didn't surprise her now. "The ranch isn't worth your life."

"Maybe not. I didn't want to face the truth, Kate. Your mother loved me for what I was—a cowboy—but I wasn't happy with that. I wanted to be a big shot. A 'baron.' I was on my way when I met Clayton and Cordelia. I wanted her in a way I never wanted your mother. I knew she would never love me in the simple, undemanding way your mother did, but it made me want her more. I tried to make her want me. Do you understand?"

Kate stood stock-still. What wouldn't she give

for her childhood image of him to stay intact, but it sank deeper into a hollow spot in her heart. Yet she knew she shouldn't hold it against him if he had been desperately in love with Cordelia, a woman who exemplified everything he had ever dreamed of. She knew what it was like to be desperately in love.

"There's more I have to tell you, Kate." She waited, fearful now that he might tell her something about Will she didn't want to hear. "I never would have killed Will. I shot him that day because I'd lost my control and because I had to back up my threat. I had to put the fear in you, Kate. My own life depended on it."

Kate's bewilderment was evident as she tried to make sense of what he was saying. Apparently, he knew nothing about Will's being wounded and disappearing. "What do you mean? I don't understand."

It was painful for him to admit his dealings with Kincaid, and putting Kate up for barter to save the ranch, but he told her everything. When he was finished she sat down hard on the chair in the corner. She was repelled by what he had done, angered and hurt even beyond tears.

Many minutes ticked by. Then her father spoke again, surprising her with one more revelation.

"I'm leaving Cordelia."

"What?" A strangled sound of disbelief came from her throat. It was the last thing she had expected. He would never leave Cordelia, except through death. Hadn't everything he'd just done been for her, in the name of love?

"There's no need to stay here in Denver," he offered resignedly, sighing. "No need to try and start over with her. She was my ruination and she won't ever change. She wouldn't understand all this—but now I do. She's pregnant, Kate. It isn't my child, but that part is not what . . . what caused me to decide to leave her. I finally saw the truth. I saw that I could never make her happy."

He quit talking then, obviously exhausted, or lost in his thoughts.

The talk troubled Kate and yet filled her with relief. He had finally come to his senses about Cordelia, even though he still loved her. "Where will you go, Dad?"

"Kincaid thinks he's going to take my ranch—lock, stock, and barrel. I aim to shortchange him in any way I can. I know how you feel about us and I've got no right to ask, but I was hopin' that just this once you would step over to my side."

Kate waited. The expression on her face never changed. "What do you want of me?"

"This time?" He finished the sentence for her, knowing what she was thinking. "I want to round up what's left of my cattle and head them south. Take everything that ain't tied down. Kincaid still thinks I'm going to come up with the ten thousand, but I'm not even going to try. Might as well take what I can and run with it."

"He may come after you."

Diering shook his head. "No, there isn't enough to make it worth his time, but it's enough to give me a fresh start somewhere else. All I want is what I had in the beginning. A place big enough to support myself. A place that isn't run on borrowed money. A place below the snow line."

His words were encouraging. Maybe once away from Cordelia's and Clayton's influence, and once away from the impossible goals he had sought and never reached, he would finally have some satisfaction and peace.

Diering watched her closely now, expertly reading her mind. "I wanted too much, too soon, but a man has to dream or he would never go anywhere. I know it's a lot to ask after what I did to you, Kate, but would you go out to the ranch and have the men round up the cattle for me? As soon as this damn headache quits, I'll be headin' out."

Kate's eyes observed him keenly, but something told her to give him a chance to prove himself trustworthy. "All right." She moved to the door, thinking now of rejoining Bart and the others. She was debating whether to tell her father about Will when he spoke again.

"I'm not finished, Kate."

She turned around and looked back at him. She wondered if some wounds ever healed. She felt pity for him, but he had brought so much of his troubles on himself. And deeper inside, she could not yet forgive him for the way he had used her without concern for her life or her feelings. It was a forgiveness that might take some time.

"I convinced myself that what was best for me was best for you, Kate," he said. "I'm sorry. I'm glad you were strong enough not to go through with it. I was wrong about Will, too."

Her love and concern for Will was almost more than she could bear. She looked away, not wanting to burden her father's recovery with Will's disappearance.

Diering saw the look on her face and needed to know what had caused it. "Why didn't Will come with you? Was he afraid I'd have one more bullet for him?" He preferred to have his suicide attempt mocked rather than pitied.

Her gaze on him was now one of sad strength, defiance, and determination to hold up despite the odds. She lifted her chin. "Will's disappeared. It looks like a kidnapping. From the evidence we've found, it appears he's been badly wounded. We suspect he may be dead."

There was genuine shock on his face, and then he looked about the room, cursing softly. Abruptly, he tossed back the covers and tried to sit up, but the pain in his head forced him back down.

Kate was alarmed at his unexpected movement. "What are you doing?"

"Thought I'd go help look for him." His eyes rolled back, showing the increased pain in his head. "Where've you been lookin'?"

She told him about the search. "Bart's going to get the sheriff today. I really need to go. They're probably waiting for me."

Diering's eyes were understanding; he genuinely hoped Will was all right. "I hope you find him, girl."

She nodded and left the room then, knowing that he was truly sorry not just for Will's disappearance but for everything that had happened. It eased the pain a bit, and she felt as though he might have a good chance of starting over and being happy this time. As for herself, she would have no life worth living without Will.

She stepped from the stale, darkened room and into the bright relief of the sun. As though the light were air, she inhaled a deep breath and gripped the railing by the stairs. The others were waiting in the street for her. Standing on the boardwalk talking to the sheriff was Clayton Kincaid. Kate stopped in her tracks, not thinking he would come around after the way she humiliated him at the church. But he would no doubt think of something to tell his friends to explain her behavior. When he turned his cold eyes on her, she shivered.

While she mounted her horse, he spoke to the sheriff, loud enough for everyone to hear. "You'd better go out and talk to Vaughn. He and Will have had their share of differences. Will's been accusing him of cattle rustling now for quite a while. It wouldn't surprise me a bit if Vaughn just up and got sick of it and had him ambushed, then dragged his body off somewhere."

Clayton looked at Kate, gauging her reaction to the casual reference to Will being dead. She met his cold eyes with her own, hating him more now that she knew he had only wanted her to help him gain the Senate seat. And yet, that in itself seemed like a flimsy reason and not enough to warrant keeping her father's head above water. But his ultimate goal had been to foreclose on her father, so he had been thinking much farther ahead than the campaign trail. No, everything he did was very well planned and timed. And it was all to aid him in some way.

They searched again all day, their course taking in all the surrounding ranches. With no luck and no sign of Will anywhere they went back to the CM ranch at dark, ate disheartedly, and collapsed into their beds.

Kate retired to Will's room, needing to be near him, wanting to be completely alone. The tears she'd held in check all day during the search now flowed freely. A horrible fear clung to her now. A wounded man couldn't hang on indefinitely, and it had been two days.

In the absolute stillness her mind relived everything that had happened since she met Will just over a year ago. Clayton's smug attitude about his disappearance this morning gnawed at her. If anyone seemed happy about his possible death it was Clayton. She bolted upright in bed. *Clayton.* Will disappeared on his way to her wedding with Clayton. Will was going to try to stop the wedding. What if Clayton had suspected as much and then hired thugs to waylay him on his ride into town? There had always been such a lust for power in Clayton. She'd caught so many glimpses of it when she'd been engaged to him. He had wanted to have it all, and it clearly bothered him when Will stood firmly in his path, an adversary that wouldn't back down easily, unlike so many others.

Feeling a new excitement and hope, she grabbed the robe she'd borrowed from Lorna and tore down the stairs and over to Bart's house. In a matter of minutes, after she'd told Bart, all the cowboys were up and ready to confront Clayton. But Kate doubted they would get anything out of him, or prove anything.

"If he's guilty, he'll never confess," Kate said, knowing him all too well. "We'll have to confront him with it and then see what he does. If he's guilty, he'll be making sure all his tracks are covered."

One of the cowboys spoke up. "I don't mean to be hardhearted, Miss Kate, but if Kincaid did do this, there wouldn't be much sense in keeping Will alive. We've received no request for ransom."

That was a truth she hadn't allowed herself to dwell on. She drew her shoulders back straighter and, in the glow of the kerosene lantern, her eyes reflected an implacable determination. "I look at it this way. If someone wanted Will dead, we would have found his body out there in that hollow. If they were simply common robbers, they too would have left him there. No, whoever shot him hid him. They could have been trying to destroy all clues that could lead us back to him. I don't know. But whether he is dead or alive, I'm going to find out who did it. They're going to pay. I'm going to be at Clayton's first thing in the morning."

Clayton had ridden hard, but as the first gray cast of dawn tinted the sky above Pikes Peak, he stepped down from his weary horse at the entrance to the abandoned mine. It was the one he'd purchased at a cheap price while in Cripple Creek on his campaign tour. The owners had hired a mining firm to come in and follow the rich veins of ore into the ground. They'd sunk a shaft and then dug several tunnels spiraling out from it. Then one owner had been killed in a barroom brawl, and the other owner, fearing for his life, had gone looking for a buyer. All the tunnels contained small amounts of ore, but right now Clayton wasn't interested in getting it out.

In the gray light he saw Vaughn's horse hidden in the trees where they'd made plans to meet. Vaughn had been the one handling the initial kidnapping, although he'd been careful not to hire any locals who could be easily recognized. Clayton tied his horse next to the other and then glanced around to make sure nobody was nosing around.

The mine was back in a side hill hidden among pines and aspens, a good mile away from the general diggings at Cripple Creek. It was an isolated place—ideal for his purpose.

On stealthy feet he hurried to the mine's entrance, a gaping cavern braced with heavy timbers. Inside, a voice from the dark startled him, but he immediately recognized it as Vaughn's.

"'Bout time you got here, Kincaid. I was beginning to wonder if you'd changed your mind about our little deal."

"I can't get away as easily as you." He removed one of the many lanterns that hung on nails on one of the timbers near the entrance. He lit it and quickly moved farther into the tunnel so the light wouldn't attract attention from outside. He followed the lateral tunnel as it angled down into the bowels of the earth. The cold, dark, deathly quiet surroundings bothered him, but he wouldn't be here long.

They walked into the mountain until they reached the spot where the previous mining crew had started a vertical shaft. Tunnels radiated out from the shaft like wheel spokes, enabling them to get to the gold deposits resting on the bedrock without excavating all the overlying soil. The elevator cage was a crude temporary structure. Cables raised and lowered the cage, but he couldn't operate the elevator himself. Thus he'd involved Vaughn again, promising him a large reward in exchange for his help and his silence.

Kincaid stepped into the cage and Vaughn went to the hoist mechanisms. "He's stuck back in one of the drifts off the first level," Vaughn said. "Just like you instructed. But I got to warn you." He hesitated and got Clayton's full attention. He felt the piercing eyes that tolerated no mistakes, no weaknesses. "The boys banged him up pretty bad. I suggest you wrap up your dealings with him as fast as you can. Matter of fact, he may be dead right now."

Kincaid came back out of the cage and stalked to Vaughn, grabbing him by the shirt collar. "What are you talking about? I said to just rough him up."

"Well, how was they to know he'd go to firing on them? He tried to make an escape. He took a bullet, and then one of the boys got a little heavy-handed. Listen, Kincaid. It ain't my fault. I wasn't there, remember?"

Clayton silently cursed and shoved Vaughn backward into the hoisting gear. "For your sake, and all those boys you hired, he'd better still be alive when I get down there. Just remember, Vaughn, your money is waiting when I get back up here."

Vaughn nodded. It hadn't occurred to him to leave Kincaid down there, but the idea wouldn't be a bad one. Vaughn didn't care for Chanson—accusing him of cattle rustling and all—but if the truth were known, Kincaid was the lowest form of life, next to a snake.

When Kincaid was in the elevator cage, Vaughn carefully sent it down the shaft to level one. Clayton stepped off into the tunnel and held the lantern up high to illuminate the damp walls. There was always water in the mines, it seemed. It came from some subterranean source. Down below, at the very base of the vertical shaft, was a sump where the seepage water collected. From there it was pumped to the surface through a hose running up the shaft. He would eventually put this mine back into operation, so he had to keep the water from rising.

He moved along the dank passage until he reached a drift, a horizontal tunnel at right angles to the main tunnel. When he reached the end of it, he saw Will's prone form. Concern at seeing the lifeless shape rose inside him as he drew near. Horrified, he saw the dark splotch of blood covering the entire side of Will's shirt. His plans had gone awry when Kate had run from the church, but he had found a way around that. Now, if Will were dead, his plans would be lost forever. He stepped closer and, with the toe of his boot, nudged the lifeless man.

Slowly, with great effort, Will opened his eyes from the faraway place where his fevered mind had settled. The blackness of his underground world was pleasantly lit by a golden aura of light, and for a moment he wondered if he'd died and had found the gates of heaven. Then the light moved and he saw Clayton Kincaid's face. He moaned and weakly drew a hand up to shield his eyes.

"I must be in hell," he managed. "And you're the gatekeeper."

"Always a sense of humor," Clayton said and then squatted down next to Will, setting the lantern on the floor next to him. "I suppose you'd like to know why you're here."

"Not particularly. I'd like to know how long you intend to make me stay, though."

"Just until I get what I want," Clayton replied

and then added for emphasis, "Or until you die. Whichever comes first."

"You got Kate. Isn't that what you wanted?"

Clayton had already considered that. Even though he didn't have Kate, he could still use her as his ace in the hole. "Yes, Will. Kate and I are now married. She's been my bride for one night. Of course, I had to leave her to attend to this business, but she was more than happy to see me go. It seems she's still in love with you."

Will tried to think through the dark mass of confusion in his brain. He knew he couldn't live much longer without food or water and with his body in this condition. The bullet wound and the broken rib were glazing his mind with continual pain. He tried to figure out Clayton's motive, but he gave up, unable to sort out the fleeting pieces of ideas.

"What do you want, Clayton?"

"I want what I always wanted, Will. I want the CM ranch. And now, just to add some honey to the top of the pot, I want the Kate Meline mine. Basically, I want to break you. You are an arrogant bastard, and I want you down on your knees."

Will couldn't smile, although Clayton's demands reached his fevered mind on a humorous chord. "I'm glad to hear you don't want much, Clayton. It should be easy...to strike up some kind of deal. You've got me on my back, so you don't...have far to go to get me...to my knees," he said, out of breath.

Clayton's lips pursed. He couldn't help but admire Will's sense of humor even in the face of death. "Would you like to hear my proposal?"

"I wouldn't want to disappoint you...by saying

...no." Will licked his lips, wishing he had some water.

Clayton laughed. "It's very simple, actually." He pulled some papers from his pocket. "I've drawn these up. It says that you are giving me everything you own in payment of a long-standing debt you owe me—money over the past ten years to keep the CM ranch running. And in exchange, I let you out of here and give Kate a divorce so you and she can be together at last."

The words sifted into his brain and he tried to keep his thoughts orderly. He tried to remember just what it was he *did* own. None of it was very clear. "I don't owe you any money."

"Only you and I know that. It's your life, Will. And from what I can see of you, you may only live a day or two longer without medical help."

"No. It won't work." He paused for long moments in between sentences as his mind tried to sort it all out and his lungs reached for air. "I could turn you in. I'm sure...you thought of that."

"You won't. Not if you want to live. Besides, once these papers are signed, it's just your word against mine. You see, I've had a chance to fix my record books for evidence that you owe me a tidy million. You could come back to Denver and try to cause trouble, but a penniless man wouldn't be able to do much fighting against a senator who has your indebtedness in black and white."

Will could see he was a loser no matter what he did. "What guarantees do I have that you'll divorce Kate?"

Clayton smiled. Will thought he looked more sinister in the yellow glow of the lantern. "You'll just have to trust me, Will."

Will closed his eyes again. It made the thoughts sharper in his mind. He had no choice, but yet if he did as Clayton wanted, what guarantees did he have that Clayton would let him out of this hellhole? None that he could see. He would simply be cutting his own throat. No, he had to bide his time. Maybe there was someone out there missing him, looking for him. With some time, maybe they could find him.

"Get out of here, Kincaid. Your deal stinks."

Disgruntled, Clayton stared at Will for a full minute, realizing the man wasn't thinking clearly in his condition. Slowly, though, he pushed himself to his feet, taking the lantern with him. Will's eyes were closed again, effectively dismissing him. He hated to admit it, but he was more than a little worried that Will wouldn't live much longer. If he didn't get him to sign the papers soon, it would be too late. He had no intention of ever letting Will up out of the mine, but he had to get his signature.

"All right, Will. I'll leave, but you'd better think about it. I'll be back to see if you've changed your mind."

"Bring some water, will you?"

"It may not do you any good by then."

The light Will saw through his closed eyelids faded until there was only the blackness he had become used to. The sound of Kincaid's footsteps receded, getting fainter and fainter until they were gone completely. The sound of the constant drip of water returned and with it the perpetual ticking of his watch, which he remembered to wind even if the time wasn't correct. They were noises that could drive a man crazy, or they were noises that were the last links to life and sanity. It simply depended on how a man let them affect him. They had come to be company for him, soothing lullabies that assured him he was still alive.

He saw her face. It leaped into his mind suddenly, pushing all else aside. His eyes flew open, but seeing only blackness, he closed them again, letting her remain there in his imagination and his memories. Oh, how he wished he were with her. Her gentle hands could soothe this incredible pain that was getting harder and harder to bear. Her kiss could wipe away the agonies, and even if he were to die, he could die in peace in her arms. At least she still loved him. He didn't want to think of her in Kincaid's arms, so he quickly erased that idea from his mind. Instead, he remembered the thrill of that first time with her that would remain forever in his mind.

Chapter 24

Dawn had barely lit the sky when Kate knocked on the door of Clayton's mansion. She braced herself for the reception she'd receive, but the English butler seemed to be expecting her.

"I've come to collect my things. Is Clayton in?"

"No, Miss Diering. He left yesterday morning for Cripple Creek. He said he wanted to look at a mine that he plans to put into production again. He won't be back for several days."

His absence was a new blow. She had so wanted to confront him with her suspicion. Now they were back to square one with nowhere to turn. But she wouldn't accept the idea that Will was dead. She would never believe that until she saw it herself. "It's just as well," she replied, finding it difficult to conceal her tremendous disappointment. "I can get my things and leave."

The butler stepped aside. "Your things, Miss Diering, have already been packed into the trunks you brought. If you have someone to carry them away for you...?"

It didn't surprise Kate that Clayton had ordered her personal belongings hauled away. "Yes, I've brought some men to help me." The butler looked past her at the rough lot of cowboys sitting in the wagon in the drive. She motioned for them and the butler stepped aside.

Bart and two of the men from the CM followed her into the mansion and up the stairs. Once inside her old room, she said, "There's one thing I have to do before I leave." She looked at Bart and then down at her finger, pulling off the engagement ring that, until this morning, she had forgotten she was wearing. "I'm going to leave this in his office. He'll be able to cash it in for a goodly sum, or give it to some other prospective bride. I'll meet you in the wagon."

She hurried down the stairs now, anxious to be out of the mansion for good, thankful that her clothes and personal items had been packed. She informed the butler that she had to return something of Clayton's, and held up the ring. The butler nodded understandably and didn't object when she went into Clayton's office.

It was a room in the house she had come to hate, for it reminded her so much of the millionaire. Everything about it reeked of his presence. An ample supply of his Scotch kept the glass-doored cabinet full, and below that in drawers were several boxes of his cigars. The room was heavy with the smell of them; a smell that never went away and one she had come to dislike because it was associated with him.

She walked to the desk and was preparing to set the ring atop a ledger when she noticed the label on the ledger: "Loans Outstanding—Foreclosures." Her curiosity to see what her father was in debt to him for prompted her to open the large book. It was bolted together on the ends so pages could be added or taken out without affecting anything else. Feeling nervous now, she kept glancing at the closed door, wondering if the butler would come to see what was taking her so long. To cover her tracks she opened the top drawer, found a piece of note paper and a pen. If the butler came in, she would say she was writing a message to Clayton. She then went back to skimming the book until she found her father's name.

As she read through the columns she was flabbergasted at the years of Clayton's support. Money had been lent for every imaginable thing, mostly living expenses. The figure at the end was more than a million dollars. Kate was just getting ready to close up the book when one page fell back and opened to the C's. Will's name stood out bright and bold. Amazed, she scanned the columns that covered ten years of loans. She shook her head in disbelief as she read, for she simply couldn't believe Will owed the banker that kind of money, if any. Will hated Clayton. He wouldn't go to him for help. And she knew he banked with a rival firm.

Then she began to see a chilling similarity between her father's ledger sheets and Will's. Rapidly, she compared the two. It was peculiar that the dates and the loan amounts were nearly the same on every entry, with only a slight variation of the dollar amount and the dates. The total at the end was also very similar.

Not understanding, but feeling the two were connected somehow, she lifted the bolts just enough to slip out the pages that were all together. Folding them in thirds, she tucked them inside her riding jacket, just over her hip. Then, leaving the ring atop the ledger, she left the room. She bid

Oliver good-bye, thanked him for helping her when she lived at the house, then left the Kincaid mansion, hopefully for the last time.

She had Bart stop at the doctor's office. Quickly, she went in to speak to her father, who looked better and was sitting up in bed. He seemed very happy to see her.

"I've left a message for the cowboys to round up your cattle," she said. Then she got right down to business, pulling out the near identical sheets. She told him what she'd found and asked him what he thought of it. He admitted that he owed Kincaid exactly what was on the pages, but he scoffed at the other pages containing Will's name.

"This is a joke, Kate. I seriously doubt Will owed anybody. Besides, he did business with the other bank. I don't know what Clayton's got up his sleeve, but it looks like he's used my sheet and simply altered the entries. It looks like he's trying to blackmail Will."

"Except Will is missing."

"Yes, but it's starting to make sense, especially if you know Kincaid as well as I do. We're going to Cripple Creek. Get Will's men and the sheriff. Find out who handles his legal and accounting affairs and check this debt sheet out with them. I'm getting dressed and coming with you."

Will had had some time to think. Normally, it wouldn't have been so hard for his mind to sort out the things Clayton had proposed, nor would it have taken him so long to formulate his reply. But in the silent blackness he'd finally decided what he would do when Clayton returned. He knew

Clayton would return because he wanted the CM too badly not to.

Will was burning up. His clothes were soaked with his perspiration. His hair and face were wet and sticky. Despite the raging fever that clutched at his mind, he was cold, shivering in the chilly air, desperately wanting a blanket. He had tried to curl up in a ball, but the pain in his side became too fierce. The bleeding had stopped now and he was thankful for that. Still, his intuition told him he didn't have long to live. He'd listened to the ticking of the pocket watch but he had no way of knowing how long he'd been here. It seemed days, but he knew he couldn't live for days without water. Kincaid knew it, too. He'd be returning soon.

Will focused on the sounds in the mine. He listened for Clayton's footsteps, but as the clock ticked away and the water dripped incessantly, he felt his mind giving in to the fever. He fell asleep for indeterminate lengths of time. It was fitful sleep and he awoke from nightmarish dreams in which everything was enlarged and out of proportion. But a fragment of his mind remained in touch with reality. He still recognized some things; mainly people, their faces looking down at him, wearing concerned expressions. And yet, when he reached out for them, they would disappear into the solid blackness and the strange shapes and forms surrounding them and him.

Always there was Kate. Once he reached out and touched her face and her hair and it seemed she was really there. She had laid a buffalo robe over him and for a moment he was so warm. Then, as a ghost would do, she smiled and vanished, leaving him more alone and colder than before.

Then he heard the sound. It intruded on his visions and he forced his mind to focus on it. The footsteps came closer and then the light appeared. In his mind he drew up his hand to shield his eyes from its intensity, but then he felt his limbs still lying heavy at his sides. With a concentrated effort he lifted an arm that was like deadweight and blocked the blinding glow from his fever-sensitive eyes.

"I see you're still alive, Will. Have you thought about my proposition?"

Clayton looked odd in his derby and without his unbiquitous glass of Scotch and cigar. He was straight and collected, as always, his knowing blue eyes as sharp as arrowheads.

Will tried to speak, but his mouth was so dry that his tongue had swollen. And then, in answer to his previous request, Clayton put a canteen to his lips and poured water into his parched mouth. He wasn't sure if he was imagining again, but the cold liquid revived him, even though it set him to shivering worse.

"Have you decided to sign the papers?" Clayton asked again.

His voice sounded so hollow and far away, as if it were coming down through a great tube. Will had not intended to play by any rules or conditions that Kincaid might lay out, but he had formulated some plans of his own. They were there in his mind, but he could never relay them in words, which was fine, because they were things he didn't want Kincaid to know.

"Yes, I'll sign." He saw Clayton smile and immediately take bright white papers from his coat. "On one ... condition."

Clayton's hand stopped in midair. "You're in no position to be dictating terms, Chanson. You could die any second."

Will smiled, and then realized he wasn't sure he had smiled. Anyway, the smile was in his mind. "Exactly. If you don't ... do as I say"—he hesitated and waited several minutes to get his breath— "you will never get the CM."

Clayton was irritated. His crafty blue eyes sparked with impatience. "What is it?"

Each breath Will took, each word he spoke was agony. He wasn't even sure that what he was thinking was coming out in the words he intended. He groped for that piece of his mind that still retained a bit of lucidity, but it wavered, like reflections in a pool.

"I won't sign ... until I'm out of here."

"You don't trust me?"

Will shook his head negatively.

Clayton stood up, knowing he had better move swiftly or he would miss the chance for which he had been waiting and planning for so long. "Very well, but I don't have anyone to help me get you out of here. Do you think you can walk?"

Will nodded. It was a struggle, and Clayton thought Will would pass out several times from the pain, but he finally got him to his feet and, with Will's arm over his shoulder and one of his arms around Will's waist, he half dragged and half carried the bigger man out of the drift, down the tunnel, and to the elevator cage. Clayton was winded and his heart was thudding violently from the effort as he lowered Will into the cage. Will couldn't stretch out, and as he sat down his face contorted in pain before he slumped over. Clayton realized he had passed out.

He gave the signal for Vaughn and the elevator cage began its ascent. When the cage stopped, Vaughn helped to get Will once again lying flat. "The thugs you hired nearly killed him, Vaughn," Clayton said. "If he dies before I get these papers signed, I swear to God you'll pay dearly."

"Why did you bring him up here?"

"He wouldn't sign the papers without the assurance that I'd set him free."

"You'd be slitting your own throat if you did."

Clayton poured some water on Will's face and watched him fight through the grogginess of his extremely high fever. If he didn't work swiftly, he knew he could lose Will to unconsciousness permanently.

"Not necessarily," Clayton replied. "He could tell everybody anything he wanted, but no one would take his word against mine, especially if I have proof that he owed me money."

"But people are going to find out about his kidnapping, and when you come along with these papers, they might get suspicious."

"I'm not an idiot, Vaughn," Clayton replied calmly. "I've thought of all that. The papers are dated two weeks ago. It'll be his word against mine, unless you or one of your stupid cronies squeals."

"You pay us like you said you would, Clayton, and we'd have no reason to do that. You know how I feel about Chanson always accusing me of rustling."

"Were you?"

Vaughn was indignant. "No," he said, then admitted sheepishly, "But my boy was. I finally sent him up to Montana before he got me into trouble."

Will opened his eyes. The light had scattered the darkness and it lay only on the perimeters of his vision. He saw another face—Vaughn's. He shoved the new surge of thoughts from his mind; it was simply too much to think about.

Clayton was there again, hovering over him. There were flashes of white—paper, and a long slender stick. A pen. Clayton shoved them at him, put the pen in his hand. Then they both helped him to a sitting position and he could no longer keep the pain inside, it slipped out through parted lips in a groan. He steadied his head from the white flash that stabbed at his mind.

"Sign the papers, Will, and I'll get you to a doctor."

Even in his fevered mind, Will didn't believe that, but he had to take a chance this one time.

"If you want to live, if you want Kate back, you'd better sign."

Kate. Yes, he wanted Kate back. He'd do anything for her. His hand began to move across the paper. There was something hard beneath it, and as if in a dream, he saw his signature progress in a scrawl across the bottom of the page. Then he dropped the pen and they laid him back down.

He saw Clayton smile, gleefully. Will closed his eyes. He heard their talking but he wasn't listening anymore. Then they were moving him again. He wished they'd leave him alone; the pain was worse when he moved. He was back in the elevator cage with Vaughn when realization dawned. He struggled back up from the fever and lunged for

377

Kincaid, who stood there smiling. Then, from behind, he felt his head explode and once again his world went black.

"Get him back down there in the tunnel until I can dispose of him later," Clayton said. "He won't live much longer now, anyway. And just to make sure, I'm going to turn the pumps off down in the sump. It'll take a while, but the water will rise and drown him, if the fever doesn't kill him first."

Vaughn stared at Clayton in disbelief. A new respect and a new fear of the banker surfaced. He himself talked big, but to actually commit a man to death in such a gruesome manner was another matter. "Turning the pump off isn't necessary, is it?"

Clayton shrugged. "It'll get him out of his misery sooner."

"You'll be asked questions when you present that paper. You can bet your life Tyler Chanson won't let it lie."

"He won't be able to prove anything. Will's disappearance will be attributed to his great depression over losing his ranch and the Kate Meline mine because of his bad debts, not to mention thinking he had lost Kate. He'll have just left the country and nobody will ever find a trace of him again." The moment of satisfaction at his cleverness vanished and his eyes hardened. He snapped at Vaughn. "Now do as I say so we can get out of here."

Vaughn's thoughts were muddled as the elevator cage lowered him to the first level. He was a big man but it was still difficult dragging Will's lifeless body from the cage and into the tunnel. With the lantern still shining from the cage, he carried Will down into the tunnel, away from the shaft, until the light of the lantern no longer reached. He laid him down on the cold ground.

He didn't feel right about leaving Chanson here to die. He wasn't the most honest man in the world, but he wasn't a damn killer. But this made him an accomplice and he couldn't see where he had a choice. When Kincaid had come to him and asked him if he wanted to get even with Chanson for flinging false accusations, he was more than willing to rough him up a bit. But this—this was more than he had ever anticipated and he knew Kincaid for the true color of his skin.

He turned back to the light and then, before his eyes, it disappeared. He started to run to catch it as the elevator cage moved up and out of his reach. He screamed and yelled, but as he reached the opening to the shaft he halted, watching the trailings of golden light and life climb upward out of his reach. With fear gripping him, he turned and raced back to Will, reaching him just as the last shadow of light disappeared, dropping them into a blackness that fell down over them like a great shroud. He started to breath faster as panic overwhelmed him. He heard Will moan and the sound drew him back to reality.

"Will!" He clutched for the man at his side.

Will saw the blackness and smelled the dampness of the cave. "I blacked out."

"He made me put you back down here and then he went and left me stranded. We're gonna die down here. He's going to turn the sump pump off."

The only thought on Will's mind was what a lying bastard Kincaid was. Then he forced himself to think again, difficult as it was.

"Will you help me out of here, Vaughn?"

"Hell, yes, if I *knew* a way out."

"There's a glory hole in this mine."

A confusing reply came back to him. "Glory what?"

"A hole, an opening to the surface . . . off the first level. Are we on the first level?"

"Yes."

"I didn't realize it until . . . I knew which mine I was in. Find it. Do you have . . . matches?"

After a brief hesitation and the sound of rustling cloth, the reply reached him in the dark. "Yes."

"Take our shirts . . . make a tight ball. Use our belts . . . damn it . . . I can't think . . . make a light . . . get some help . . ."

"Okay, okay." Vaughn got the picture. They had to get out and Will was in no shape to do anything. It was up to him. But even if he found the glory hole, there were no guarantees he'd be able to get out of it.

On Kate's right was Ellis Kingsley, the sheriff. On her left was Rory James, Will's legal advisor whom she'd met in Cripple Creek. When he'd seen the damning ledger sheet, he wasted no time boarding his horse and joining the posse. Along with them were Bart Russell and the other men of the CM ranch. Bringing up the rear was her father, pale and in pain from his head wound, but determined to be a part of this expedition, to make Clayton do some explaining and hopefully find Will.

They rode hard for Cripple Creek but Kate's love and determination overcame any tiredness.

It didn't take long to discover where Clayton's mine was. As they neared it, they dispersed and rode in smaller groups, surrounding it. They saw two horses staked to aspen trees displaying the vivid yellow colors of early fall. Kate had a strange, intuitive feeling that Will was here. In her dreams she had seen him in a dark place. He'd reached out for her, and then disappeared. She was sure Clayton was behind it all. He was the only one who would have a good reason for keeping Will from getting to the wedding. And, from the looks of the ledger sheet, he had some other plans in store for Will. She knew his devious mind, and knew that no evil was too great for him to tackle.

They dismounted and the men drew their guns, not knowing what they might encounter but wanting to be ready. With Kate in the lead beside the sheriff, they entered the main entrance to the mine. There were a row of kerosene lanterns at the entrance as they picked up several and lit them. Despite their efforts to be quiet the sounds of their movements and booted feet rang loud in their own ears and Kate worried that the noise might give warning to Kincaid.

An idea occurred to her, and Kate held out her hand, stopping the party of men. She motioned for them to gather around. In a whisper she said, "Let me go in alone. I have a feeling Kincaid may say more if he doesn't feel threatened. You wait just out of sight, but keep in earshot."

Her father stepped forward. "No, Kate. I don't like the idea of you going in there alone. If he's guilty, he could take desperate action."

She glanced back down the dark tunnel that went deeper into the mountain. Her heart was thudding hard and fast. She had to find Will and there could be no wrong moves. Her feelings were strong that Kincaid was involved, even though she didn't have proof. "I know Clayton. Besides, he can't escape unless he knows a back door out of this place." She shivered involuntarily. The sooner she could get away from the confining, heavy rock walls the happier she'd be. But she had to find Will first, or die trying.

They were silent as each considered her idea. She could tell by the looks on their faces that they had sympathy for her. None of them believed Will was still alive. They had not been convinced that Kincaid had had anything to do with his disappearance. "Blackmail and extortion are his games, Kate," the sheriff had said. "Murder really isn't his style." But Ellis Kingsley didn't like the millionaire any better than most who knew him, and he had come along on suspicion of kidnapping, if nothing else.

At last, they agreed to her suggestion. She turned away from them to proceed along the tunnel, but her father's hand on her shoulder stopped her. He held out his revolver. "You may need this." She nodded, looking into eyes that now mirrored his regret—but hope, as well. Then, holding a lantern in one hand and the revolver in the other, she advanced into the narrow entrail of the earth.

The tunnel opening became wider and higher. Cautiously, she stepped into a huge granite cavity, a geode or natural room in the geological structure of the mountain. She saw Kincaid operating the hoisting equipment for the shaft. He wore an unusually gleeful smile on his face. He was alone.

She stood motionless until the elevator cage halted at their level. It was empty, except for a lit lantern.

"Testing out the equipment, Clayton?"

He whirled. For a second she saw a mixture of emotions flash over his face, but at seeing who had startled him, they all quickly disappeared. He collected himself, unintimidated by her, just as she had known he would be. His thin, straight lips thinned even more as he smiled in his arrogant way. "And what brings you here, dear Kate? Surely you didn't decide you wanted to marry me after all?"

"I came to get Will."

She read his expression again, trying to see if her hunch was correct. He covered his initial surprise quickly, but she moved farther into the granite room and set the lantern on an old wooden chair. She moved her other hand and he saw the big Colt revolver she held at her side.

Clayton's eyes narrowed on her. "I take it you haven't found him yet."

"You know we haven't, because you know where he is, don't you, Clayton?"

His blue eyes were veiled, but she saw something there that told her she was correct. "What's your plan, Clayton? If you kill him, how will you ever collect that money he owes you?"

This time his cunning gaze faltered. A shred of alarm lingered. "Now, how would you know about that, Kate? That was just something between Will and me."

Kate patted the pocket of her jacket. "I have the ledger sheet right here. I also have those belonging to my father. My guess is that if I don't give you back these ledger sheets, you'd never be able to foreclose on my father or Will, because these are probably the only copies you have."

"You're wrong. I have copies at the bank."

"But Will's was personal, just between you and him. You said so yourself. And my father's was, too. I doubt the board members of the bank would have approved of carrying my father for over ten years. As a matter of fact, I doubt they would have even lent the money to him in the first place. But you did, out of generosity, and from your own funds. If was your way of slowly but surely sucking up every piece of ground surrounding Denver."

Clayton shrugged as he moved toward her. "So what is the point, Kate. Do you have one?"

"Yes. After comparing the ledger sheets, I noticed a great similarity in the two. My father says he did owe you the money, but my hunch is, you made others with Will's name on them just to blackmail him, to get the ground that you can't get any other way."

He lunged at her. She pulled back and lifted the gun, but he was too quick and had her by the arm, knocking the gun to the ground. He twisted her arm behind her back and drew her up against him as he directed her toward the elevator cage. "How clever of you to figure out my plan, Kate. But there's more to it than that. With Will as my captive, I have used you as a pawn again. He thinks I married you, and all I had to do was assure him I would divorce you if he signed over everything he owned to me. In other words, the CM ranch and the Kate Meline mine."

He shoved her into the elevator cage and put the retaining bar across the front. "Now I'm going to send you down to join him. The two of you can live happily ever after."

He turned toward the hoisting works, when, from out of the shadows, the posse of men emerged, forming a line that effectively blocked the only exit. With guns pointed, Sheriff Kingsley said, "That was a nice confession, Kincaid. Now I'm taking you in on the charges of kidnapping, extortion, and blackmail. For your sake, Will Chanson had still better be alive or we'll add first-degree murder to that."

For the first time, Kate saw Clayton Kincaid frantic. He hesitated, swaying a bit, not knowing which direction to take. He spotted the gun on the floor but Bart Russell had seen it first and, just as Clayton dove for it, Bart's foot covered it. The foreman shoved the barrel of his .44 right into Kincaid's temple. The banker slowly straightened.

"Now," Bart said. "Where's Will? You'd better speak fast or I'll blow the top of your head right into these granite walls."

Kincaid backed up, trying to get away from the cold metal pressing into his skull, but Bart moved right along with him. Finally, he gave in, but still not relinquishing his superior attitude despite his predicament. "He's on level one, but it doesn't matter what you want to charge me with. You'll never win in court, and I'll still come out the victor. You can't take the CM or the Kate Meline from me. He signed it over, and it's all legal."

Rory James propelled his barrel-chested, six-foot frame forward and pushed the sides of his suit coat aside in a cocky stance. "You lose all the way around, Kincaid. Looks like Will pulled a fast one on you, too. Will doesn't *own* the CM ranch, nor does he own the Kate Meline mine."

Clayton's face fell with disbelief. His eyes darted from Rory to the sheriff and then to Kate. "You're lying. Of course he owns them both."

"I'm afraid not," Rory said, feeling his own bit of glory at squashing Kincaid a little deeper into the dirt for what he had done to his friend. "The CM belongs to Tyler Chanson until Will's thirtieth birthday in January. As for the Kate Meline, I transferred the title several months ago to Kate Diering at Will's request." Then, ignoring not only Kate's shocked expression but Kincaid's belligerent efforts at denial, Rory turned to the men, and with a forward motion of his arm in the direction of the mine shaft, said, "Go get Will."

The men flew into action. Kate's father happily took over the guarding of Clayton, relishing holding a gun to his head. Kate, Bart, and Kingsley went down the shaft, while Rory James operated the hoist. The other men lit out for Cripple Creek on a gallop to get a doctor and a wagon to transport Will.

As the elevator cage stopped at the entrance to level one, Kate stepped out first, holding her lantern high and moving quickly now through cold darkness, her hopes high. And then she saw him. The initial shock from seeing his blood-stained body halted her in mid-stride, but then on running feet she went to him and dropped down on her knees at his side. He was without a shirt and shivering, yet his skin was burning up. The perspiration from a fever covered his face. The ugly wound in his side was difficult to look at and one quick glance told her that even with rapid medical care, he might not survive the brutal treatment.

She put her hand on his cheek gently, and another on the black mat of hair on his chest. She spoke in a frightened whisper. "Will. Will, it's Kate." Unable to control the knot of emotions inside her, a sob reached her throat and tears began to flow. "Will, you've got to be all right. I love you. Oh, please, Will, don't die."

The movements of his eyes beneath his eyelids gave her hope. And then, slowly, with great effort, as if he had traveled from a great distance deep inside his mind, he emerged into consciousness and opened his eyes.

"Kate?"

"Yes, Will. I'm here."

"Kincaid?"

"We've got him in custody."

"Vaughn... gone looking for the glory hole..."

The men exchanged glances and set out down the tunnel after Vaughn. Then, in her kneeling position, she bent over Will, covering his upper torso carefully with the warmth of her body and the loving embrace of her arms. With her cheek next to his, her salty tears washed away the heat of his fever and she whispered in his ear, "It's all right now, Will. I'm here, and I'll never leave you again."

Epilogue

Will and Kate sat in the buggy outside the courthouse and watched the law officers take Clayton, Vaughn, and the other hired thugs away to the penitentiary to serve their sentences. As the people filed out of the brick building some of them stopped by the buggy to congratulate the newly married Chansons on their victory.

Bart leaned against the wagon wheel and Lorna stood next to him. "You kept it a damned good secret, Will. None of us even suspected the ranch wasn't yours yet."

"It was an agreement I made with my father when I was eighteen, Bart. The ranch was mine in every way except in name. I ran it the way I wanted to, made the decisions. If Dad was satisfied with what I'd done here, then he would relinquish the deed to me when I was thirty," Will said, not wishing to relate all the details to the spectators. "I guess he figured I'd have my life together by then." He looked at Kate sitting next to him. The love in his eyes was evident to everyone watching. "And I surely do now."

Rory James stepped forward, extending a hand to Will who accepted the handshake heartily. "Thank you for what you did in there, Rory."

"Sending Kincaid to jail was worth all the gold in the Kate Meline to me." He changed the subject, knowing Will was anxious to get away from Denver with his new bride of two weeks. "I hear you're off on your honeymoon?"

Will gladly took the cue and gathered the reins in his hands to prepare to go. "Yes, we need to get home and pack. We're going to Texas. Kate's never met my family."

Rory moved back away from the buggy and the others did the same. They bid the young couple farewell and hollered best wishes after them as the buggy moved away. After they were out of town Kate looked up at him. "You outdid yourself on my wedding gift, Will. Why did you give me the mine while I was still engaged to Clayton?"

Will smiled in his mischievous way and then looked down at her. "Because I kept the hope that your love for me would prevail."

"You knew me better than I did."

Unexpectedly, they heard a shout and a lone rider approached them. The man stopped in the road. As they drew closer, Kate recognized her father.

They pulled the buggy to a stop next to him. "I hope you won't mind that I wasn't at the trial," he said, pushing his hat back from his forehead to reveal the small bandage still covering his head injury. "We're headin' south today. I think we can make it to New Mexico in a couple of weeks."

Kate was proud that he'd gone through with his plans. He wouldn't have to pay Kincaid back the debt, but he wanted his slate clean to start a new life. Cordelia had fled to Chicago, not even staying to be at her father's trial. Of course, the humiliation would have been too great.

Will looked south and could now see the dust rising from the hooves of the cattle Diering was taking. "Thanks again, Tom, for being there to bring Kincaid in."

Tom sized up the man who was now his son-in-law. Will was as tough an opponent as Clayton had been. He could also be just as deadly and in a way that was just as subtle. "I was wrong about you, Will. You were always a better man than I, and I'm happy to have you for my son-in-law."

"A man is what he wants to be, Tom."

Diering nodded, realizing the wisdom in the words. He wished he'd had as much when he was that age. But now, at the age of forty-six, he was, once again, going to be what he wanted to be. His gaze shifted to the Navy Colt strapped on Will's hip. His dry lips twisted into a half-smile. "I see you've taken to wearing that thing all the time now."

There was a joking quality in Diering's tone and Will matched it. "I figured you might have one more bullet in yours."

Diering smiled, satisfied with the response. He pulled his hat down tighter on his head, an action indicating he was getting ready to leave. "Thanks for letting me borrow a few of your cowboys, Will. Now, you two, don't be strangers to New Mexico."

He wheeled his horse around and lifted an arm in farewell. They returned the wave, knowing that if they were ever to see him again, they'd have to go south. He was leaving Colorado and the pain of its memories forever.

Kate snuggled closer to Will, happy to see the

change in her father. When he was once again a small stick figure in the distance, she said, "I'm a little nervous about meeting your family, Will."

He looked down at her, surprised. "Why? They'll love you just the way I do."

A teasing smile played on her lips as she looked up at the love in his sapphire eyes, shaded but not hidden by the wide brim of his big hat. God, how she loved him. "I'm just afraid they may notice."

"Notice what? Kate"—he pretended exasperation—"don't dangle things in front of me. What are you getting at?"

She laughed. "I'm afraid they'll notice I'm already carrying your child and we've only been married two weeks."

Will pulled the team to a halt and stared down at her. Then his shocked expression turned into a smile. "Cripple Creek?"

She nodded. "What do you think? Will they still welcome me with open arms?"

Will drew her closer against him. An all-new love for her augmented the one that already existed. For a moment he thought about the child growing inside her; a living part of each of them; a human being to carry on their lives and pick up where they left off.

"How can they not understand, Kate?" his lips whispered against hers. "They have lived it all before."